PAINTER OF THE DEAD

PAINTER OF THE DEAD
Copyright © 2020 by Catherine Butzen.

Originally published in 2015 as *The God Collector* by Samhain Publishing. This edition completely revised and reedited for Thinklings Books, LLC.

Cover design by Nada Orlic.

Thinklings Books
1400 Lloyd Rd. #552
Wickliffe, OH 44092
thinklingsbooks.com

Shades of Immortality, Book #1

PAINTER OF THE DEAD

Catherine Butzen

Thinklings Books, LLC
Wickliffe, OH

PROLOGUE

The security guard sat filling out a time sheet when the door opened behind him.

"You took your damn time, Jay..." he began.

It wasn't Jay. A handful of gray powder blinded him, and his deep, hacking cough cut off his next words. The powder clung to him, filling his lungs, its sickly-sweet scent overpowering. In the space of three breaths, he was unconscious.

Black-and-white monitors lined the small room, displaying feeds from all over the Oriental Institute. The man double-checked them. Nobody was about to disturb him—especially not Jay, who was sleeping off his own dose under a table in the employee cafeteria. The man plugged in a small laptop and made a few artistic tweaks to the security system.

The powder's effects would wear off within fifteen minutes, and the guards wouldn't remember a thing about their blackouts. Not enough time for a full-scale burglary, but more than enough to make the changes he needed. He typed quickly, tongue between his teeth. Patience, patience, and time management were the keys. They always had been, but modern technology required a little more patience than he was used to when doing this kind of work.

In two weeks, the new collection would arrive. Once the Institute actually had the items in hand, its new procedures would go into effect, and the system would be virtually unbreachable. Unless, of course, he had first arranged a way in for himself.

Behind him, Hank snorted in his sleep. The man smiled. Falling asleep on the night shift was regrettable, but not impossible. Besides, how much could've gone wrong in fifteen minutes?

There. With a final keystroke, he sent his bundle of code spiraling off into the system. When he came back, his door would be ready for him. And the servants would be there in the darkness, waiting to answer his call, just like they should have been a long, long time ago.

CHAPTER ONE

...I gave the priest the whole story, reminding him of his
promise of silence, and asked him what I should do. He
said to me, "If you are insane, pray for healing. If you are
telling the truth, begin a diary. No gods will help you in
this."

– Excerpt from the Steen Papyrus,
circa 1400 BCE (fragment)

Transforming the main hall of a natural history museum into a party
venue wasn't easy, but the planning committee had done a heck of a job.
Long strands of lights hung from the second-floor balconies in glittering
loops, the statues of the Muses near the ceiling had been cleaned and
polished, and flickering lamps in cobalt-and-gold shades lit up the dozen
round tables arranged in front of the central dais. A pack of skeletal *Struthiomimus sedens* stood proudly on their pedestal, their black fiberglass
bones touched with glossy yellow-white in the lamplight. Behind them
loomed the massive figure of Little John, a near-complete Tyranno-
saurus unfazed by the party going on under his huge feet. Dozens of
guests circulated in black ties, their laughter and conversation muted
slightly by the sheer size of the hall.

Theodora Speer glanced down, checking her hands and dress one
last time for flecks of paint. She had worn a plastic smock while working
and had checked herself over when she'd finished up, but being
surrounded by so many well-dressed people had started her worrying
again. Paint stains, like spinach in your teeth, tended to be invisible until
the moment of maximum embarrassment.

Nothing. Good. She smoothed down her eggshell-white dress and tried not to look nervous.

Waiters circulated, carrying trays of champagne and, in a nod to the upcoming festive season and the chilly November weather, hot cider. Theo took a glass of cider and carefully sipped as she glanced around, trying to spot her coworkers.

Every year the museum gave a party for its most generous donors, and certain staffers were selected to attend. Their job was to make friendly conversation with the people who funded their work and, hopefully, to keep the donations flowing for another year. Theo wasn't entirely sure why the art department had been tapped for the job this time; the people who designed murals, posters, and resalable pop art for the gift shop didn't usually rub elbows with the paleontologists and doctors.

"Penny for your thoughts?"

Theo jumped and reflexively clutched the glass to prevent spilling her cider. That voice, at least, she recognized.

"I wasn't thinking much of anything, Aki," she said, turning to face the dark-haired man. Akeela Lee was an abstract impressionist who dabbled in surrealism when he was bored and who considered ragged T-shirts the height of fashion. Seeing him in a tuxedo was like seeing a clock melt. "Just letting my mind wander. You look good."

"Only under protest," Aki responded, tugging at his bow tie with a momentary grimace. "I thought we were past the point where society required that we kill ourselves to meet a standard of beauty."

"Society doesn't require it; publicity does," Theo pointed out.

Aki yanked on the bow tie again. "Poh-tay-toh, poh-tah-toh."

"If it's bothering you that much, get rid of it and go for the free-spirited artist look. I bet half the guests don't want to be dressed up either."

"No can do. Schechter made a point to tell me, specifically, about the dress code." Giving up on the bow tie, Aki tucked his hands into his pockets with a sigh. "On the other hand, it means I get to be the Asian James Bond for an evening. Lee. Akeela Lee."

"Sandy must've liked it."

Aki's gaze flicked across the room, settling quickly on Sandra Navarro, a slim, dark-skinned woman in a flame-colored evening gown. "I don't know. I didn't ask."

"Of course not." Theo finished her drink and set the glass down on one of the tables, from where it was instantly whisked away by a waiter.

"You're just a nice colleague with a healthy respect for her work, right?"

That got a scoff from Aki. "So I'm taking it slow. Big freaking deal. And if we're going to be talking about awkward personal stuff—"

"Nice transition."

"Thank you. If we're going to be talking about awkward personal stuff, what about you? I keep expecting to come in in the morning and find you sleeping under your desk. Hell, I'm surprised you even turned up to this." He raised an eyebrow at Theo. "You need to have more fun."

"There's a flaw in your argument. Two flaws, actually." She ticked them off on her fingers. "One, implying that I'm here voluntarily. Two, implying that forced socializing with my coworkers, not all of whom are as adorably weird as you, qualifies as fun."

"Still not an answer. Don't tell me you couldn't have weaseled out of this."

"Publicity." That one word was sufficient to sum up the whole situation, and Aki nodded knowingly. Who could fathom the mind of Publicity?

The art department of Chicago's Columbian Exposition Museum of Natural History often fell victim to the plans of Mariana K. Schechter, PhD, and her public-relations team. The artists agreed that it wasn't fair. Members of the scholarly departments—the historians, anthropologists, and archaeologists, the preservation experts and librarians—rarely had to deal with Dr. Schechter. They made the discoveries and showcased the pieces of history that drew in the crowds.

The art department, on the other hand, was responsible not only for gift-shop fodder, banners, and murals, but also for the general aesthetics of the place, including that sticky and indeterminate requirement—"child-friendly." Theo had frequently crossed swords with Dr. Schechter over what was and wasn't allowable in a public space. Unfortunately, Publicity had won their last bout after a parents' group complained about the heavily armed and fearsome-looking Aztec warriors on the wall in the children's annex, and Theo had been forced to concede that Publicity usually knew what it was doing.

Still...

"Why does Publicity even want us here?" Aki insisted. He was naturally inquisitive, especially when it came to things he didn't like having to do. "They're fired up for Treasures of the Middle Kingdom, up to the point of Egyptianizing the annual party. So when they invite the trustees and board members to a shindig, they trot out the entire Egyptology Department, the Ancient Religions guys...I think I saw the Cultural Anthropology team leader buried in the hors d'oeuvres. And I saw that jackass Zimmer glaring at some old lady who was checking out the naked warrior bronze. But the people who design brochures?"

"Brochures for the exhibit," Theo pointed out. She had to admit she was curious too, but after the Aztec warriors, she was trying not to rock the boat. "And of course they've got Zimmer here. The patrons probably like seeing the head of Security around. It tells them we're serious about protecting their investments."

"You mean Publicity's serious now. If that Collector doesn't get caught soon, they're going to have a collective heart attack."

Theo shushed him. "You know we're not supposed to talk about that. Didn't you get the memo?"

"Four times. I think Security has it in for me." Aki tucked both his hands into his pockets. "Come on, lighten up. If you really think there's anybody here who hasn't heard about that whole thing, you're delusional. The minute the papers gave the guy a name—"

"I know, I know. But I don't want to get fired. Do you?" Theo hoped nobody had overheard them. The Columbian had its own specialized gossip networks, and talk flowed freely enough most times, but it was widely acknowledged that talking about the Midwest's recent spate of museum thefts was a bad career move. Nobody wanted the high-powered donors thinking the Columbian might lose the items they had helped it buy.

Fortunately, she spotted a distraction. Sandra Navarro had been buttonholed by the head of the Margrave Foundation and was sending out subtle but clear signals for help.

Theo nudged Aki. "Go talk to Sandy."

Aki frowned. "What? Why?"

"Trust me. Go talk to her." Theo gave Aki a gentle push. "Be her artist in shining armor."

It took Aki a moment to catch on, but when he did, he stepped up to the plate. Taking two champagne glasses from a passing waiter's tray, he hurried across the room and neatly inserted himself between Freddie Margrave and Sandra, offering each a glass. Bond, indeed—the man could be smooth when he wanted to. Sandra's expression of relief was noticeable, though she changed it to a smile when Margrave looked her way. Judging by her expression, Margrave had been talking either golf or marital infidelity.

Thankfully, there wasn't much time left for socializing. Within moments, an army of waiters appeared from the sidelines, carrying stacks of dishes and silverware. As the guests chatted and sipped their drinks, the waiters—moving with the trained precision that made it a spectacle worth watching—whisked fresh cloths and place settings onto the tables and transformed the scene from lounge to dining room. Place cards were set out, and a tantalizing aroma stole into the air. Dinner was about to be served.

Now the circling groups took on a purposeful air. The board members and wealthiest donors moved toward the dais, while the hoi polloi casually found their place cards. The waiters melted into the shadows at the edge of the hall, to be replaced by wine stewards bearing drink lists and more champagne.

Theo found her assigned spot. To her surprise, she was at one of the mid-level tables with a professor of art history, a prominent (and wealthy) modernist sculptor, and a name she vaguely recognized but couldn't place. Well, that explained it—Dr. Schechter always arranged these events as carefully as Caesar had managed his legions, and she wanted someone from the art department for this group.

Aki and Sandra had been placed a few tables over with a group of dour-looking men in suits. Clearly, the doctor was deploying the charm-ers where they were needed the most.

Taking a seat, Theo surveyed the people joining her. Professor Greg Applebaum from Culver was a tousle-haired blond man who looked much less comfortable than Aki in his tuxedo and bow tie. The sculptor Sinai—one name only—was lounging in his chair, watching the gathering with alert eyes. Theo didn't know much about him, though she would have bet good money that that would change by the end of the evening.

The third member of the group surprised her somewhat. He was tall, six foot two at least, with deeply curved lips and neatly parted, graying black hair that reached to just past his earlobe. His brown eyes were slightly tilted, not quite almond-shaped but near enough to be noticeable, and fringed with charcoal lashes. Faint lines in the corners of his eyes and in the creases by his fine-bridged nose completed the look; he could have been anywhere from an over-stressed thirty-five to a carefree fifty.

The thing that drew Theo's gaze, though, was his skin. It was a coffee color and should have had a touch of copper in the yellow-tinted light of the table's alcohol lamp, but instead there was a soft blue-gray under-tone she had never seen before. It was as if the normal red notes had been washed out and replaced with indigo.

If I painted him, Theo thought, *I'd begin with purple ochre.* Not a color that normally cropped up in her life portraits. She rubbed her thumb against her folded knuckles, wishing for a pencil.

The man turned and caught Theo's stare eye to eye. Awkward. She felt her cheeks warm and instinctively lowered her head, trying to make herself unobtrusive.

It didn't work. "I'm sorry, I don't think we've met," the man said, holding out one broad hand. "I'm Seth Adler."

"I—nice to meet you, I mean, Mr. Adler," Theo said, trying to maintain her composure. The words came out rushed. "I'm Theodora Speer. I'm one of the artists here at the Columbian."

Seth Adler's eyebrows rose at her first name, but he smiled and didn't comment on it. The hand that Theo shook was hard and strong, with square, blunted fingernails and calluses discoloring the tips of the fingers. They were old and thick, their shade lighter than the rest of his skin. *Purple ochre*, Theo agreed with herself, *but desaturated. Faint warm tones, blended and layered...cadmium yellow, but never enough to hide the blues underneath.*

"It's a pleasure to meet you, Ms. Speer. I've always admired what the artists here do for the museum."

Had he? The name was familiar, but Theo still couldn't place it. The man didn't seem to be a professor, and the way he talked made her doubt he was another painter or sculptor. A banker or lawyer, then, likely one with an affection for hiking or extreme sports, judging by the calluses and muscled shoulders. Maybe his name was on one of the donor plaques in the lobby? It would explain the familiarity.

"Well, I'm glad to hear it," she said, trying to strike the right note between formal and friendly. Her words were coming more clearly now, which was a relief. "We're mostly here to help put it together. The history and science are what's really important."

"Never underestimate the role of the artist," Professor Applebaum interjected with the fervor of an academic dog seizing a favorite intellectual bone. "The ultimate expression of a society's cultural values, and criticism of same, can be found in the artistic expression of everyday pursuits—"

Sinai yawned. "It sounds boring to me. It doesn't take much talent to see things that are already there, after all. Not the kind of thing an artist should do. No offense intended," he added, nodding to Theo.

"I'd say I do the same thing you do, Mr. Sinai," she said as mildly as she could. Now her face was warming for a completely different reason. "We both make things to express an idea or an image, and we get paid for it. I'd say the difference"—*is that you probably make seven times what I do*—"is that you work to your own schedule."

"Art is worthless unless it says something new," Sinai responded. His tone was as mild as Theo's, but she guessed that he wasn't nearly as ruffled as she was. He had the air of someone who was speaking from certainty.

"'Fraid we'll have to agree to disagree," Theo said as a waiter approached their table with the wine list. Sinai was well-known, both as a painter and a sculptor, and Theo had seen and admired his installa-tions, but that didn't mean she had to enjoy arguing with him about whether her own work actually counted as art. Instead of continuing that line of conversation, she took the wine list and let the talk carry on with-out her.

The three men provided an interesting study. Sinai was at ease with the waiter and his companions, ordering easily, while Applebaum's politeness couldn't quite conceal his awkwardness when he tried to tip the waiter. Artist and art historian, somehow opposites.

The third man didn't fit with either. The relative ease of his manner was at odds with the lines of his form: his shoulders and back were held stiffly, as if he were afraid of being caught doing something he shouldn't. She wondered if she was imagining it, but when she followed the line and silhouette of his broad form, watching the way the shapes shifted as he moved, she realized she was right. It wasn't so much how he moved as how he didn't. Sinai's shoulders were relaxed, Applebaum's pulled for-ward slightly as if he were trying to duck into himself. Mr. Adler was tense and still.

The waiter turned to Theo, distracting her from her thoughts. "Your choice, ma'am?"

"Just water, I think," she said, handing the list back to him and mentally thanking the universe for the intervention. Being caught staring again wasn't going to make a good impression on the patrons. "I have to work later, and I don't want to push my luck."

"And for you, sir?" the waiter continued. Mr. Adler had barely glanced at the list.

"The Arras Blanc," he said. "You have to work later?"

It took Theo a moment to realize that the question was directed at her, he'd changed gears so quickly. "Well, I don't have to," she said, flicking a stray wisp of blonde hair behind one ear to cover her confusion. "But I want to. We're planning the main mural for Treasures of the Middle Kingdom, and I'm sure you know how big projects go. The minute I turn my back, I think of something I should've done instead."

"Treasures of the Middle Kingdom," Mr. Adler repeated slowly. "The artifacts are from the Eleventh and Twelfth Dynasties, I believe. It opens at the end of December, doesn't it?"

"And it has the mummy?" Professor Applebaum interjected. There was a genuine smile on his face, and Theo couldn't help smiling back more widely this time; the man was clearly an enthusiast. "The tubercular specimen with the anachronistic burial?"

"You'll have to talk to the Egyptologists about the details, professor," Theo said. "I just paint them." Not that she hadn't studied every scrap of information she could get her hands on about the planned exhibition—or about Egypt in general. Theo always had time for a culture that equated images with magic. "But yes, the mummy and its funeral goods. It's one of the most unusual things we've ever done, and definitely one of the biggest. Practically every department we've got is involved somehow."

"What's so special about this mummy?" Sinai said. "You've got whole rooms full of mummies in the other exhibits. Was this one a king?"

"They don't know what it was," the professor cut in, his hands flat on the table as he leaned forward in his excitement. "Nothing about it suggests royalty. But it was buried with thousands and thousands of *ushebtis*, the little figurines meant to serve the gods in the next world. It's the largest ushebti cache discovered, ever. A very rich burial in a very small tomb with a very sick mummy."

That drew raised eyebrows from Sinai. "Ahh," he said. "There's a story here, isn't there?"

"Any chance of a curse?" Adler said. There was a touch of dry humor in his voice. "That's usually what stories like this are about."

"No curse that we know of," Theo said. She knew plenty about the shabti statuettes and their mysterious inscriptions, but she wasn't sure how interested the whole tableful of donors was in Egyptian minutiae. Applebaum was clearly into it, because he'd described them using the academic *ushebti* rather than the everyday *shabti*, but the other two might be bored stiff by the topic. She settled for middle ground. "But it's a definite deviation from the historical record, and that's almost as good. Add that to one of the best-preserved Twelfth Dynasty mummies discovered in a long time and, well, everyone's very excited about the possibilities."

Mr. Adler relaxed as conversation began to flow, but that didn't mean much. Something about his lines bothered her: the tension in his shoulders and back, the odd angles of his nose and cheekbones... He had interesting lines, that was for sure, and his palette begged for a portrait in oil pastels.

Once, she glanced up from the table to see a familiar figure standing at the edge of the hall. Mark Zimmer, the new head of Security, a lean man in his late thirties or early forties with striking red hair and a tendency to stare at people as if he were trying to X-ray them. He'd gotten a reputation for anal-retentive efficiency, but nobody complained too much about his strictness when he was around to hear it. With a museum thief making headlines—especially one flashy enough to get himself a colorful nickname—increased security was a necessity.

Zimmer didn't look happy, which hardly surprised Theo. The donors' party always concluded with a behind-the-scenes tour of the museum's workshops, and having several dozen unvetted persons prowling around and poking at things was probably high on his list of worst-case scenarios.

As she watched, he swept his gaze toward her table. She could almost see the wheels turning as he ticked off the people: Applebaum—not a threat. Sinai—not a threat. Her—cleared. Adler—possibly suspicious? He moved on. Apparently, Adler hadn't pinged his radar too much, though Theo would bet Zimmer'd be coming back their way soon enough.

Theo saw him twice more during the second and third courses. She wondered vaguely if he was going to eat, but her attention was diverted by Sinai and Applebaum starting a loud argument about disease in art.

By the time the dessert plates were taken away, she hadn't gotten them to agree, but she had at least persuaded Applebaum not to shout. Nobody wanted to hear about gout over their ganache.

At that moment, a murmur of conversation rippled through the room, and heads automatically turned. On the dais, a middle-aged man stepped up to the microphone, a smile on his sharp face. As near as he ever got to a smile, anyway.

Dr. Wayne Van Allen, curator of the Columbian's Egyptology Department and the man whose pet exhibit was keeping Theo's and Aki's teams busy. The museum staff could guess the content of his prepared remarks: "Welcome," "glad you could make it," "here's what we're planning to do in the next year," "please give us more money." Still, Theo lent half an ear. It wouldn't make a good impression to be seen not paying attention.

"Welcome, ladies and gentlemen," he said. His voice was flat and soft, though he seemed to be making an effort to sound lively. Theo kept her head aimed in Dr. Van Allen's direction, watching the movement of her tablemates in her peripheral vision.

"We're gratified to see so many of you," the curator went on, "especially since this coming year is going to bring us a lot of surprises. Thanks to your generosity and the hard work of our museum staff, we'll soon be ready to display a unique set of treasures. Artifacts from a period of Egyptian history that public perception often overlooks."

As Dr. Van Allen continued, sketching out their plans for the exhibition and giving the donors some background on the Eleventh and Twelfth Dynasties, Theo took the opportunity to sneak a few more peeks around. Though he effected a pose of bored detachment, Sinai was definitely listening: The idea of the lost periods of history seemed to intrigue him more than he would let on. Professor Applebaum, on the other hand, had tuned out, and Theo guessed that he was growing tired. Being talked to—or at—seemed less to his taste than an active conversation. Or argument. Out of the corner of her eye, she could see Aki and Sandra at their table, their heads close together as Aki sketched something on the tablecloth.

Something flickered to her right—a glint of gold, moving sideways and too quickly to be the ripple of a banner. Theo turned her head slightly and met the eyes of Mr. Adler. He had taken out a pocket watch—yes, a real pocket watch, the kind of old-fashioned affectation that the bankers and lawyers loved—and was checking the time as discreetly as he could.

When Theo caught his gaze, he gave her a small smile and flicked his eyes toward Dr. Van Allen. She smiled a little herself as she under-stood—like Professor Applebaum, he didn't enjoy being talked at, but he was trying to be more discreet than simply zoning out in his seat.

"...including a complete reconstruction of the burial chamber." This drew murmurs of approval from the donors, and Dr. Van Allen inclined his head to the room at large. "While the focus of the exhibition is the treasures of the period, we are honored to be able to exhibit the mummy of tomb THS2 as an integral part of the story. The so-called 'leper mummy': a man who lived with a terrible disease four thousand years before he had a prayer of understanding it—and who was buried under very unusual circumstances. We look forward to sharing with you what this ancient artifact has to teach us.

"And now for the final event of the evening. On the back of your place cards, you will find a group number. Each group will be personally escorted around the museum, behind the scenes, for a firsthand tour of the most important and secretive parts of our work. Please don't hesitate to ask your guides about anything that interests you—the Columbian is proud to host all of you who have made our efforts here possible."

Theo breathed easier after she turned over her place card and con-firmed that it was blank. The donors would have been placed in groups, but someone might have failed to turn up and left her guiding one of the tours.

Aki and Sandra, along with half a dozen other museum employees, were waving and calling out congenially to the people who had been assigned to them. Theo envied them their ease, not their job. Not when she still had a mural to finish planning.

As people began to rise and find their groups, she nodded to the fellow members of table five and climbed to her feet. She wobbled on her heels but didn't fall.

"From the escape attempt, I take it you're not leading a group?" Adler said dryly. "No fool, you."

Be nice to the guests; don't make the Columbian look bad; relax. "I'm just part of the team," Theo said, lifting the hem of her dress to prevent stepping on it. Damn shoes. "There are so many talented people here already that I couldn't add anything to a tour tonight. You're in group...six?" He nodded. "That's probably Aki's group. He's the painter I mentioned earlier; incredibly talented, and not even thirty either. He'll be able to tell you so much more than I could."

Sinai was saying something to Professor Applebaum, and she took the opportunity to slip out while they were distracted. As for Mr. Adler, it would probably be better if she didn't get caught staring again. He would be looked after—Dr. Schechter's genius for social arrangements would see to that—and Theo, having done her duty, could escape with a clean conscience.

CHAPTER TWO

Underneath, where the ink and paint had been scraped away, there was only blank papyrus. But then Bet shook ash and some special powder over it, and the images stood revealed. I ordered him to teach me the trick, but he would not. Scribes must have their secrets, he said.

- Excerpt from the Wilkinson Texts,
circa 1000 BCE (fragment)

The Columbian Exposition Museum of Natural History was laid out in a grand classical style, with one massive hall at the center of the ground floor and a dozen smaller galleries branching off on either side. It had been a real triumph of planning to make the echoing hall comfortable enough for a sit-down meal, but Theo still slipped away from the party with relief.

One particularly ornate pillar fronted a niche for a security door. She scanned her ID and went through, pulling off her heels as she did so. One of the security guards nodded to her as she passed an intersection, stopping his automatic reach for his walkie-talkie.

Being behind the scenes at the museum was like going backstage at a theater. Out front it was all elaborate displays set against the seemingly ageless stone, a backdrop of history with the modern elements never quite overpowering it. Back here, the museum's lifeblood ran through painted concrete corridors lit by harsh fluorescent lights. There was no clash of decoration because there was no decoration.

Farther on, beyond an old-fashioned steel gate, was one of the massive freight elevators that helped the place run smoothly. They were constantly in use during the day, carting supplies between floors as one traveling exhibit was broken down and another constructed. At night, with the massive building quiet, Theo could catch a ride straight to her floor.

She could hear chattering in the distance as she closed the grate of the freight elevator. Theo pressed the button for the top floor—the artists' loft—and breathed a slight sigh of relief as the doors closed before any groups could join her. She felt a twinge at the selfishness, but she was also fairly sure that if she got stuck in an elevator with a donor, she'd wind up accidentally getting her department defunded.

The elevator rose and rose and rose. The gates on each level were closed but the doors beyond them were open, and Theo caught glimpses of the museum coming sluggishly to life as she climbed upward. The Columbian was like an iceberg: ninety percent of it went unseen. She spotted scenery painters, robotics technicians, document preservation specialists, and an associate professor of botany arguing with a man who was wheeling a giant stuffed gorilla into Oversized Taxidermy.

A couple of people waved or nodded as she went past. Theo responded in kind. After eight years as a volunteer and employee at the museum, she knew many of the behind-the-scenes people. They were families and societies unto themselves.

The upper workshops of the Columbian had been chipped out of several combined spaces long after the rest of the building had been completed, and the loft was twenty feet high on one wall and thirteen feet on the other. Small skylights on the angled roof could let in sunlight, but in the middle of the night they were like black mirrors. Two windows, each covered with steel bars to prevent anyone accidentally going skydiving, gave the loft a bisected view of the lake shore.

The room itself had been pulled, rather awkwardly, into the twenty-first century. Deep blue carpeting and slightly paler paint covered the hundred-year-old wood and plaster. Small offices lined each side of the aerie, filled with mismatched pieces of old furniture and displaying whiteboards with schedules and sketches pinned up around them. The rest of the space was taken up by a loose assortment of half-height cubicle walls surrounding messy workspaces. The cubes themselves overflowed with cartoons, reference pictures, personal touches, and the other things that the members liked to see. Papers, fliers, and Post-It notes were plastered an inch deep on the walls.

She liked the loft. Jokes and sarcastic commentary bounced from person to person, designers trading tips and artists criticizing one another's technique. If a new hire was likely to clash with the existing ones, it became obvious in the busy communal atmosphere.

Visitors often expected an old-fashioned artist's studio, but the world of graphic design these days was high-tech. Digitizing tablets and flatscreen monitors filled most of the cubicles, each setup boasting the latest editions of Photoshop, Illustrator, and Corel Painter. But the Columbian had all kinds of artists on staff, and many of the large cubicles had desks jammed up against the dividers to make room for easels and art boards.

Theo's own station, its dividing walls no higher than her chest, was one of the largest and closest to the door: a benefit of seniority, but sometimes bad for her concentration. A digital knight in armor rode back and forth across her monitor, carrying a banner that read *Welcome to the Art Department!*

A photograph of her parents, grandparents, and siblings was propped up next to the monitor, displayed in a worn Disneyland frame and looking like an ad for an insurance company that Cared About You. She was in the middle with her grandma Dora, just as awkward at fourteen as she was at twenty-seven. With her hooded green eyes and strong jaw, she took after Grandma, but having the two of them together in the photograph created a strange effect she wasn't sure she liked.

The rest of the cubicle at least pretended to be professional. Her calendar had every hour of every day blocked out for various projects. Next to her desk sat a small file cabinet, each drawer labeled and locked. It actually contained her secret stash of *Top Gear* and *Car and Driver*, silent testament to a hobby she could never afford, but nobody had to know that. Stacked on top of it were the *Atlas of Human Anatomy*, a pamphlet on Tuscany left over from a previous exhibit, Gardiner's *Egyptian Grammar*, and a reference book about leatherworking. The carpet was protected by a plastic drop cloth, and her easel displayed a half-finished painting.

She liked digital. It had an Undo button, for starters, which in real life was a palette knife and a lot of cursing. But for something like this, a mural being created for an exhibition of the Columbian's own, doing it old-school was important to her.

Plus, it looked better for the donors.

Humming, Theo dropped her uncomfortable shoes and kicked them under the desk. She ducked down behind the low cubicle wall and opened a desk drawer, pulling out a pair of jeans and a button-down shirt. It was the work of moments to slide into the jeans and whip the dress off over her head. Shirt, smock, hair in a bun, dress into the desk. No point in wasting expensive paint by getting it on her good clothes.

The design she was working on would become the final mural for the new Egyptian exhibit. It would be a...well, she didn't consider anything her masterpiece, but there was something in it that made it special. Normally she worked on it in the dedicated studio area, but she'd had to bring the design out into the open for the donors to see. Hopefully they would like it. If only she could make it something worth being liked.

Motion! That was the trick, the thing she always chased. It niggled at her when nothing else could. Motion on canvas, motion in pigment. It was one of the elusive qualities that made art great, that made someone stop and stare at a Winslow Homer or an incredible, incomprehensible Escher.

Tongue between her teeth, Theo surveyed the painting as it stood, gaze skating easily over the familiar shapes and shades as she asked the inevitable question. *Will this do?*

Not yet, but it might. It was a layered scene: two darkly tanned Egyptian men in simple white kilts were dragging a papyrus-reed boat up onto the shore with their backs to the viewer, while a third secured a basket full of fish. Behind them the Nile flowed, broad enough that the far bank faded into a mass of soft colors and stippled strokes.

Towering over the boatmen and obscuring the far bank was the green-painted funerary barge of a king. Golden eyes were set on the barge's prow, and the figure of the king's gilded coffin blazed with light atop it, but the boatmen didn't glance up from their work.

There was potential for motion, if she could grab it. The wind stirred the men's kilts; the smaller of the two boat-haulers was bent almost double, his back straining as he dragged on the sodden craft. A bend, a stretch, a touch of light—maybe she could—

The rattle of the elevator disrupted her concentration before it could take hold. "Not tonight, hon," Theo reminded herself. Tonight she wasn't likely to get much done, not with people running around and asking questions.

But that didn't mean she was going to ignore her responsibilities. People attended for more than the parties: They wanted to see the museum at work, and Theo had her part in that. When a group of five patrons was escorted into the aerie, she looked over her shoulder and waved to them before loading her palette with orange and titanium white.

To her surprise, Aki wasn't leading them. Jem Vladashvili, a student intern, was at the head of the group instead. Theo could make out a few shapes from the corner of her eye, but she concentrated on her work while Jem gave his spiel. The second boatman, the straining one, had real potential—the folds of his kilt were damp with sweat and water, but something about its curve and stretch was telling Theo it wanted to move. The quality of light and texture was the key here. She folded yellow, orange, white, and a pinprick of pink together, creating a rich golden tangerine that layered beautifully into the existing colors of the kilt and showed where the light of the setting sun shone right through the fabric. It was beginning to come together.

Jem's voice floated past as he gestured. He had a thick Russian accent, but he spoke slowly enough for everyone to understand him, and Theo knew he was favoring the patrons with his almost-sweet smile. "This is where we are designing the many pictures for inclusion in the new exhibitions. Theodora is always planning the important new murals, and Akeela—he is not here in the loft now—he is always planning many of the other pictures we are needing, such as for our brochures and signs. We are working here for a long time, and it is a very good way to make the pictures for what the museum is needing."

"I thought murals were bigger," a female voice said. "That's just a canvas. My painting class uses those."

"The mural must be created before it is made in larger size for the wall," Jem explained. Theo could feel the patrons moving closer, and keeping her back turned was no longer diplomatic. She stepped aside to let them examine the painting for themselves, and tried not to fidget while they did.

The patrons murmured over the canvas, and one of them poked the surface of it, drawing an inadvertent squeak of alarm from Theo.

"Please, no touching," Jem said before Theo could say anything. "It is not good to touch the painting before it is dry and ready."

One of the visitors piped up with a question about the funerary boat. Jem fielded that, and the other questions that followed, while Theo tried to figure out where to put her hands.

Finally, the party drifted off, led by Jem. From the sound of things, he was telling a story, and a ripple of laughter accompanied the group down the hallway. Bless Jem for his people skills.

The light shifted and she squinted. Fresh shadows had fallen on her palette, turning her lovely tangerine gold almost brown. Someone was standing behind her, and they were blocking her light.

Putting on a friendly smile, she turned. "Excuse me, may I help—Dr. Schechter?"

Mariana Schechter was a short, sleek platinum blonde in her fifties. Tonight she was wearing a copper-colored gown with a matching emerald bracelet and choker set, and her spike heels put her nearly at eye level with Theo. As usual, though, the height disparity seemed to go the other direction—underneath the soft waves of carefully styled blonde curls, Dr. Schechter had a stare like a razor.

Standing behind her was Seth Adler. He had his hands in his jacket pockets and was looking around the loft with a sort of cautious curiosity. His gaze lingered on the painting for a long moment.

Theo's heart gave a flip-flop. Dr. Schechter tended to hobnob at the dais level, sweet-talking local politicians or wealthy art collectors into sending more funds the Columbian's way. If she was here in the loft with a random guest— Oh no, had he complained?

Had Theo crossed some strange invisible line? And there were hundreds—no, thousands—of artists and graphic designers who'd be ready to take her place....

She swallowed, her mouth dry. "Evening, Dr. Schechter, Mr. Adler. Sorry, you startled me for a second there."

"Quite all right, Theodora." Dr. Schechter half-turned and took a step back, clearing the line of sight between Theo and Mr. Adler. "I was hoping I'd find you here. I'm sure you've already met Mr. Adler?"

"I...oh yes, at dinner." This didn't sound like the beginning of a reaming-out, but if there was one thing Theo had learned early it was that life always had another disappointment in store. "Is there something I can help you with?"

"Yes, actually." Dr. Schechter gestured toward both of them, as if she could make them move closer to each other with the sheer force of her interpersonal skills. "Mr. Adler was put with Akeela's group, but he's very interested in the art department and was hoping for a private tour."

A private tour? Thanks to the security concerns surrounding the collections, that almost never happened. But if Dr. Schechter was authorizing it...Theo glanced at Adler, curious, and found golden-brown eyes fixed on hers.

Her fingers loosened on the paintbrush as she met his gaze. She'd been wrong. Not curiosity. Caution, yes, but not curiosity. He was seeing everything he had expected to see, and yet he wasn't at ease. She wondered what he was thinking. Maybe she could ask.

"No, it's not a problem," she said. Dr. Schechter was watching. "I might not be the best person for this, though. I mean, I don't normally give tours."

Dr. Schechter gave Theo a nod. "I realize that this is unusual, Theodora, but Mr. Adler has clearance from security," she said. "And given his areas of interest, I thought you would be the best choice to show him around. He's done so much for your department."

Theo's confusion must have shown because Dr. Schechter elaborated, "Mr. Adler is the direct controller of the Neith Trust."

Oh.

Oh.

The Neith Trust was the longest-running endowment in the history of the Columbian. Everyone in the department knew the story. Rachid al-Adhur, an Egyptian Muslim educated in London, was among the first men to endow the museum when it was founded in 1895. The elderly al-Adhur had been outraged by the destruction of Egyptian antiquities and had dedicated a large portion of his fortune specifically for the museum to use in restoring tomb-painting fragments in their collection. In the 1930s, the Trust had been expanded by al-Adhur's son to include the recreation of old works, and soon most of the art department—and part of the Egyptology group—was funded by the Trust.

Al-Adhur's family, now the Adlers, had kept it going for more than a hundred years. They'd carefully stewarded their money through the generations, buying slow-growing but reliable businesses and investing heavily in property. They never seemed to act out in ways that would draw negative attention and were generous to a fault with their contributions to reputable institutions. The perfect donors, in fact, if one hadn't been there in front of her.

Theo tried to covertly survey the loft, wondering if there was anything she should have covered up or gotten rid of. If the controller of the Neith Trust thought that his money was being misused, she was dead.

Dr. Schechter was watching her. A response seemed to be in order. Theo swallowed again and hitched her friendly expression back into place.

"I had no idea," she said. "I'm not used to donors being, you know, human."

She immediately flushed and fought the urge to cover her face—*So much for looking professional, Theo; he's gonna think you're a flake*—but while Dr. Schechter flashed her a sharp look, Mr. Adler gave a small smile. It was an odd expression, a minor tilt of the lips that looked out of place on an otherwise placid face. Something about it tugged at her memory, but she wasn't sure what.

"Guilty as charged," he said. "I'm sorry I didn't say anything earlier. I wanted to talk to someone and get a sense of how things were in the department, so I asked the doctor to point me toward an interesting employee. Forgive me?"

"Oh, absolutely," she said, trying to keep her tone equally light while mentally scanning every word that had passed her lips in the past three hours.

"Doctor," Adler said, "thank you for the introduction. I believe you set a time limit of one hour for this tour, correct?"

"That's correct," she said.

"In that case, I'd like to get started at once so we don't keep Miss Speer here too late. Would you excuse us?"

Dr. Schechter probably wasn't used to being dismissed, but she handled it with grace. "Of course," she said. "Theodora, take Mr. Adler down to see the mummy, won't you? And be sure to check in with Security when you're finished up here. Good night, Mr. Adler." And she strode away, steady on her high heels despite the thick carpet, leaving Theo and Mr. Adler alone in the loft.

Theo crossed her arms, trying not to look as nervous as she felt. Her parents knew how to handle this kind of thing. Local politicians, newspaper critics, and prominent academics were bread-and-butter to them, but her memories of their dinner parties mainly consisted of staring at her plate and trying not to say anything that might embarrass them. What now?

Well, at least Dr. Schechter had given her a place to start. "All right, Mr. Adler," she said, cleaning her brush. "Would you like to meet our star exhibit?"

"Please," he said. "Lead on."

* * *

The mummy was officially designated THS203, but people who work with the dead have to have a sense of humor, and it had acquired a number of nicknames since moving into the preparation lab. Somebody had taped a reworked version of the THX1138 logo to the door, and the mummy itself had been referred to in various internal memos as Tiny, Doorstop, Turkey Jerky, and the Sixth Ranger.

Most of the names were apt. THS203 was well-preserved, but what had survived wasn't a sight for a weak stomach. Unwrapped from the crown of its head to the middle of its chest, it resembled an insect emerging from a flaky brown cocoon. The bandaging had flattened its nose, and its jaw hung loose, no longer kept in place by torn leathery cheeks and lips. Years of tuberculosis had ravaged it before it had gone into the tomb, and its partially unwrapped arms were twisted twigs.

"There it is," Theo said, resting her fingertips on the glass. Nobody outside of the preparation lab called THS203 "he": though technically male, it was more fossil than human. Easier to think of it as an artifact than a corpse. "Meet THS203. Number Three to friends."

Mr. Adler stood next to her, gaze fixed on the dead man behind the glass. His hands were back in his pockets, but his back was ramrod straight. Theo waited a moment to see if he would say something, then tried to fill the silence as best she could.

"It's amazing it's in such good condition, really. People first learned about the THS2 tomb when its pieces started appearing on the antiques market, back before the Columbian was founded. Number Three and his grave goods have been bouncing around collections for the last century or so, and it took forever for us to get as many pieces as we have. Now we can finally display them together. It's going to be a great exhibit, I think."

A muscle tightened in Adler's cheek.

"But it is in good condition?" he said. "Will it last much longer, out of its tomb?"

"We're taking care of it," Theo promised. "It was pretty lucky as far as mummies go. One collector partially unwrapped it and took the amulets hidden in its bandages, but most of those were tracked down and bought back into the collection. Stored in low light, in an airtight and sterile environment...it could last forever."

That seemed to satisfy Adler. His gaze lingered on the mummy's face for a bare moment before skating away, focusing on the half-undone wrappings.

"The amulets," he said. "Will they be returned to the mummy?"

"They'll be on display in the same exhibit." Something was bothering Adler, but she wasn't sure what. "It's a fascinating collection. There's the heart scarab and the *djed* pillar, of course, standard burial amulets, but we don't often see male mummies buried with an Isis knot amulet. The *tyet.* It's considered a woman's symbol, usually. Though, of course, it does symbolize resurrection. Some of the experts here think it must have been a gift from his wife..."

She faltered slightly. Adler's gaze was still fixed on the mummy.

"It looks unusual," he said finally.

"Strange?" Theo guessed.

"Repellent."

Not Theo's first choice. Drawings were important when even a weak camera flash might damage an artifact, and Theo had spent hours in the preparation labs, sketching the mummy and its collection of artifacts. To her, THS203 was like an insect breaking out of its chrysalis. The owner of the body had once believed that he was moving on to the next world, and the specimen they examined was what he had left behind.

Adler, though, didn't seem to be in the mood for a discussion like that. He seemed to be waiting for the mummy to justify itself: get up, walk around, give them both a reason for its presence there. And when it didn't, he turned away from the glass as if his low opinion had been confirmed.

"I'm surprised you don't like it," she said as genially as she could. "I thought your family was very involved with the preservation efforts."

"Financially only," Adler said, leaning his back against the glass. "I do some networking for valuable pieces on behalf of the museum, but aside from my great-grandfather, none of us has known much about the actual excavating and caretaking. That was one of the reasons we set up the Trust."

"Well, you've made a lot of excavators and caretakers very happy people," Theo pointed out. She couldn't help a prickle of worry at the expression on Adler's face. Was he feeling sick? How many glasses of wine had he had at dinner? She couldn't remember.

"You know, we don't have to hang around the lab if you don't want to," she said. "Would you like to see the other THS2 artifacts?"

"In a minute." He half-turned for another look at the mummy. "What do you think of all this? Does the exhibit seem like a good idea to you?"

Theo was taken aback by the question. "Well, yes," she said. "This is what it's really about, isn't it? History. Helping people come face-to-face with the past."

"The past, yes. But Dr. Van Allen wasn't talking up the past so much as he was talking up that mummy. Bile fascination for a corpse." Adler's eyes darkened. He looked at Theo as if asking her for help. "It's not right, Miss Speer."

"That's not it at all," Theo said bluntly. She probably should have been more diplomatic, but he was asking her to say that their work wasn't worth anything. Never in a million years. "It's true we're excited about the mummy. And Dr. Van Allen talked it up to the donors because, frankly, there are some in that crowd who do come here for the dead bodies." Or naked statues—the upstairs bronzes tended to get their glazes rubbed off in pretty specific places.

"But I have friends in Production," she continued. "They're working with a forensic artist to reconstruct what Number Three here would have looked like in real life. The guys in Interactives aren't just making a copy of the tomb; they're building a scale model of the riverboats those fishermen I painted would have been rowing. We made copies of the amulets buried with the corpse. Number Three wanted to live forever, and if we do our work right, we can help it do that. We can take people out of"—she held out a hand, pointing to the flat, white-painted walls and the sheer glass and the security camera blinking endlessly—"all this. Bring its world back for a little bit. Help us remember. We shouldn't forget where we came from, or we might not know where we're going."

Mr. Adler cocked his head, studying her. Theo could feel an instinctive blush rising again, but she met his gaze and studied him in turn. Some of the lines in the corners of his eyes and mouth smoothed out.

"You really believe that," he said. His voice was quiet. It didn't sound skeptical or insulting—*Oh, you've got to be kidding me; that sounds so stupid*—an attitude that occasionally reared its ugly head.

"I do," she said. "It's important work."

"But do you think it's the wisest thing to do?" he said. His eyes turned back to the still form of THS203, lying there in his climate-controlled cabinet, with his frail arms crossed over his brittle brown chest. "One of the risks of the past is that people romanticize it. Curses, monsters, bloody battles, star-crossed lovers—that sort of thing. That's what they want to see, not potsherds and shabtis."

"And they get it," Theo said. "A lot of history isn't much different from that. There really were battles, dangerous plans, and star-crossed lovers. And because there were, we owe it to them to be honest about what happened." She swallowed a sudden lump in her throat. "If we don't, then what's the point?"

"But that's not all there was," Adler interjected. "And when people see this stuff, they become convinced the past was a theme-park ride. Do you think you can show the lovers and the planners accurately, Miss Speer? Can you bring them back to life?"

The fluorescents of the lab were harsh on his colors, bleaching the remaining warmth out of his skin and casting blue-gray shadows along the sharp lines of his jaw. It reminded her of a course she had once taken in sumi-e ink painting. For a moment she wanted to touch him, wondering if he would feel like skin or paper under her fingers.

He clearly didn't like the mummy in front of him, but the art department was relying on him and his money, and he'd delivered. And he wanted to know: Was it worth it? Were they doing good work? Or did they only perpetuate stories for entertainment? Oh, they were real stories, no doubt about that, but did they do much good?

"I'm going to tell the truth," Theo said. "There's so much we still don't know. But we can try to get it right."

"That's a good answer," Mr. Adler said. He threw another glance at THS203. "Are you listening?"

"God, I hope not," Theo said with a grin. Some of the tension began to bleed out of the room. "If it finds out what the lab boys call it, it'll be out for blood."

"I don't know about that. Mummies aren't like what they are in the movies, you know."

"But you still don't like them?"

"Just because I'm not afraid of being killed by something doesn't mean I'm obliged to like it."

Theo watched him, wondering about his choice of words. She'd never said he was afraid, but maybe he'd been thinking it anyway. Whatever he was thinking, though, it was clear that THS203 with his sad smile wasn't going to be a happy topic of conversation. "Well then," she said, "the good news is that we have plenty of other things to see. How do you feel about taxidermy? They should be prepping large snakes tonight."

"Hmm. Watching animals being skinned is more of a before-dinner activity, I think."

The way he delivered the words—completely deadpan, as if he were discussing a matter of national security—coupled with that strange quirk-of-the-lips smile, made Theo's stomach do an odd flip. Stupid nerves! This was definitely more of an Aki gig.

"In that case, how about we go"—she picked a direction at random and pointed—"back that way. Prep A and B are taking care of some shab- tis from Number Three's cache, and they're absolutely beautiful."

He nodded to her. "I always have time for beautiful things. Lead the way, Miss Speer."

CHAPTER THREE

The friendship of a scribe is not to be discarded lightly, I
think. For it is they who will write my prayers when I am
gone, and I do not want to die forever for the sake of a
careless slip of a pen.

- Excerpt from the Wilkinson Texts,
circa 1000 BCE (fragment)

The whole hall was in motion. It had been divided by temporary walls,
and teams of eight or twelve men called out to one another over the buzz
of electric saws and cursed the electricians who skittered between them
with orange extension cords. There was a busy energy in the air, and
drifts of sawdust littered the floor in the unfinished areas, giving the
space a delicious woodsy scent that made some of the artists sneeze.

The first of the gallery rooms had been effectively finished. The
walls were painted a warm sandy color, fading to tarnished gold at the
base, and a dais for the full-sized Nile rowboat had been built. The
carpet hadn't yet been installed, but Theo knew that the intended shade
was a deep blue-green, chosen to perfectly match the colors of the water
that she had painted. Visitors would feel as if they were knee-deep in the
river, sandy banks rising up on each side. It was perfect.

The one thing lacking was the mural itself. One long wall was left
primed but unpainted, and it was here that Theo, Aki, and the team went
to work.

The completed painting had been scanned and mapped with a grid.
Using a projector, they overlaid painting and grid onto the wall, marking
the squares and lines with faint pencil that would disappear entirely
under the paint. The grid would be projected again when the base colors

had been finished, giving them areas to concentrate on for detail work, but for now they painted in broad strokes.

This was the best part. The artists worked quickly, laying down the most basic shapes of flat color: blue here, green here, yellow on the bank, and a blob of blue-black that would eventually become a fisherman's hair. Backmost layers first, let it dry, and then the next above it. This was not the time for detail.

Theo almost galloped up the stepladder, balancing a small can of blue-gray with her left hand as she drew broad swaths of color across the wall. Behind them, fans were aimed at the wall to help the paint dry. Wisps of Theo's hair fluttered in the breeze, and she tucked them under her plastic shower cap, leaving a smear of blue near her hairline.

Aki was talking again, naturally.

"All I'm saying is it's sad," he insisted from his spot in the far corner of the mural. "Your parents jet off to Taos for Christmas and leave you watching their house? They couldn't even take you with?"

"Believe me, I'd rather do it this way," Theo replied. She finished filling in the shape of a wave and reached for the palette loaded with deeper blue-green, stippling the fresh color onto the wave. "They're going to be doing dinner parties and rubbing elbows. Mom's got a Christmas present all picked out for some guy who runs a super PAC. It'll be a lot better in Deerfield."

Aki shook his head. "Lame."

He said something else, too, but Theo didn't register it. Patches of cinnamon brown, the base flesh tone for two of the men, could take the white of the kilt. Motion, maybe? She'd had good results in the original painting, but had never been entirely satisfied by the shape she'd achieved. Now she could try again.

She was reaching for a small tube of white when an incoming commotion broke through her haze. Several heads turned toward the entrance to the gallery. Mark Zimmer, the chief of Security, hurried through the crowd toward the door, with a couple of his guards trailing behind. Somebody—somebody who shouldn't be there, to judge by the commotion—had entered the gallery. Theo felt a poke of surprise when she recognized him.

He was in gray this time, a shade almost identical to the sleek, iron-colored streaks in his hair. In the strong light of the gallery his skin held more warmth, this time with the touch of copper that should have been visible on the night of the party, though the blue undertones were still there. As she watched, he maneuvered easily around the minefield of sawhorses and scaffolding that littered the hall. Two more security guards trailed in his wake but weren't stopping him, so the artists and builders let him through.

Zimmer didn't take kindly to people strolling into an area closed to the public. "Can I help you?" he said, crossing his arms.

"Seth Adler," Mr. Adler said calmly. He handed Zimmer a folded piece of paper. "I arranged with Dr. Schechter to view the construction of the new exhibition. I think a message should have been sent?"

Zimmer opened it, glancing back and forth between Adler and paper. "Checks out," he said. Theo smiled a little at that. Translation: "Okay, the administration says you're authorized and I technically have to listen to them, but I wish they'd quit letting outsiders run around backstage, goddammit." She liked that Zimmer understood that people worked late and so made accommodations to the security schedule, but if he could've kept the collections safe by locking people out of the museum altogether, he'd have done it in a heartbeat.

"Don't worry, Mark, he won't make a mess," she said, putting one hand on her hip and leaving behind paint fingerprints. Both Zimmer and Adler turned at her words. Zimmer didn't seem thrilled at the interruption.

Adler's lips quirked in something not quite a smile, but close. Shining droplets flecked his hair and shoulders where snowflakes had melted.

"Miss Speer," he said, raising one hand in a half wave of greeting. "Hard at work, I see." He took in Theo's mussed hair and paint-spattered plastic coveralls, and to her surprise, the almost-smile grew. "You're having fun."

Aki elbowed Theo, but she ignored him. "You know how I feel about my job, Mr. Adler," she said. "I always have fun. Are you here for another look at the mummy?"

"Never," Adler said. "But I wanted to see things when the museum wasn't on its best behavior. It took time for my schedule to clear enough to allow it." He stopped at the edge of the tarpaulin, inclining his head.

Theo shifted, unsure of what to do with herself.

"And maybe take you out to lunch," he added.

Oh.

Her first instinct was to break eye contact. Maybe find something else to talk about, or cover up her sudden confusion by dropping something. But dropping something in front of Mr. Adler wasn't going to look good for her or the department—oh damn, she was turning red, wasn't she?

She played for time the best way she could think of and made a show of studying him mock-seriously. Though the overall picture was as sleek as it had been at the gala, this time there was a telltale rumple around the edges: a scuff mark on one shoe, the worn leather of his wristwatch band, the droplets of melted snow. He looked less like the million-dollar donor and more like the man she was itching to sketch.

"Thanks for asking nicely," she said, silently ordering herself to act normal. "That actually sounds great. I have a break in about forty minutes, okay? If the paint fumes haven't killed us by then."

"I'll meet you at the southern staff entrance," he said. He nodded to her and moved past, still trailed by the security escort, and disappeared into the next section of the hall. The gazes of the artists turned back to Theo, who could feel her blush deepening.

"You do realize that you don't have to cooperate with the donors on everything, right?" Zimmer said dryly.

"I know," Theo replied. She fiddled with her paintbrush, trying to calm her nerves. "Relax. I'm not going to embarrass the department or give away the security codes, all right?"

"I know," Zimmer said. "I passed around the rules for worker-patron interaction three months ago, and you're smart enough to remember them. What mystifies me is why you're so calm about it."

Theo sighed and turned back to the wall, deliberately putting her back to the Security chief. "It's lunch, not the invasion of Poland."

"Lunch with the controller of the Neith Trust," Aki pointed out as he swung by for a fresh brush. "Who, by the way, has more money than either of us will ever see and spends it on sponsoring us. You can't expect me not to make fun of that."

"Self-deprecation doesn't fit you, Aki," Theo said. "How about you and Zimmer both stay out of my lunch plans?"

"Only if you promise to tell me everything. Stock tips, for example."

* * *

Theo shucked her paint-spattered coveralls and checked her reflection in the dark mirror of the nearest sleeping computer monitor. There was still the smear of paint near her hairline, which she removed with an alcohol wipe. Aside from that, she was…acceptable. Sighing, Theo fluffed her limp blonde hair, then asked herself why she cared. Business lunch meant businesslike, not pretty.

Seth Adler was waiting outside, right where he'd said he would be, flecked again with fresh snow. The lead-colored sky sifted down flurries, and drifts were already accumulating on the hoods of the parked cars. The flakes melted when they hit the sidewalk, though, leaving damp spots on the concrete.

Theo huddled into her blue parka, but managed a smile as she stepped out into the cold. "Hope I'm on time," she said. "I had to go up to the loft to get out of my suit."

"You're punctual," he assured her. The cold seemed to be affecting him more than it did her; his cheeks were bright red. "I was early. Shall we?"

"Sure," she said, tucking her hands deeper into the jacket's pockets. "What were you thinking? I usually throw a Hot Pocket in the caf microwave, but I don't know if that's your kind of thing."

"I was thinking of the Chancellor, actually," Adler said. For a moment, Theo thought he was going to take her arm, but if he'd considered it, he'd changed his mind. Instead, he led the way to the parking lot, Theo following a step or two behind.

"The what?"

"A restaurant in the Loop. It's old enough that nobody minds the pub décor, and just expensive enough to keep people from feeling uncultured about eating food that tastes good."

"Mind if I ask what your definition of 'tastes good' is?" Theo tactfully avoided mentioning the issue of payment, although her enthusiasm had dimmed at *expensive*. She was more than willing to pay her share, but mentioning how pricy the meal might be was tacky.

He won back points, though, by giving his reply careful consideration. "The problem is, there's really no way to describe it without sounding like a double entendre."

"A lot of meat, huh?"

"Something like that."

"Well, I appreciate you trying not to be sleazy, but I did go to art school." She gave him a bit of a smile back. "An accidental double entendre is nothing compared to the stuff the second-year graphic design students got up to."

He surprised her by laughing, a hoarse chuckle. "So I hear. Mr. Lee talked quite a lot about it. Too much, in fact."

Her smile faded. "He does that," she agreed.

"I'm sorry," Adler said quickly. "Are you two—?"

"We're—" she began, but stopped. Adler's poker face was good, but he hadn't mastered the art of friendly disinterest. "We're friends," she said.

"I see." He tucked his hands into his pockets. "I'm sorry. I shouldn't have joked about another member of the cabal. Like the Marines? Offend one and you offend them all?"

"Actually, that's the Code of the Freaks," Theo said. "But no, honestly, I don't want you to get the wrong impression of the art department. We like to make fun of each other, but we're not...*flakes*, I guess."

Adler drew to a stop, and Theo bumped into him. The blush came back in full force and she took an instinctive step backward, but Adler just looked over his shoulder. "Slippery this time of year," he said. "Are you all right?"

"I'm fine," Theo said.

* * *

The Chancellor was a strange blend of restaurant, pub, man cave, and shrine to Chicago. Waiters and waitresses sported Al Capone T-shirts, and each wall featured a wide-screen TV showing a mix of sports and news broadcasts, but the dining room was all dark-wood paneling, dignified leather upholstery, and linen napkins. Black-and-white prints from the city's history crowded alongside movie posters and headshots of famous gangsters. Theo recognized a few shots from the museum's own archives.

It actually looked like the kind of place she would like. Theo and Aki had spent more than their share of evenings doing shots in Loop bars, especially on holidays when traffic gridlocked the whole city and there was nothing to do but drink festively colored beer and watch the police round up their fellow drunks in funny hats. It had a settled-in feeling, and there didn't seem to be a dress code.

Adler nodded to the on-duty bartender, who waved them toward a table in the back. Evidently her escort was a regular.

"What do you think?" he said, sounding...awkward? A little, though it took her a moment to recognize the emotion from him. "Do you like it? We can go somewhere else if you're not comfortable."

Theo smiled, touched. "It's great," she said, picking up the drinks list from the table. "I can't believe I've never been here before. I spend so much time in the Loop, but it seems like I'm always running into things I've never seen before."

"Keeps life interesting," he said. "That's a good thing, isn't it?"

"Not always," she pointed out. "I'm pretty fond of dullness, myself. Artists with interesting lives usually seem to die by the time they're thirty."

"Cheerful thought," Adler observed with a twist of his lips. "I hope you're not planning on cutting off an ear."

Theo touched one earlobe. Today her earrings were silvery curlicues with a pale-green chip of crystal in the center of each spiral, and she ran her fingertip over the metal, tracing the elegant curves there. "Never happen," she said. "I like jewelry too much."

Adler's gaze followed her finger, and she saw his eyes widen. There was a moment of silence between them before Theo quickly lowered her hand and looked back at the drinks menu. Was she flirting? Oh no, she was flirting. Mentioning jewelry at the same time too. *Classy, Theo. Meet a nice guy and make him think you're after his money.*

He didn't seem to think that, though. She wondered if she could make him laugh again.

More small talk, this time about the art department itself. Their restoration and re-creation plans interested him more than she'd thought they would, and he kept coming back to the subject of the shabti collection. When would they be on display? How many of them? What did she think of them?

"We're lucky to have them," she said, but his curiosity prompted her to add a little more. "Dr. Schechter or Dr. Van Allen could probably tell you more, though. I just paint them."

"Dr. Schechter is too slippery. Every time I speak to her, I feel as if whatever she says has footnotes I'm not being permitted to see. And Dr. Van Allen...isn't very approachable."

"So you want me to squeal on my bosses," Theo deadpanned.

"Precisely." His expression was perfectly, beautifully serious.

"Oh. Well, why didn't you say so? The tyrannical regime of the

Schechterites must be ousted."

Adler spluttered into his drink, but it wasn't a full laugh. She grinned at him. "Although we'll need to talk about something else too," she added. "So I won't have to lie when the higher-ups ask me what we were discussing."

Adler gave that due consideration. "What sort of topic? Politics? Entertainment? Controversy?"

"No controversy. Too controversial. How about the weather?"

"What can you say about the weather in Chicago? 'Day 56: Still freezing. Distinct bouquet of dead fish.' Baseball?"

"I thought we said no controversy. When the Sox won the pennant, Interactives wouldn't talk to Taxidermy for over a week. News? The economy?" She caught his grimace. "Oh, right. That's probably like mentioning Macbeth to an actor, right? Do I have to turn around three times to break the jinx?"

"I'll forgive you if you promise not to mention it again." Adler gestured as if he were warding off the Evil Eye, getting a laugh from Theo. "Family, perhaps? You must have stories."

"If you want to be bored to death," Theo said. "The Speers are nothing to write home about. Except my grandma Dora was a Goldwyn Girl back in the day, and doesn't that embarrass the hell out of my mom. How about the Adlers? It must have been strange, growing up with this huge family legacy."

"Not particularly." He drummed his fingers on the table, mulling over his words. "It feels normal, really. All families have expectations, don't they? It's rather…" Theo waited expectantly for the next words, but he stopped and offered her a crooked smile instead. "You know, I don't have a way to end that sentence without putting my foot in my mouth. What about your family?"

"It's nice to know I'm not the only one with chronic foot-and-mouth disease," Theo said. "I'm the eldest of three—there's me, Edith, and Godfrey."

Adler looked amused. "Your parents like old-fashioned names, don't they?"

"Sort of." Theo crossed her legs at the ankle and made herself comfortable in the booth. "Grandma Edie, Grandma Dora, and Great-Uncle Godfrey pooled their savings to buy Mom and Dad a house back when they were newlyweds, and my parents promised to name kids after them in memoriam. Mom used to tell me that if she'd had a choice, I would've been Jennifer Amanda. How about you? Got a sister?"

"No, it was just me and my brother."

"And where's he now?"

"He got religion," Adler said.

Theo leaned back, wondering if she'd touched on something sensitive, and he shook his head. "No, not in a bad way. He was my closest friend when I was little, but he never wanted to be involved in"—he waved a hand vaguely, encompassing not so much the restaurant as the world—"this. He passed away a few years ago."

Theo winced. "I'm sorry. I didn't mean to bring it up."

"Don't be. He had a good life." Adler took a sip of his drink. "He was a good man, if a little bit too, eh, concerned for my soul. Besides, I'm the one who brought it up." He grimaced. "My mistake."

"I'll say." She leaned forward. "See, you've got me curious. You don't like talking about family, so you mentioned it? I'm pretty sure Freud would have something to say about that."

"Oh God, not Freud," he said, shaking his head. "Help?"

He ran a hand through his hair, looking awkward enough that she was willing to help him. It was hard to be nervous about talking to him when he'd walked into a conversational trap he himself had set.

"All right, I think we've done enough talking to satisfy my bosses," she said, taking a few olives from the appetizer plate. "How about we forget Freud and talk about something that won't embarrass either of us?"

"Yes. Please." Adler took a sip of beer and settled back in his chair a little. "Tell me more about that mural you were working on. Most of the exhibits have murals framed on canvas, don't they? But you were painting it directly onto the wall."

"Well, it's about practicality, really," she said. Adler still hadn't touched the appetizers—another detail for her mental portrait. He hadn't eaten much at the party, either. Maybe it was a question of comfort and personal boundaries. "When it's a traveling exhibit, like King Tut's treasures, the large graphics that go with it will be printed on fabric and displayed stretched on a frame. It's a cheap way to fill up your wall space. But while Treasures of the Middle Kingdom is going to go on the road later, it's something we put together ourselves, not a loan. It needs to make an impression."

She shrugged. "When you print a painting on fabric, especially when you're blowing up a smaller image to, say, ten feet by twenty, it loses a lot of vibrancy and detail. Printed versions can go on the road, but for this...for this, it has to be perfect. It will be perfect."

"And what happens to perfection when the exhibit closes? Will it be painted over?"

"Probably. Or scraped off." His brow furrowed at that, and she shrugged again. "It depends on whether they reuse the dividing walls they built. If not, the whole thing might go into storage, but if they need the walls for another exhibit it'll probably get scraped."

There was an odd look in Adler's eyes that she couldn't decipher, and she wondered if she'd said the wrong thing. It wasn't as if the mural were somehow unique or special; it was a copy of a picture made for the exhibit. Maybe he was objecting to the waste?

He didn't say anything, though, and for a moment she struggled to fill the gap in the conversation. "I know it sounds strange, but it's really not," she said as lightly as she could. "We're used to it. Every painted-on mural goes on a temporary wall anyway. To paint an actual wall, we need special dispensation from the museum's board of directors."

The corner of Adler's mouth twitched. "Is the bureaucracy really that bad?"

"It's not the bureaucracy—it's the building. It's not such a big problem in the newer wings, but the main body of the museum was built out of a hall from the World's Fair in 1893. It's considered a historic site, and the Heritage Association gets really picky about whatever we do. Last month someone taped a cat poster over our dumbwaiter door, and the whole department got angry letters."

"Why does the art department have a dumbwaiter?"

"Our loft used to be part of the offices for the big cheeses of the Fair, and they had big dumbwaiter shafts built in so people could send up hot dinners while they were working late. Ours still works too," she added. "The tray's gone, but the pulley and rope are pretty strong. If someone needed to hide something in a hurry and didn't mind breaking it, they'd drop it down the dumbwaiter shaft and get in through the ground-floor panel to clean up the mess later. Apparently, it was a really popular way to get rid of illegal booze back in the twenties."

Adler laughed for real this time. For a moment his posture loosened, and the taut strain went out of the lines of his form; with shoulders relaxed, he looked younger than before. His eyes had a warmth the rest of his colors didn't—halfway between tawny and auburn, with a glint of reflected light in them that bypassed her mental Pantone charts and went straight to whiskey. Old whiskey, the good stuff that could make your head swim if you weren't careful with it.

Oh, damn, this was a dangerous line of thinking. Clearly Aki had been right about her needing to get out more.

It had been a while since she'd been to lunch with a man who wasn't Aki. Her last relationship had ended by mutual consent when both of them realized that they were sticking together purely out of boredom and inertia—not the stuff dreams are made of. Throwing herself into her work had been one way to stave off loneliness and avoid getting herself into another mess. But if she was reacting like this because a donor was good-looking and friendly, then she had good reason to pull herself back. This was how flaky artists, not professionals, acted.

If she wasn't professional, she wasn't anything.

She was answering one of his questions about the department's reconstructions of tomb paintings when a flash of color caught her eye. It was gold—no, too brown—bronze, real prehistoric bronze, not a color typically found in Loop bars. She turned her head as she tried to catch the source of it.

It was one of the TVs. It was showing a news broadcast, the voices of the anchors almost drowned out by the noise in the dining room. Inset behind the two reporters was a picture of an ancient bronze shield, looking vaguely familiar and out of place next to the coifed pair.

"—taken a shocking turn," one of the reporters was saying. "Sources within the university's administrative branch have informed us that far from being the simple act of vandalism originally believed, the events of last night were a deliberate attack on one of the city's oldest institutions."

Theo's stomach clenched. Adler cocked his head curiously, and she realized that she'd trailed off in the middle of a sentence. "I'm sorry," she said. "The news—"

His gaze followed hers to the TV, and his jaw tightened. The screen was showing the front of a familiar stone archway.

It wasn't her museum, but she knew it anyway: the Oriental Institute of Chicago, known for its collection of artifacts related to the ancient Near East. It was an odd place, quiet and dim, its galleries filled with out-of-the-way corners where a girl could get comfortable with a sketch pad.

The news crawl below the image was talking about crime statistics, and the reporter made that face they made when serious stories didn't involve murder or anything else exciting.

"—detected the alarm shortly after three o'clock," she said, "by which point the collection had already been emptied. Shards of stone were found on the floor of the gallery, but we don't know at this time whether the stolen items have in fact been destroyed—"

Theo took a deep breath. "Not another one," she whispered. The waiter refilled her water glass, but she didn't touch it.

The camera was panning across what she recognized as the Hall of Syria. It was a wreck: cases smashed, statues toppled, a rare early Christian manuscript slashed to pieces. The reporters talked on, discussing distraction tactics and whether the Collector—if this was indeed his work—harbored some kind of hatred for museums. "Someone goes to this much effort to make a mess, I'm thinking there's got to be serious issues there," one of them observed to the other, who nodded.

The screen cut to a commercial, and Theo finally turned away. A dull ache was throbbing in the back of her neck, and she massaged the muscle with the heel of her palm. It helped to have something to do with her hands.

"Jesus," she murmured. The images seemed to be burned into her brain. The Collector had wrecked items he couldn't steal before, but this... She pressed her fingertips against her eyelids, making starbursts erupt in her vision.

"So..." Adler's voice was quiet. "The Collector?"

"The Collector," she managed to say. "Or someone like him—her? Them?"

"I'd heard stories," he said, toying with his fork. His eyes were fixed on her, though, and that tension was back in his shoulders and stark lines. "It's unavoidable in certain circles these days. A cat burglar who attacks collections of Eastern artifacts and destroys what he can't take. Though the Columbian's board of directors has seemed eager to reassure its donors that everything's secure."

"We've been fine so far," she said. "We have a good security team. But I—I don't think anyone's gonna be too happy. Someone'll hear about this"—she jerked her head toward the TV—"and it'll be on the grapevine in minutes. They'll be double-checking everything, setting up new checkpoints." She shook her head. "It's gonna be a mess."

For a moment, there was silence between them. Adler's hands were flat on the table as he leaned forward slightly, the pressure leaving paler patches under his skin, and a few lines appeared in his face as his jaw tightened. Theo took a quick swallow of ice water and tried to get her nerves under control.

It didn't work. The Columbian had done a lot of business with the Oriental Institute, co-sponsoring shows and making trades of certain artifacts. The thought of THS203 sprawled half-out of a cracked case, its bandages ripped, made her throat close.

"I should go," she said. "I'm sorry, I probably should. The museum takes this kind of thing very seriously."

The words sounded canned, but they must have made some kind of sense because Adler nodded. "All right," he said. "I hope this won't cause trouble for your department."

"I wish I could promise it won't."

She tried to ask for the check, but Adler insisted on taking care of it. He seemed concerned about her reaction to the news and asked a few times if she was feeling well. Her hands trembled as she and Seth drove back toward the museum.

Work on the mural had stopped. Five team members were gathered around Jake Stiegler, who was streaming footage from a local news site through his phone. Aki glanced up as Theo slipped in next to him. "How was your date?" he whispered.

"Fine, and it wasn't a date. I came back as soon as I heard." She nodded to the phone. "How'd you guys hear?"

"Document Preservation heard it first. They passed it to Anthropology, who passed it to Egyptology, who passed it to us." Aki shook his head. "The board probably knows by now. Ten bucks says the exhibit gets postponed while they reevaluate everything."

Theo grimaced. Postponed was one step from canceled. If the board thought the museum's security was in danger of being compromised, they would be willing to lose the revenue of a big exhibit if it meant protecting the rest of the collection. Six months of work down the drain.

She watched the newscast as long as she could stand it, but that wasn't long. The images of smashed cases and destroyed relics did something strange to her stomach. "I'll be back in a few," she murmured to Aki. "I need to go check on something."

"Saying hi to your friends?" Aki whispered back.

"No comment."

* * *

She wasn't in the labs so often these days, but she'd spent plenty of time on sketches there a few months back, and she still had fond memories of the place. Her boys were right where she'd last seen them, arranged on shelves in a climate-controlled cabinet, staring calmly back at her.

"Hey there, guys," Theo murmured as she patted the glass. The three dozen statuettes looked back and didn't answer. Like always.

They came in various shapes and sizes, all obviously handmade by someone without much technical skill. Skill, though, wasn't what made the experts so excited. The sheer number and variety of the shabtis, especially in an early Middle Kingdom burial, were unheard of. The thirty-six in front of her were barely a fraction of the cache.

Aki knew she had a fondness for the little guys, but he didn't share it. *Geez, no wonder,* he'd said when he found out. *Men who don't talk back.* She'd rolled her eyes at him and left it at that.

It was almost impossible to explain that the shabtis did talk. Sort of.

Seven were the classic mummiform shabtis, hands crossed over their chests, their bodies bound into stiff, upright shapes and scored with shallow lines to indicate the shapes of the bandaging. Formulaic spells were etched into their bodies, calling on the gods to favor their owner. The next four were unusual specimens: unpainted clay figurines in the shape of overseers, more spells chiseled into their bodies. The rest were soldiers in various poses of drawing a bow, tying a sandal, kneeling to pray, or fastening a cloak. Every single one had the lines of crude hiero-glyphics etched into its back or its chest—the thing marking them as part of the same cache.

The academics had several theories about how the shabtis had been made and why and by whom. Models of workers were common grave goods in the early Middle Kingdom, but almost none had been made of this type of clay, and they never featured the unique prayers that were carved into these specimens. Dr. Van Allen himself had been seen to raise an eyebrow over the subject.

But to Theo, veteran of art school and project deadlines, they looked like end-of-the-semester work. The sculptor had been making a few of this, a few of that, and then throwing in a couple of yet another type and hoping numbers would make up for the fact that he appeared to have been drunk when he was writing the hieroglyphs. Three of the little guys had gaping holes in their chests, with dimpled marks in the remaining clay where a wad of organic matter must have been stuffed to pad them out.

Working fast and working sloppily, then, but determined to make as many as possible. In the afterlife, these shabtis would come alive and serve their master. It literally was a matter of life and death.

But being sloppy wasn't their fault, was it? They didn't mean to hurt anyone, and they certainly hadn't given anyone trouble. Smiling, she patted the glass again, bonding with that ancient sculptor.

"Been there and done that, brother," she said softly. She bet he'd be happy to know how long his work had lasted.

She leaned her forehead against the glass and looked into the eyes of the closest shabti. He was in soldier form, holding a bow and arrow. Half of his face had sloughed off years ago, leaving a single eye with a dot of Pacific-blue paint in it. Given the other members of the collection, she guessed the soldier had been made early on, when the sculptor thought he had more time to spend on the details.

The face was crudely modeled, with a stub of a nose and no mouth at all, but something about the tilt of the one eye and the low, relaxed shoulders spoke to Theo. The model looked...amused, almost. In a calm way. He wasn't exactly having a ball, but he was in a good place and taking things as they came.

With a few details, an anonymous man four thousand years ago had made something that could evoke emotion in her. It might not have made it to the realm of the gods, but the shabti still had life.

"Good for you," she told it.

CHAPTER FOUR

I didn't think it was history when I was doing it. I thought I didn't want to die or have my expedition declared a failure by my king. Later, the libraries would tell me different—that it was a historic moment, a turning point in world affairs. Historic moments always smell like shit and dirt.

- From the personal journal of Aelfred the Black,
circa 1191 ACE (fragment)

The morning dawned gray and cold. A fresh inch of snow covered the city, fat flakes drifting down lazily on the chilly wind off the lake, and Theo put on two jackets before leaving her apartment.

The whole city seemed reluctant to wake up. Traffic on Lake Shore Drive was sluggish, and the holiday cheer scattered throughout the Loop seemed tired and shrill against the gray sky. The keycard reader on the Columbian's south staff entrance had an actual icicle hanging from it.

Inside, the museum was sluggishly beginning its day. Pipes groaned and creaked as extra heat pumped through to bring the place back to life. Theo shared the elevator with a man holding a tray of dead pine martens. The smell of formaldehyde was overwhelming, and she tried not to breathe too deeply as the elevator made its agonizingly slow crawl up to the eaves of the building.

The loft had the air of a wake. People gathered in small clusters and talked quietly, their expressions grim or worried or simply confused. The board had convened; now it was time to wait and see.

Theo sipped her coffee as she opened her email. Twelve messages, most of them work related: a list of the winners of the employee raffle, an angry note about a missing lunch cc'd to the entire top floor, a message from sadler@adlerfinancial.com, and three new security bulle-tins. Wait, what?

Theo eyed her inbox, trying to decide which of the messages she wanted to open first. Personal issues versus professional issues...tough call. She closed her eyes and clicked randomly.

```
From: Mark Zimmer <security01@columbian.net>
To: All
Subj: Re: Security bulletin 2.0

Addendum to previous bulletin—

REMINDER: All forms of social media are considered
"issuing a public statement." Even if your profile is
set to Private, somebody will find a way to share it.
Until further notice, please DO NOT discuss the so-
called Collector robberies, museum security, or
internal museum policy of any kind in public venues
such as Facebook, Twitter, etc. For a partial list of
prohibited topics and venues, see the attached file.

Please remember that this is not an infringement on
your freedom of speech or a, to quote Mr. Lee's last
mass email, "Nazi-like" restriction. Information
publicly available is a tool for potential thieves,
and we have to be prepared to deny them anything we
can.

Call the Security office if you have questions.
```

She scrolled through the other messages. The remaining bulletins held no surprises, mostly reminding everyone of the rules. Employees must wear IDs prominently displayed and be prepared to offer addi-tional identification when questioned by authorized personnel. Nobody was to say anything to the media. The Security office would be conduct-ing an internal review, rescreening everyone with access to sensitive areas and especially valuable items.

That last item added another pound or two to the lead weight in Theo's stomach. Her access rating was fairly high, thanks to that time spent in the prep rooms sketching mummies and shabtis. Granted, a security review wouldn't turn up anything more damning than a couple of college fines for paint-spattered dorm rugs, but that didn't mean Theo wanted the hassle. Knowing that someone was sitting there pawing through her records made her flesh creep.

Shaking her head, she closed the emails and finished off her calorie-laden coffee. Maybe those personal issues wouldn't be so bad. She opened another message.

```
From: Seth Adler <sadler@adlerfinancial.com>
To: Theodora Speer <tlspeer@columbian.net>
Subj: Lunch

Miss Speer—

I'm sorry that our lunch yesterday ended so abruptly.
Is there a chance we could give it another try? I
enjoyed talking with you. Please call me.
```

And, at the end, a standard text signature with home, office, and cell numbers attached.

Theo sat back in her chair. Around her, the loft came to life as the furnace heat permeated the last cracks of the building. Someone was humming circus music—either an attempt at distraction or a coded act of aggression toward Stiegler, whose coulrophobia was legendary. Life went on.

Theo knew she wasn't a very insightful person. If she had been, her last relationship might not have ended with a whimper instead of a bang. But though she'd never expected to really understand someone like Seth Adler, it was beginning to bother her that she couldn't.

But she remembered the way Adler had looked yesterday. Hard angles and lines, contrasted subtly by the suit that showed a little wear and the droplets of melting snow dotting his hair and skin. The wry humor, the small smile, the strange attitudes he wore in his body that disrupted the image of the sleek businessman.

She ducked her head and covered her face with both hands. Her cheeks were warming again, and there was a strange tremulous sensation in the pit of her stomach. She needed perspective on this, or she'd do something stupid. Time to call in the cavalry.

"Hey, Aki!" she called over the low cubicle wall. "Adler wants me to go out with him again!"

"Woo-hoo! Is he gonna put out this time?"

Theo rolled her eyes and, knowing her friend, waited. Footsteps moved toward her and Aki's head popped over the edge of the cubicle.

"Seriously, though," he added conversationally, "from the way you were acting yesterday, I thought it was a massive disaster. Do you really want to try again?"

"I don't know," she said, looking up at Aki. "I mean, I like him—sort of. He's funny when he unbends. But he's a donor, which means spending time with him is dating inside the workplace. Technically. And I think I kind of flaked out at the end when I heard about the robbery..."

She let her head sag into her folded arms. "Argh! I'm confused as hell, Aki. Help. I don't think Zimmer's security alerts covered this."

"Huh, I'm surprised. He covered everything else." Aki came around the cubicle wall and perched on the edge of Theo's desk. "Hey, did you hear we can't use Facebook anymore? My mom's gonna be pissed about that."

"No, we just can't discuss the robberies or the museum on Facebook. Are you gonna help me or not? I'm at a loss here."

"Tell him dinner instead. You two seemed to get along a lot better when there was wine involved."

"And how the hell do you know that?" Theo said archly, mock-offended.

Aki stretched. "You're not the only one who can eavesdrop, remember. People get an eyeful of goofy ol' Aki and figure he doesn't have a brain in his head. I saw Adler playing with his pocket watch and you were actually smiling at him."

"Stalker."

"Nah. Think of me as more like a bodyguard." Aki picked up the family photo in the Disneyland frame and made a face. "FYI, you should get rid of this before Stiegler has a shit fit. Huron was singing 'It's a Small World' while you were at lunch yesterday, and they really got into it."

"Focus, Aki," she said wryly. "Please. So you think I should suggest dinner?"

"Yep. More distractions, plus wine. And if he turns you down, bonus—no more conflicting feelings."

"That's a little sneaky of you, Aki. I knew we were friends for a reason." She took back the photo and put it facedown on the desk, obscuring the offending cartoon characters. Aki hopped down off the desk, and she shooed him away before turning back to the computer.

```
Dear Mr. Adler,

That sounds good to me! I should be the one apologiz-
ing, though—it was me that ran out on you. I promise
it won't happen again. :)
```

Unfortunately we have to finish up the exhibition
prep ASAP, so lunch outside the museum really isn't
an option right now. If you've got time after 6 PM,
though, we could go grab a working dinner someplace
near.

Theo Speer

Not perfect, but it would do. Send. With a sigh, she pushed her chair back and cracked her knuckles, working out the kinks in her fingers and wrists.

The most recent layers of paint were curing downstairs, and would be for most of the morning. Since the delay was unavoidable, she was automatically slated to help with the inevitable last-minute ephemera of every massive exhibit: posters, brochures, wrangles about photograph resolution and saturation, and the hundreds of other little things that made up a museum experience.

As she flipped through her to-do list, the email window lit up.

I like that idea. Maybe if we move fast enough, our
jobs won't be able to drag us back.

Tonight isn't possible, but how about tomorrow? I can
pick you up at the museum at 6:15.

Italian this time, maybe? With no televisions on the
side, I promise. S.A.

"Surprisingly not disastrous," Theo murmured as she typed her acceptance. Her stomach still felt a little queasy, but she did her best to ignore it.

Fortunately for her peace of mind, she was kept busy all morning. Yesterday's commotion had disrupted the painting schedule, and now they were in a rush to finish the mural before their tight pre-exhibition schedules became too hopelessly skewed. By eleven o'clock they had laid down most of the mural's color patches and were ready to do detail work.

Theo was eating lunch at her desk when the department started buzzing again. Administrative emails, mostly from Egyptology, were flying with wild abandon. Only a handful had been accidentally cc'd to the entire museum staff, but that was enough for everyone to know that the board had come to a decision.

As Theo finished her burrito, a crowd gathered by the door. Someone had come in. She caught a glimpse of a short man and a shock of graying hair.

Well, that meant one thing. She scrunched up her burrito wrapper and dropped it in the trash. The denizens of the aerie gathered around Van Allen, and Theo joined them. Aki was already there, his hands coated with charcoal from sketching.

"What's the word?" Theo whispered. Aki shrugged.

Dr. Van Allen called for silence, and the grumbling artists and technicians gradually settled down. As short as he was, Theo could barely see the top of his head through the small crowd, but she could hear him clearly enough. It was impossible to judge his mood from his words, though. Unlike Dr. Schechter, who would attack a new project with the tireless energy of a bloodhound on the scent, Wayne Van Allen always had the same blank façade for whatever was presented to him.

"Attention, please," he called out, and the last of the talkers quieted. "Thank you. First, allow me to say that the work you've been doing has been very encouraging. The exhibition is ahead of schedule, and I can say with confidence that it's going to make quite the impression once it opens."

"But," Aki muttered.

"But there's been a change in the exhibition materials."

Aki elbowed Theo, and she gave him a quick shove back and hissed at him to be quiet.

"The museum recently engaged in a series of negotiations with Oxford University, which is conducting a study on tuberculosis in pre-New Kingdom mummies. In light of recent events, we've agreed to offer them THS203—"

A babble of protest broke out before he could continue. "Bogus!" Aki yelled, and half a dozen of the others agreed. Theo didn't try to stop him; she was thinking the same thing.

Mummies were getting rarer every year. A good specimen, especially one with such a strange background as THS203, was invaluable. A tuberculosis study could mean anything from noninvasive scans to active dissection, which would as good as destroy the specimen.

Either way, it was leaving them with no mummy and no centerpiece for the tomb re-creation. Everything the lofts had been working on would need to be altered, reshuffled, or redone completely. Maybe the exhibition wasn't being canceled, but Dr. Van Allen's announcement was going to mean scrapping half of the work they'd already completed.

The curator held up his hands for quiet, and the loud complaining reluctantly subsided. "I know this is going to make more work for us," he said, adjusting his glasses. "But this decision hasn't been made lightly, and I promise you this is going to be good for the whole museum. As an incentive for offering the mummy, we've been guaranteed the first pick of the Pompeii artifacts coming out of Florence in the next year."

That got a murmur from the assembled artists and workers. Pompeii was a hell of a draw, and the historical society in Florence was producing new macabre casts of the ancient victims. A Pompeii exhibit, especially on a semi-permanent basis, could go a long way toward keeping the museum in the black.

"So…overtime, right?" Aki said, crossing his arms. The technicians wouldn't be too happy about that; they'd already put a lot of time and effort in on the project, and running new wiring for parts of the gallery would be a pain in the ass. The artists, on the other hand, were more than fifty percent independent contractors and needed every hour they could justify billing.

"Overtime," Van Allen confirmed. "Two of the interactives are being moved to cover the wall, and the remaining space will need a simplistic mural. With so little time, we won't be able to order prints or plaques, so anybody who's free to join a gridding team, let your group leaders know now. Speer, I trust you can supply our mural needs?"

He said it mildly, ordering a painting as if it were a pizza with extra cheese, but Theo could see her scant spare time vanishing down the drain.

"To replace the mummy?" she said, frowning. That whole display, replaced with another mural? It had to be good, and it also had to be done quickly. "On the west wall…"

She could see the layout in her mind's eye, the setup the department had been working on for weeks. Without the mummy itself, the important element of immersion would be lost. She had to come up with some way to pull them back into the ancient world. It was Empires of India without the life-size elephant, Travels with Early Man minus its mammoth-tusk hut. Something to pull the visitors into the world, something in two dimensions that would make them feel as if it were in three…

"The west wall," she repeated. Not a light bulb, but a spark nevertheless. And on the east wall...oh. Oooh.

"I think I have a couple of ideas," she added slowly. Van Allen raised an eyebrow at that. "But I'll need to get to work now, so someone'll have to take my spot on the first mural team. I can get you the prelims tomorrow, okay?"

"Tomorrow morning." There was slight but noticeable emphasis on the second word. "We have to be practical."

"Is that what they're calling it these days? 'Practical'?" Aki muttered in Theo's ear as the group broke apart. She swatted him lightly on the arm, but it was an automatic reaction; her mind was focused on other things.

Three dimensions, walls, staring eyes. Potentially eerie, but also potentially fascinating. She picked up her tablet and began to sketch.

A few minutes later, her computer pinged. She had email. Apprehensive, she opened the message.

```
From: Akeela Lee <ajlee@columbian.net>
To: art peeps list <tlspeer@columbian.net,
jknorth@columbian.net, jlvladashvili@columbian.net,
ptstein@columbian.net, rtfenicki@columbian.net, znmc-
mann@columbian.net>
Subj: pompeii?

Ten bucks says it's not just ths03 going AWOL. Board
meetings just to trade one mummy? Yeah right. Bet he
wants to get as many exhibits off grounds and out of
the museum as possible so there won't be liabilities
when stuff gets stolen.


From: Jared North <jknorth@columbian.net>
To: Akeela Lee <ajlee@columbian.net>
cc: art peeps list
Subj: Re: pompeii?

Who cares?


From: Akeela Lee <ajlee@columbian.net>
To: Jared North <jknorth@columbian.net>
cc: art peeps list
Subj: Re: pompeii?

>Who cares?
```

> Everyone, genius. Work is going to get a lot harder
> to come by soon. How's your resume?

There was more, mostly passive-aggressive sniping between the team members, but Theo didn't read much of it. Though the loss of THS203 had been tempered by the possibilities for fresh designs, Aki's commentary had put dark thoughts into her head.

If the museum's response to the Collector threat was to batten down the hatches and trade away some of their more likely targets, then they probably wouldn't be accepting many new exhibitions either. And without a constant rotation of shows requiring new designs, brochures, and graphics, much of the art department—including Theo—would be superfluous.

Looking for a distraction, she checked her voice mail. Her mother wanted to know if she'd heard about the robbery, and whether she was still going to watch the Deerfield house for them while they were in Taos.

Theo texted back a plural affirmative and tried not to think about what she'd be doing for Christmas. Maybe she could have friends over to the house? They could buy a couple of cases of the cheapest stuff they could find, like they had done when they were in school. Ringing in the birth of Jesus with a hangover sounded good.

If her friends weren't doing anything for Christmas. Which was about as likely as the Collector spontaneously turning himself in.

With a sigh, Theo turned back to her new designs. 'Twas the season for getting her ass in gear.

And for breaking dinner dates. The sight of the open email tab reminded her, and her heart sank at the thought. Sending another email changing her mind might make it appear that she'd panicked. After a moment's hesitation, she picked up her cell phone and dialed the number from the email footer.

"Seth Adler," came the brisk voice. He sounded somewhat distracted.

"Mr. Adler?" she said. "This is, uh, this is Theo Speer."

"Morning, Miss Speer. I got your email." There was warmth in his voice. "I hope you didn't have your heart set on anything too popular. At six o'clock in the Loop, you'd have better luck getting a ringside seat at the Colosseum."

"Nah, I'm flexible. But—well, I'm sorry, Mr. Adler—"

"Just Seth, please."

"Uh, Seth. I'm sorry, I can't make it." Theo cradled the phone awk-wardly, tucking it between her jaw and shoulder as she picked up her stylus again. "Everything's gotten crazy, and they need me here for at least the next week. I don't know if we can meet up anytime soon."

"What happened?" Adler sounded worried, and Theo heard a screech of tires from the other end of the line. Talking while driving; and from the sound of it, he'd pulled over abruptly. "Is this about the break-in at the Oriental Institute? Are you all right?"

"I'm fine, and the museum's fine." She couldn't quite keep a small smile off her face. "There've been changes to the exhibition, that's all. Our friend Number Three had to duck out early, and they need me to draft a new mural to cover the spot where his sarcophagus would have gone."

"'Duck out early'?" Adler repeated. He still sounded worried, but covered it with a veil of light humor. "Seems somebody's been reading from the Book of the Dead. Do you need help catching a runaway mummy?"

"I don't think anyone could stop it this time." Theo selected the eraser tool and rubbed out a problematic area. "Number Three's been called up by the Oxford Egyptological Society. They're doing a big study on tuberculosis in pre-New Kingdom mummies, and one of the speci-mens they'd planned on using was withdrawn by its owner." She rear-ranged her grip on the stylus and began to sketch again, outlining the familiar shape of a human body with quick, easy strokes. "The Colum-bian's offered it to Oxford in exchange for a lot of Pompeii stuff every-one's been panting over."

"What a waste," he said bluntly. "Whose decision was this?"

"That would be the board." She filled him in on the latest devel-opments and rumors. "But it's not that bad, really. We still get the tomb goods—and if they decide the mummy's not what they need, or finish the scan without needing to autopsy, we can have it back." Six quick lines, curved and bunched, created the rough shape of a coffin. "It's really tough to get mummies for studies like this these days, since so many of them are owned by governments that don't allow invasive procedures. And we get the Pompeii stuff and Number Three back if we're lucky." She shifted the phone to her other shoulder as the man began to emerge from the digital lines. On a whim, she threw down the first shapes of his face: long, flat nose, generously curved mouth, weary eyes. "But that means I'm on overtime. Rain check?"

"Of course." The tension had ebbed out of his voice, and she could hear the revving of the car's motor as he pulled back onto the highway. "How's next Monday?"

"Perfect."

She ended the conversation feeling somewhat more relaxed. Monday was a few days off, but by the time it came around she would have a lot less on her plate. Then she could focus on this whatever-it-was with Mr. Adler. Seth.

For now, though, she needed to find her copy of Gardiner's *Egyptian Grammar*. The new painting presented a different angle on the burial chamber, and the visible inscriptions would be different. Was it "n mwt.f dt" or "m nwt.f dt"?

The book turned up underneath a stack of printouts. Sighing, Theo unearthed it and flipped through the dog-eared pages. Her desire for accuracy was a double-edged sword: It sometimes left her squinting at rows of near-identical symbols and desperately trying to find a photograph of the burial chamber that wasn't blurred or shadowed.

Okay. "M nwt.f dt" it was.

Theo didn't speak ancient Egyptian. She knew the alphabet and a few phrases and vocabulary words from the exhibition texts; that was all. But the syllables were like music, and music was a step away from color. She pinned each syllable to a color and painted them in the back of her mind, memorizing the matches and clashes and what they meant to her.

Life was confusing. Men were distracting. But color? In the world of shade and tone and tint, Theo was in control. She let out a breath she didn't realize she'd been holding and settled down to work.

CHAPTER FIVE

The galley started taking on water, and for a moment, I saw her. She looked like somebody's mother, her eyes streaming or maybe just blacked. Nobody's pretty when they're losing, I suppose. So much for Greek gods.

*- Excerpt from unknown work,
circa 30 BCE (fragment)*

Theo yawned and put down the stylus. Aside from her, the loft was deserted, leaving her alone in her cubicle's bubble of light. The flatscreen monitor displayed a multicolored tangle of sketched lines spread out over half a dozen layers, each color and layer keyed to a different arrangement.

After half a dozen attempts, she found an arrangement that felt natural. Time to start building: the straggling shapes of professional mourners, the slightly bent form of a priest in the mask of Anubis, the pair of slaves struggling to support the coffin. A private funeral with few attendants.

But that was only part of it. Theo let a tired smile cross her face as she sat back in her chair, imagining it. In her painting, mourners and priests toiled to see the anonymous man buried, but across the room the real shabtis would be lined up in their stiff little rows, with cracked faces aimed toward the mural. Visitors would be the same size as the painted people, letting them meet those priests and mourners eye to eye. And when they turned away from the mural, there would be the shabtis. Watching the watchers.

Standing, Theo flexed her spine and stretched. Something cracked, something else popped, and Theo let out a soft sigh. It was almost eleven o'clock at night, and after a long time hunched over the tablet, her back was partially cramped up. Pain couldn't shake that sly sense of accomplishment, though.

She should pack it in for the night. But did she have to? With the finished image already complete in her mind, reference books open around her, and color charts fanned across the desk, it felt like the necessary tools were in place. What she needed to do was make the colors and shapes move.

Her brain fizzed with what felt like hundreds of ideas jostling to get her attention. This was the best part of any project—the moment when the first hurdle was complete and she felt like she could do anything, before the inevitable frustration and annoyance set in. She didn't want to let the feeling of excitement go.

But if she worked much longer, she'd be useless in the morning. And worse, she might do something stupid while sleep-deprived, like delete her own files. Theo massaged her cramped right hand and saved her design one last time. She really did need sleep. Driving home was going to be interesting; that was for sure.

Maybe one more stop first.

Gathering up her sketchbooks and flash drive, she finished shutting down her workstation and stood. The nighttime loft was a maze of low walls and high ceilings in deep shadow. It was a perfect place for a zombie attack, if that was your idea of a good time. Theo's imagination briefly filled the corners with crouching monsters, but it was a perfunctory nod to the darkness—it was hard to scare herself when she was so tired.

She settled her laptop bag on her hip and rattled down the loft staircase toward the elevator. There was a guard stationed next to it, and he nodded to her as she flashed her ID. She recognized him—Yuri Vladashvili, Jem's American-raised cousin who'd sponsored his student visa. He looked tired, as the night shift usually did, but he gave her a wave anyway. She waved back. Yuri was a nice guy.

She followed the familiar path on autopilot. Left, left, down the stairs, right, and she was in Preservation.

The labs were different from the loft. Here, state-of-the-art equipment was set against sterile, white-painted walls on tables swathed in protective plastic, making it look like a sci-fi movie set. There were two subdivisions: Preparation and Restoration. The handful of shabtis intended for the display had had their display mocked up a few days before, but they were still in Restoration and Theo could access them with a swipe of her card. She picked up the pace, eager to see if the figurines could add fuel to her spark of inspiration.

She rounded the corner and stopped short. She wasn't alone.

For a moment, she didn't recognize him. The man was tall and broad-shouldered, with straight black hair that came to just under his ear and a build like a career soldier. He wore heavy trousers with several pockets; a long-sleeved shirt in dull, dark gray; lightweight boots; and latex gloves. There was a duffel bag slung over his shoulder, half-filled with something bulky. And he was standing in the corridor in front of the prep lab, a lock pick in his hand.

Theo froze and the man turned. The fluorescents bleached any remaining warmth from his skin, leaving it a gray that was almost blue.

"What—"

Her hands flexed unconsciously, and her grip on her bag slipped as the lock pick fell from the man's grasp.

"Mr. *Adler*?"

Before she could get out another word, Adler grabbed her. One arm looped around, pinning her to him, while the other hand came down hard over her mouth. Theo yelled and tried to bite, but he gave her a shake and Theo was cut off by her own yelp.

"Don't say anything!" he whispered. His eyes glinted unnaturally in the low light of the corridor, and the hand over her mouth shook. "Don't say a word, Theo!"

Wait. What? *What?* Theo squirmed, trying to twist free, hoping that she would get loose and make him explain himself. There had to be a reason why the controller of the Neith Trust, the dry-humored man with the sleek suit who joked about his family issues, was standing in the prep lab with lock picks. It didn't compute. Seth Adler did not do this.

But he was. Theo looked into the dark eyes, wondering what she had been thinking. How had she not seen that he wasn't on the level? Was she that stupid, or was he that good?

"What are you doing?" she whispered behind his hand. Adler's shoulders hunched and he loosened his grip a little.

"I said don't say anything," he whispered. "There's no time. I need your card."

"My what?"

"Your card, your access card, the one that gets you into the labs! Where is it?"

Her ID was hanging loose on its lanyard, but the security card was different; she hid it in her wallet, tucked between her library card and a snapshot of her sister Edith's firstborn. Its magnetic strip would get her into every secured zone in the museum, provided she was cleared in the central computer.

"It's..." She hesitated. "I need a hand free."

He let her right arm loose, and she reached for her wallet. Her fingers trembled as she touched the plastic card. The second that card was swiped, it would open the door—but it would also record its use in the security system. Seth Adler didn't need to get into the lab for a good reason, and the system would know it was Theo who had let him in.

"Why?" she managed, half-afraid and half-incredulous. "Why are you doing this? What the hell do you want in there?"

"I need the mummy," Adler said quietly. "The mummy and the shabtis. Give me the card, Theo."

When Theo didn't let go of the card, Adler snatched it from her fingers. Theo grabbed for it, but Adler muscled her out of the way and swiped it through the scanner.

He was distracted. Theo sucked in a deep breath and lashed out.

Her foot hit the back of his knee, and he stumbled hard, almost falling. It was enough for her—she ducked away and ran for it, her shoes clacking noisily on the waxed tile of the hallway. She heard a grunt of pain, and for a moment, her heart leaped. She had done it; she had gotten away. She could get to the security desk and call the cops on the donor who'd lost his goddamn mind—

Then a hand clamped down on her arm, and Theo lurched, biting down hard on her tongue as she was yanked back.

"Let me go!" she shouted, and Adler cursed in a language she'd never heard and covered her mouth again. *Dammit dammit dammit, so close!*

"Don't even think of it," he whispered harshly. "Theo, you have no idea how important this is. If you stop me, we're both dead!"

She bit him hard this time and he recoiled, blood welling from the teeth marks as he pulled his hand away. She'd got him right through the gloves. Her mouth filled with the taste of latex and something sharp, almost like clay, and she spat the blood onto the floor.

"Stop it!" he hissed.

"What the hell is going on?" she said. "You're hanging around in the museum and trying to steal a mummy! You're a donor, for God's sake! A trustee!" She knew she was gaping disbelievingly at him, but there was no other possible reaction. Part of the situation still wasn't processing. "Aren't you rich enough?"

His face contorted. "You think this is about *money*?"

"What else—"

"Life and death." In one quick tug, he hauled her back toward the prep lab. The door was hanging open, and she knew that soon, the timed alarm would trip. If she could delay him for a few more seconds...

But he seemed to know that trick. He pushed her into the lab and closed the door sharply behind them, sending the dropped access card skittering across the clean white floor.

In the half-light of the dimmed lab, the world looked strange and out of balance. The dim blue glow of the lights on the machines deepened the illusion of ink as black pooled in the hollows of his face. Only his eyes picked up the highlight of cold indigo, glinting as if the ink hadn't yet dried.

Theo could hear the soft whooshing of the cooling and dehumid-ifying system, pumping fresh air through the lab and filtering particles out of the atmosphere. It was like the room breathed—in, out, in, out—slow and regular, unlike the rushed, frantic creatures that intruded on it. The dim blueness barely touched the mummy in its clear plastic coffin; and as their shadows moved over it, some horrible part of Theo thought the mummy was the one breathing.

Seth broke the illusion. He snapped the light on and pulled Theo across the room, toward the mummy's chamber. Theo clawed at the hand holding her, but her short, blunted nails caught on the latex glove.

He scooped up the access card and held it out to her. "Open it," he ordered.

Theo balked. "Why me?"

"I need my other hand free. I know you can open it, Theo. Please."

Theo blinked hard, trying to keep her eyes from watering, and took the card. Her fingers slipped on the plastic as she swiped it across the scanner.

Everyone knew the rules. THS203 had to be kept at a constant temperature with no moisture in the air that could possibly start the mummy's shriveling or decaying. It was kept in a vacuum-sealed tube most of the time, but when the specialists were working on it, it would be laid out in the clear coffin. Theo had had to do a six-day course on artifact handling before being allowed in the lab to sketch. Nobody had thought someone would actually try to steal the mummy, so the code for the case was the same as the room itself.

"Oh God. Don't touch—"

Too late. Adler unrolled a fleece blanket from his duffel bag and briskly wrapped the mummy up in it, dropping brittle flakes of ancient bandaging onto the floor as he handled it. Theo flinched and almost recoiled when Seth swung the mummy off the table.

"Here, hold this." And with no further ado, he dumped the swaddled mummy into Theo's arms. She staggered, almost dropping it. It was lighter than she had expected, eerily so, but the smell of old paper and ancient incense and leather…no, dried skin…assaulted her. Her stomach lurched.

Damn it to hell. He knew that she could never drop the mummy, not when all of them had been drilled over and over about how to handle the precious antiquities.

"You son of a bitch," she spluttered, struggling to balance the stiff burden without breathing in its choking must. "You can't do this!"

"I have to." Adler yanked back the fleece covering the mummy's head and looked it in the face, dark eyes to dark eye sockets. The mummy's eternal lipless grin seemed almost sad now, smiling in the face of its newly uncertain fate. As Theo struggled with the stiff corpse, Adler covered its head again. Flakes of bandage and ancient hair drifted to the floor.

"Stop it!" Theo hissed, horrified. "You're going to destroy it!"

"It's dangerous," Seth said. "And I'm doing what I have to do. Keep hold of it and follow me, Theo."

"Like hell I will!" she snapped.

"Theo." His gaze bored into her. "I need to get this done, tonight, or horrible things are going to happen. Please. I didn't want you to be part of this, but you are now, and I have to make a decision. Bring the mummy."

Theo blinked hard. Tears, whether of anger, frustration, or pain, might drip on the mummy. "You're still not making sense."

"Please bring the mummy, Theo."

She made the mistake of taking a deep breath. The cooling system sent out a puff of fresh air, blowing the musty smell of the mummy back into her face, and she choked and almost dropped the thing. "Can't we stop?" she managed to say, dampness beading in her eyes as she struggled to breathe. She jerked her head back to keep the tears from falling. "Stop and think for five seconds. Please. Why are you doing this?"

He didn't answer, just rearranged his grip on his own bag, jaw set.

"You've spent so much time and money helping us. We talked about preserving the past—"

"And that's what I'm doing." He pulled on her shoulder, forcing her to move to avoid dropping poor, awful THS203. "Preserving something and preventing disaster. Not that I've done so well at that so far, it seems."

It was a short walk from the lab to the artifacts restoration bay, but to Theo it felt like miles. She kept glancing up at the security cameras, wondering why the guard desk hadn't noticed anything yet. How could they not have sounded the alarm? Seth Adler was robbing the museum, and nobody was doing anything!

Seth Adler is the Collector.

More shabtis stood where they'd been on the night of the party, lined up in neat rows. Their crumbled faces stared blankly at Theo, withholding comment or judgment. For a moment, as the shadows moved over them, their tilted smiles and blank eyes mirrored Adler's. A powerful urge to smash the smirking statuettes overwhelmed her, edging her vision with red. She sucked in another breath and tried to focus.

Adler knew what he was there for. He bypassed racks of shining jewelry—perfectly restored, less fragile and easier to carry—and made straight for the shabtis. Burdened by the mummy, Theo couldn't run, and she watched in helpless fury as he wrapped each shabti in a twist of cloth and dropped them into his duffel bag.

Then the phone rang.

Both of them jumped, nearly dropping everything. The yellow light blinking on the lab phone meant that it was an all-lines call, and Theo's heart leaped. Finally!

"What's that?" Adler whispered.

Theo swallowed.

"Security check-in," she lied. "If no one answers, they'll know something's wrong."

Adler let out a short, frustrated breath, and Theo knew he was weighing his options. *Let me answer it,* she silently pressed. The call would have gone out to all secured internal lines, but once the receiver was picked up, the system would pinpoint every line that answered. It was supposed to help locate lost after-hours guests or guards whose walkie-talkies weren't working. *Come on, come on.*

"Answer it," he said. "Keep it short." Theo nodded and picked up the receiver.

"This is Theo Speer," she said conversationally, sandwiching the receiver between her ear and shoulder so she could maintain a grip on the mummy. Her arms were beginning to ache, and she tried not to think about what would happen if she dropped or damaged the thing. "It looks like no one answered the all-call. Is everything okay?"

"No!" the voice of Mark Zimmer, security consultant par anal, came back. "Speer, what the hell's going on? Why are you in Restoration? The system's been on the fritz—we only got it back online a minute ago—and the alarms on that floor are screaming!"

The alarms were screaming? Maybe whatever Adler had done to the system was wearing off. Either way, it was good news for Theo. "All quiet here," she said, trying to figure out how to warn Zimmer without the crazy thief realizing what she was up to. Pig Latin probably wouldn't do the trick.

Said thief was uncomfortably close now. He'd pressed his head close to hers, straining to listen in on what Zimmer was saying, and Theo had no time to put the mummy between them as some kind of dehydrated chaperone. She felt the rasp of coarse skin and stubble, and the warmth of his breath on her cheek. He smelled like old leather and male sweat—salty and coppery and brassy, the smell of how new blood tastes. Theo's cheeks flamed, and she could feel her heart skip a beat. Oh goddammit.

"Stay where you are," Zimmer was saying. "Somebody's definitely loose in here. I'm sending a security team up for you now, got it? Stay put."

Adler cursed as Zimmer hung up. "This wasn't supposed to happen," he muttered. "I swear, Theo, this wasn't the plan. It was supposed to be simple."

She didn't know what to say to that. He sounded sincere, but he was still doing—what?

"Look," Theo said softly, trying to ignore the persistent ache in her arms. "Things could be worse. You can wait for the team with me, and we'll tell them you snapped because of stress. You must be able to afford a really good lawyer. Or you can leave and I'll tell them that I didn't see your face. I wouldn't tell—thieves aren't allowed to patronize the museum or give grants to the art department, and we really need that Trust—"

That was evidently the wrong thing to say because Adler turned his dark gaze on her. Her heart gave another flip-flop as he let out a short, hot breath. "The art department."

And then he said, *"The air shaft,"* making Theo want to groan. Never before had her eager talkativeness gone so badly wrong. The unguarded, secret air shaft, left over from its dumbwaiter days.

The mummy was yanked out of her arms and the bag of shabtis thrust into them. Adler tucked the mummy under his arm and grabbed Theo with his free hand. "Just a little farther," he whispered. "We're going up."

They went up. Feet slapping on the concrete stairs, breathing harshly in the close corridors, they climbed toward the sky. As they turned on the third landing, Theo realized that he was following the same route she'd taken from the loft to prep. Was that why he had attended the donors' party, then? To scope the place out? She felt sick and stumbled for a moment.

Adler braced her easily with one arm, balancing the mummy with the other. The muscles stood out hard under the rumpled cloth. Not a banker's arm. How could she have missed these details when she'd met him?

She kept her ears open as they hurried along. She kept hoping to hear the clatter of the guards' feet on the concrete, but Adler moved like the devil was at his heels, and Theo was dragged along in his wake.

The aerie was as she'd left it. Her chair was pushed out, and her disorganized office supplies cast strange, spiky shadows onto her desktop, thanks to a lamp she'd forgotten to turn off. The loft looked the same as it always did at the end of a long day, when it was her alone with her thoughts. So much for peace of mind.

Adler found the dumbwaiter shaft easily—a plain, white-metal panel, standing out sharply against the esoteric mess of posters and project blueprints that the art department layered onto its walls.

"I see it's been painted over," he said, twisting the latch. "Did you get special dispensation from the board to do that?"

It was such a familiar thing to say that Theo started. For a moment, he was back to his former self—the small quirk of the fluid lips and the inquisitive tilt to the head—as if he were planning to dodge work and wanted to know if she was up for it.

He watched her for a moment, the latch in hand, seemingly waiting for a response. She clutched the shabtis and said nothing.

"All right." The humor disappeared as Theo failed to respond. He yanked hard, pulling the panel out from the wall. As he peered down the shaft, though, he recoiled. Apparently, he had forgotten the sheer, fifteen-story drop.

Theo saw his eyes dart to the old spool system, the bungee cords dangling down into the shadows of the shaft, and her stomach lurched as she realized what he was contemplating. Before now, the whole experience had had a horribly dreamlike quality. Now she knew, without asking or making a conscious decision, that someone would die.

"Don't be crazy," she said softly. "Please. It's not worth it."

He turned to her, and something in that dark stare made her shiver. *Dammit dammit dammit dammit!* Panic had a lot to answer for.

"It isn't," he said. "Not forever, anyway."

He pulled the bag of shabtis out of her hands. Theo stumbled, instinctively grabbing for them, but Adler knew what he was doing and had them in his hands before she could tighten her grasp. He opened the bag and seized a shabti, seemingly at random, his fingers trembling as they gripped the ancient clay.

As Theo watched, he raised it to eye level. His lips parted, and she heard the softest of sighs as he breathed on the little thing.

"Don't be crazy," she repeated, almost without realizing it.

Seth didn't answer.

He'd locked the door and had her key. She had to stop him. She reached for the shabti, but he dodged her hand, snake-fast. As she fought to reach something, anything, he strung the first artifact from the bungee cord and sent it sailing down the shaft.

"Give…them…back!" Theo panted as Seth blocked her grab again. "That cable's as old as the museum! It'll break! You'll die, and they'll be *destroyed!*"

He grabbed her arm and Theo stamped hard on his foot. He lurched and his grip loosened. She stamped again, and he grabbed her other arm and pulled her away from the wall.

The layout crew had their own alcove with an industrial printer and a cutting table, away from the dumbwaiter panel, and Adler made use of it. He pushed Theo, and she stumbled enough for him to force her down onto her knees. Before she knew what was happening, her wrists were zip-tied around the leg of the heavy cutting table and Adler had stepped away. His face was pale and drawn, his expression unreadable.

"Theo..." He looked down at her, lips parted, seemingly trying to find words. "I didn't mean... This wasn't the plan. I swear."

Theo grunted as she tried to shift the table. It wasn't bolted down—if she could lift it, she could slide the zip tie off the table leg—

But the museum never threw out anything if it could save money by keeping it, and the cutting table was a massive metal beast with a scratchproof stone top. She got her shoulder under one end and heaved, breathing hard through clenched teeth. Pain shot through her arm and back as the edge of the table dug hard into the skin there, wrenching her downward even as her trembling legs forced her upward.

Her knees gave out and she slumped back onto the ground, sweat streaking her forehead. Adler turned his back to her and was busy at the dumbwaiter door, attaching the bag to the cable.

Something rattled on the edge of Theo's hearing, and her heart leaped. It was a familiar sound, almost too familiar for her to recognize if the shaft opening hadn't amplified it. It was...oh please...the rattle of the freight elevator coming up.

It was slowing. Stopping. One floor below. They had to find her before he could get away. Taking another, deeper breath, she pitched her voice as loud as she could: "Zimmer! Help! We're up here!"

Adler swore. His hand slipped on the cords, and a dull boom echoed up the shaft as the bag banged against the side of it.

"I'll drop it!" he said, rounding on her.

Theo met his gaze and held it.

"Not right now, you won't," she rasped. "You want them too much. Zimmer! Help!"

He hissed in wordless frustration as he hauled on the cords. More clangs and clatters echoed up the shaft. Theo froze, tensing at the sound, her heart breaking for the dead man and the little figures in the bag.

Adler took the pause to finish feeding the last of the rope through the spool. It unwound and spiraled down out of sight.

Theo tried to yell again, but Adler moved first. He crouched down in front of her and clamped his hand over her mouth, pressing the back of her head into the side of the table. She snarled and tried to bite him again, but he'd learned his lesson and kept his fingers out of range of her teeth.

"Please," he said softly. "Try to believe me. I have a good reason."

He smelled like leather and dusty old cloth. This close, she could see the subtler details in his face—the small folds in the corners of his eyes and mouth, the deep color of his irises, the smattering of graying stubble across his jaw. The skin lay close over the tendons and muscles of his neck, and Theo's brain automatically threw out a note from her anatomy studies: *Dehydration sharpens features.* His lips were dry and cracked.

For a moment, she searched his face, looking for signs of the Seth Adler she'd met before. He looked like a man with a terminal illness, his expression drawn and horribly sad. No, not sad: resigned. Theo cataloged the face as she always did, checking off the shape of his features and the set of his mouth, and part of her brain stirred and said, *He's serious.*

"Then let me go," she said against his hand, her voice hoarse. "Please. Give it back and things can go back to the way they used to be."

"I can't. I'm sorry." His hand went to the back of Theo's head, winding into the tousled blonde hair. His gaze was fixed on hers, his expression begging her to understand. "Theo, I was going to…I wanted to talk to you. It was going to be different." His thumb traced the shell of her ear, skating lightly over the skin. "I was going to be someone different." He cradled her, breath warm against her face. "I swear."

"You didn't have to be someone different," she said. "I liked the one I already knew."

His lips parted. Those eyes—God, she felt like she was watching something being destroyed. A sculpture smashed. He was so close to her.

Then the elevator rattled, and Theo came to her senses. She recoiled from him. His face twisted, and he fell back and climbed to his feet.

"I told you," he said. "No choice now." There was color in his face, and his breath was coming hard and fast.

Theo's world spun, and she felt like she was about to fall off the edge into space. *What the hell happened?*

Before she could summon up any words, Seth stumbled to his feet and shucked his jacket. He bundled it up and dropped it down the shaft, his hands trembling. Then he moved to Aki's cubicle.

Her friend's desk was littered with painting supplies, and Seth flicked through the jars and tubes with a grim sureness. He hesitated a split second before seizing a large square bottle full of clear liquid.

"Don't," Theo managed to say. "Please."

He didn't look at her. His face was pale, but he uncapped the bottle and drank it down.

Part of being an artist was knowing how to use the tools correctly. What to do, what not to do, what could mix, what was dangerous. Theo had been called unimaginative and stupid, but she was nothing if not methodical in her work. The man who'd robbed her had just drunk the most toxic paint thinner they had.

He gasped out a short breath that cut off abruptly. Blood appeared on his mouth, staining his teeth an incongruous pink. He tried to keep standing, instinctively fighting, but the stuff was made to do its work well and Theo knew that it was already too late.

A ragged scream tore out of her as Seth Adler fell to his hands and knees. The blood was coming faster now. Theo could hear the voice of her freshman biology teacher: *Soft tissues aid in the absorption of chemical solutions, ensuring the substance's complete distribution throughout the body.* She yanked on the zip tie, knowing she had to get free, had to do something! Tears streamed down her face as she watched him kill himself.

Dust drifted from the hand clutched at his throat. He was incredibly dusty now, his clothes coated with fine, gray-brown particles like the samples the field researchers brought back from the Theban tombs. Blood trickled from between his lips, moving slowly as it soaked up the powder.

The dust poured from Seth now. It coated his body, turning his black clothes ash-gray and his skin the color of granite. He shuddered as his muscles clenched, and the grayness fell from his twitching fingers and left trails in the air.

And then there was nothing but the dust, and Theo couldn't restrain another scream as Seth Adler's dying body collapsed in on itself.

Hair, skin, and bones vanished into the cloud that filled the air. It spread and stained everything it touched, leaving streaks on the floor. In seconds, there was nothing left but a pile of clothes on the floor.

Theo tried to breathe, and her lungs rebelled. Her throat seized as the dust coated her. She coughed and spat, coughed and spat, tears becoming mud as they trickled down and mixed with the clay powder on her cheeks. She crouched there in the center of the loft, unable to wipe the dirty tears away, unable to breathe, unable to yell or curse or do anything but reach desperately for air that wouldn't come.

"Theo!" someone called. Theo tried to respond, but the dust seemed to be everywhere. She wept and choked and fought to speak.

"Theo!" Yuri Vladashvili was kneeling next to her. Theo blinked through the burning tears, trying to place him. Yes, Yuri. Jem's cousin, the one who mocked him mercilessly for his stilted English, while Jem repaid the favor by teasing the American-raised Yuri about his awful Russian. Yuri, who liked *CSI: Miami* and had a habit of eating Circus Peanuts on shift.

Yuri, who waved at her when she was clocking out for the night. Yuri, who was normal.

"Yu—" The name was cut off by a violent spasm of coughing.

Other security guards streamed past him, Maglites and batons at the ready. She thought she recognized Mark Zimmer—did that man ever sleep?—but she was gasping for air, and the thought was driven out of her head.

Yuri cut the zip tie around her wrists and caught her as she pitched forward. The rough plastic had rubbed her forearms raw, and blood beaded on the surface of her skin.

More guards were filling the loft, choking as they inhaled the strange dust. One of them, his hand over his mouth, had found the dumbwaiter. His shout sent the others scurrying over, shining flashlights down the shaft. "Nothing," one of them said, grim-faced.

"What about the mummy?" Theo demanded. She tried to stand up, but her knees were cramped and weak, and she almost collapsed onto Yuri. His breath smelled like Circus Peanuts.

"Haven't found it," he said, patting her back helplessly as she had another coughing fit. Another of the men shook his head and moved away from the shaft.

She swallowed another cough. Her voice was gravelly and hoarse, but at least she could breathe. "But it should be down there. At the bottom. I saw him drop it!"

"Who?" a voice said sharply. Mark Zimmer came up on her other side, taking her weight off Yuri's arm and helping her sit down on the workbench. His motions were solicitous, but there was an urgency to his tone. "Who, Theo?"

"Seth. Seth Adler—the Neith Trust guy." Theo breathed in deeply again and tried to ignore the expression of disbelief on Zimmer's face. "He grabbed me and took my pass card. Made me help him carry the mummy and the shabtis. He dropped them down the shaft, and..." Turned into dust? "I don't...I don't know. He must have drugged me."

"You look drugged. Hell, you look half-dead." Zimmer was pale, and there was a hard twist to his mouth. The dust matted his red hair, turning it almost tan. "Is he still in the building? Did he say where he was going?"

"No...no, I..." Theo rubbed her face, wincing at the pain in her wrists. "I don't remember. He didn't say..."

It was impossible to think straight. Her head was spinning, her throat ached from her convulsive coughing, and her muscles protested from the dragging. Nothing made sense anymore.

Zimmer seemed to realize that. "Just tell me," he said quietly, "and you can go lie down. Is he here?"

She shook her head. "I think he's dead."

"What do you mean?"

"He...he fell apart. Disinterred." She bit her lip hard, trying to force herself to think clearly. "I mean disintegrated. He turned...turned into dust."

Even as she said it, she knew she could never say it again. Zimmer's face was a stark mask of disbelief and anger, but at the words "turned into dust," his jaw almost dropped. Even the words themselves tasted wrong on Theo's tongue, like she couldn't believe she was saying them. A robber *disintegrated?*

"He must have drugged me," she repeated. "He covered my mouth. Maybe there was something on his gloves?" None of this was making sense. Stop the world, please; she wanted to get off. "He made me, made me get him into the labs. He threatened to wreck everything if I didn't. He took THS203 and some of the shabtis. Wrapped them in cloth. Then he dropped everything down the dumbwaiter shaft and—and I guess he roped down. I think he's the Collector."

One of the security guards sucked in a breath and got a big lungful of dust for his troubles. Zimmer motioned the rest of them back and snapped a couple of code words into his radio before turning back to Theo.

"Why did he want them?" he said. He was trying to be patient, but Theo could see that he was tugging at the leash to get information. To do *something.* The police would be here shortly, but minutes after the crime had been committed, Zimmer needed every detail he could get. Theo did her best to focus.

"He wouldn't tell me. He only said it was a matter of life and death." Zimmer's expression was skeptical, so she jerked her head toward the door. "Check the lab. He must have left fingerprints. Or blood. I might've bit him a little."

Zimmer's expression softened at Theo's strained sarcasm. "Just stay there," he said before thumbing the radio again.

"Kennedy! Are the cops here yet?" A crackling voice answered in the affirmative. "Tell them to break out the biohazard gear if they have it. The perp dropped a powdery substance all over the place, and it's making a hell of a lot of people cough."

"Hey, boss!" one of the guards shouted. He was kneeling next to one of the tables, sifting through the dust that Seth had left behind. Fabric came to light: pants and a shirt, pockets filled with tools. Latex gloves were lying where they'd fallen, filled with more gray-brown powder. The guard's face was a picture as he gingerly lifted one of the discarded socks.

"Put that down!" Zimmer snapped. "Nobody touch anything, understand? If there's a speck of DNA, I want the lab guys to be able to find it."

Theo wondered vaguely if Adler had mad cow. Or another prion disease, really. Something that would cause people to catch it if they breathed in his dusty remains. She remembered breathing in smoke, smoke and ash, the one time her parents had grilled outside. Dad had almost set the house on fire.

"C'mon." Zimmer put a hand on her arm. "As soon as the cops take your statement, I'll have someone get you home. You're going to be okay."

His hand rested on one of the bruises Adler had left on her arms, and the dull ache wiped out the sensation of touch. She had to have been drugged, she knew, because nothing was feeling real anymore.

"I'm sorry," she said softly. "I don't think I'm gonna be real helpful."

"That's okay." He squeezed her arm, five points of harsher pain breaking through the throb of the bruising, and the room seemed to come into sharper focus. "He's going down for this. I promise."

"I don't want…" What did she want? She didn't know. She left the sentence unfinished and muffled another cough.

CHAPTER SIX

The fire raged up the hill, untamable. So much old wood
in the city—we knew we couldn't stop it, but the gods
knew we had to try. And where was the emperor? I don't
know. These things should not happen when rulers are
just.

– Excerpt from unknown work, vellum sheet,
circa 1200 BCE

The squad car dropped her off at the door of her building. Officer Hunt
put a hand out, offering quietly to escort Theo up, but she shook her
head and clutched her bag. She had to get home, now, and get out of her
dusty clothes and pretend that the evening had never happened. She
ignored the officer's well-meant reassurances and bolted for the door.

The apartment was a standard white-walled bachelorette pad,
distinguished mainly by its location on the edge of the South Loop and
the astronomical rent that went with it. In the three years she'd lived
there, though, she had managed to stamp her personality onto it. One
wall of the living room had recently been turned into a landscape scene
(still unfinished—she hadn't taken the protective plastic off the furniture
in eight months) and the others had had reproductions of famous
artworks painted straight onto them, complete with trompe l'oeil frames.
It was one more area of her life where Theo spent her time up to her
elbows in varnish, but she enjoyed it: for work or for pleasure, she loved
painting. Being home, surrounded by the comfort of her own work and
the images of the Masters' greatest pieces, cast a momentary sense of
calm over her.

Her cell phone rang, shattering the peace. Theo fumbled reluctantly to answer it. The caller ID blinked at her. Aki.

Answer? Ignore?

Ignore. Aki was one of her best friends, but she couldn't handle talking to anyone right now, let alone someone who was a habitual bundle of energy and sarcasm. Her hands trembled slightly as she turned off the phone and dropped it onto the bookshelf.

She half sat, half fell onto her plastic-covered couch, and a small cloud of dust arose. Dust, dust, Seth Adler turning into dust, Seth Adler practically kidnapping her, Seth Adler holding her and asking her to forgive him...

Oh hell, everything hurt. She buried her head in her hands, and her shoulders shook.

With the horrible dust clinging to her clothes and the bandaged places on her wrists where the zip ties had drawn blood, Theo shuddered and failed to force down another sob.

The smell was everywhere. That dry, earthy smell on her clothes and hair and the fresh gauze on her wrists, tickling her throat and turning her next sob into a cough. Staggering to her feet, she stumbled over to the bathroom and yanked the door open. Her torn nails caught on the fabric before she managed to drag her shirt over her head.

No point in waiting for the water to heat up. It streamed down over her, turning dust into thin clay liquid that stained her bra and glued her soft slacks to her legs. She squeezed her eyes shut and faced into the spray, letting the freezing water soak into her hair and skin and remaining clothes. The tape holding her bandages in place flapped loose under the spray, and the gauze slithered to the floor in a sodden heap. In seconds, half her body was numb.

She didn't know how long she stayed there. The water began to turn warm. With shaking hands, she mopped the remaining grime off her face and dumped shampoo into her tangled hair. Her scraped fingertips stung, and the water that ran over them turned pinkish as the crusted blood began to dissolve. She was grateful for the ache; it gave her something to focus on. The smell of apple shampoo began to overwhelm the smell of the dust.

Finally, Theo turned the water off and crawled out of the shower. The bra and slacks went straight into the trash. Too stained to wear again, she told herself. Wrapping herself in her fluffy bathrobe, she wandered into the living room.

Something itched in her hands, under her skin. Her fingers twitched. She hunched her shoulders as she sat down on the edge of the couch, flexing the fingers and trying to make the sensation go away.

She needed to do something.

What did people do in this situation? Theo didn't know. Minutes ago, she'd been almost crying; now, everything felt dim and unreal, as if she were sensing the world through a thick layer of gauze.

It must be trauma, right? People got traumatized. She leaned forward, knitting her fingers together, and rocked back and forth as she tried to think.

Sleep would be good, but she was too wired. She stood and took three steps, her wet hair scattering droplets of water on the carpet as she walked. Vaguely, she thought about the scenes she'd painted. History had plenty of war and horror. She should be crying, shouldn't she? She should be devastated, wallowing in the depths of emotion, tearing out her hair. She should be sad. But she felt...nothing.

Her motions were on automatic. Go to the spare bedroom, which served as her home studio these days. Slide a smock on over the good bathrobe. Pull a canvas from the rack. Paints, paints, paints. She reached for gold without quite knowing why. Not enough sleep, maybe.

No point in sketching. This wasn't going to be good. She prepared her palette in a haze, stared at the unprimed canvas for a moment, and then drew a single streak of eggshell white down the center.

The colors flowed in a ribbon through her mind. Eggshell. Titanium white. Dove gray. Antique gold. Alizarin crimson. Purple ochre...

* * *

Hours had passed. Her head sagged, and the end of her messy braid dipped into the paint tray. The sharp smell of yellow ochre filled her nostrils, jerking her awake again.

Light seeped in through the frosted windows of the workroom. Paint was drying on the tip of her brush; she'd fallen asleep standing up, and she hadn't realized it. On the easel, a mess of colors and shapes resolved itself into something strange.

If Theo wanted to be exact, it was Klimt's *The Kiss*. Everybody had a favorite painting, and that was Theo's; the lush gold and the cascading shapes created movement that she ached to capture. But standing back from her easel, she knew that Klimt had definitely not intended it to be seen in this way.

There was one person in the painting, and that was Seth Adler. Instead of a woman, his head was bowed over the gnarled figure of THS203. But his grip was already failing, because he was falling apart: the skin peeling away, the bones crumbling to powder, his form disintegrating. His head was whole; his neck was rotting; his chest was withered scraps over yellowed bone. From head to toe ran thousands of years of age, beginning with simple decay and ending in dust immeasurably older than the ancient corpse he was clutching.

The brush fell from her hand and bounced, leaving crusts of dried paint on the carpet.

Later, after a few hours of sleep, she would probably recognize it for the amateurish crap it was. She hadn't sketched, just splashed paint right onto a raw canvas like a freshman. Half of it was blobs of color. But faced with the image in the early morning light leaking through the gaps in the curtains, she sank to her knees and buried her face in her hands.

It isn't fair. The thought whined in her head, the least attractive aspect of one's inner child, but she couldn't repress it. It wasn't fair. Why was this happening? What the hell had he been thinking?

Her eyes burned. Tears squeezed out from between her lashes. Ordinarily, she would have forced them down, wiped them away, told the world she had allergies—anything to keep from being seen as another flaky, immature artist. Anything to prove she was serious, dammit. But alone in her own home—frustrated and confused and angry and in pain—Theo succumbed to humanity and let herself cry.

* * *

Safe. For what felt like the first time in a century, Seth took a deep breath and let himself relax. There it was, the monstrosity, nicely trussed up in the coffin he'd prepared for it. It leered at him, its teeth speckled black with the ritual powder he'd sprinkled over it for good measure.

It had been a simple recipe, but one of the only ones he knew. If he'd made it right, the stuff would keep the mummy isolated from the world: until the next sundown, its spirit would be barred from its body. He hadn't expected that body to be much of a threat in the first place, but he believed in being prepared.

Seth stepped back from the coffin and heaved the huge lead-lined lid into place. The coffin itself was concealed inside the shell of a plain couch, with a multicolored blanket thrown carelessly over it. There were other spots prepared—hideaways where he could stash that damn corpse where it would never be found. For now, though, he had to stick with the couch.

He couldn't leave immediately. The police visit had made that clear enough—Theo Speer had obviously told them everything. The fact that he wasn't in custody right that second meant they hadn't taken parts of her story too seriously. Such as his death. They must have thought she was unhinged with shock, so they'd merely questioned him.

But while he probably wasn't in trouble now, he would be if he vanished so soon after the theft. He'd have to behave as if nothing were wrong. Except, of course, that he was alarmed and unhappy, thanks to the completely unfounded and distressing accusations leveled at him by a woman he'd thought was friendly. Maybe his lawyer could hint that she might be a stalker.

No, that was Seth, wasn't it? After all, he was the one who'd been silently watching her. He hadn't had a choice about it, with a gaze locked in place and body paralyzed behind the thick glass, but he could have chosen not to go farther with it. Could've talked to another member of the staff, or withdrawn himself from museum business altogether now that the items he needed had finally been collected.

But the urge to see in the flesh what he'd glimpsed through false eyes had been difficult to resist.

Now he was in the position of actually knowing the person he'd had to use.

Theodora Speer was a fascinating one. At the party, and at lunch too, she'd been reserved and a bit wary. But in the labs? She loved the shabtis; there was no way to get around it. A little of it had crept through when she'd talked to him, telling him about their plans for the exhibition.

Bored. That was it. Bored to death. Her focus on color, her need to record and remember everything—the way she grinned when she talked about Aztec warriors or dumbwaiters... She struck him as someone who wanted to explore a world beyond paint and public relations.

He was a bastard, doing this to her. But he couldn't let that make a difference. Protecting himself and the mummy had always been his first priority. If the Columbian's people pressed him, he could threaten to defund the Trust, and that would keep him safe enough.

The goddess might disapprove, though. He silently prayed that

Neith wouldn't hold it against him.

But no matter what she thought, Seth would have to carry on. He'd spent a long, long time hunting down the mummy and its tomb treasure, and now that he had them, he intended to keep them. It was, after all, a matter of life and death.

The next move was obvious. He could wait for a while and then move out of the city, taking his collections with him. The patron-of-the-arts character could quietly die off in Chicago where it belonged. He might even change his name again; after a long time as Seth Adler, it might be time for a switch.

Then what? said a persistent voice in his head. Find the mummy, find the lost shabtis—that had been the plan for so long. The Trust, the identities, the details of lives lived. What came next?

Maybe he should stay Adler. He wasn't a young man anymore, not by a long chalk, and he didn't relish the idea of uprooting and starting again as someone new. He hated the cold, but he was used to the city. And in this global age, the world could come to him.

He had the mummy now, didn't he? Locked away where it couldn't be found or used against him. Why not enjoy himself for once? A patron of the arts could get respect in certain circles, and he already had a life here. Perhaps he should stay and take another stab at a lasting relationship.

And there came that thought again, and Seth squashed it firmly before it got too comfortable in his brain. He had to be desperate if he was still thinking about Theo as anything but a possible obstacle. After all, she'd likely named him to the police in a case of what was either grave robbing or grand larceny. Seth knew he'd bought a lot of trouble from that quarter.

Was there such a thing as grand grave-robbing? Grave larceny, maybe? There had to be a term for it. English was such a mutable language.

It's not just language, she'd said, her back to the glass. She'd been talking to one of the preservationists while the clay slept, but the fire in her words had jolted him out of his sleep. *It's never just about language or art or religion; it's about magic. How these elements blended together and created something new, right in the middle of the desert. That's something we don't have, I think. Art is art and language is language, and magic, well, we're too grown-up for it. Right?*

Hell. *Hell.* He growled and kicked at the base of the faux sofa. It was completely petty and did nothing but make his foot hurt, but the pain distracted him. He groaned again, hunching over and hopping in place, nursing his aching toes and cursing in three languages, two of them dead.

Why was she haunting him? A few images and half-remembered words snatched unawares through glass—it was too little for anyone to actually care about. It had been a long time since he had last been with a woman—but was it long enough to make him lose his control and act as stupid as he had tonight?

He didn't know, and it gnawed at him.

But there was the fire that had woken the clay. Language and art and religion and magic, she'd said, and perhaps had never quite understood what that implied for her.

Theo's eyes lit up when she painted. Theo hungered for knowledge. Theo had camped out in his brain and refused to leave. She shouldn't be an issue, but she'd made him laugh, and she lived in a world that was too small for her vision of it. Seth had laid his plans, and she'd stepped in and made him question them.

He wasn't going to sleep well tonight.

CHAPTER SEVEN

The priest was using a speaking tube to make the statue
of the god give prophecies. I threatened him, telling him
it was a sacrilege, but he wasn't afraid. "The governor
allows it," he said.

How am I supposed to make him believe the truth? I
can't say why I believe because it sounds mad, and I can't
show why I believe because I can't afford it. Well, it's his
business, but I don't think his god will be happy when
they meet.

– Excerpt from the Jurisprudence of Diokles,
circa 910 BCE (fragment)

Simon and Garfunkel were singing "A Hazy Shade of Winter" from the
iPod dock. Theo wasn't sure why she'd picked it, or why it was on her
playlist in the first place, but it had an upbeat tempo and it almost fit
what she could see.

The scene outside her windows was picture-postcard perfect. Snow
drifted down slowly in plump, fluffy flakes, and the sidewalks looked
almost pretty with a fine layer of white over the ice and gray slush. A
Salvation Army Santa Claus had installed his kettle outside the big
bookstore, lending a distinctly Norman Rockwell quality to a scene
already filled with holiday decorations and charming Americana.
Perhaps the political poster in the Indian restaurant's window was a
touch discordant, but overall, the scene would have fit a Metropolitan
Museum print or a retro calendar.

Theo leaned back and gently began to knock her head against the
window.

She'd never been susceptible to cabin fever before. Her parents had
learned early on that forcing her to stay in her room was a punishment

with no teeth in it. Alone, with paper or a book or her own thoughts, she could concentrate on the worlds and images swirling in her head.

This time, though, those images weren't ones she wanted to spend time with. And even her parents had never left her in her room for three days straight.

Three. Nice round, mythic number. Three days for Jesus to rise from the dead; three sons setting off to seek their fortune; three seasons in the Egyptian calendar. After three days in the apartment, three days since the robbery, someone should have arrived bearing answers. That's the way it should go, right?

With a sigh, she rested her forehead against the cold glass. It'd be nice if things worked like that.

Well, if the universe wasn't going to provide her a miracle, she would have to make her own. Theo clambered down off the window seat and grabbed her phone from its place on the bookshelf. The very first name in her contacts list: Aki Lee. Four missed calls.

The phone rang once in her hand, and she picked up.

"What the fuck?" Aki demanded bluntly, his voice crackling over the bad connection. "Seriously, Theo, what the flipping fuck? Why haven't you been calling me back? Are you all right?"

Sighing, she sat down and leaned her back against the bookcase. "I'm fine, Aki," she said, relief welling up in her chest. "I'm sorry I haven't been answering your calls. It's...I've been busy. Do you have time to talk?"

"You think you've been busy? I'm trying to do two big redesigns at once, and my inbox is full of emails from the art squad pestering me for details of whatever the hell went down in the loft." Computer keys rattled in the background. "Jared North is driving me insane, by the way. He's convinced you killed a guy. You didn't, did you? Because I owe him fifty dineros if you did."

"Redesigns? Aki, are you back in the loft?"

"Nope. The whole department's been closed since whatever-it-was happened. The loft is taped off, and everyone's security clearance has been revoked while they check our logs. I'm waiting to hear if I'm gonna get fired or not. Seriously, Theo, what the fuck?"

"You're gonna have to be more specific, Aki."

"You know what? I'm not having this conversation over the phone. Are you home?"

"Yeah."

PAINTER OF THE DEAD   83

"Coffee. Your place. Half an hour, and you'd better give me some-thing to tell North or he's gonna claim he won. That fifty is going into my vacation fund, goddammit."

When he was worked up, Aki used profanity like punctuation, and Theo was grateful for the familiarity. "Okay, but I've only got instant. I've been stuck waiting for a verdict myself, and I'm pretty much out of…everything, really."

"I'll bring it. My mom sent me a bag of that fancy coffee they fish out of cat shit, and I'm not drinking that by myself." There was a rattling sound as Aki grabbed his car keys. "Hang tight, I'll be there in thirty."

"Wait, Aki—"

The phone cut off, and Theo set it down. Okay, then.

In fact, it took twenty-seven minutes before her doorbell buzzed. Theo opened the door and Aki stalked in, looking as frustrated as she'd ever seen him. His hair was ruffled instead of stylishly disheveled, and he was wearing an olive-green T-shirt and cargo pants. He dropped a bag of coffee beans into Theo's hands and flopped down on the couch, looking like he wanted to break something.

She carefully sniffed the coffee before putting it in the grinder. "All right," she said as she hit Blend, "talk. What's going on at work?"

"Well," he began, slumping farther down on the couch, "I got an email from Zimmer on Tuesday night that you might 'need a friend.' You didn't call me back, so I guessed you were sulking or something. Then when I came in to work on Wednesday morning, my card wouldn't swipe through. I talked Security into letting me in, but the loft was taped off and one of Zimmer's flying monkeys was standing there telling me to go home. Nobody was giving us answers. Stiegler got into an argument with the guards and almost slugged a guy. He needs to lay off the caffeine. Some people left 'cause, hey, free day off, right? But you hadn't turned up yet."

He shook his head as Theo poured the fresh grounds into the coffeemaker.

"Finally, Van Allen turns up and tells us there was a robbery, and the art department was implicated. Mummy's gone, shabtis're gone. We had to go home and wait while there was a security check. I got Yuri to talk to me, but he said it was somebody you know, and that the guy disappeared into thin air. Which isn't helpful." Aki eyed her. "So, yeah…it was Adler, right?"

She sighed. "I refuse to answer on the grounds that I may be incriminated."

"So it was him."

"Pretty much." Theo poured two cups of coffee and brought them over to the couch. "He...he drank paint thinner and turned into dust. Or that's what I saw, anyway."

She paused, waiting for the sarcasm, but Aki just shook his head and took one of the cups. After taking a sip of her own, she told him the whole story.

Most of it. He didn't need to know about that strange moment between them.

"Maybe he wanted to ruin the exhibit," she finished, shaking her head. "But I think it's more than that. He had some kind of fixation—kept talking about life-or-death situations."

Aki snorted. "If he wanted to ruin the exhibit, he screwed up. We're actually supposed to keep working in our downtime, prepping new stuff focused on spooky crap. Publicity sent over a whole text package for a new brochure about curses."

"That's crazy," Theo said, cradling her coffee cup. "They don't have the mummy anymore. They lost a lot of the shabtis. What are they going to do?"

"Capitalize on a big story, obviously," Aki pointed out. "C'mon, you know what the publicity game is like. The weird burial already fits the whole 'woo-woo Egyptian curses' deal, and now someone manages to steal the mummy and vanish?"

Theo didn't say anything, but Aki winced. "Sorry, I didn't mean to make a big deal out of it. Look, the point is, people love a car crash. Everyone wants to know why that mummy was stolen. They're going to go ahead with the exhibition. The display's gonna be called 'The Tomb of the Lost Mummy.'"

"People love a car crash," Theo repeated. "Is that why I still have a job?"

Aki sipped his own coffee, grimaced, and stood up to get another packet of sugar. "No, you still have a job because it wasn't your fault. That guy would've gotten into the lab no matter what, and probably would have gotten more if you hadn't been there."

Her friend was carefully avoiding using the name of the thief. She wasn't sure if she was angry or not, but part of her was relieved that he wasn't pressing the issue.

"Plus, you would have serious grounds for a wrongful-termination suit," he added, effectively spoiling the moment. "They don't want to get sued 'cause of you."

"Nice one," Theo grumbled into her coffee. "I was feeling encouraged for a couple of seconds there."

"I didn't mean it like that and you know it." Aki finished emptying his third packet of sugar into his cup. "There're a few armchair Rambos who swear they would never ever, ever have let this happen, they'd have broken the thief's neck with their bare hands, but nobody believes 'em."

Theo snorted at that image. "Sandusky?"

"And Meyers. The John McClanes of the tech department."

"Believe me, if I could have nominated one of them to take my place, I would've." Theo leaned sideways, resting her head against the cool glass of the window. Far below, a car horn honked and someone yelled about blind drivers—just another morning in the Loop. "Aki, please, be honest with me. How screwed am I?"

Aki frowned. "I'd say...forty percent. Like I said, they don't want to give you grounds for wrongful termination, but there are already rumors that you had more to do with it than you're letting on. Be careful."

Aki's departure left the apartment feeling a little colder for Theo. The museum thinking that allowing her to continue doing her job, the only thing she wanted, might somehow endanger it—that was a nasty thought. How could empty space feel so stifling?

* * *

The museum was teeming. Normally on a weekday morning in December, there would be a few dozen visitors scattered around the great hall in tour and school groups. Today, there were hundreds lining up for tickets and pestering the harassed-looking docents about the antiquities on display. Somebody had put an oversized hockey jersey on Strewth, the leader of the *Struthiomimus* pack, and a group of Canadian tourists was taking pictures in front of him and his packmates Wilbur and Lenin. The café under the Pangaea display was doing brisk business, and their jacked-up prices were being willingly paid by visitors chilled by the walk along the windswept lakefront. With the running and shrieking children, the cheerful babble, the smell of hot coffee, and a local news outlet doing a puff piece on curses, the solemn halls of academe had taken on the air of a street fair.

"Holy cow," Theo managed to say. Museums had been losing attendance for years, to the point where her parents fussed about whether she would still be employed in five years' time. But it seemed that a whiff of curses, a touch of crime, could draw the public back. That's entertainment, chum.

She undid her scarf and fumbled for her ID card before remembering that it had been taken away as evidence. Sighing, she joined the line at the security desk, falling in behind a couple of women who had apparently misplaced a purse in one of the galleries. They were chatting easily—one describing a good trade she had made in an online game, the other making appreciative noises—and with the comfort of longtime friends.

For a moment, Theo blanked out and let the noise wash over her. It hadn't been long, but she desperately missed the camaraderie and comfort of the loft. She needed that moment, even if the chatting friends weren't hers. She needed to enjoy a few seconds of normality.

As the line shuffled forward, a shout broke Theo's concentration.

"Hey, Speer!" the voice called, and Theo looked up, startled back into the real world. Yuri Vladashvili was hurrying toward her. The two women stopped their conversation and glanced at Theo, clearly wondering if she were being caught by Security for something nefarious.

So much for the moment. Theo turned to face Yuri. "Morning," she said. "I heard things were going well here and I wanted to have a look..."

"I'm sorry, but Dr. Van Allen doesn't want you back upstairs yet," Yuri said with a sympathetic grimace. Theo's heart sank. "The loft is still taped off, and everyone's been told to go home until further notice."

"But what about the exhibit?" she insisted. "If we're going forward with it, I need to prepare that mural."

Yuri glanced around, clearly spotting the eavesdropping women. He shook his head and took Theo by the arm, towing her away from any curious onlookers and toward the gate into the big hall. The guard on duty spared a curious look for Theo, but he waved them through without comment.

"Graphics really aren't a priority right now," Yuri confided. "This is all rumor, okay? But somebody up top is getting pissed off about the new visitors being interested in the crime. We've been told not to give them details or admit that anything happened. Basically, they've got bigger fish to fry."

Theo wilted. She understood it—intellectually, anyway—but viscerally, it felt like a punch in the gut. When it came down to brass tacks, the whole thing was still an embarrassment, no matter how much they were insured or how many new visitors the controversy attracted.

"Forty percent screwed," she muttered, remembering Aki's words. "It figures. But isn't there someone I can talk to? Some way I can get into the loft for a bit? If the exhibit is going forward, then we've got to figure out what to do with that wall. I can design it at home if need be, but it has to get done, and I need to get my stuff from upstairs."

Yuri hesitated. "What would you need to get?" he said.

"References. Mainly the facial reconstruction that Egyptology commissioned and a copy of the exhibition bible. I know, I know, it's not supposed to be let out of the museum before the opening, but I'll need it." She tugged on the end of her braid as she thought. "And the sketchbooks I had stored in the loft. They have my work on the coffin and the shabtis."

"I told you, we can't let you up there." He shook his head. "Look, though...maybe I can get you in to see Mr. Zimmer. He might be able to work something out. I mean, he was there when it happened. Wait here."

"Thanks, big guy." She gave his arm a quick squeeze. "It means a lot to me."

Yuri was gone for more than half an hour. Theo waited in the great hall, making herself as comfortable as possible on one of the benches and watching the crowds while she tried not to worry or fidget.

The patrons moved on, oblivious to her, and she found herself oddly comforted by the sight. The museum was alive, it was relatively undamaged, and business continued despite the petty drama of the robbery and the violated aerie. The chattering of hundreds of voices blended together, echoing off the marble and reverberating in the higher reaches of the hall itself, creating a comforting background rumble that made it impossible to feel alone. She should spend more time down here, she told herself. Take the time to actually enjoy the place.

She was so engrossed in the sight, watching the people, that when Yuri abruptly reappeared at her elbow, she jerked like she'd been electrified. "Jesus," she breathed, trying to calm her racing heart. "Don't do that!"

"Sorry, Theo," Yuri said, looking abashed. "I didn't realize you were so zoned out. Look, I was able to get you a few minutes with Zimmer. Make it quick, okay? He's really busy with the new security rules."

"I can imagine," she said, keeping her tone neutral. Her heart was still pounding, and she cradled her right arm, phantom pain flickering through the bruises and scabbing there. Poor Yuri seemed to realize why she was so spooked, and his face fell. She sucked in another breath and offered him a smile: she hated to see him worry.

Yuri swiped his card and held the door open, very gentlemanlike with an exaggerated bow, and Theo's smile was genuine as she swished past him and curtseyed.

The Security office was in a state of controlled chaos. Everyone seemed to be on the move, doing five things at once, and Zimmer's door was locked. Yuri knocked and called out, "It's Speer!" The door opened quickly.

Zimmer looked like he hadn't been getting enough sleep, but he retained an air of professionalism. He ushered Theo into the office and, dismissing Yuri, closed the door behind both of them. Theo gingerly sat on the edge of the one visitor's chairs.

"Coffee?" he offered, but she shook her head. "More for me, then. It's been an interesting week."

"Which is why I'm here," Theo said. Zimmer raised an eyebrow as he went about refilling his mug. "I was wondering if there's been any progress on finding the thief—or his body, anyway."

"If you mean the mummy, no," Zimmer said. "If you mean Adler, he's not dead. The cops found him at his townhouse an hour after the robbery. Security footage said he'd been there all night."

Theo's stomach clenched and her expression must have shown it because Zimmer shook his head sympathetically.

"He's not dead?" she said carefully.

"If he's dead, he's being unusually talkative." No cream, but plenty of sugar for Mark Zimmer, she noticed. A man after her own heart, in that regard. "Our cameras had been fed a loop. Ever since *Speed* came out, that trick's gotten harder to pull, but professionals can still manage it. We didn't get usable footage from the lab or Restoration. And when the cops talked to Adler, they found a guy who'd been home. No witnesses but his security system, but there were no signs of tampering. At this point it's your word against his."

"And his weighs more."

"You were scared. Disoriented." Zimmer sipped his coffee as he settled back into his chair. "Nobody's likely to press charges, but you have to understand that we've got no proof it was Adler in the loft."

"Do you think it was him?"

He looked at the desk, avoiding her gaze. "I'm not paid to speculate. My job is to protect the antiquities, not figure out how donors think."

"All right. If he isn't involved, does that mean I can get back to work? There's too much to do, especially with the star attraction missing."

"I'm sorry, but I can't upgrade your security status until the loft is cleared and unsealed."

"What about working from home? Can I do that?"

He hesitated at that. "You know, you could see this as a vacation. I know it's rough, but you could take advantage of free days off...." Theo let out a soft breath, and Zimmer shook his head. "What I mean," he continued, "is that you don't have to work. You were attacked. That's more than enough reason to take time off."

"But I don't want time off!" Theo exploded. "I want to do my work! I've been here for six years; I've never had a security violation; I play ball with the other departments! Why can't I work at home? If we're going to get this exhibit off the ground, if we're going to shove this in that son of a bitch's face, I have to help!"

She stopped, panting. So much for being professional. She was throwing a tantrum in front of the Security chief, and a Pet Rock could have told her that wasn't the way to get her clearance back.

But Zimmer didn't seem about to throw her out of his office. Instead, he sagged and rubbed his forehead. "You know," he said, conversationally, "I almost never get anyone in here who actually wants to do *more* work. It's refreshing."

"I'm sorry; I shouldn't have shouted," Theo said, face red, "but I mean what I said. I need to help out on this, Mr. Zimmer. I'll give you any documents you need, anything you require to fast-track my background check or whatever it is you're doing. But if this exhibition gets pushed back because this jerk decided he wanted a four-thousand-year-old corpse for his living room décor, I'll...I mean, we'll look bad. The museum will look bad."

"I think you were being more honest with 'I'll,'" Zimmer responded. "But workaholics typically don't do things to jeopardize their jobs." He pushed aside a manila folder. "Listen, I can't authorize you back in the loft. And it's too late for you to do anything more on Treasures. Your work has already been divided up among the other artists, and the mural is going to the printers the day after tomorrow. The exhibition is going to open on time."

Theo's heart sank. Replaced.

"But if it helps," Zimmer continued, "the board wants you at the launch party. I can authorize you for that."

"I know it sounds weird, Mr. Zimmer, but I don't think a party is going to compensate for being kicked out of my department." Theo's voice sounded hollow. If they could pull everything together without her, what did that make Theo Speer? Expendable, for starters.

It was a selfish thought, she knew. But for so many years, art had been all that gave Theo a place in the world. She was of average height, average intelligence, average looks—but she loved colors and shapes and textures, and she poured her love of those things into pictures, in hopes that it would make bygone worlds a little more real. She was good at her job. She *was* her job. She'd hoped that she had made herself indispensable to the Columbian. Apparently not.

Zimmer didn't seem to realize what was going through her head. Good. The last thing she needed was the Security chief thinking she was insane.

"You're not being kicked out," he said. "You're on leave for a while. Anyway, the launch party's going to have a lot of journalists there, and I know Dr. Schechter would love to put a sympathetic face on this story by introducing you to them. You might be able to get publicity, sell your own work that way."

"I'm not sure…"

"Look," Zimmer said. "Come to the party. Schechter's people might be worried, but you've seen the crowds." He ran a hand through his tousled red hair. There were dark circles under his eyes; those crowds were clearly a nightmare for him to deal with. He caught her expression and chuckled. "Yeah, yeah, I know; I complain about it. But it's money in the board's pocket, and, no matter how they feel about it, you're right in the middle of the whole mess. Everyone on the standard press invite list has already RSVP'd, and it's not because they're dying to learn about the Middle Kingdom. Come to the party, and the people upstairs will calm down."

Theo wavered. But Zimmer had always been straight with her, and though she didn't love the idea of a party, she needed to get back into the swing of things. It would be an opportunity to socialize with the loft people she hadn't gotten to see, at the very least.

"All right," she said, crossing her arms. "Maybe if I'm good I can get my access card back. Is it still at six o'clock?"

CHAPTER EIGHT

Wine, more wine than I've ever seen, and the Greek honey brew, militites. Fortunately there were no Greeks at the celebration—I've no stomach for their philosophy these days. Not a drop of beer to be found, though, which made it a very poor party...

- Excerpt from the Iudex Diary, author unknown,
circa 300 BCE (fragment)

The Treasures launch party glittered. The lights were on high in the whole museum, turning the dark windows into gold-tinged mirrors. A huge banner of the mummy's colorful mask hung over the entrance to the exhibit, smiling faintly down at the milling partygoers. The information desks had been moved to create a special open space for statues of the gods, all gleaming-white fiberglass with gilded eyes.

And there they were again, the waiters with their trays of drinks, as sleek and inhuman as they had been on the night when it began. And here was Theo again, in shoes that pinched, circulating with a glass of wine in hand and making small talk.

Only this time, people actually wanted to talk to her. With the attention centered on the loss of the mysterious mummy, Publicity had been thrilled to get Theo to turn up.

There was no eggshell-colored dress this time. People actually wanted to talk to her, and she couldn't find comfort in trying to blend. At least, that was what she'd told herself. But when she'd opened her closet that afternoon and looked at the dress, Theo knew she couldn't wear it ever again. The last time she'd worn it, trouble had come into her life in the form of a tall man with whiskey-colored eyes....

She'd shoved it back into the closet, taken herself down to Michigan Avenue, and spent money she couldn't afford on a brilliant scarlet dress that flowed like water when she moved.

It helped her simulate a confidence she didn't feel. She seemed to be the only one who needed it: her coworkers looked self-assured or even excited.

And why shouldn't they? The party was the culmination of months of hard work, and they were ready to relax and enjoy the fruits of their labor. They'd gone the distance, done the job, made their mark—pick your cliché. She hadn't. And maybe letting herself stand out would show the board she had nothing to hide.

And when she got home, she knew her own work there wouldn't be an escape. The motion of her painted figures was slowing, the oddities of them fading; if the muse had descended, she'd clearly decided to cut her losses and ascend again, leaving Theo's studio littered with yet more half-finished paintings.

The would-be Klimt was still there too, and, no matter what she did with it, it wouldn't leave her alone. She was beginning to think that the smartest thing to do would be to throw it out. Its presence made her brain itch.

A ripple ran through the crowd as the door of the gallery opened. Docents lined up by the entrance, smiling like runway models as they handed out audio-tour headsets and pointed curious guests to various parts of the exhibit. Theo sighed and toyed with the stem of her wineglass, pressing fingerprints into the clear surface and then trying to put her fingertips back in the same places again, like a bored kid playing with the wet rings on a restaurant table.

"How're you holding up?"

The voice made her jump, and she almost dropped her glass before she recognized it. Zimmer: wearing his one official work party suit, his fiery hair smoothed down.

"Fine," she said. "Okay, a little jumpy, I guess," she admitted as Zimmer gave her a skeptical look. "A lot jumpy. But I'm pretty sure that's normal. How's the party? Catch any criminals yet?"

"Not yet," he said, taking her arm and gently shepherding her away from the crowds moving toward the docents. "Plenty of rule violations, though. I caught two of my guys betting on whether or not we'll get anyone trying to grope Ta-weret."

"It's a topless statue," Theo said wryly. "What're the odds of it *not* happening?"

They fetched up by the buffet. Theo nibbled at a red-velvet cupcake, trying to avoid dropping crumbs on her dress. Zimmer finished his drink, meaning he was actually off duty for the evening. A stickler like he was wouldn't drink if he might be called on to tackle someone looking at an exhibit funny.

"You okay?" Zimmer said curiously, picking a cookie off the buffet. "You seem distracted."

"Mind's wandering, I guess," she said, shrugging and stepping away from the cupcake plate. Drowning her sorrows in calories wasn't the way to go. "It happens, sometimes. Brain goes on safari, sometimes it comes back with an idea."

He smiled a little at that. He had a nice smile, though it was a bit awkward. Like he didn't use it much. "And has it?"

"Jury's out." She brushed the last of the crumbs off her hands and smoothed down her dress. "It's been doing that a lot lately."

"I know the feeling," he said as he unwrapped a chocolate cupcake. "Sometimes it's hard not to let your mind wander, especially if you're trying to deal with a problem that makes no sense."

Her stomach dropped. "You mean the robbery?"

"Not much else to talk about around here." Zimmer took a bite of the cupcake and made a face. "We got the lab report on the dust, by the way. Powdered clay, mixed with an unknown organic compound—some kind of biomatter, probably offal. No toxins, just a distraction."

"So he went to a lot of trouble to steal something he can't fence and to not hurt anyone doing it," Theo said. No sense in mentioning disintegration; that was more of a headache than she wanted anymore. "No sign of a drug? Hallucinogens?"

Zimmer shook his head. "Nothing, but it's not surprising. If it was in gas form, it would've broken down and dispersed pretty quickly. They didn't find anything in your skin and hair samples, but that doesn't entirely rule it out."

She breathed out. She wasn't crazy. She'd been drugged, and though there was no evidence of it, it was still a perfectly reasonable conclusion.

"What about the clothes he left behind?" she said, carefully avoiding the use of specific names.

"Clean. No DNA."

"And my access?"

"Tentative," Zimmer said, not quite meeting her eyes. "I'm working on it, but the police prefer to keep all angles covered until the perp's caught. I can give you this, though."

He fished in his pocket and pulled out a plastic swipe card. "This'll get you into the loft once, to retrieve your things. You can do it anytime; there're extra cameras up there now, so you won't need an escort."

"Thanks." She took the card and tucked it into her clutch. Mark Zimmer letting a tentatively cleared individual into the back corridors by herself? Either hell was freezing over, or he really did trust her. The knot of tension in her stomach loosened.

"Speaking of escorts..." Zimmer glanced at his watch and frowned. "I have to walk the perimeter in the exhibit. Care to join me?"

"Oh...no, not right now."

She wanted to see the exhibit, eventually. It was what she'd been working toward for more than eight months: sketching, planning, arguing, erasing and starting again, putting in overtime on everything from the biggest murals and banners to the gift shop T-shirt designs. But with her little guys no longer on the shelf and poor THS203 gone and her mural replaced, what exactly did she have? Selfish thoughts, maybe, but she couldn't go in right then.

"I'm gonna go say hi to Little John," she said. "The poor guy hasn't been getting any love since the docents started dressing up the *Struthiomimus* pack."

"All right, suit yourself," Zimmer said. "Don't get trapped by the reporters. Remember, the Columbian's official comment is 'no comment.'"

He strode off into the crowd, purposeful and quick. The guards at the exhibit's entrance recognized him and stepped aside without asking for his ID. Instead of going in, he stopped and had a quick word with them. It was much too far away to hear, but Theo got the impression he was calling them on the carpet for not checking to make sure he was still him. She turned away, not waiting to see him go in.

Little John was a replica, but he made an impression. He stood frozen in midstride, jaws gaping, on the hunt and ready to chomp down on the nearest juicy animal. For almost twenty years, he'd been the center of attention in the main hall; families had lined up to photograph themselves with him, pretending to run away or push each other in front of the rampaging king of tyrant lizards. But recent renovations hadn't been kind to him. The *Struthiomimus* pack, lurking behind him with their hockey jerseys and Santa hats, had been stealing his spotlight.

Theo gazed fondly at him. She could imagine the sinews and muscles filling out the skeleton, but she could also imagine the poor alpha predator being snickered at by the skeletal prey he was oblivious to.

Few people stopped to look at the silent monster. The new exhibit held their interest instead, and dark-gray fiberglass was a weak competitor against glittering gold and carnelian.

So much gold. No matter what, she couldn't seem to get away from gold. The Scythian exhibit would be opening soon, with her team's painting of the gold-encrusted chieftain's burial.

A patch of darkness moved on the far side of the skeleton. The hall's marble was a pale gray that looked yellow-white under the floodlights and dove-colored in the shadows, and there was no reason for that dark patch to be there.

It moved slowly, lurking in Little John's blind spot. There were tinges of blue in it, slate blue and ivory gray...a tie that was a strip of stark white...all topped with coal-colored hair and skin that cried out for purple ochre.

One heel skidded out from under her, and Theo braced herself against the base of the skeleton.

What? How did he—?

She had to be seeing things. Imagining, maybe. She needed to focus. There was no way he would be here.

But why not? The investigation was ongoing, and it wasn't as if the cops had taken her testimony seriously. She shouldn't have left in the part about seeing him disintegrate. But if he was here, that proved they weren't interested in pursuing the charges.

And he was, after all, one of the sponsors of the exhibit.

Of course he'd be here.

Lurking on the other side of the T-Rex. While the other sponsors were elsewhere.

She was going to kill him.

Theo slipped again as she lurched into motion, but she wasn't going to let her damn shoes stop her. There, on the other side of Little John, was the man who'd nearly ruined everything. He was the reason

THS203 was gone and, with it, the museum's chance at the Pompeii specimens. He was the one who'd taken the shabtis, endangering the work of the ancient artist she'd thought so much about. And he'd added insult to injury by asking her to forgive him, like he thought that would make everything okay! Self-righteous bastard. She'd have his head on a platter.

She rounded the platform, and Seth Adler came into view. He'd stopped and was looking up into the tangled bones of the huge skeleton, hands tucked into his pockets.

He looked different. The faint lines around his eyes had been smoothed away, and the gray streaks in his hair had an odd yellow undertone to them: bleached in, no longer natural. If she looked closely, she would probably see dark roots. He looked younger, healthier, and more put together—unfairly so. It seemed he'd been relaxing and having work done while she was hiding in her apartment, scared and confused.

"Miss Speer," Adler said, never looking away from Little John, "the exhibit is lovely."

"Mister Adler," Theo ground out, trying not to actually growl. Maybe she was taking her cue from Little John.

He turned on his heel and looked her in the face.

A chill ran down her back as she met his gaze. "What the hell do you think you're doing here? Why aren't you skipping town with your haul and leaving my damn museum alone?"

Her eyes burned, and she forced down the flood of anger with an effort. They were alone on the far side of the skeleton, but sounds carried in the wide hall—and she didn't want to be seen picking a fight with a patron. Hell, if Adler decided to lodge a complaint, she might be turfed out. But it was hard, horribly hard, not to remember the pain in her arms.

"*Your* museum?" Adler said softly. Theo's fists tightened by her sides.

"I'm not going to argue semantics with you. Leave." The next word came out with some difficulty. "Please."

Adler recoiled, moving a quick step back at the venom in her tone. "Theo! Not here. There has to be something—"

"Like what?"

"—something I can say—"

"How about 'goodbye'?"

"I'm trying to explain—"

"Explain *what?* Robbery and assault?"

"Listen to me!" he hissed. Theo took a step back, surprised, but her fists were still clenched and ready. "I didn't want to do it either, do you understand? I've spent years helping build this collection! But circumstances—circumstances weren't favorable." He wilted, his sudden burst of anger spent. "I had to make my move."

For a moment, Theo's rage abated. He was sagging, his eyes hooded, deep lines appearing in his skin as his face fell into a mask of exhaustion. He looked...worn. Weary. He looked old.

Then common sense reasserted itself, and the sting of eyes fighting back tears brought the dust cloud of the nightmare back to her. Theo set her jaw and refused to let herself think that way. She had to stand her ground.

So he looked sad. Big deal. He had also burgled the museum, possibly ruined her career, and made her more miserable than she had ever been in her life. Another crack appeared in the dam, and she took a step toward him, keeping one hand on Little John's base to steady herself. She was so angry that her knees were shaking, and she needed the feel of the cold stone to help her focus.

"You," she said softly, "are asking me to understand—and forgive—what you did. Understand and forgive your breaking into the museum and destroying invaluable artifacts. Not to mention hurting me, almost ruining the exhibit, and wrecking the loft. I could lose my job because of you. And you want me to feel sorry for you." She took a deep breath, fighting for calm. "How many ways do I have to say no?"

"I'm sorry I hurt you...and for everything else too." Theo could see Adler's hands clench. "But I'm trying to tell you that that's not the way it is. Can't you believe me?"

"No. I can't. You stole that mummy!"

"It belonged to me!" he snarled. His eyes were two sharp points of light in the dark hollows of shadowed sockets.

Theo was too angry to be nervous anymore. "No. It didn't. You helped get it for the museum, but with our money and for our collection. I don't care what kind of fucked-up fixation you have—you wanting it doesn't make it yours!"

"You don't have all the facts, Theo. And you're not letting me explain." His lips were tight, his expression drawn. "There's more to it than that."

"More to what? You drugged me!"

"I didn't."

"Then how did I see—"

"Me die?"

Theo stopped, mouth half-open. Emotions flooded her, rage and hatred, joined by confusion, frustration, sadness, and a kind of fear she wasn't sure she could explain or name. Adler's words, their speaker utterly set in his convictions, were a slap in the face. How could he not get it? How did he not realize ruining the collection wasn't something he could explain away? Tears pricked again, staining her cheeks with the remnants of her cheap mascara.

"Enough," she said as calmly as she could, wiping away the tinted tears. Adler's expression was strange—almost confused, his eyes tracking over her as if trying to figure something out. Well, that was his business. Theo was done. "I can't do this, Mr. Adler. I just… Please. Go away. I know what you did, and you haven't said a thing to convince me it wasn't a plain old robbery. Have a nice time at the exhibit, and don't forget to visit our gift shop." She turned on her heel.

"Theo—"

For a moment, the rage flared again. "That'd be Miss Speer to you," she said without turning around.

"Here."

There was a rustle of cloth, and Theo looked despite herself. Adler was drawing something out of his pocket. A handkerchief, white linen with SRA embroidered on it.

His expression was conflicted. But the only thing he said was, "This might help."

Wise words. If he'd said, "You look like you need this," Theo might not have been able to keep her new, fragile calm. But after staring very deliberately at the handkerchief, she took it and mopped her face, leaving inky streaks of Long & Lashious on the soft cloth.

"Waterproof, my ass," she muttered to nobody, and Adler's mouth quirked. The expression vanished quickly, but she'd spotted it.

"Things don't always do what they say on the label," he commented.

She met his eyes again, trying to show him she still wasn't scared. Hell, she wasn't. Anger and exhaustion had wiped out any chance of that. "Yeah. You can never trust anything to act like it's supposed to."

"Subtle." Dry as the desert.

"But true." She folded the handkerchief neatly before handing it back. His forefingers touched hers, rough and blunt but no longer coarsely callused, the skin smooth and supple instead of worn like a middle-aged man's. Her skin tingled, and she could feel the warmth rising in her face again. "Enjoy the exhibition," she said quietly.

"Theo," he said. His fingers folded around hers, and she didn't pull away. She could feel the fine muscles shifting under the sleek form of his hand, warm and real. Her heart ached, and she didn't know why. Her lips parted.

He cupped her face in his hands and kissed her.

Her breath caught in her throat. His hands sank into her hair, broad fingers threading through the pale blonde as cautiously and tenderly as if he were holding the gold she painted so often. Rough lips ghosted over hers, tentative for a second before taking the plunge.

Somehow, she was in his arms. Warmth—warmth and a shuddering need—coiled through her as she pressed against him. He dipped his head, trailing a kiss down her neck and lightly scraping the pulse point there. Theo let out a low moan.

The sound surprised her and yanked her back to reality. With a yelp, she slammed her palms into Adler's shoulders and pushed him away.

Clearly Aki was right—too much time at work, not enough time dating.

Adler looked dazed, his color high, and Theo knew she had to look the same. The son of a bitch could kiss; she'd give him that. But…

"Theo—"

"Miss. Speer." She turned on her heel, her jaw clenching. Bastard. Bastard. *Bastard.* She heard him shift behind her, a few faltering steps before he stopped again, and she kept walking. She had to, or she would do something she'd regret.

The other side of the T-Rex wasn't far enough. The other side of the hall wasn't nearly far enough. She went straight for the nearest security door and swiped her pass with a trembling hand. She didn't feel better until the door was closed behind her.

* * *

This city. This godsdamned, freezing necropolis of a city was doing horrible things to his head.

Snow crunched under his shoes as he stalked across the parking lot, trying to ignore the voices of the other departing guests. The sky was deep indigo, not a star to be seen, and the lights shining down on the parked cars tinted the ice a dirty orange. Despite three layers of clothing, the wind whipping off the lake bit him right to the bone.

As if it had heard him, the wind picked up, raising a flurry of new-fallen snow and sending it whirling around his feet. Seth thrust his hands deeper into the pockets of his overcoat and tried desperately to think warm thoughts. Sun; sand; a broad, flat river sliding along placidly in the warmth of summer. For a moment, he thought he could smell the rank bogs of the shallows, and he fought the urge to close his eyes and enjoy the memory. The asphalt was treacherously icy.

With a sigh, he pushed the memory aside. As nice as it would have been to be someplace else—someplace where they saw snow once every hundred years—it wouldn't help to pretend. No matter how much he'd rather be overseas than stuck one more day in this cold, evil, cold, confusing, cold...

His car chirped as he unlocked it, gloved fingers fumbling awk-wardly with the keychain remote. Forget staying. Once he could disappear without drawing too much attention, he'd pull up stakes and move somewhere quieter. And warmer.

But the worst part was that he knew he was trying to distract himself.

Evidently, he was getting senile in his old age. It was the only expla-nation for the way he'd been behaving these past few days. He should have knocked Theo out before she'd seen too much, let her convince herself she'd imagined him as the thief. They could have had a laugh about it later. He hadn't needed help carrying everything, so why had he made a mess for himself by involving her? It could have been easily avoided.

Yet he hadn't wanted to. A man who'd lived a long life had so much more to lose; and if he'd been sane, he'd have doubled down on his efforts and put the mummy and the shabtis first. But he actually *hadn't wanted to*. He'd chatted with her, laughed with her, liked seeing the world through her eyes. She thought about colors and professional reputations and the beauty of what was, to her, history.

There was more too. The body he lived in knew what it had seen before his spirit had entered it. Normally such memories were just darkness, but this one had scraps of words and images there.

It's okay, little guys. Everyone has shitty friends at one point or another. You'll get there.

He could see her: face blurred by weak memories and half an inch of plexiglass, her hair a smear of white-blonde as she leaned against the case. There was a smile there, he thought, as she talked to him…it.

That's the problem, right? she'd said. *Bullshit. Some guys don't know how to behave.*

What do you think? she'd said. *Should I do it?*

Don't worry, little buddies, she'd said. *We appreciate you. Been there, done that.*

She probably didn't realize she'd been doing it. Muttering to herself, muttering to the shabtis, talking to them while she sketched them in their stiff rows. She had no idea what they really were. Not something she could be blamed for, since no man alive knew it. But thanks to what she was and how she did her job, she'd come closer to the truth than anyone in a long, long time.

The thought ate at him. All things considered, he barely knew the damn woman, but the shabtis did, and that bled through their link until Seth didn't know what he was doing. Their clay had awakened to her voice, and they cried out for her.

He might have guessed the hearts were a bad idea. But he'd seen the experiments done, again and again, and nothing else had worked…and he'd wanted to live so badly.

With a groan, Seth slammed the car door behind him. The Mercedes purred as the engine turned over, stark-white headlights stripping away the orange-tinted shadows. The snow on his coat began to melt into droplets, and the warmth of the heater and the luxurious seats clashed with the residual chill of the winter night, making him shiver.

He had to get out of the city. Soon. A few more months, at most, and he could put it behind him. Hopefully.

* * *

The loft was quiet. It was too big and open to completely block off with crime-scene tape, but flags were wound around several pillars and pieces of furniture, reminding onlookers that this was part of an active investigation and they shouldn't linger. The computers were off, the supplies left where they'd been dropped on the night of the robbery. A darkish smear near the bottom of the scuffed table leg might have been blood, but Theo decided it wasn't. There was no sense in jumping to conclusions when it was probably a discoloration in the metal.

It wasn't right, seeing the loft like this. Her mental image of her workspace was lively, full of colors, motion, arguments and accidents and pressure. The robbery had turned the artists' aerie into a museum piece, preserved at the moment of whatever it was that had happened. Like Pompeii or Palmyra.

She glanced down. The dust was gone, and from the streaky marks, the carpet had been recently vacuumed. Collecting evidence.

Her tablet and laptop bag were gone, left in the prep lab and likely impounded for examination by the police. But tablets always broke at the worst possible times, and Theo had learned to keep a work-grade spare in her bottom drawer. She fished it out and settled into her chair, hesitating a moment before firing up her desktop computer.

She probably should have waited for a better time. But she had to retrieve her files, right? Only someone using a museum-authorized machine could access their shared server, but it was easy to download the files and email them to herself.

Theo's head ached. It had been a long, exhausting day, and she needed time to process everything. Probably time to go home and get some sleep. She stared at the file for a moment, then moved the mouse to the X in the corner of the screen.

It would've been a good design, really. A little stiff now that she reexamined it, but maybe if the priest's hand were resting more naturally...?

With a sigh, Theo leaned over the tablet and erased most of the hand. This wasn't going to leave her alone until she fixed it.

As she dug into the problem, sketched out the new lines, a sort of peace settled onto her. The world narrowed down to a sequence of colors and forms, each complex in their own way, each demanding attention and care. Deviations a few pixels' width could skew a line, killing the motion she was trying to capture. It was something she had to concentrate on, because she alone could make sure its world didn't go wrong. It was nice to have a problem she was capable of solving.

Her thoughts were interrupted by the sound of the rattling elevator. Figuring it was Aki or Jem or one of the others, she didn't look up from her work. Between the residual aches and the buzzing in her head, it was hard enough to focus, and she couldn't spare the brainpower.

Footsteps came toward her cubicle. It wasn't Aki or Jem, though. A blur of red caught her eye and she turned, curious despite herself.

Mark Zimmer had loosened his tie and his suit jacket was gone. He carried a metal case under his arm, about the size of an encyclopedia volume.

For a moment, she wondered if he was about to fire her after all. Maybe he'd learned something. Maybe they'd gotten access to some unhacked security footage and seen...something.

A heavy feeling settled in her chest. She shifted, trying to keep her eyes on her work and vaguely hoping that he would disappear. Unfortunately, he instead moved closer. For the first time she noticed that he smelled like sandalwood cologne.

"I was talking to the other donors, and I might have put the pieces together. Theo, I need you to do something."

Her hand twitched, smearing a line. "What? What kind of something? Am I getting kicked out of here?"

The Security chief smiled, and the expression looked more uncomfortable than before. He never had learned how to make himself entirely likable. The pleasant look didn't compute on him, but Theo felt a surge of affection for the honesty of it. He didn't want to be here any more than she did.

"No, nothing like that. It's not a nice thing, though." He shifted his grip on the box under his arm. "I talked to the police handling the investigation, but there's nothing solid yet. They've questioned him, but the police seem to think there's no reason to probe further. They want hard evidence; gut feelings or witnesses don't count."

Ah. He wanted something, and he had to be playing this tune at least partially for her benefit. But good cop, bad cop worked for a reason, and if even a little of his emotion was genuine, she was grateful for it. After spending days feeling like she was going insane, it was nice to think that someone else believed what she'd said.

But those thoughts were dragging Theo away from the most important part of the conversation, the one he'd perhaps hoped to slip past her while greasing it with sympathy. "Mark," she said as evenly as she could, "what do you need me to do?"

"He's holed up in his place. His townhouse. Ever been there?"

"No," she said, "I haven't. He lives in the Gold Coast, doesn't he?"

"Not quite. Three floors of a skyscraper in the Loop." Zimmer's tone was definitely disdainful this time. "He says his family's owned the property since the Great Fire."

"I live in the Loop too," Theo pointed out. If he was going to crucify Seth Adler, it had better be for something he couldn't also catch her on. There were plenty of legitimate reasons to hate the man, besides his living arrangements.

"Not like this, I bet. Guy's rolling in it, and he's got no damn reason to do what he did."

"He said it was a matter of life and death." And why the hell was she repeating what he'd said? Was she trying to defend him, or just making sure he was pilloried for the right reason? Maybe that time spent painting contorted faces in execution scenes had left her jaded.

"It's a good line," Zimmer said, tucking one hand into his pocket. "It's easier if he can make it sound like he's doing it for a noble cause. Did he say what was life and death about it?"

"Not really, no. He kept saying I wouldn't understand. And when I ran into him tonight"—she didn't miss the flicker in Zimmer's gaze at that—"he said he was reclaiming what belonged to him. He seemed to think it was a moral issue."

"Sounds like a vigilante."

Sleeplessness had its effects. For a moment, Theo's image of Seth Adler acquired a cape and cowl. He already had the all-black wardrobe, she thought wryly.

Trying to shake herself out of her odd mood, she turned back to the tablet. "It's not my job to figure out what's going on in his head," she said as the stylus tip swooped across the plastic. "I think I'll settle for 'he has issues.' So what does this have to do with me, Mark? You keep dancing around the issue."

"I think I can pin him, but I need information first. It all relies on whether or not we're onto him." Zimmer laid the metal case on the workbench, its thud resoundingly dull and final. "If he is the one who robbed us, he's going to skip town as soon as possible, and we'll never get a chance to take him down. The Adlers have a reputation for being secretive anyway, so it's hardly a sign of guilt if he doesn't spend a lot of time outside. His business practically runs itself; he gets a bundle because it's still his, but it's not as if he needs to go into the office every day." Yes, that was definitely disdain in his voice. "And I don't have a legitimate reason to go see him myself."

She should have seen that coming. "And I do," she said. Not a question.

"I did see him hitting on you tonight, Theo." Zimmer crossed his arms. "I need you to be the inside man. Woman. Go visit him, check on him, tell me if he seems nervous or knows we're onto him."

She scanned Zimmer's face, looking for a hint of an ulterior motive, but there was nothing that she could see. He looked worn and unhappy to be in the position of making the request.

"I could," she said neutrally.

Zimmer raised an eyebrow.

"But it'd be suspicious as hell. He came on to me, sure, but I accused him of being the thief who tied me up and nearly destroyed my career and a bunch of other highly fragile things. Me casually dropping in on him isn't exactly believable."

"That's where I mostly need your help," Zimmer admitted glumly. "This isn't exactly the kind of thing I planned on when I went into the security business. A honey trap—"

"Make that a Trojan horse, Mark, or I'm out of this right now."

"Okay, Trojan horse. But there has to be a reason for you to visit him. Something you can tell him. Maybe you can apologize to him?"

"It's not going to happen." She picked up the stylus again, gripping it hard enough to turn her fingertips white. "I know what I saw."

"Can't you lie?"

"No. I can't. He has a bad habit of figuring me out." A thought struck her. "What about a painting?"

Zimmer frowned. "A painting? Like offering to do a portrait of him?"

"Not quite." Her mind was racing. She could get rid of it! A legitimate reason to put it and him out of her life in one cleansing moment. The thought made her feel warm inside. "I did a quick painting, in the days after the—you know, the loft thing. It's complete shit, but it's about him, and he likes that." It was hard to keep the bitterness out of her own voice. "I'll bring it to him with a *vade retro*." Zimmer raised an eyebrow. "You know, 'get thee behind me, Satan'?"

"Stick to English, I think. Confusing him won't get us anything at this point." Zimmer raked a hand through his hair, thinking. "That could work, Theo. That could really, really work." His eyes were bright, and he was almost grinning, an oddly boyish look on the man's sharp face. Theo found herself smiling back.

"Take him the picture. I've got a panic button for you in here"—he tapped the surface of the metal case—"but I don't think he'll try anything. I'd like to give you a bug to plant, but a paranoid bastard like that probably checks for 'em, and we don't want to get caught out for illegal surveillance. The cops have me looped in, and they're following separate leads; I don't want the museum to lose his money because we did something careless. Just get him the picture, make with the evaluation, and then skedaddle, okay?" The rough-and-ready façade had fallen away, leaving an excited, smiling man with a drawl in his voice and a light in his eyes.

Theo couldn't share his enthusiasm. But the opportunity to get rid of the painting? Maybe not *vade retro*, but closure. She liked the sound of that. Get it out of her life, get him out of her life, and leave the rest of it to the authorities.

She'd left the picture in her spare bedroom, quietly drying on its easel. It should be done by now. A quick layer of clearcoat, then, and she could have this over with.

CHAPTER NINE

Pepy cast the wax men into the fire, and there was a great cry, and the armies of Kush began to melt as if they too were wax. And when they had melted into the sand, their blood watered the earth, and it became red and fertile. And so Pepy's magic saved the lives of the people of the Nile.

- Excerpt from "The Deeds of Pepy," Egyptian fairy tale, circa 2200 BCE (fragment)

As Theo got out of the cab, a gust of wind whipped up, catching the broad portfolio and turning it into a sail. She struggled as the wind almost snatched it away. It figured—the damn painting had caused her so much trouble already, it was trying to get one last lick in before she could throw it out of her life. Growling in frustration, she dragged the portfolio back down and jammed it under her arm, mentally daring it to try anything else. Aki might put up with this from his paintings, but Theo was not in the mood.

This was it. Ten minutes in and out. Drop the painting, try to gauge Adler for Mark, get the hell out of there. She was done with hallucinations, with being drugged, with people using her, with stolen antiquities, with nightmares about patrons turning to dust, and with men who didn't make sense and followed her through her dreams.

She hadn't gotten much sleep.

Now that Theo was almost at the end of her majestically long rope, with the fraying knot in sight, she was ready to cut the whole business loose and pretend none of it had ever happened.

Seth Adler occupied the top three floors of a medium-sized skyscraper not far from Michigan Avenue. Information on his personal life was surprisingly scarce (he didn't even have a Facebook page), but from what Theo could gather from the museum's archives, the American branch of his family had made out like bandits in the aftermath of the Great Fire and owned loads of property in the Loop ever since. His deceased father, Faruq Adler, had supposedly lived in the same building. More than a century of privilege, power, and wealth, facing one confused artist.

She half expected a doorman in a fancy uniform, but there was only an echoing marble lobby, a set of elevators, and several carefully placed security cameras. The elevator buttons for the first twenty floors were marked inside like any other place, but at the top of the list was a black button with white lettering: *Penthouse. Please Hold.* The lens of another camera winked from the corner.

It was a completely sensible precaution, but it annoyed Theo anyway. The world seemed to keep dropping obstacles in her way. She jammed her thumb down on the button and held it, ignoring the whir of the camera as it focused on her. After a moment, she planted her free hand on her hip and tapped her foot, a broad theatrical movement that substituted for other, less professional gestures.

After a long, long moment, the camera whirred again. There was the barest hint of a jerk, a rumbling noise, and the car rose as smooth as butter. So unlike the rattling, old freight elevator at the museum. Being rich had its advantages, it seemed.

All right, all right. Resenting someone for their elevator was pushing it too far. She took a moment to breathe deeply and did her best to tamp down on the unreasonable anger. Yes, she was here for a confrontation—that was enough to be worked up about, without seeing evidence of his guilt in building fixtures. This whole business had been beyond rough, but it was putting edges on her personality that she didn't like.

Professional, professional, professional. She used the word as a mantra. Whatever else had happened, Theodora Speer was a professional.

The elevator glided to a stop, and the doors slid open. Hoisting the portfolio bodily, Theo stepped out with it held between her and the world beyond, like a shield. She didn't know what she expected—brushed steel-and-glass modernity? The heads of artists on pikes?

After staring a moment, she lowered the portfolio and shook her head. Never let it be said that Mr. Adler didn't know what he liked.

Stretching ahead of her was an enormous gallery with recessed ceiling lights and polished wood floors. The turn-of-the-century inset bookcases and vaguely Art Nouveau fireplace spoke to a prior existence as something else, perhaps a library with a drinks cabinet and a mantel to display old regimental colors. But the second floor of the three-story penthouse had been cut out entirely, leaving a broad, high-ceilinged hall that didn't belong there. At the far end loomed a steel-and-glass staircase that descended from the third floor and turned at midlevel to touch down facing the long gallery. An enormous window backed it, but the panes were tinted to keep out most of the sun.

The bookshelves were half-covered by hanging cloths, and the walls were cluttered with what looked like decorative weapons. Brighter-colored fingermarks on the wood betrayed the presence of dust, and the floor's clearcoat was old and streaky.

But Theo's eye was drawn past them. "Gallery" had been the right word, it seemed. What she had at first taken for pieces of random furniture resolved themselves into wood-and-plexiglass museum cases, a dozen or more on each side of the room.

Gripping her portfolio, she moved closer. The cases were filled with ancient junk.

A glance showed her a jade sword hilt with its blade long rusted away, a half-rotted straw basket with a brownish stain on the bottom, a folded piece of gray-green cloth marked with what looked like a heavily stylized X in undyed gray, and an iron circlet with crude thorns cast into the metal. A few feet over, a crest of the Emperor Valerian sat on the remains of a fourteenth-century Mongolian saddle, while a mummified monkey gazed sightlessly out with its back to Theo.

She tried not to stare, but it was hard. It was as if Seth Adler had opened an encyclopedia at random and picked items from whatever culture his finger landed on.

The walls were more organized. The hanging cloths were actually faded banners, and racks of polearms and swords hung alongside them in what seemed to be a vaguely chronological order. The arrangement was broken up at irregular intervals by mounted pieces of stained glass or wrought iron. Art was random and, for the most part, unfinished and uncoordinated. On the north wall, what looked like a Mies van der Rohe original sketch clashed rudely with a graceful sumi-e painting of a galloping horse.

It was massive, and it was schizophrenic. Wealthy amateur collectors typically focused on one or two specific eras and favored large, impressive pieces that would justify the money spent. This, though, was like something compiled by a hoarder, with no distinction between trash and treasure. He might be the kind of enthusiast who saw the worth in the old.

Still, she couldn't imagine only one man choosing to display it all. Was it a family obsession? If so, the other Adlers must have been as strange as Seth, and maybe stranger. She was glad she'd never met them.

Not that there wasn't genuine treasure mixed in, which made it all the more odd. Collecting random junk was one thing; Theo had seen stranger stuff on TLC. But the jade hilt or...she moved closer, curious despite herself...yes, a small pouch of coins, open to display the unmistakable profile of Gaius Julius Caesar, were items worth keeping. There were tapestry squares, clay hieratic tablets, an ornamental gauntlet with a twelfth-century Venetian prayer etched right into the metal.

Footsteps yanked her out of her reverie. A dark shape was coming down the stairs, oddly quiet despite the oh-so-modern floating glass steps. Theo tightened her grip on the portfolio and firmly reminded herself why she was there. The panic button was a reassuring weight in her pocket, and the broad portfolio formed a shield between her and the owner of the history junkyard. She was ready.

She wished she'd brought her sketchbook. Theo Speer's *Jerk Descending a Staircase.*

At least the jerk in question wasn't as neatly groomed as he used to be. The formerly put-together Seth Adler had come apart: shirt rumpled, tie loose, shades of gray bleeding into the background like overthinned watercolors. His shoulders hunched slightly, but his head was up, and there was a distant cast to his features.

"Miss Speer," he said. Finally, he'd gotten it right. "Can I help you?"

Theo shifted, keeping the portfolio between him and her. "I want to show you something."

"I'm fairly sure you're required to exclusively contact me through my lawyer," he said, stopping a step or two above the floor. "You made it very clear at our last meeting that you wanted nothing more to do with me."

He seemed ruffled but not panicked, as far as she could tell, with no obvious signs of being about to skip town. Mark would be happy to hear that.

"It's pretty simple, Mr. Adler," she said softly. In the lifeless gallery, surrounded by ancient things, some of the fire had gone out of her stomach. "I need to get something off my chest. Once I'm done, you're never going to hear from me again."

"Do you mean that?" he said. His gaze swept over her, lingering on the portfolio and the hard set of her jaw, and he moved a step or two closer. Theo let her grip loosen, and the edge of the portfolio thudded against the floor.

"Always do." He wasn't wearing shoes, she noticed; his footsteps had been quiet for a reason. Barefoot, though, he was still a good six inches taller than Theo.

"After you robbed the museum, I had an idea." Adler opened his mouth, possibly about to deny the allegation, but she kept talking: "I know, I know, *habeas corpus,* and I don't see any evidence that you habe the corpus, but you can't tell me what I did and didn't see. The good news for you is that artists are supposed to be insane, so nobody will pay attention to me. So I wanted to get rid of this"—she nudged the portfolio with the toe of her boot—"because to be honest, it's probably the best and worst thing I've ever done, and having it around is scaring me. I want it gone." She swallowed.

"Th—Miss Speer," he said softly. His expression was still tense, his posture stiff, but his hands were tightening on nothing and there was a strange note in his voice. "I'm not sure I can help you get rid of—"

"You're not *helping me get rid of it.* Think of it as taking responsibility for what you did." Theo snapped open the clasps on the edge of the hard-shelled case, the clicks of metal on plastic amplified ominously by the echoing gallery. It felt good, protective, like loading your revolver while the man in black was riding up Main Street. "Weren't you the one talking about being repelled by mummies? Well, you inspired me."

The case fell open and Theo, in one swift movement, snatched up the canvas and turned it to face Seth.

She'd done more work on it. It was still crude, but its lines were crisper, its form more realistic. It had been easy to make the mummy; Theo had whole sketchbooks full of her exhibition work. The man himself had been harder. There was a point, it seemed, where even purple ochre failed.

"Enjoy," Theo said shortly, shoving it into his hands. A lump was rising in her throat, and she knew she had to get out before she said something she would regret. This was over. "If you want another one like it, call my agent."

There was a yelp and a curse—rolling and guttural, a language she couldn't place—as Adler almost dropped the canvas. Theo turned on her heel, her cheap boots leaving black marks on the floor. She could hear his breathing, harsh and echoing, half-muffled by the painting that had been thrust into his chest. Served him right.

She made for the elevator, not quite running but definitely not walking either. It wasn't that far. She could make it.

"Theo?" His voice had an odd note in it, half-angry and half-questioning, but she ignored it. *Keep walking, keep walking*, she chanted to herself. Like seeing your ex in the supermarket—don't stop to talk or you'll wind up in a world of uncomfortable. Pretend you don't hear.

"Theo!" Louder this time, tinged with something like fear. Her steps faltered unwillingly. "Theo! What did you do?"

Heart racing, she clenched her hands by her sides and turned. Part of her expected to see him bearing down on her... But no. He'd halted in his tracks and dropped the painting. It lay facedown on the floor, quite innocuous, but Seth Adler was backed away from it with wide eyes.

"What did you do?" he repeated. With the blood draining from his face, he looked almost gray with fear. "You could have killed me! Get rid of it! Get rid of it now!"

He fumbled in his pocket, and Theo was about to retreat when she saw the lighter.

Paints were horribly flammable, and that wasn't the least of it. Her heart raced as she remembered where she was: dry air, cloth hangings, varnished wood floors...and in the middle, an oil-soaked bomb in the form of the best and worst work of her life. And Seth Adler about to set it off.

Moving faster than she knew she could, Theo bounded forward and slapped the lighter out of his hand. It went skidding across the floor, the metal making comical plinking noises as it bounced off the hardwood.

Adler recoiled from her, and Theo stumbled. His hand flashed out to catch hers and she gasped, lashing out with her other arm. Her short, ragged nails dug into the back of his hand. He let out a grunt as he lost his hold, and Theo lurched forward to land on her knees on the hardwood. Footsteps thudded as Adler retreated hastily.

"Dammit," she breathed, bracing her hands against the floor. "What was that?"

With an effort, she sat back on her haunches. Adler came into view, moving gingerly. His face was twisted up in an expression she couldn't quite name, but she thought there might be guilt there. He held out a hand, but she ignored it and got to her feet.

"Could have killed you?" she echoed, trying to keep her breathing steady. Adler's hair was rumpled, lying in curls of black and gray against his undone collar, and the pulse in his throat was rapid. She swallowed again and pulled her eyes away. "It isn't that bad. I know I'm not much with the more abstract schools, but a little Klimt never hurt anyone."

"Don't tease," he said. The words came out rough. "Why did you paint that?"

He was holding his left hand at an odd angle. Two of the fingers were wrenched, and Theo's fingernails had left bright-red lines on his skin. She'd hit him hard enough to injure him. His good hand still flexed automatically, and his shoulders were hunched, as if he was prepared to jump at any second. The painting lay where it had fallen, but his gaze kept flicking back toward it.

"I was angry," she said as evenly as she could. She blinked, trying to focus as she massaged her arm. He wasn't making much sense. "You robbed the museum. I needed to do something, and I didn't have a photograph of you to rip up."

His eyes narrowed. "So you do know. How did you find out?"

"Know what? I thought it would feel good to get it out of my system!"

Seth was mirroring her actions, massaging his own injured hand. Not badly hurt, though: the purplish marks were fading at the edges, the swelling of the wrenched joints beginning to subside. As she looked, the last of the bruises vanished into the skin.

He stepped back and picked up the painting. Little beads—dried blood?—fell from his hand as he flexed his fingers. The torn streak left by her nails was already gone.

"Why did you paint me like this?" he said after a long moment. "This worshiping figure. This isn't me, Theo. It's chaotic."

Chaos. Pieces clicked, and something dropped in her stomach. She thought of her poor shabtis—frozen in their poses of work or worship, their limbs stretched out and stiff if age hadn't broken them off—all gone.

There were rules for those tiny creations, and there were rules for their painted brethren on tomb walls. All arms and legs had to be visible. The face displayed in profile, no distortion of the form. The body was whole, sacred, and must be untampered with, or disaster could result. So the Egyptians had believed. It was crucial to maintain order and reality in their art, because art, words, religion, and magic worked together to hold the line against the forces of chaos. They must have order, or every-thing would be destroyed.

The beads from his hand had bounced far on the smooth hardwood. She picked one up and rolled it between her fingers.

"You honestly believe that?" Theo said. The nodule between her fingertips didn't crumble, and its surface was smooth and matte. "So you tried to burn it? God."

His hold slipped, and the painting slid a few inches through his fingers.

"I know I'm no Matisse, but you still can't burn my painting just because you think it'll bring you bad luck." There, that sounded sensible of her, didn't it? "It's the principle of the thing."

"Some things deserve to be burned." He dropped the painting, kick-ing it away. The canvas skidded across the room and bumped into the wall. "Burn it. Cut it up. Paint over it. I don't care. But it can't stay that way, and it can't stay here."

"Why not? Because you don't like Art Nouveau? Or are you trying to get me out of here before I realize your blood turns into clay?"

His eyes widened. "What do you mean?"

"Artist. I know clay when I feel it." She crumbled the bead between her fingertips and flicked the dust off. It felt good to say it out loud. "Old clay too. Montmorillonite."

"My blood—"

"Your blood turns into clay, Seth."

"But it—"

"*It turns into clay.*" She met and held his gaze, putting her anger and confusion and fear into her eyes as if she could pin him to the wall with the force of her stare. Like sticking a butterfly on a card. "At this point, there aren't a lot of lies you can tell me. So are we going to keep dancing around the issue?"

Another frozen moment passed, and Seth wavered. His eyes

dropped for a moment, and his shoulders hunched. The taut lines of his body created pools of shadow that washed him out.

"Tell me the truth," Theo said. Her lips felt numb and the words came out slurred, as if they were trying to keep her from getting herself into more trouble. Mummies, shabtis, curses, robberies, life and death, paintings, and blood that turned into clay. "I'm ready to listen. Please, tell me the truth."

He paced a few steps, stopped, and glanced back, his fingers twisting reflexively. They were, Theo noted vaguely, completely healed. He swallowed.

After a long moment, he straightened his back and faced her again as best he could. "It sounds insane," he said.

"Which'll make a nice change from how dull the last few weeks have been." She kept her gaze fixed on him. He looked like he wanted to run or sink into the ground, and though she wasn't sure she'd blame him for it, it wouldn't be happening on her watch. "Tell me the truth," she repeated softly.

The dead man in front of her struggled to find the words. His lips twisted.

"I suppose you could say," he began slowly, "that I've been stretch- ing the truth. I'm not from around here."

"I guessed that," she replied. Her eyes never left his face. "Where are you from?"

"Waset." A pause. "Thebes."

She took a deep breath. "I think the question is…*when* were you from Thebes?"

He never blinked, but the dark eyes seemed to flinch. "I was born seven years before the ascension of Amenemhat the First."

Theo took another breath. She put a hand on the wall, her fingers splaying against the smooth surface. Her brain automatically threw out the information, culled straight from the museum's exhibition bible. Twelfth Dynasty, right at the beginning of the Middle Kingdom. Circa 1991 BCE, if you believed the most common estimates. More than four thousand years ago. A time before cavalry or iron weapons.

It shouldn't be believable. If she hadn't seen what she'd seen in the loft, she would have written the whole thing off as delusion. If not for clay blood and dying men turning to dust. Either it was true, or she was losing her mind.

But in her life, her brain was the one thing she really had. If she were insane, she wouldn't even have that. She couldn't accept that thought.

"And you"—Theo cleared her throat—"you're that mummy?"

"Was." He paused for a moment, searching for words. "Old wine in new bottles."

"Old soul in new body?"

"Exactly."

"It's a good story," she said. "Do you have proof?"

Silently, Seth held his hand up for her to examine. She stared at it, searching for any sign of marked skin. But there was nothing. She touched it.

Her fingers folded around his. The skin was coarse but unmarked, the old scars she'd seen at the party gone as cleanly as if they'd never been there. His hand was warm and strong, with none of the teeth marks she knew she'd left. The webbing and ball of the thumb were whole, despite the skin that had been torn not so long ago.

"Nothing heals that fast," she said.

"You're right," Seth said. "Nothing can."

"New bottle?"

"Old wine."

"Very old," Theo murmured. Her eyes stung, but to her surprise, a bitter smile edged its way across her face. "And to think I was intimidated when I thought you were, what, in your fifties?"

"We'll split the difference," he said softly. "The new body is about thirty."

"Really?"

"I promise." His thumb traced the side of hers, flesh lightly gliding over flesh. "Young and healthy."

She swallowed. "Mr. Adler, are you trying to seduce me?"

Oh God. Faced with a man who claimed to be more than four millennia old, his long, dark fingers wrapped around hers as he transfixed her with his stare, and the first thing that came to mind was *The Graduate*? His expression was knowing, and she resisted the urge to slap herself in the face.

"Are you feeling particularly seduced?" he responded.

"Not exactly."

"Good." His tone had a twist of wryness. "That would make things awkward."

"That's right; I'm way past thirteen," she said. "So what were you? A priest, right? Condemned for love?"

"You've been watching too many movies. And for the record—I've been wanting to say this since the party—those mummy films are garbage. None of that ever happened."

"I know," she said. "I mean, who ever heard of someone coming back from the dead?"

Seth stepped back, seemingly gauging her mood. His eyes flickered over her, and Theo's hand felt chilled with the loss of his touch. She sternly ordered herself to focus and tried to ignore the pounding of her heart.

"What were you?" she repeated softly. "Tell me, Seth. Please. Give me anything to prove that we're not both going insane."

He let out a slow breath. "I was the son of the governor of the Crocodile District," he said. "Downriver from Thebes itself. Beautiful land, very fertile. My brother and I became trusted servants of the great Amenemhat. And I had the honor of marrying the pharaoh's grand-niece."

Of course. A mummy man had to have a connection to a pharaoh, didn't he? Nobody ever claimed to be a reincarnated peasant from nowhere. Her bullshit detector pinged. "Right," she responded. "So was she the great love of your life? You transcended death for her, right? Or are you going to disavow her dramatically?"

"I didn't love her," he said flatly, "because it was a political match. But we were good friends, and she was my wife and the mother of my children. You should know when you're crossing a line."

"Have a heart," she said. "I'm taking a lot on faith here. Maybe I was wrong and people do heal that fast. I'm just a flaky artist—what do I know about this stuff?"

Seth looked down, his jaw tensing. "I answered your question, Theo. I told you the truth. Are you satisfied?"

"No."

"No? What else could you want?"

"Everything," Theo said. Seth pulled back another pace, his expression openly wary and distrustful.

"Okay, maybe I didn't put that right," she continued quickly. The words stumbled over themselves as they raced out. "I don't want to blackmail you or steal your magic potion or anything. But if you're

telling the truth, if you really are some kind of...of ancient mummy..."
She shook her head, still unable to believe what she was saying. "Then
you're the only person—the only person alive today—who remembers
those times. If this is a lie or a hallucination or something, it's such a big
one that you can't expect me to let it go."

She shivered. Colors and textures tumbled through her mind: old
gold, cool blue-green, startlingly red ochre painted onto yellow plaster or
dabbed into the hollows and crevices of low relief. "You could know...so
much. Don't you get how many questions there are?"

His expression was unreadable. "Questions?"

"How you lived. What you did. What you believed." She swallowed.
"How you're here."

"I believed in the gods that watched over us all. But how I'm
here...that was my brother's work." He shook his head. "He was a great
priest, one of the greatest I ever knew. He made the shabtis for me."

"Is that..." she began.

Seth nodded, his eyes dark. "He wrote a prayer to say over them,
and another to cut into them. 'Words spoken by the son of Merenptah.
This is a vessel for him, and will become as him through his will. A savior
of the *ka*, a form to cast the *sheut*—'"

"—'a home for the *ba*,'" Theo whispered. Nobody outside of the
department knew about those inscriptions. It was a battered line of
hieroglyphics, pieced together from the few remaining marks on dozens
of statuettes, but the professors had been incredibly excited about it.
Nothing had been published yet; they were quietly planning a study of it
and its potential impact on the modern view of funerary customs. There
was no way he could know it. Unless...

"I believe you," she said. Finally. It felt like a weight had been lifted,
and she breathed out, terrified and exhilarated at the same time. She
believed him. She accepted, somehow, that the dark-eyed man standing
in front of her was something that she knew shouldn't exist. It scared
her, but it freed her. The worst had happened; what could be stranger?

"You believe me?" he asked, his voice oddly uneven.

"I believe you," Theo repeated. "You're not normal." Another smile
began to appear in spite of herself. "And I just won a prize for understatement."

"I'll admit, I've never been called 'not normal' before," Seth said, "I
think. I don't remember it all."

"Well, you know me," she said, wrapping her arms more closely around herself. The stillness of the gallery pressed in around her. "I always was pretty good at saying the wrong thing."

"I don't know about that," he replied with a smile of his own. "'I believe you' was pretty good."

Against all odds, she found herself smiling back at him. A warm feeling settled in her chest, along with a twinge of nervousness. Motion, pure motion, was there if she could grab it. He was a foot from her now, his hand near hers, a flush in his face coloring his high cheekbones.

"So you wanted the artifacts so you could stay alive," she said. *Focus, Theo.*

"'A vessel for him, and will become as him,'" Seth recited. The words had a rolling, sonorous quality, like a chant in church. "The tomb was my cache, my place of sanctuary, where the shabtis were hidden. But it was robbed in the 1880s, while I was in India. I set up the trust as a cover and spent years tracking down everything."

"And that night in the loft"—she was proud her voice faltered only a little—"you breathed on one of the shabtis before you sent it down the shaft. You died upstairs—"

"And came to life downstairs."

A man dying of tuberculosis enlists his brother, the priest, to create fake bodies for him. Something to hold his soul in the real world. An ancient Egyptian man does this, knowing that his entire world is constructed around the eventuality of death, and that he was going against every rule his universe is based on. Order versus chaos, and trying to hide from the afterlife was the absolute essence of chaos.

"So when you found them," she said, "you thought you had to steal them back. Them and your mummy."

He flinched at the mention of the mummy. She saw a flicker of apprehension in his gaze, and she knew she was on the right track.

"You need the mummy," Theo continued. Seth didn't say anything, but he couldn't hide the emotion in his eyes. "The body is the home of the soul and must be preserved. As long as it exists, the soul can continue." Her head shot up. "That's why you took it!" she burst out. "I told you it was going to be used in the study—"

"And possibly dissected," Seth said flatly. "I might not be wearing it anymore, but I have a certain fondness for it."

"You said you didn't want to do it that night," she said. Seth relaxed a fraction, but his gaze stayed fixed on her, both cautious and defensive. He seemed to be waiting to see which way she'd jump.

Theo stepped back, running a hand through her hair and breathing deeply. "This is big," she said, half to herself. Putting it into words was hard, but with every word that she added to it, it took on more solidity in her mind. "This is...this is something so big I can't even say how big it is. I can't—I mean, I can't make you give them back. Not now."

The words felt strange. To admit straight out that she wanted to let someone keep something they'd taken from the museum burned, though these were definitely extraordinary circumstances. She didn't see people come back from the dead every day, after all.

At that thought, she let out a short bark of laughter, drawing an odd look from Seth Adler. "I'm sorry," she said. "But this wasn't what I planned on when I went to art school."

"It wasn't what I planned on when I took my commission from the Minister of War," Seth responded dryly. "Though at the time, my concern was mainly with advancing my family."

"You must have been scared," she said suddenly. He raised his head slightly, lips parting a little. "To try and make yourself a magic body."

Seth looked down. "Terrified," he said. "I thought I was cursed." His voice was hoarse. "I prayed every day. For a year. The aches got worse and my family began to collect my burial goods."

"'A very odd burial,'" Theo quoted, remembering the conversation at the donors' night, "'and a very sick mummy.'"

"I didn't do anything!" he burst out. "I paid my dues; I was faithful to my wife; I honored my gods and my family! There was no reason for the gods to do that to me!" His fingers flexed, clenching instinctively as if he were trying to find a way to fight the memory. "I thought they wanted me dead. One sacrilege was hardly an overreaction. I wanted the long life that had been stolen from me.

"Good men don't earn much. Accolades when they live, but cheap stelae when they die. If I didn't make a plan, I was going to die like a slave. No more war, no more seeing my family grow, no more chances to earn glory for my name or bring victories for my king." He turned again, angry, but not at her. "So I went to my brother. Shabtis were said to become whatever we wanted in the next world—so why not shabtis that could return me to this one in a new body? Meren called it sacrilege, but we did it anyway. Why should a cursed man care if he offends the gods?"

Theo shook her head. "What a mess," she said. There didn't seem to be anything else she could say. Seth let out a short laugh.

"Definitely not normal, eh?"

"No. Not normal." She tried not to think about the light in his eyes. His breath was coming faster, anger seeming to fire something in him. He moved closer, and Theo's heart thumped as he put his hand on her forearm. For a dead man, he didn't feel very cold.

Speaking of not normal...

"What was your name?" she asked.

This time, Seth didn't hesitate. His gaze was fixed on hers. "Anhurmose."

She turned the word over on her tongue. A name for the mummy. A name for the man in front of her.

"Anhurmose," she repeated. "Anhurmose."

"I like Seth better," he said. She shivered as his warm breath touched her face.

"I like them both," she told him. She did, despite the insanity of it all. Poor mute, sad-smiling THS203—all he'd wanted to do was live forever, and in a way, he'd managed it.

Seth was something else. She still had reasons not to trust him, especially over the robbery. But he was also something that she had literally never encountered before, and that night in the loft had torn her customary realism to shreds and given her motion on canvas like never before. She wanted to see, do, and know more. She wasn't forgiving him for everything that had happened, but understanding blunted the edges of her anger.

"Really," he said gently, "you don't have to lie, Miss Speer. I haven't exactly made your life easy."

"Theo," she said. "And easy...no. Interesting?" She moistened her lips again. "Yes."

"Is interesting a good thing?"

"It's a change," she murmured. "Change is good."

"Theo." The shadows made deep pools of darkness under his eyes and in the hollows of his throat. He was a bas-relief, a sculpture from a time when the world was both more and less civilized. Her brain screamed that she was about to do something incredibly dangerous, that there was no point in moving further when she knew she was going to get in over her head. Her body threw other images at her: the warmth and tantalizing roughness of his lips, the taste of motion that cascaded across the canvas after she had known real fear. God, one incident and she'd turned into a thrill junkie.

She wanted that back again. And if it ended in tears, wasn't that what artists did? Chased heartbreak for their work?

"Seth," she said, "interesting is a very good thing."

It was barely a kiss, just a brush of her lips across his as she stood on tiptoe, a touch that lasted a frozen moment. But something struck, a match flared, and Theo's heart shivered. She could feel Seth's pulse pounding hard in the skin beneath her hand.

It seemed to release something in him. His hands went to her jaw, thumbs stroking over the skin there as he pulled her closer and deepened the kiss. His need was raw, palpable, a little desperate as he held her. Theo's lips parted without thinking, responding to the need there, letting him past one more barrier. His tongue touched hers, sending another spark of heat skittering through her, and she curled her hands into the fabric of his shirt.

He murmured her name again as they separated. His color was high—redness in his cheeks, lips kiss-bruised, and eyes bright. Their gazes stayed locked, his skin warm against hers.

There it was again. The shifting of the world, the sense of movement, still figures somehow alive in spite of being paint and pigment. It wasn't intoxicating—it was enervating, like the moment before the big drop on the rollercoaster. Her still-life world was jolting into motion. It would be so easy for it to go wrong, but for once, there was something there to go wrong.

"That wasn't smart," Theo said after a long moment.

"No, it wasn't," Seth admitted, his voice rough.

She moistened her lips again and stepped back a pace or two, trying to pull everything into focus. The motion began to still as sanity reasserted itself. "Four meetings, two kisses," she said. "And you've got me doing it too."

"I'm a bad influence," he admitted with a touch of humor. "Forgive me?"

"Maybe. If you're willing to trade."

He raised an eyebrow. "Trade what?"

"Call it compensation," she said. "You wrecked my exhibition, and now you've handed me this idea of someone who's been alive for four thousand years. The ultimate primary source." She tugged on her braid, thinking. "I know professors who would pay millions to pick your brain for half an hour."

"It's not that simple, Theo." He frowned. "Four thousand years is too much to recall. If I didn't write things down sometimes, I'd never remember where I'd been. My memories of Egypt are stored in the clay, but everything beyond that fades."

"Then tell me about that," she urged. "Tell me about Egypt. Tell me about anything. Sounds. Images. Colors."

"I can't, Theo. Not—not yet." Some of the remaining warmth faded from his eyes. "It's difficult to explain."

She put a hand on his arm. "I swear I'm not going to tell anyone, Seth. But one thing. Please. One thing that I can take to prove that you lived four thousand years ago."

There was a long moment of silence, and Seth's gaze was leaden and unreadable. Finally, he dropped his head, unable to meet her gaze anymore.

"My tomb," he said. "I've looked at the excavation records. You've got most of it. But there's another chamber—on the northwest side, sunk into the slope. It's hidden behind the mural of Apep. Inside, there are ten more shabtis, grave vessels with models of food and drink, two jars of beer, five loaves of bread, a jar of honey, a chisel one of the workmen dropped, and a badly misspelled copy of the Book of the Osiris-Name. It's what those professors would call the Coffin Texts." The corner of his mouth twisted. "My scribe was good, but his spelling was not. I didn't realize that until 1938, did you know? I read an analysis of my own tomb inscriptions. They said I must not have been very well liked, to have such an amateur writing on my walls."

He looked at her again. "Is that enough?"

"It is." The words left her in a whisper, but they carried weight. It was. It was something the museum's people in Egypt could confirm. And it was also something that people would question if she revealed it and it turned out to be true—or untrue. Lots of angles here, directions she wasn't used to thinking about. Still... "I think it is."

CHAPTER TEN

You have wandered for too long. Think of your corpse and come home.

- From the "Tale of Sinuhe,"
circa 1960 BCE

It was impossible to tell what time it was. There were no windows or clocks in the bedroom, lending the place the air of a comfortable tomb. Theo sighed as she rolled over, stretching out the aches in her muscles. Her rumpled shirt had left crease marks in her skin, and she'd kicked the blankets off the bed.

Memories came creeping back, slow and awkward, and her face reddened in the gloom. She'd been kissing a man. Kissing Seth Adler, the source of her current trouble and the inspiration for her weirdest work yet.

Her bag lay where she'd dropped it by the edge of the bed. Reluctantly, she reached out and flopped over to it, fumbling through the contents for her cell phone. The glowing display told her it was almost six o'clock in the morning.

Staying over had probably been a mistake. But the exertion of their struggle, and the sheer overwhelming nature of the revelation Seth had shared with her, had worn her out. Seth had offered a guest bedroom—with a locking door—and she'd accepted.

Her sleep had been deep but plagued with strange dreams. She had the oddest sensation that someone had been calling her name, asking for...something she couldn't remember.

Focus, she told herself sternly. It would be time to get up soon, and she had things to do.

For a start, she had to call Zimmer.

Groaning, Theo let her head drop into her hands. Zimmer would be waiting for her report. If he thought something had happened to her, he might tell the police, and who knew what would happen next.

It was plain that she would have to lie, and the thought made her stomach twist. Twenty-four hours earlier she'd been solidly on Zimmer's side, ready to help him expose a psychotic, drug-fueled art thief. Now she didn't know where she stood. If she tried to explain it to the Security chief, she doubted he'd listen. Mummies? Blood turning into clay? History straight from the horse's mouth? Not the best way to guarantee her job security, especially not when she didn't even have her full clearance back yet. She would have to come up with a damn good lie.

The thought made her horribly uncomfortable. Sitting there in the gloom of the bedroom, she felt like a gullible tool.

At least I didn't sleep with him, she told herself, as resurgent disbelief fought against the memories of clay droplets and disintegrating bodies. That, at least, was a sentiment that could apply to either side. Whether he was an accomplished liar or a...*thing*...she shouldn't have gone as far as she had. Let alone talking late into the night and then sleeping over. There was common sense at stake here, although that felt like the one thing that had been in short supply lately.

Sighing, Theo swung her legs over the edge of the bed and straightened up, trying to move quietly. Early or not, she wasn't going to be able to doze much longer in Seth Adler's home. She listened at the door, wondering if he was awake, but heard nothing besides the low humming of the central air system. Safe. Tugging her shirttail down, she opened the door and stepped out into the hall.

Seth was where she had left him, laid out on an enormous tan couch and fast asleep. His arms were neatly by his sides, his legs pulled together, a blanket tucked around his still-dressed form.

Moving as silently as she could, Theo stepped closer and peered at him. His eyes were shut tightly and his breathing was shallow.

He lay so still it took her a moment to spot the evidence that he was alive. There was a pallid tinge to his skin and the veins and tendons stood out sharply, as if moisture had been sucked out of the flesh. Shuddering, she turned away. Watching him certainly wasn't going to do anything for her peace of mind.

Unsure of what else to do, Theo returned to the broad gallery. It looked very different now. With the great ceiling lights dimmed, only a few bluish strips lent faint illumination to the assembled collection.

One of the banners was crooked. Her portfolio case had been shoved haphazardly onto a recessed shelf, hiding both it and the lethal painting. The painting's skid across the floor had peeled several layers of pigment off the canvas, scoring it deeply and destroying part of both figures. Yet Seth still hated having to see it. She tweaked the banner back into place, hiding it completely.

It was almost funny in its strange way. The person who collected these things had experienced chaos like she could never imagine, but he was afraid of a simple picture. Four thousand years of danger and death were nothing compared to four hours with oils.

Feet padding noiselessly on the sleek wood, she moved to the nearest case and peered in. There was the old, faded piece of greenish cloth with the undyed X showing on the top. In the darkness, the green was washed out, leaving the remnant gray-black with a nearly white symbol on top. With a start, Theo realized what it must have been originally—dark seaweed-green dye used instead of black, since faded over the years. Hundreds of years, if her reading of the symbol and color scheme was correct. Which meant it wasn't an X.

"Hospitaller," she murmured, sketching the shape of the cross with her fingertip against the glass. "Of course." No surprise that the leper mummy had gravitated toward the great doctors of the Crusades. They'd ultimately become pirates too, which had probably appealed to the military part of him. Had this been his, then? Or did he just collect flotsam and jetsam?

The case was set close to the wall, next to a recessed fireplace that clearly hadn't burned anything in years. A few more items were displayed on the mantel: a medieval German helmet, a moth-eaten glove, a curved knife on a wooden stand. The knife's hardened leather hilt was stamped with a set of initials, but the whole thing had a thick coating of dust.

There was a creak behind her and she stiffened. The quality of the silence had changed. Someone was awake.

Breathing out, she ran a finger over the hilt of the knife and wiped away some of the dust. She'd seen weapons like it before.

"What is it?" she said anyway, brushing away a little more. The colors began to come through: the dark gray of worn steel, the initials

R.A. It was an old weapon, but it had been well-used. "Who was R.A.?"

"Rachid al-Adhur," came the voice of Seth from behind her. "He had quite the interesting life before he founded the Trust. That's a Khyber knife."

"From your time in India?"

"The most recent sojourn, yes." Seth leaned against the doorframe, watching her. In the low, cold light of the trophy room, the remaining warmth in his colors faded away. He might have been a tinted marble statue.

"And the knife?" she asked. She wiped away another spot of dust, exposing an old crack in the leather of the hilt.

"The knife was a gift while he was playing the part of a Hassanzai of Tor Ghar. Rachid found it necessary to adopt a new persona for a while."

"I'll bet he did." The knife looked worn. It had been used, a lot, and then cleaned one final time and put away in a trophy room to gather dust.

He found it necessary; *he* founded the Trust. Despite surrounding himself with pieces of history, Seth seemed to have closed himself off easily from his former lives.

Or perhaps not easily. She didn't know much about the Hassanzai, but late nineteenth-century India hadn't been a good place for people with divided loyalties. War and rebellion raged across the continent. Now, though, it was all gone. Dust gathering on an old Khyber knife, its aged leather set as hard as wood, the people it might have killed names in textbooks.

Everything passed, and the heat of politics and religion and colonial warfare became lines in a history book to some. Even something that could force Rachid al-Adhur to adopt a fake identity—an imposture within an imposture, carried out by a man who couldn't die—would eventually vanish.

If this was really true, then everything was impermanent to him. Everything she took for granted, like the country she lived in and the rules and morals her world ran on, would pass. And he'd live to see it, and learn the new rules in turn. *Sic transit gloria mundi.*

She couldn't imagine what that was like. But the motion, the blurriness that it must lend to the world itself, made her thoughts spark.

"I'll bet he did," she repeated, and turned away from the mantel to lean against the case. She rested her arms on the top of the glass as she

leaned down, examining the strange garment. The tails of the shirt she
wore fluttered in the soft breeze of the air system, and she knew Seth's
gaze was on her. "You know, we had an exhibit on the courts of the
maharajahs not so long ago. 'Opulent' doesn't begin to describe it. How
did Rachid like that?"

"He didn't care." Seth moved around to the other side of the case,
mirroring her posture with his own and meeting her eyes as he leaned
over the Hospitaller tunic. "He didn't have the kind of life that put him in
the palaces of the rajahs and ranis—not when there were so few left after
the Mutiny."

"You mean the Indian Rebellion?"

He shrugged. "Six of one. People died."

"As they typically do in mutinies and rebellions." Theo stepped
away from the tunic and moved left, toward the next case. This one
contained everything golden: more gold coins, an aged gold torque in the
old Celtic style, and a gold-plated cigarette case with a date and inscription that were worn down to almost illegibility. She thought she caught
the number 1901 on it, but it was hard to tell through what looked like
acid damage. "That was when the empire really started coming apart.
You must've seen that coming. You're an old hand at this, after all."

Seth circled around her, padding almost noiselessly on the smooth
boards, before stopping opposite her again. He rested his fingertips
against the glass this time, poised above the sleek curve of the torque.

"Nobody can see the future," he said softly, his eyes once again
locked on hers. "And it's hard to see an empire dying if you're one man
on the edge of it. No matter how many times it's happened before."

Theo swallowed, but kept her voice calm and level. "Is that what
you've learned from four thousand years? That you don't know anything?"

"Not quite," he said. "But it's a good start."

He reached across the case and, softly, slid his hand down her forearm and over her wrist. Her fingers curled around his without quite
meaning to, and he ran the edge of a thumbnail over the pad of her palm.
"The problem with people, Theo, is that we're never as wise or as strong
as we think we are. That was the first thing I had to learn. I don't know if
I've learned anything since."

"Sure you have," she said. "I notice we're not speaking Kemetic."

He gave a wry smile at her teasing tone. "Learning a new language isn't that hard when you have no alternative. And given that I've been speaking English for about three hundred years, I'd flatter myself that I have some knowledge of it."

"Really?" She drew back her hand and circled around to the next case. There was another piece of folded cloth there, less ragged than the Hospitaller tunic and dyed what must have once been a beautiful shade of red. She leaned over the case, propping herself against it and letting her back settle into a deeper curve. Her breasts, modest but peaked in the cool air of the room, rested against the chilly glass.

Seth's dark gaze followed her every move, but this time he didn't move with her. He stayed there, tracking her with his eyes—hungrily, she thought, with a hint of caution. He knew a game was being played, but he didn't know where he stood.

"Really," he said. "It was a difficult change. But learning English isn't much, next to building a house or manning a ballista. I've always managed well." He reached across the space for her hand again, but Theo slipped around the case and turned to the rack of spears and polearms instead.

She ran one forefinger over the dull edge of a halberd's blade, hyperaware of Seth's piercing stare at her back. "Well, you'd have to," she said softly. "You're not supposed to be here."

He was still by the last case, his hands resting on it. The dim light touched the edges of his fingers and palm, leaving the rest as dark claws against the glass. "Am I not," he said, his voice hoarse.

"You aren't." She traced patterns in the dust with the tip of one finger, moving slowly, almost idly. Her words were light and calm. She had him, she knew, in the palm of her hand. "You should be dead. But here you are, Seth Adler, the financial superstar, in your nice suit, surrounded by relics of those centuries in between. You shouldn't be here, but you are. Somehow. And you can't tell me that's been easy."

"Maybe not." Seth stretched out his hand and brushed his fingertip over the dusty halberd. He was closer to her now, his skin inches from hers, his eyes glints in his shadowed face.

Her mouth was suddenly dry, but she forced herself to focus. "And if it isn't easy," she said, "then when I ask about it—please, Seth, tell me the truth."

She wiped away the pattern with a sweep of her thumb. "You don't have to lie to me. I can't use your words against you. I need...I need to know, sometimes."

Seth's gaze darted over her, his mouth twisted into a tight line. Then his hand dropped from the blade and came to rest on her shoulder, gently stroking the ball of his thumb over the taut line of her collarbone. The warmth and closeness of him, against the coldness of the room, drew her like a nail to a magnet.

The kiss was deeper, harsher than before. She drank it in and fought for more, her hands curling into the fabric of his shirt, her body pressed against his. There was a hitch in his breath as her legs parted slightly, and he pulled her closer, stroking one hand over the curve of her hip and thigh.

"Di djed nebet," he murmured into her ear, his voice somewhere between a laugh and a sob.

Djed. She knew that word. She pressed her lips against the corner of his mouth, feathering kisses there, as his grip on her tightened. He whispered the words over and over again, like a prayer, and she wrapped herself into him and held him as he prayed.

"Hey," she said quietly. "Look at me, Anhurmose."

He shifted, but never got the chance. A shrill buzzer cut through the cold room, and a bright-blue light winked on at the end of the hall, making him jump and pull away.

"Hell!" he muttered. "The elevator."

Theo's back stiffened, and she instinctively yanked down on the hem of her shirt. It was like a shot of cold common sense straight to the back of the neck—someone else was possibly about to enter the equation, and there she was, pantsless in a man's art gallery. Not a phrase or a position she'd ever anticipated, and not one she was prepared for.

What are you thinking? she shouted silently at herself as she ran for the stairs. Seth was moving over to the elevator control panel on the wall, but she still didn't have pants on, and that was the thing that concerned her the most.

She had reached the bedroom and was scrambling into her jeans when the intercom flicked on.

"Police!" a voice buzzed. "We have a warrant to search these premises."

Theo froze. For a moment the world seemed to spin off its axis, making her stumble as she fought to rearrange it into sense. She sat down hard on the bed, tangled in her own jeans, as the voice repeated its demand.

He must've had the whole place wired with the intercom speakers, she thought vaguely. Wanted to know who was coming to visit. Smart man.

What were the police—? Why—? Oh no. Was this because of her? Had they finally decided to take her testimony seriously?

The thought galvanized her. Sprawling across the bed, half-dressed, Theo grabbed for her bag and fumbled through it. Receipts, ChapStick, and allergy medicine went spilling across the carpet before she finally found the panic button. She pressed it.

One moment. Two. Heart-stopping silence, nothing but the buzz of the intercom and distant banging noises from the elevator shaft. It didn't seem that Seth was letting them in, but that wouldn't last long. There were fire stairs, but could they be locked? Could he control that too? No Loop skyscraper was built to withstand a police siege....

She pressed the panic button again and again, but nothing happened. Cursing, she dropped it and fumbled with her bag, trying to finish pulling her pants on and grab her cell phone at the same time. Outside, the shouting went on.

"Come on come on come on..." she whispered as she dialed Zimmer's number. It rang—her heart leaped—

Voice mail. Her stomach dropped.

The knocking came again, louder. A voice called out something she couldn't quite hear. The bedroom door opened.

Theo spun, phone in her hand. Seth was standing in the bedroom doorway, pale and hard-eyed. He was fully dressed already, and held a pair of gloves and a scarf in one hand.

"We have to go," he said. "Come on. I have a way out."

"Wait!" she said. "There has to be a mistake. I thought they weren't going to investigate what I said!"

"Clearly they've found new evidence," Seth said tightly. As distant bangs echoed through the elevator shaft, he led her back into the gallery and over to one of the racks of polearms. He seized one of the grips and twisted. There was a grinding click, and a section of the wall swung out. Lights flickered on, illuminating bare cinder-block walls and a steep concrete staircase.

Seth's expression was pained and grim as the secret door opened. "I can't get caught, Theo. Not at this stage."

For a moment, she considered telling him to go. She'd stay, right? She hadn't done anything wrong.

Except being caught in the apartment of a man she'd previously accused, during the middle of a police raid, while the man himself had apparently vanished into thin air. No matter which way you spun it, that wasn't good. Her one lifeline wasn't picking up his goddamned phone. And Seth, with his knowledge and warm hands and desperate murmurs in her ear, was poised at the edge of a precipice. His eyes begged her to make a choice.

Grab the motion, Theo.

The staircase smelled like stale air and paint. She grabbed his arm and pulled him through the secret doorway. As it clicked closed behind them, the pounding feet and yells were abruptly muffled. Only their breathing echoed in their ears, harsh in the small space.

It was clearly meant as a secret escape route, nothing more than that. There was one single fluorescent light on each landing. It felt closed in, like an old gallery. Nobody had been here in years. There wasn't even dust.

After four flights, the stair ended abruptly at another small door. Theo flattened herself against the wall, heart pounding, as Seth fumbled with the lock. The door clicked open with well-oiled silence, and the two of them hurried through. They were in a white-painted hallway with a janitor's closet ahead of them. Theo knew a maintenance hall when she saw one.

No time and no words. Seth had clearly been afraid something like this would happen, and he'd set up an escape route for himself, but he only owned the top floors. Their Batman exit ended there. Fire stairs now.

Twenty floors, forty flights, forty turns. They moved without speaking, their feet thudding on the painted cement steps. High above, the police might have already broken in. They would be ransacking the place, looking for him. Finding the artifacts, finding the painting, finding evidence that he had been there minutes before. Finding the receipts and pills that she'd dropped.

Theo's throat seemed to close, and she stumbled on the last step, almost crashing into the wall. Her heart was banging so hard it felt like it would crack her ribs, and black spots danced in front of her eyes.

"Theo," Seth whispered, his voice hoarse and harsh in the confined space. "Theo, *djed—*" His hand touched her back, one broad thumb stroking a line down the center of her spine.

Djed. The word he'd said before, in the trophy room. It had tickled her brain, but with his hand on her now, neurons sparked and made the connection. Djed: one of the hieroglyphs in the tomb art, one of the many she'd memorized and reproduced again and again. Djed, backbone. Djed, strength.

The moment of thought yanked her out of the worst of the crush. Breathing deeply, she rested her hands against the wall, forcing herself to focus. Get to the bottom of the stairs.

Get out. Call Zimmer and find out what the hell was going on. Don't panic. *Djed.*

"Djed," she repeated, pushing off from the wall. "I hope so. Let's go."

* * *

She seemed to think it was a command, or maybe a spell. Was it? He wasn't certain anymore. Everything had gone awry.

They hit the bottom of the stairs moments later, Theo catching her breath, him silent. High above them, the police would be turning his home of ninety-seven years upside down. If they thought to check everything, he could be dead sooner rather than later—but for now, they had to keep moving. A free Seth Adler could eventually find his shabtis and disappear. One in custody couldn't.

He pulled Theo into the building's first-floor health spa. One of the lockers in the men's room was always closed; no key had ever been cut, and he didn't need one. A twist of his fingers popped the lock out.

It was small, as his caches went. A duffel bag on the floor of the locker contained two thousand dollars in cash, a phony ID, and a hooded parka for a quick change of appearance. After a moment's deliberation, though, he tossed the jacket to Theo. As much as he hated the snow, he wasn't the one who'd get frostbite.

She accepted the jacket wordlessly. Something about her seemed to have shifted, but he wasn't sure what. She was numb, maybe, but not lost. Had he made a good choice, offering her the chance to come along?

Of course, he told himself. *The police might learn things from her about me. Keeping her close keeps me safe.*

Djed, though. The word had sprung to his lips of its own accord. The phrase he'd spoken in the penthouse above had ritual meaning, not merely as a sentence but as a form of invocation, and he barely knew why he'd said it. If the gods were watching, something like that was unlikely to be a coincidence. And the thought that the gods might be moving him to do anything—good or bad—at this moment was much more terrifying than the prospect of losing his new life.

"Where now?" she whispered as they reached the security door. "What's the plan?"

He didn't reply, just thrust the door open, and the two of them tumbled out into a fresh snowbank. It was a service alley, but the new snowfall had covered over the garbage and Dumpsters with a clean white powder that showed clear footprints. Seth stamped back and forth, muddling the tracks as best he could.

When she realized what he was doing, Theo lifted the lid of the Dumpster. She hauled out two bags of garbage and tore them open, spreading the old newspapers and food scraps everywhere. In seconds, the clean white blanket of snow was obliterated and their tracks destroyed.

Despite his adrenaline and creeping fear, Seth felt a prickle of admiration. It had been a long, long time since he had been running from anything in deep winter. He nodded to her, unsure of how exactly to phrase what was going through his mind, but Theo didn't seem to need a response. Her shoulders hunched as she faced into the wind, and her face was blank.

The service alley was clear, but several squad cars were parked at the front of the building. In seconds, Seth and Theo were two more commuters in the endless whirl of the Loop.

They were far enough from the Magnificent Mile that the shopping traffic thinned out. Instead, the people around them were tourists and workers, bundled up for the quick rush between buildings or from their job to the subway. Starbucks was doing brisk business, and commuters at bus shelters huddled over steaming cups of expensive coffee.

If anyone looked their way, they would assume that Seth and Theo were taking a quick jaunt across the street for a drink or a meal. Nobody who lived or worked in downtown Chicago would pay attention to them anyway: in a city of two million souls, there was safety in solitude, and making eye contact in public meant inviting unwanted attention.

Theo didn't say anything until they were six blocks away from the building. Seth silently offered her his arm, giving him a chance to pull her a little closer and murmur in her ear.

"The first twelve hours are the most important if I want to get out of the country. I have to reach my caches, and then the airport—"

He paused as Theo stiffened. "I don't know if I can take you with me, but I can try. If you want to."

Theo made a face. "What? No. The airport's a bad idea." Seth stopped for a moment, surprised. "They'll be expecting that," she added, tugging him into motion again. "Unless cop shows have lied to me, your assets are going to get frozen once they declare you AWOL, and maybe mine too. You won't be able to buy a ticket or charter a plane."

"I've done this before. Trust me."

"Since September 11th? Since you were a suspect in a major robbery, complete with police breaking down your door?" Theo rested her arm against his shoulder, acting like she was cuddling up to a boyfriend. "I hate to be cliché, Seth," she continued in a near whisper, keeping her expression calm, "but this is bad. How often have you been raided?"

"Not in a hundred and thirty years. Listen to me, Theo. I know what I'm doing. You can come with me if you need to—I'm sure they're checking on you as well."

"It's not that, Seth," she said calmly, only a faint hint of strain in her voice. "This isn't about me. Okay? You can't rabbit."

"Why not?" he said.

Minutes ago she had been soft and warm to the touch. Now she felt almost as cold as the city, and her muscles were tight under her skin.

"Because someone set us up," she whispered. "Leaving the country isn't going to solve that! We need to figure out what's going on, and why those people came to your house."

Seth tightened his scarf, more for something to do with his hands than anything else. Who cared why the police had come? People acted irrationally, and that was one of the few things that never changed over centuries or continents.

"Take it from someone who's been around a long, long time, Theo," he said. "It's better to get out while you have the chance. The hysteria usually dies down in thirty years."

"That's your tactic? Wait for everyone else to die or give up?" The idea seemed to horrify her, though she was keeping her tone level.

"Is that a problem?" he said tightly.

"In this century, it is," she responded. A gust of wind raked over them, carrying the smell of smoke and dirty snow, and she shivered violently against his arm. "People have a lot tougher time vanishing off the grid now. How much harder do you think it'll get in a couple of decades? If this doesn't get fixed now, someone's going to jail. And not all of us have extra lifetimes to waste."

For a moment, anger flared. He had seen, done, and endured more than she ever had or ever would, and she was telling him what to do. Never mind art or magic—this was his business, and for centuries he had run and survived to run again. She couldn't understand what was at stake here.

But djed, he'd said. Djed meant more than stability. It was backbone, order, *ma'at* against the unholy chaos of *isfet*. Strength. Perhaps Neith was trying to tell him something, if her power could touch this frozen stone city.

"In that case," he said slowly, and with great reluctance, "what should we do? We can't stay on the street."

She grabbed his arm. "Come on. You've missed a lot of things in your ivory tower, and one of 'em is the best way to be anonymous in the world. Can you trust me?"

"I—"

His hesitation was more than answer enough, unfortunately, and the way her face fell made his chest ache. But what was he supposed to say? Yes, he trusted her because he liked her. That didn't mean he could be careless about his chances. Anyone with a brain would say the same thing.

Djed. Di djed nebet.

The lady gives me strength.

"I don't know," he said. "But I trust that you mean well."

"Close enough." She tugged on his arm. "Let's go catch a train."

"What?"

"You heard me."

There was a set to her features that he had seen before, but it took him a moment to place. It was the look she'd had when he saw her in the loft that first night. A look that said, *Stand back; I know what I'm doing.*

She ducked into a nearby pharmacy and emerged five minutes later with cheap knit hats, scarves, and an off-the-rack parka. "Camouflage," she said when he pointed out that the cold couldn't harm him much.

"Everyone's wearing stuff like this, and it'll make you harder to spot."

Once he was attired to her satisfaction, hat pulled down over his hair and a scarf over his nose and mouth, she pointed him toward the nearest Red Line subway station. There were security cameras in the station, but with fresh snow sweeping across the lakefront and freezing wind howling through the steel-and-glass canyons, nobody would pay attention to two more bundled-up commuters.

As they waited for the train, Theo filched a day-old newspaper out of a recycling bin and divided it up. "Nobody makes eye contact on the subway," she said in a low voice, handing him the Arts & Entertainment section. "With the suit and the parka, you're like a hipster professor. No one'll notice you."

"I hope you're right," he muttered as he took the paper.

"I hope I am too."

CHAPTER ELEVEN

I have not treated any god with disrespect. I have not cheated anyone. I have not done what the gods hate. I have not caused anyone to do harm to another. I have not brought suffering upon anyone...

- Excerpt from the "Negative Confessions," Papyrus of Ani, circa 1250 BCE

They switched trains seven times before Theo started to feel safe. What she'd told Seth was mostly true: dressed as they were, nobody would look twice at them, especially on a weekday. Still, there were security cameras in the stations, and it wasn't until they'd thoroughly fouled their trail that she relaxed.

The truth was the CTA was a temporary solution at best. They'd dodged the police, but what had set the police off in the first place? Theo's knowledge of law enforcement stopped at *CSI* and the top stories on the cable channels. She would've used her phone to check the news, but she'd left it behind in Seth's apartment, and none of the headlines on display at the newsstands helped her out. And after hours on the train, crisscrossing Chicago three times, they were tired and worried. They needed to go to ground while they figured out their next move.

After a lot of hard thinking, though, Theo came up with one possibility.

Aki Lee lived in a twentieth-floor apartment on the very edge of a gentrifying outer-Loop neighborhood, right on the line between middle-class quiet and yuppie paradise. The building was old-world elegance for the first five floors, but at some point in the 1970s the roof had been pulled off and fifteen stories' worth of a sheer gray façade tacked on. If you squinted, you could almost pinpoint the spot where the rents started to rise.

There was no doorman, but the front door was locked and there was a buzzer. Theo's thumb hovered over the button as she hesitated.

"You should probably talk to him alone," Seth murmured. "I get the impression he won't like me."

"The theft didn't help," Theo pointed out. "But for what it's worth, I think he was suspicious before that."

Seth tilted his head. "Very observant of him."

"No, he just thought you wouldn't put out." Seth's expression was priceless, and he opened his mouth to reply, but Theo pressed the buzzer before he could say anything.

After several long moments of silence, the panel crackled. "What?" a tired voice demanded. "Mom, not again!"

Mom? Seth mouthed, confused. Theo hid an unexpected smile and responded.

"Aki, it's me."

Another moment of silence, this one shorter and infinitely more awkward.

"Theo?" Aki said carefully. His voice was rough with sleep, but that didn't hide the confusion in it. "Theo, what the hell?"

"It's a long story, Aki." Theo hugged herself, trying not to shiver. It was 4:00 p.m., and the temperature was dropping as the sky darkened. "Please, I swear I'm not gonna get you into trouble, but you have to let me in. I've been outside for hours, and I'm freezing my ass off."

The outcome was never in doubt. Seconds later, the intercom buzzed and the door unlocked. She slipped through sideways and Seth followed her, looking reluctant. This, after all, wasn't his turf.

The trip up to Aki's floor was silent, and neither of them looked at the other. Seth peeled off his gloves and made a show of reading the Maximum Occupancy sign and fire hazard warnings posted in the elevator. When they reached the right floor, they exited and Theo motioned him out of sight before knocking on Aki's door.

The door wrenched open to reveal a wild-eyed, disheveled Aki in sweatpants and a Rhode Island School of Design T-shirt with an unmentionable mascot. "What the fuck?" he whispered as loudly as he could. "Where have you been? What are you doing here? I had cops coming by an hour ago, asking me if you were on drugs! What's going on?"

"It's a long story," Theo managed to say. "Can I come in?"

"Yeah, yeah, of course." He stepped aside. "I'll make coffee. You obviously need it."

"Not only me," she said. "I brought a friend."

Seth stepped around the corner and met Aki's stare. "Hello," he said calmly. Aki flinched, his jaw clenching as he stared at Seth. Then, to Theo's surprise, he moved back and motioned for them both to enter.

The door had barely locked behind them before he pounced. Seth had half a second to raise his hands when Aki slammed into him like a deranged linebacker and knocked him to the floor. Skull met floorboard with a sickening thud.

Aki landed on top and grabbed Seth in a choke hold. Seth broke it easily and tried to roll Aki off him, but the angle was awkward and Theo could see fresh blood, already browning into clay, spotting the floor where his head had struck. Aki jammed both thumbs into the hollow of Seth's throat, cutting off his air.

"Stop it!" Theo shouted. "Stop it, both of you!"

"Are you kidding?" Aki grunted. Seth grabbed Aki's arm in a bone-breaking grip, and the smaller man's face went white. He dug his knee into Seth's stomach, drawing a short, sharp gasp of pain from him but not enough to break the other man's hold. "This guy—Ow! Mother-fucker!"

Theo had never seen a rolling ball of flailing cartoon limbs in real life before, but it was obvious that they were about to turn into one. Seth was stronger and had lifetimes of experience, but Aki was scrappy and incredibly angry, and the two of them were pummeling each other relentlessly. In seconds Aki's mouth was bleeding and Seth's hand sport-ed a brand-new bite mark. Neither paid attention to a word Theo said.

"Goddammit!" Theo yelled. Grabbing a half-empty pot of cold coffee off the table, she threw it over both of them. It brought them up short.

"Fuck," Aki said, shaking droplets out of his hair. "That's *disgusting.*"

"Will you listen to me now?" she demanded. "Or can you at least leave the dick-waving contest for later? Aki, I know, I should have mentioned I had him with me. But there were reasons. Something huge is going on here, Aki, and it's made a giant mess. You have to trust me. Please."

There was a moment of hesitation on Aki's face, but it was a fraction of what Seth's had been. Theo and Aki had known each other a long time, and Theo had always been the calm, stable one, the Hobbit to Aki's Dwarf. She didn't cheat, steal, or break the law, and she definitely didn't lie to her friends.

"Son of a *bitch,*" Aki said, but he let Seth up. The two men were still glaring at each other, and both had fresh bruises forming.

"We're not going to be here long, Aki," Theo said quickly, forcing their attention back to her and breaking the stare-down. "But we need to find out what's going on, preferably without getting arrested. The cops came to Seth's place this morning, and I don't know why. Have you heard anything?"

Aki turned, scowling. "Have I heard anything? I heard them saying you helped this asshole rip off a bunch of Egyptian artifacts from the museum last night! Jewelry, a couple of statuettes, that kind of thing. They found your prints at the scene."

Theo's stomach gave a lurch at Aki's words. For a moment, his face was distant and unreadable. "Aki, you don't think I—?"

"Hell no. Anybody who's heard your riff knows the museum's your life. You wouldn't." Aki didn't look at Seth, but there was venom in his voice. *"Him,* on the other hand...?"

"Jewelry and statuettes." Seth snorted at the thought as he wiped cold coffee off his parka. "I've been supporting the art department and networking artifact purchases for years. If I wanted antiquities, I'd buy them, not break in."

"I've seen rich people do way crazier things than pull a heist." Aki crossed his arms. "My mom put me through school making chicken-wire cages for millionaires who liked wearable sculpture instead of clothes. Anyway, it was Theo"—he turned his skeptical eye on Theo, who frowned back at him—"who fingered you when the mummy and the shabtis were ganked. The police were saying you might've been working with a couple of professional art thieves, or maybe pulling an insurance scam."

Seth's face froze, his expression remote and statue-like. "That's not—" he began, his voice brittle.

"It's a very long story," Theo broke in. Aki was open-minded, but he likely wouldn't be too happy with an explanation involving the truth. After all, even if he didn't believe the mummy business, Theo would still be confirming for him that Seth had stolen from the Columbian. "Aki.

Please. You know I wouldn't be here if things weren't desperate. Just, please, trust me and Seth for a little bit, and let us lie low here for a few hours. Okay?"

There was another frozen moment of silence, and Theo's heart dropped. Finally, though, Aki gave a short, curt nod, and the two men took a couple of steps away from each other. Theo let out a soft breath and slumped a little, settling onto the arm of the sofa.

"All right," Aki said sharply. He straightened his back and crossed his arms, the picture of alertness and immovable rigor. "But not for long. I'm technically hiding criminal suspects, and you know they'll come talk to me again. Being your friend and all. What the hell's going on?"

"We were framed," Seth said bluntly. "That's the explanation. The stolen artifacts were from the Middle Kingdom exhibit, weren't they?"

"Yeah. Shabtis, mostly."

"So someone who wanted them earlier was taking advantage of Theo's accusation. While she and I were out of the way, the remainder of the cache could be burgled. Her prints would be easy to find; she's left them all over the museum. Our someone would know that."

Aki's brow furrowed. "Someone like who?"

"We don't know," Theo said, aiming the words at Seth. He stared back, immovable. On the train she'd spilled the story of Zimmer and the panic button, but she hadn't been able to back it up by calling the man himself. She'd left her phone in Seth's apartment, and on her advice, Seth wasn't using his. He'd ditched it in a trash can in Chinatown.

Aki wasn't buying it either. A spasm passed over his features as he visibly weighed his options. He could believe his friend's bizarre story and risk becoming an accessory to grand larceny, or kick her out and risk the possibility that she might be telling the truth.

The spasm passed, and he nodded once. "Okay," he said. "One night, okay? One night only. When I said I like to live life on the edge, I meant more like the extreme rock-climbing, flaming JELL-O shots kind of edge. It's mostly fun when you're not actually doing anything illegal."

"Well, at least we never did anything illegal," Theo said. She leaned her head back and closed her eyes, trying to organize her racing thoughts.

"Speak for yourself," Seth murmured. Aki made a warning noise, something like an angry cat, and Seth turned on his heel and walked away. Theo heard the balcony door slam, and opened her eyes reluctantly.

"Aki?"

"Yeah?"

"You've never gone rock-climbing."

Her friend laughed. "The elevator here breaks down three times a week. Same thing."

She wondered if Seth could really deal with someone like Aki. Easygoing, wry without being bitter, matter-of-fact about his own strengths and weaknesses. Unassuming. Someone who could be that way because he'd never really been in any kind of danger or feared for his life. In that, Theo and Aki were a lot closer than Theo and Seth.

But she'd kissed Seth and watched him die. Now he was here because he was following her suggestions, trusting the advice of an amateur solely on the basis of their connection and her familiarity with the modern world. Seth trusted her enough to change his plans. That meant something.

Her tired body was reluctant to move, and it took a real effort to get herself off Aki's comfortable couch. "I'll be back in a few minutes, okay?" she said as she stood. She felt Aki's eyes on her back as she went out onto the balcony and tried not to wonder what her friend was thinking.

The balcony door was glass, but Aki had draped a printed Indian blanket over a curtain rod to keep anyone from looking in or out. Brushing the blanket aside, Theo stepped into the night.

The cheap parka didn't fit Seth, but he was wearing it anyway. His scarf was a band of white that seemed to cut off his head from the dark-clothed body. He had his gloves back on, and the slick black leather was the one part of it that suited him. In the orange-purple light of the city he was a statue again, like the black-glazed Anubis that guarded so many tombs. Silent and watchful. He leaned on the balcony railing and watched the city lights, and Theo watched him.

"I hate this," he said after a long moment. "I hate winters here. Nothing ever gets warm."

Theo moved over to the railing. "I'll bet," she said. "This winter's worse than usual, though."

"Can't be more than zero out."

"Been that way for a while. It's a bad time of year for this kind of thing."

That got a bit of a rueful smile from Seth. "Running?"

"Yeah." Theo huddled into her coat. "It's probably harder on you, though. You kept the charade up for a century, and it's been spoiled."

"I'm sorry." The words came out awkwardly—not insincere, but unaccustomed to being used. Theo guessed that Seth didn't have a lot of people who might warrant such a thing. "I'm sorry you were dragged into this. None of it was supposed to happen this way." He swallowed. "I didn't know you were working that late. You weren't meant to be involved."

"I know." Theo turned to him, meeting his eyes. "If I hadn't gone down to say goodbye to the shabtis, I wouldn't have seen you."

"Or if I hadn't been seated at your table at the party, I wouldn't have recognized you." Seth shook his head.

That brought her up short. "Recognized me?" she repeated. "That was the first time we met. Wasn't it?"

"Not exactly." Seth shook his head. One gloved hand lightly touched a fading scar on the ball of her thumb. "You cut your hand in the prep lab months ago. Someone dropped a jar, and you were helping to clean it up. That was the first time I saw you."

"But there were only a couple of people in the lab that day. You couldn't have been there. How did you—" She stopped. There had been eyes watching her, but not human ones. "The shabtis are conscious?"

Seth shook his head. "No, not really. But magic—my kind...really, the priest's kind—is bound up with names and images. You spent so much time there, talking to them as if they were real. It had to make an impression."

"Images and names," she said softly. "The essence of a real thing."

"So Kemet believed." His free hand was idly tracing lines in the snow on the railing. She thought she saw an ankh, but he wiped it away before she could be sure. "And, well, the shabtis are images made to become real things. So treating them like the thing they were made to represent and become... It gets a little tangled. I'm not explaining this very well, I know. I was never the priest. I could barely read or write. This was my brother's job, or my scribe's."

Theo's face reddened. She definitely remembered talking to the shabtis, reassuring them about the exhibition, joking with them, telling them they were handsome. The statuettes had been in storage for a long time, after all. The exhibition would've been the shabtis' first chance to be presented to the public. Talking to the little guys had felt natural.

Once, for the heck of it, she'd planted a kiss on the cabinet. Why not? She was always good at entertaining herself when she was alone, but she didn't know if they had the same skill. It must not be fun to be stuck in a glass box. But they'd been stolen again....

Seth stiffened as Theo put an arm around him, and he looked down at her in surprise. With their differences in height, she couldn't comfortably drape the arm across his shoulders, but the waist did almost as well.

After a moment's hesitation, he pulled her closer. Theo let out a quiet sigh and relaxed into his arms, doing her best to share her warmth. A shiver ran through Seth, and for a moment, she thought she heard his breath hitch in his throat. He lowered his head, resting his chin on her hair.

"Too cold," he said after a long moment. His voice was deep and hoarse. "Next winter, I'll take you to Egypt. The weather's sane there. None of this fucking snow. I can show you where Itj-Tawy was, and my burial site."

"We can't," Theo murmured. "Nobody's supposed to go there right now. Politics and all."

"To hell with politics. I have more of a right to see Kemet again than anyone else. If you want to go, I'll take you."

Theo took in a slow breath. *He means it*, she thought.

It was too soon for this kind of thing. They were fugitives, caught in a mess that she couldn't begin to figure out. Common sense banged her over the head again, telling her she was being an idiot, she was leading him on, she was going to get herself killed over someone she barely knew. But she had grasped at something, some elusive quality of motion in life that had been lacking before in hers, and she couldn't blot out this picture now.

"We'll figure something out," she said.

They stood like that for a long time, sharing their warmth and looking out on the lights of the frozen city, until a shout from Aki shattered their reverie.

"Theo, you have to see this! There's more about the robbery o—" He stopped at the balcony door, seeing the two of them together. His eyebrows shot up, but he didn't comment, which Theo was grateful for. She was too wrung out to argue with him.

"They're running the story again," Aki said, leaning against the half-open glass door. "I thought you'd want to see it. It's pretty crazy stuff."

That was an understatement. The museum robbery was a nice, dramatic story without uncomfortable political or religious angles, and the TV news channels were eating it up. Theo's odd behavior during the first theft was dragged out, this time with a Mata Hari twist: What had she really seen? Was she in on it? Seth was officially wanted for the robbery, with Theo suspected of being an accessory to grand larceny, but both of them were being sought by the police.

Theo groaned and sat down hard on the couch, letting her head flop back in exhaustion.

Seth, on the other hand, was firing questions at Aki. Did other broadcasts mention anyone finding the mummy? (No.) Did Aki know of anyone else who might believe Theo's innocence? (Yes, a few.) Had there been word about Seth's accounts? (No, but they wouldn't exactly reveal that on TV.) Finally, Aki snapped at him, which made Seth frosty.

Theo's growing headache wasn't thanking either of them.

"But why would this happen?" she said for what felt like the millionth time. "By themselves, the shabtis aren't very valuable. It's easier and cheaper to make fakes!"

"Maybe it's the Collector?" Aki suggested, leaning forward. He had territorially claimed the spot on the couch next to Theo, leaving Seth to the love seat. Few men can sit regally in a cushiony armchair with a blatantly hostile '70s pattern, but Seth somehow managed it. His mask was back in place, and to sprawl like a normal person would have been acknowledging weakness in front of a non-ally.

"Maybe," Theo acknowledged. "He does target Egyptian and Eastern collections in general. But why?"

"I dunno. Let's ask him." This with a glare at Seth.

"I," Seth said slowly, "am not the Collector. If I merely wanted shabtis, I would have bought them."

"Which doesn't explain why you stole ours weeks ago," Aki said. "Theo, why are you hanging around with this asshole, anyway?"

She let her head flop into her hands. "It's complicated."

Seth looked at her now, his expression tense. Her heart thumped hard in her chest as she weighed her options, much as Aki had done less than an hour before. She could tell the truth to Aki, who deserved to know what he was getting into. Or she could protect Seth's secret, which had to be one of the biggest discoveries in the history of the human race.

"He's being blackmailed," she said finally. The words felt like they were being dragged out of her. "He's been receiving anonymous threats. People breaking into his home, forcing him to help them rob the museum. He thinks the Collector is actually someone who works in the museum business and wants a scapegoat—"

"Zimmer," Seth cut in. That got both Aki's and Theo's attention. His face was grim and lined: the thought seemed to have aged him, bringing back a few of the years he'd been cheating. "Mark Zimmer sent her to talk to me yesterday. He gave her a panic button but it didn't work, and when she tried to call him for an explanation, there was nothing. I'd bet good money Mark Zimmer is involved in this."

"Aren't your accounts probably frozen?" Aki pointed out.

Seth glared. "Do you have an actual objection to the idea?"

"Yeah. It's stupid." Aki crossed his arms and matched Seth glare for glare. "Why would Zimmer steal anything? Theo already said the stuff's pretty much worthless unless you're really plugged into the black market. It's not like there's a big demand for dead guys and little clay dudes."

"Which ignores the obvious answer," Seth said. His lips were pressed into a thin line. "What if Zimmer knows what the shabtis can do? He could be after their powers."

Aki gave him a "what the hell?" stare, and Theo stiffened in her seat. "Seth," she said, "you don't have to talk about that. I think we're confusing Aki."

"No, I think we do." He sounded resigned. "Theo, if we don't lay our cards on the table, your friend won't be able to help us. And I think we…need help."

It was a short explanation. At the end of it, Aki turned his disbelieving stare from Seth to Theo, almost waiting for both of them to burst out laughing. "Am I being punked?" he said after a long moment. "Theo, this guy is so full of shit. Tell me it's a joke."

Theo sighed again. "I'm sorry. It's not," she said. Her regret was genuine. At least she didn't have to let her blackmail lie get too far, but that wasn't much comfort. "I saw him disintegrate, Aki; I told you that. And there was that 'organic dust' on the floor of the loft, remember?"

"Bullshit." Her friend's face was pale. "Show me the proof, or I…I don't know. You have to go."

Theo and Seth exchanged glances. Then Seth took a craft knife from the piled-up art supplies on the table. As Aki gawked, he neatly and efficiently slit his own wrist.

"What the fuck?" Aki yelped. "This guy thinks he's the Terminator! Theo—"

But the blood was already drying, the slashed veins closing. Beads of clay broke away from the wound and landed on the carpet.

Aki took it a lot better than Theo had, she had to admit. He looked at her, then at Seth, then at her, then at Seth again. Color drained out of his face, and his pupils dilated. For a moment he sat frozen, his eyes darting around the room, as if he were trying and failing to process what he'd seen. He nodded.

Then he grabbed another knife off the table and drove it into Seth's side.

Theo leaped to her feet, heart in her mouth, but Seth just grunted a little. As Aki stared, Seth pulled off his jacket and rolled up the edge of his shirt. The handle of the knife stuck out between two ribs, bobbing ever so slightly with each breath he took. After a moment of deliberation, Seth extracted it.

Two inches of the blade were covered in cadmium-red blood. He held it out to Aki, who shook his head, backing away a few steps. The knife made a dull clunk as Seth dropped it onto the table, and more shards of clay scattered.

"Good aim." Seth tucked in his bloodied shirt. "I'll need to borrow something clean to wear. And if you're going to stab me again, give me a few seconds of fair warning so I can break your wrist."

"Jesus Christ," Aki said, more out of a need to say something than anything else.

"Are we finished?" Theo cut in. Her hands trembled, and she crossed her arms, hiding the telltale shaking. "Aki, look, we're not crazy. Okay? And believe me, Zimmer may be a good guy, but there're a lot of people who'd pay if they thought they could learn to do that."

Aki shook his head, seemingly emerging from a trance. "All right," he said. "This could be a bad trip, but, whatever, let's say for argument's sake that this is happening. And that there's magic statues that can make guys not die. How the hell would anyone, especially Zimmer, know about it?"

"Anyone who can read my priest's script knows part of the story," Seth said. Clay dust was smeared across his sleeve. "'This is a vessel for him, and will become as him through his will.' But it would take a real leap of imagination to guess the whole of it. Even my tomb paintings don't say everything."

"Would they work for Zimmer?" Theo wondered, trying not to worry at the way Aki had winced over "my tomb." "They look like you— sort of," she amended, remembering the slender and withered mummy. "And Zimmer's sure as hell no son of Merenptah."

"If you are who you say you are, and that's a big *if,*" Aki said, "then your father would have been born at least four thousand years ago. That's a lot of time for the family to go forth and multiply. If Zimmer is a distant relative, sort of a Farnsworth to your Fry, couldn't this Egyptian Rare Candy bug work for him?"

Seth blinked. "What?"

"Cultural references," Theo translated. "He wants to know if it's possible."

"It could be. But that hinges on not only knowing him to be a descendant of either myself or my brother, but also on him knowing he was and realizing he could use the shabtis. It's a long shot."

Theo tugged at her braid, thinking. "I don't know," she said. "Zimmer...Zimmer's a good guy. He's pretty rule-bound, but that's not a bad thing in the security business. It could've been someone else, as long as they worked for the museum." Both men looked blank at that, and Theo shook her head. "The news said the thief took the stuff in Prep D, remember? Those are the last of the ones that were never LoJacked. There's no way some random thief would know that particular group would be easiest to move."

"Still rules out most of the departments," Aki put in. "Paleontology couldn't tell a shabti from a hole in the ground, and they'd probably prefer the hole. Write off anyone from CompTech. Astronomy, head in the clouds. Art History and Library, maybe, but I wouldn't make book on it—"

"You've made your point," Seth said. "Now please, stop the puns."

"For a guy who says he lived through the craziest periods in history, you sure are uptight," Aki pointed out. There was something strangely ironic in being catty to an ancient Egyptian, but Theo wasn't in the mood to appreciate it.

"Guys," she said wearily, "don't. Please. We need a plan."

Aki scowled, but Seth picked up a pencil and began making notes on a discarded sketch pad. "We have to assume my legal assets are no longer available to me," he said, "and I imagine yours are not either. If we're going to get anything done, we'll have to reach one of my caches. I've been maintaining a storage locker under a fake identity, and it should still be secure. Once we have more in the way of resources, we can make plans." He glanced up, and the whiskey-brown eyes fixed on Theo. "If you're...amenable."

Theo was torn. There was something between them, something powerful, but she wasn't sure what it actually was yet. Need for motion had taken her this far, but part of her wished he would vanish and take the next choice out of her hands.

Even if they did stay together, could she vanish with him? Should she? Life on the lam was no way to go, especially when the longer she stayed gone, the worse it would be when she was eventually caught. What a mess. What a fucking mess.

"Nobody knows where I am, or if I'm guilty for sure," she said slowly, out loud. "It'll be the authorities' word against mine. And they don't know the museum as well as I do. We might be able to find more information about the real thief."

"And he loses his advantage," Seth finished. His eyes brightened. "Perfect. We'll visit my cache first thing in the morning, and then start looking for clues."

"Quit planning for her," Aki growled. "Theo. Look. I'm not gonna turn you in, but this is crazy, even for you. You're not a PI or something. And this magic stuff, it's just...*kooky*," he finished lamely.

"It leaves options," Theo said. "If I turn myself in now, that's it. But if I help you now, I can still turn myself in later."

"And she may not be a PI," Seth added, "but I know a few things about staying hidden. Get me to my cache, and Theo and I will be safe for at least a few days."

"You're both nuts," Aki muttered, but he didn't raise any more objections. Theo could see the questions in his eyes, though. *Seth has money, connections, and supposed mystical powers, so why would he want to spend them helping Theo? Sex?*

There's that, Theo's level stare replied. *But I'm also the one stopping him from running away this time.*

"Both nuts," Aki repeated, shaking his head. "But at least you'll have something to talk about. C'mon, Theo; I'll put you in the guest room. There's a foldout couch in there for the Mummy here too." He raised an eyebrow. "Unless you two would prefer to share?"

Theo's face flushed. For a moment, a warm ochre tinge colored Seth's face. "The couch is fine," he said coolly.

* * *

In the morning, Aki gave them a makeover.

"Are you sure you're not my gay BFF?" Theo said as he brushed temporary dye into her long blonde hair. Aki's eye-roll was clearly visible in the bathroom mirror.

"You're not funny," he said. "Stop trying."

It somehow didn't surprise Theo that Seth turned out to be familiar with the art of disguise. She found herself giggling—an unexpected but welcome sensation—as the men discussed age lines and highlights. Immature? Very. But it sure felt good.

When the work was finished, Theo doubted her own mother would have recognized her. Her skin had an unhealthy yellow cast and her hair was a dull, mousy brown, the kind of color that had to be natural because people rarely chose it on purpose. For extra security, it had been curled badly. "You see someone with a horrible haircut, and that's all you remember," as Aki had put it. Tinted eye shadow gave her mutable green eyes a touch of blue.

After Seth made good on his threat of taking a new shirt, Aki saw it as a challenge. He dug through his closet and the building's lost-and-found, finally turning up a ripped pair of jeans and a Detroit Tigers warm-up jacket that almost fit. Seth's expression was priceless, but after an obvious struggle (and a quick rinse cycle) he put them on.

Aki shook his head again as he looked them both over one final time. "You look like someone's parents about to hit the bars," he said frankly. "No one will notice you, at least until Imhotep gets you to his cache." He shrugged, and his eyes grew distant. "Take care of yourself, Theo."

"I will, Aki." She squeezed his arm. "Thanks for your help. I'll see you on the flip side."

Without another word, the pair slipped out.

CHAPTER TWELVE

Gods are bastards.

- *Graffiti at Thebes,*
date unknown

It was eight o'clock in the morning, but the sun was low and the city remained bathed in purple and orange shadows. The wind came in gusts, sending eddies of fresh snow whirling around their ankles. Beside her, Seth's head was down, his eyes fixed on the pavement. One does not tread lightly in city slush.

"So this cache…" she said, breaking the silence of the frozen morning. "It was obvious you didn't want to elaborate in front of Aki."

"He makes my fists itch," Seth said bluntly. "And we're better off trusting as few people as possible. This cache isn't big, but it's the largest I have in the city, and it has tools and materials that will be helpful."

Theo nodded, tugging on the collar of her parka. She'd layered two shirts underneath it for quick changes, but she was starting to think that had been a mistake. Sweat collected quickly in the cheap fabric. "In case you needed to disappear?"

"When I needed to disappear," Seth responded. "The original plan was that once I had the…supplies, I wanted to leave town. Go traveling. See more of the world."

Supplies. Seth really hadn't spent a lot of time outside his ivory tower; he sounded like he was talking about drugs.

Theo wondered what kinds of odds and ends he had seen fit to hide. Probably some of his shabtis, and maybe more of his past-life artifacts that couldn't go on display in his home. Something, at any rate, that he wasn't comfortable with anyone seeing. There was a lot of that for him.

Contemplating this, she didn't pry when Seth fell silent. The pair of them walked side by side down the street, companionably quiet, their breath clouding in the chilly air.

Theo didn't know how much she could help him, but she could see that being on the move might be doing him good. Running had to be a habit formed to protect his secret, and facing a problem rather than avoiding it might speak to his core self. And every time she'd used his real name, his color had risen.

She didn't know where she was going, or what would become of her life, and that scared her—but it also warmed her to see him stepping up. She wished she had her sketchbook.

The city was grudgingly awakening, its cars slow and infrequent, as if the machines themselves didn't want to get moving. The *Sun-Times* and *Tribune* had already been delivered, their weight leaving cracks in the ice they'd landed on. At bus stops, commuters tucked themselves into the corners of the plastic shelters, to get as far from the wind as possible. Seth and Theo joined the crowds under the heat lamps at the Red Line stop, shoulder to shoulder with strangers who gratefully shared the warmth while refusing to make eye contact or say anything. Everyone was lost in their own world.

The O'Hare airport sprawled on the far edge of town. Seen from the air it was a mix of modern and colorful, skewed buildings surrounded by acres upon acres of dull-gray industrial lots and parkways—a blob of Monet in the center of a Mondrian. Hundreds of businesses lived and died on those lots, serving the vast complex of the airport. It was busy, anonymous, and rarely open to pedestrians.

The recession of the 2010s had left many buildings vacant, but at least one sector was still going strong: the self-storage lots. People going to or coming from elsewhere always needed to store things, and the competing outfits openly advertised Private Units, No Questions Asked.

Seth led Theo to one of the many forgettable storage buildings. The units were divided into blocks of six, accessible from either inside or outside, and the guard at the gate accepted Seth's fake ID without batting an eye. He gave them both a perfunctory looking-over, mumbled the schedule in a rote recitation, and went back into his guard shack to doze.

Seth threw Theo a small smile and fished out a key on a blue-plastic key chain.

"Part of the emergency kit?" Theo said quietly once they were out of the guard's earshot.

"Never leaves me."

He slipped his arm around her and pulled her into the building. Inside, it was all slick tiles, sputtering fluorescent lights, and solid, locked doors—like a high school on a day off, Theo thought wryly. Their footsteps echoed as he led her down the hall and stopped at one of the many doors.

"It's more than Kemet," he whispered in her ear as he unlocked it. "I had to save what I could. I can't show you everything, not now, but I want... You have to see what I mean."

He ushered Theo into a dark, stuffy room and closed the door behind them. It was warm, and Theo immediately began to sweat. "Paid for a heated unit, huh?" she said a little breathlessly as Seth locked the door behind them and fumbled for the light switch.

"Of course. The things here could be damaged—" A rolling, consonantal curse, hard k's and slithery s's, escaped as he banged into what sounded like a metal shelf. "I can never find... Theo, would you... Ah!"

Light blazed, the joyless yellow-white of more harsh fluorescents. Theo flinched, automatically shading her eyes. *Wonderful things*, Carter had said when he'd first opened King Tut's tomb. She half expected to be blinded by the dazzle of gold.

The unit wasn't enormous, but Seth had made good use of the space. Against one wall was a low couch, obviously custom-made, with a few cushions sporting an embroidered design of lotus flowers. There was a spindle-legged table and a matching chair that looked almost Greek. Carefully stacked on a low shelf were scrolls of yellow-white paper (onionskin? Not vellum or papyrus, these days) and a writing board shaped for propping up in a cross-legged man's lap. Several of the scrolls showed wear and would have unrolled completely if not for the shoe-laces tied around them. On the walls, though—

"Jesus Christ," Theo said involuntarily.

"Among others."

They were gods. Dozens of gods. Gods in every possible style and from every imaginable religion, from gilded figures of Odin and Zeus to ivory Inuit sea goddesses and grimacing Pacific spirit masks. A dozen handmade Egyptian gods sat on a special shelf reserved for them, with old and new copies of sacred symbols—the ankh, the knot-of-Isis tyet like the one his mummy had carried, the Eyes of Horus and Ra—

arranged in front of them. There was Jesus, all right, looking odd and small amidst the colorful assembly. The gods crowded the walls, and their eyes watched Seth and Theo and gave away nothing.

Place of honor was given to two-foot-tall twin statues. One was impossible not to recognize: Anubis, on one knee with his hands resting on his thighs. He had been carefully carved from a single piece of wood, smoothed and sanded and lacquered black, and his eyes glinted with gold and mother-of-pearl inlays. The other Theo couldn't quite place. She wore an elaborate shield-shaped crown and carried a bow and a quiver of gilded arrows. There was a covered metal bowl placed between them, and its edges were blackened from years of fires.

"Neith," Seth said reverently, nodding to the goddess. It took Theo a moment to realize that the nod was actually a truncated bow. "Mother of the sun and archers. I named the art trust in her honor. She was my patroness."

Theo's gaze stayed on the other statuettes. Next to that motley crew, Neith and Anubis seemed positively benevolent, though perhaps that was part of the point. "What about them?" she asked quietly. The eyes were making her nervous; she couldn't shake the feeling that they were judging her. "I didn't know you worshiped… Is that one Aztec?"

"Yes, that's Tlaloc." Seth inclined his head to the statuette, which had oversized staring eyes and prominent fangs. "And next to him, Itzpapalotl. I don't worship them, but these are gods whose hospitality I've enjoyed over the years. They could have annihilated me any time I crossed their borders, but they didn't."

His voice was rough. "They're mostly forgotten these days. I keep lists, copying them over and over again, so I don't forget. And I burn incense to them."

One by one, Theo picked them out. Sedna, with her children the sea creatures. The African Mami Wata. The hand symbol of the god of Israel and Jacob, and more she couldn't begin to name. So many gods, so many lands visited and lives lived.

A shiver ran through Theo. He remembered them and gave them honor in thanks for their mercy to him. It sounded ridiculous. Collecting gods like that, old gods, when everyone knew that they were nothing but stories that ancient cultures made up to explain things…

Really? a voice whispered as Theo felt the blood drain from her face. There stood a man who lived because of gods, or powers, unknown to her. What other creatures were out there in the darkened corners of history, hiding the way Seth had? Every story she'd read about them, gods and monsters, crowded her mind and crept in behind her eyes. Why not? *Why not?*

A strangled cry escaped from her throat as she turned on her heel and made for the door. She didn't have the key. For a crazed second, panic seized her completely—the dozens of eyes were fixed on her, watching and judging, knowing that if she didn't give her pound of flesh, they'd have no reason to let her live. Gods were evil, petty things with powers that she'd never be able to face—

She flattened her back against the door. Seth's eyes were wide with alarm, one hand reaching toward her, but for a moment the one thing she could see was that host of staring faces. Her gaze was locked on theirs. Her jacket collar clung to the skin of her neck, and she realized that tears were running freely down her face, mixing with the perspiration brought on by the hot, still air. Her heart pounded; her world shrank to her and those staring, judging gods.

Then darkness fell and the faces vanished. Theo let out a gasp, a half sob, as the eyes winked out of existence. They were still there, she knew, but in the dark she could only feel metal at her back and hear her own harsh breathing echoing in the enclosed space. The gods were gone. She was safe.

Breath touched her ear, and a pair of arms enfolded her. "Theo," Seth whispered hoarsely. His grasp was almost painfully tight, but she didn't care. "Theo. Djed. Are you all right?"

She couldn't reply. If she thought about the eyes, the staring powers beyond her comprehension, she would go insane. She needed the here and now. Desperate, Theo flung her arms around Seth's neck and pressed her lips to his in a wild and clumsy kiss.

Sensations flooded her. There he was, warm to the touch, skin flexing under her fingertips. His day-old stubble scraped at her cheek, sending millions of tiny shivering feelings—painpleasure-painpleasureholdme—flickering through her quick as thought. His lips a smooth curve, an enigmatic smile that was ruined when he came to life, responding to her need—

She could feel his heart pounding wildly under her hand. Hot blood, a tremor in the hands as her legs automatically began to part, the hiss he gave in the back of his throat and the shiver of pleasure as he moved that eager kiss down her neck, nipping at her collarbone... She moaned, clutching those sensations to her, clinging in the darkness to the things that made him human.

"Don't be afraid," he whispered against her lips. "You owe them nothing. They can't touch you."

As he said it, his breath hot against her skin, she felt the fear begin to drain away. Slowly, so slowly, she began to relax in his arms. She'd stood between him and Aki, between him and the human authorities; he was trying to stand between her and the gods. She breathed again, murmuring something even she didn't understand as the tension unwound. Her heartbeat began to slow.

"Can you face them?" Seth said quietly.

Theo drew in a breath.

"I think so. Wait!" She didn't want him to reach for the light switch just yet. "Listen." Her words felt awkward, and she struggled to grasp them. "I don't...I don't want to be watched. Or used. I'm not theirs."

"They don't have that kind of power," Seth said. "Not here, not now. But when I finally do stand in front of the judges, I want to begin my negative confession with 'I have not refused homage to those who sheltered me.'"

"You're a good man," she said.

When the light flicked back on, the eyes of the gods didn't seem quite so judging.

Fortunately, Seth didn't give her an opportunity to dwell on it. He knelt down and began hauling several fireproof boxes from under the couch. Each one of them had been triple-locked, with hieroglyphic symbols Theo had never seen before painted onto the lids and sides. Seth worked the locks skillfully, opening each without a single click or scrape.

She stared. The boxes contained everything she could possibly imagine needing for a life on the run: multiple passports and driver's licenses, more skin and hair dyes, pieces of concealable weaponry that Theo couldn't name, prosthetics enough to build three or four different faces, bank cards, social security cards, and—holy hell, that was a lot of cash.

"You put a lot of thought into this," she said, sorting through the documents. "There's at least three identities here."

"You never know when one won't work," Seth responded. "Some

are better than others. I had to use different forgers for each type and name, and few of them are up to the best standards. But I learned a few things from them." He extracted a smaller box from the largest one and opened it. Inside were several ID badges from federal agencies. None of them had photographs or the final stamps applied.

"I can't fake working identities on short notice, but a convincing-looking ID from the government is usually as good for anyone unofficial. Give me a few hours, and I can make you something useful."

Swiss Army Seth? She didn't doubt he could too.

"Are you going to do it right now?" she said as he sat down at the spindle-legged table, box of materials in hand.

"There's no time like the present," he said. "I'm sorry, Theo. Will you be all right for a few hours?"

She nodded. He turned away and got to work. As she watched, he began to cut one of the cards apart, gently raising the outermost laminated layer to get at the chip implanted in it.

Too bad she hadn't brought that sketchbook. Looking for something to do, Theo let her curiosity get the better of her and picked one of the scrolls off the shelf. Definitely modern paper, probably from a specialty art store, but the writing was in hieratic. The penmanship was casual and broad: lines wandered, characters ran into each other, and Greek or Cyrillic symbols cropped up here and there. It had clearly been written for the scribe's eyes only, with no concern for whether anyone else could read it.

"What are these?" she asked, not really expecting an answer. At least she knew most of the symbols. Not enough to understand, but enough to see distinctive repetitions and patterns in the text. She squinted at the paper, picking out the hieratic version of the basket hieroglyph—the hard K. Then the mouth R, and the horned-viper F. She murmured it aloud, trying to find where the vowels would fit.

"Cleopatra VII Philopator," Seth supplied. He glanced at the scroll and pointed the tip of a razor blade at the back of it. Turning it over, Theo found a series of numbers like a library card-catalog ID.

"It's my diary," he added. "Well, parts of it. I keep trying to maintain one, but I don't have the patience to write down everything and parts always get lost. I recopy them every chance I get."

"In hieratic?"

He grinned wryly. "Well, my version of it. It's the one language I never forget. I copy the diaries, seal them in a cache, or save what I can. This is the one way I can remember where I was or what I did."

Theo looked down at the scroll in her hands. It was beautiful in its own weird way, a modern re-creation of what one of the ancient papyri might have looked like when it was new. "But isn't that impractical? I mean, these things don't last forever. And people can find them."

He shrugged his shoulders at that. "Chances are that anyone who finds them won't know what it is. And I don't trust digital. It's too impermanent."

"Anhurmose, this is your life," she murmured.

Seth's eyes softened as she used his name, and for a moment, he set down the razor blade.

"Cleopatra Philopator. That's *the* Cleopatra. You knew her?"

"Not exactly. But I was a mercenary at Actium," Seth said. "I saw her for about three seconds on the royal galley. It wasn't a pretty sight."

"She wasn't beautiful?"

"I couldn't tell. And nobody's beautiful when they're losing."

Of course not. Theo had read about the Battle of Actium, when Cleopatra and Marc Antony were defeated and Egypt's future as a Roman province was sealed. It hadn't been a good time to be an Egyptian queen. "Who did you fight for?" she asked curiously.

"Octavian," Seth said. "Emperor Augustus, he was later."

"Smart man," she murmured. "You picked the winning team."

As she spoke, she turned the parchment over. Actium was, what, 30 BC? And he had been there? How many times had he recopied this parchment, preserving memories of a sea battle two thousand years past? It made her head spin.

Seth snorted, apparently unaware of the thoughts going through her head. "I picked the one that paid better and didn't have Antonius."

"But he was fighting for Egypt," Theo said. "I would've thought you would want him to win. So Egypt could remain independent, I mean."

For a moment, his gaze went blank, focusing on something she couldn't see. "It was already dead," he said. "The Macedonians claimed they were kings by divine right, but the line of descent had been broken so many times… Better no king than a bad one. At least the Romans tried to maintain order and take care of the land."

Seth was gesturing to the shelf of gods, pointing out the native Egyptian deities. "I spent time in Alexandria, but you're not going to see

Serapis here. He wasn't one of them. The Ptolemies and their people made him to keep the population under control! If I'd cast my shabtis in Serapis's name, I'd be as dead as Antonius."

Theo looked up at the gods and wondered. Someone must have invented them at some point, hadn't they? And yet Seth, in their names, was still alive. How did you tell which gods were real? Or did they become real when they were worshiped? The staring eyes were beginning to bore into her again, and she turned her back on them.

* * *

Hours passed in near silence. When the scrolls and various boxes had exhausted their entertainment value, Theo tried to find a way to occupy herself, but Seth was bent over his work and she knew what it was like to be deep in a project. He'd switched off again, she thought, irritated in spite of herself.

To distract herself from getting too annoyed over what was doubtlessly important (but did he have to tune out so completely?), Theo took a blank roll of paper from one of the shelves and, using a stick of charcoal from the makeshift brazier, began to sketch. The close heat of the room made her lightheaded, and after a while, she stripped off her outermost shirt and fell asleep.

She awoke to the sound of crinkling plastic. Opening one eye, she realized groggily that she was lying down on that strange pseudo-Egyptian couch, her cheek pressed to one of the cushions. She blinked away the remnants of sleep and raised her head. Her cheek ached, and glancing into a polished bronze mirror on the wall, she could see that the cushion's embroidery had left the shape of a lotus printed on her cheek.

The sound that had woken her was Seth. He was kneeling next to another box, unwrapping plastic from what looked like freeze-dried disaster rations. He glanced up as she stirred, and a guilty expression flitted across his face.

"I didn't mean to wake you..." he began.

"I shouldn't've been sleeping any...way," Theo said, rubbing her eyes. The last word was split in half by a yawn.

Seth rose, holding a couple of the packages under one arm. "You didn't sleep well last night, though. I could hear you tossing and turning."

"Still, I shouldn't be napping when we've got work to do," she said, swinging her legs over the edge of the couch. "What time is it?"

"About four in the afternoon." Seth turned over the packages, grimacing. "I thought we should eat something, but the only food I can keep here is the kind that won't go bad. The words 'shelf-stable' are never a sign you're about to enjoy yourself. Which would you prefer: alleged chicken or alleged stew?"

Theo stifled another yawn. "Death."

"Pick again. It's not—ah—all it's cracked up to be."

She hid a smile at the awkward slang and pointed to the package of faux fowl.

It appeared to be an MRE or Meal, Ready to Eat, the military food-stuff that had the rare privilege of its entire name being a bald-faced lie. Still, Theo couldn't deny that she was hungry, not when she hadn't had a real meal since the day before yesterday. Pilfering Aki's Chex Mix wasn't quite the same.

"You've never died, though," she pointed out as she extracted what was supposedly a chicken patty from its plastic tomb. "Not really. You said you haven't...crossed over."

"No," Seth admitted, gaze fixed determinedly on his meal. "But I'm in the house when the lights go out, you could say. Does this look like stew to you? I can't tell."

Theo recognized a diversionary tactic when she saw one, but she let it go. If Seth wanted to talk about it, he would do so in his own time, and prodding would make them both angry.

"I don't want to say what it looks like," she said, tearing her rubbery patty in half. "Mom always told me not to use that kind of language. Try this instead; yours could probably eat you."

After some persuading, she managed to make Seth accept a few pieces of her meal. He didn't seem to need more than a mouthful or two, which made a strange sort of sense to her. If she were designing a brand-new body for a soldier two thousand years before the birth of Jesus, she would want him to require as little food and water as possible. He would have to sleep less, be stronger and faster, heal better. And of course, hah, be taller. Six foot two was nothing much to modern eyes, but in the days of Amenemhat I, it would've made him a giant among men.

Looking over the rim of her bottle of water, she found herself remembering the tubercular body of the mummy. Seth, Anhurmose then, must have been in horrible pain. The vessel he had built for his soul had been an escape from that as well. And it was good for a man who was planning to live a long, long existence as a general in wartime conditions, though maybe there was vanity in it too.

As she watched, Seth tore a few scraps of chicken from his half of the ration. He tossed them into the bowl, poured lighter fluid over them, and fumbled for matches. Theo automatically looked up at the smoke detector in the ceiling, but she saw that its batteries had been removed. Having firemen break in on your burnt offering was definitely not part of the ritual canon.

The fire blazed up and died away almost immediately, burnt out after a minute or so. As it receded into ash, Seth murmured a prayer.

"You can say that again," Theo said. "So what now? What are we going to do?"

"We have to find Zimmer," Seth declared, waving away a wisp of smoke from the bowl. The meat had been completely consumed, leaving behind nothing but a thin crust of black ash. "He's our best lead right now, whether he was involved or not. Do you know anyone who could help us get back into the museum?"

"Not Aki," Theo said. "He's supposed to be working from home. But Sandy Navarro is pretty smart, and she might be willing to listen. Or Dr. Van Allen. I've known him for years, and he was head of the Classical Antiquities Department when I was interning as a scenery painter."

At that, Seth looked surprised. "Dr. Van Allen? I remember him. Short man, strange, unsociable?"

"Pot, kettle."

"I'm serious." Seth's expression turned grim, the brown eyes sharp and snapping. "He sent a request about six months ago. He wanted the Neith Trust to be extended to cover administrative and departmental costs. I didn't think much of it at the time. Museums always bleed money."

"Come on, Seth. You're not thinking he had something to do with this?" Theo almost dropped her cup in surprise. "He's the curator of the Egyptology Department!"

"He has the clearance," Seth pointed out, setting down his own cup of water. "He can read hieratic and priest's script. He would have known which shabtis were LoJacked. And he was extremely eager to have a large amount of capital funneled into a place where he could make use of it."

Theo formed a mental picture of Dr. Wayne Van Allen. She didn't hate working under him: despite his standoffishness, Dr. Van Allen had helped keep multiple departments producing. And funded, of course, though the Trust had been a big part of that. A little man, quiet enough, but relentless in his work. Leaning across, she tossed a cracker into the embers.

"It's possible," she conceded reluctantly. "But I can't see it, Seth. Curators always want money—it's like a fish wanting water. But he'd never do anything to hurt the museum. It's his life."

"Then let's see if anyone else fits the bill." Seth's dark eyes focused on her. "You know the museum, Theo. Can you think of anyone besides Zimmer who might have had a motive to help or hinder us?"

Theo closed her eyes and thought. All those weeks and months, working and visiting from department to department, she'd been pretty secure in her position. She hadn't been considering which of her fellow employees might be a thief or a would-be murderer. There were a few unpleasant types, especially in the Animatronics and Building departments, but nobody struck her as the sort of person who'd frame someone for antiquities theft.

Though there was something else.

"It has to be someone who was in the loft or with the cops," she said. No question of which night. "Someone who heard my story about you. They did it while I was at your house, and I doubt that's a coincidence. It made us look like we were in on it together, and to swing that, they had to know that I named you as a suspect in the first place."

"Not necessarily," Seth said. "Zimmer could have brought in an outsider and told them."

"Then I've got nothing." Theo groaned and ran a hand through her hair. "I'm sorry, Seth, but this isn't my field of study and we need more information. But someone profited by doing this, and I can't figure out how or why."

"So who could be the one profiting? A good principle of any mystery. Let's begin with the people you know. You mentioned this woman Sandy. Would she know how the robbery happened?"

"Possibly. Whenever something like that happens, everyone's briefed on what not to say to the press. Emails get sent out to the whole staff. You can usually work out what happened based on what you can't say happened."

"And Dr. Van Allen would know?"

"Definitely."

"Then we should contact them both. Get the story from each of them and see if there are obvious discrepancies. Check it against news and police reports. If one is clearly lying, we may have our culprit."

"How are we going to get police reports?"

This time, his good humor didn't quite reach his eyes. "You make your phone calls, and I'll make mine."

And he would have too; Theo had no doubt of that. Unfortunately, several things happened at once.

The brazier lit up like a bonfire. Sheets of flame roared up, incinerating the meager offering in an instant and sending a wave of dry heat rippling through the close room. A strangled cry burst from Seth. His whole body stiffened, the tendons leaped in his neck, the blood drained from his face. One hand was pressed to his chest and clutched the hollow of his heart as if he were trying to keep it from escaping. His knuckles were white.

"Neith, protect me—" The rest of his words were in the language of his birth. He would have collapsed if Theo hadn't dropped her food and caught him. As it was, his weight dragged her down, and she cradled him against her chest as she tried to sit back into a kneeling position. She thanked anybody listening that the smoke alarm was already out of commission. The makeshift brazier was burning so fiercely that the edges of the bowl were beginning to turn orange.

Something moved at the edge of her vision. There were almost no shadows left in the harsh light of the fire, but she could swear there was a shadow flickering at the corner of her eye. It circled the fire, moving as she turned her head, prowling like a dog on the scent. It was dark, not the gloss black of a statue or a healthy dog, but the four-legged dead black of—something.

Blood dripped from Seth's nose and eyes. Theo stifled a scream as he clutched at his face, pink lines showing under his skin where the veins had burst. She tried to grab him but he scrambled to his feet, throwing off her hands with unnatural strength. He backed up against the table, almost knocking it over, his hands clamped to his face. The blood running from his nose dried almost instantly into red Nile clay.

"Neith, protect me. Neith, shield me. Neith, protect me." English and the ancient language interwove, a bilingual chant of desperation and pain.

"Seth!" Her shout was cut off as he spasmed, crashing backward against the table again and knocking the remaining scrolls and statuettes off as one of its legs snapped. The clay fell away in wet chunks, leaving his face streaked with red-black mud.

Slowly, the shivers began to subside, and the prayers fell silent. His knees crumpled as the strength went out of them, and he toppled—collapsed, more like—slumping back against the ruins of the spindle-legged table.

Theo caught him again, trying to keep him from cracking his skull on the wall. His head lolled back, dark eyes wide and staring, tears mixing with clay to leave muddy stains.

"Seth, Seth," she whispered.

He blinked, clay beading on his eyelashes.

"Can you hear me, Seth?" Numbly, she ran through the signs of stroke in her mind: check pupils for unnatural dilation, feel joints for floppiness. Spend time in a studio with lots of chemicals, you learn to memorize the emergency procedures. But it was impossible for her to tell how bad he was. No seminar she'd ever taken had told her how to give first aid to a man bleeding clay out of his eyes.

They focused on her, at long last. The dry lips parted and the streaks of reddish clay cracked when he moved.

Tears beaded in Theo's eyes. "Seth," she repeated, her voice hoarse. "Seth, can you hear me?" The words quavered. Even if he couldn't, what could she do about it?

She cradled Seth's head, wiping away the mud with the pad of her thumb. "It's not time yet," she said softly. His stubble felt rough despite the calluses on her fingers. "Four thousand years, and you're going to die in a storage locker by the airport? So much for Mister Governor."

The lips twitched, and the remaining clay in the corners of his mouth crumbled.

Theo almost collapsed in relief when she realized he was trying to smile. The eyes focused, red veins beginning to fade from the whiteness of the eyeballs as his strange inbuilt healing took over. The fire was dying as quickly as it had sprung up, leaving behind the pale yellow light of the fluorescents. Without the blaze of flame, the world seemed dimmer and colder.

"Yu iti," he rasped. *"Yu iti haty-a."*

Theo blinked away the last tears, trying not to show how worried she still was. Seth tried to sit back up, but fresh red lines bloomed on the skin and Theo put a hand on his chest to keep him down.

He tried again. *"Gouverneur c'est...mein vater..."*

"It's okay," she said quietly. "Just focus on me."

"The governor was my father." He stumbled over the words, but at least it was English again. "I was a...a rich kid."

She wiped away a few streaks of clay. "Welcome back, rich kid. I thought you'd crossed over for sure that time."

"I think I might have." He mopped most of the remaining clay out of his eyes, grimacing at it. But his hand squeezed Theo's tighter than ever, the skin cool and slick with sweat. "Someone has my mummy, Theo."

Theo's stomach clenched. "I thought you had it hidden."

"In my townhouse." He struggled up into a sitting position against the broken table, and Theo took one of his arms, giving him something to lean on. "I did think it was adequately concealed. I used some things to hide it."

"Magic? Secret sigils?"

"Four locks and a fingerprint scanner. But I did add a few spells. Simple, but they should have turned eyes away from it. Someone found it."

"What...?" she started as she wiped clay off her hands. The red lines had almost faded, but they weren't completely gone yet. "What happens? Happened? I mean, what did they do?"

His mouth twisted. "I don't know. It felt like I was being ripped in half. It's been damaged; it has to have been. Someone—someone knew that hurting it would hurt me."

He swallowed, and Theo knew what he was thinking. Maybe THS203 might've been dissected by the tuberculosis study, but not while it was also evidence in an ongoing investigation. The only one who could've accessed it would be someone who could see through magic, and the only one getting close to it would be someone affiliated with the case.

"Zimmer?" she said. The name tasted like ash in her mouth as she said it. She'd hoped to avoid that, but it was hard enough fighting the damn shadow who'd set them up, and it needed a name. The one man with universal access to the museum, the one who'd sent her to see Seth on a flimsy pretext and failed to respond when she tried to ask for his help... His was as good a name as any.

And the actual shadow? The stalking dog? She opened her mouth to say something, but swallowed the words at the last moment. Too much going on already.

"Or his accomplice." Seth struggled to sit up again, leaning hard against Theo as he tried not to fall. She sagged back onto the couch, letting him rest against her as she helped him get settled.

His hands trembled, but he was no longer bleeding and some of the color was coming back into his cheeks.

"I guess this answers the do-they-know question, Seth."

His hand squeezed hers.

Ten minutes ago, he had been on top of the world, or as close to it as possible in their situation, and now he could barely stand. And worse, he had fallen because someone had his mummy.

No, not *his* mummy. *The* mummy. An artifact that could hurt Seth, no matter what he was doing or where he was. Someone knew what Seth was, enough to circumvent the security he'd placed on the mummy and enough to know that hurting it would hurt him. It could be an accident, but the way their luck was going, it was more likely an attack.

Seth seemed to be thinking the same thing. "We have no time left," he said quietly. "I have to find a way to get my body back."

"There can't be too many places you can hide a mummy in this city," Theo said. She hoped, rather than knew, that that was the case. "I'll make a couple of calls. There has to be someone else in the museum who'll talk to me."

"No." Seth managed to sit up this time. His color was back, and his voice was stronger. "This is getting out of hand. You need to go to the police. Turn yourself in. Tell them that I threatened your family if you didn't help me. I can drop off the radar, find the mummy myself, and disappear."

There was a moment of silence. Then Theo swept another strand of her hair aside and looked him straight in the eyes. "To hell with that."

"Theo—"

"No. To hell with that." She crossed her arms as Seth straightened up, trying to protest. "You heard me. I've been with you on this so far, Seth. If you don't want me around anymore, say the word and I'm gone; I don't stay where I'm not wanted. But if this is you trying to save me trouble or something, then screw it. You almost died in front of me. That mummy means they have a way to hurt you, and they don't strike me as the type to let you catch up with them!"

She stopped, panting. Her face burned, not from embarrassment but with the flush of anger. All the pent-up emotions of the last few days—frustration and rage and the terror of something moving and alive that she'd never quite felt before and couldn't recognize—they were rushing through her, making her shiver.

"You're serious," Seth said after a moment. He looked stunned.

"If I didn't stop at grand larceny, why would I stop now?" she snapped back. "If you're bored with me, then say it, I'm gone. But don't think you're doing me a favor by trying to send me away. Capisce?"

"You're crazy," he said slowly. A small smile tugged at his lips. "That's supposed to be your line, isn't it?"

"I'm an artist, Seth." Theo threw her arms out, encompassing the room and the mummy-man and the whole insane world in one gesture. "I paint dead things. I pretend that I can recreate the faces of ancient corpses or turn walls into portals into the past. I know the skeletal structure of a *Struthiomimus sedens* better than most people know their credit card numbers, and then I put a freaking Santa hat on it. I'm sitting in a storage locker with a man who can't die, and I volunteered to help him. I am...I am a flake. Believe me, if I were crazy, I wouldn't have a problem telling you."

She took a deep breath, vaguely aware that her hands were shaking. "Now, are we going to start hunting down this bastard or not? Because I take it kind of personally when someone tries to kill you by long-distance voodoo."

"Theo," he said softly. Something in his eyes made her stop her impassioned half-rant. "Theodora. It's an old name. Do you know what it means?"

She frowned, brought up short by the question. "Theodora means 'gift of God.' It's Greek, my grandma said. Why does it matter?"

"I met a Theodora once before." He stood up, wavering a little, and opened one of the boxes. Some digging produced a scroll, clearly one of the oldest and tied with a scrap of what looked like purple silk. The dangling tag was lettered in hieratic, and Theo picked out the letters, mentally calling them by their hieroglyphic equivalents: basket K, water N, folded cloth S, loaf T, box-stool P, quail-chick U. She tried to place the vowels that hieratic didn't have. The last symbol threw her for a moment, but certain sounds hadn't existed in the old alphabets.

"Constantinople?" she said finally.

Seth nodded.

"An empress," he said. "Theodora, wife of Theophilos. Not a perfect woman, but she loved the icons. They made her a saint for restoring the images of Christ to the palaces and churches of the Byzantine Empire."

Theo swallowed, her mouth dry. "You met her?"

"I did. I was with the Roman Empire for a long, long time." He held out the scroll, and Theo touched it as carefully as she dared. "She believed that her deity was in the images. A good name for her, to be called a gift from her god."

"It's just a name."

"Names have power." When she didn't take the scroll, he set it down on the table instead. "I was—am—called the son of the war god, and see how I turned out."

"I don't think soldiers are supposed to live forever," she pointed out. *Or run from a problem*, she added mentally, though she couldn't exactly blame him for that. Soldiers didn't usually have to deal with angry gods or eternal life.

There was something enigmatic in his expression. His features were set, glacial as they had been that night at the museum, but his eyes were fixed on hers and seemed to be asking for something. His hand rested on the scroll, toying with the end of the scrap of silk. As she watched, he wound it around one coppery-blue finger, silk folds lying taut over the smooth flesh. She swallowed hard.

"Anyway," she said loudly, forcing her thoughts back to the present, "I'm not ditching you, not now. We need a plan. This person hurt you from miles away. He has the mummy. What're we going to do?"

"Find him. Stop him." Seth shook his head. "Retrieve the mummy intact, if possible. I know this may be shocking to you, but I'd prefer not to die again."

"Damn right," she said softly. Her lips twisted in sad, bitter humor. "If you try to die on me, I'll paint you another portrait. A *Cubist* portrait."

The silk slipped from his fingers. He stretched one arm out, mutely offering something neither of them could put into words, and she went to him and curled into his embrace. His breath ruffled her hair as she rested her head against his shoulder. For a moment she let herself relax, wrapped in his arms, enjoying the closeness.

"Noted," he murmured, his voice a low rumble. His hand stroked softly over the curve of her hip, toying with the hem of her remaining shirt.

"Seth..." She pressed a kiss to the hollow of his throat, caressing the pulse point there. She could feel his heart thundering under her cheek. When she said his name, though, his muscles tensed and his hands dropped away.

"I should finish the papers," he said, and stepped back. Theo watched him, chilled by the sudden distance, as he sat down at the table again and picked up the knife. His hand shook.

The knife slid from his grip. He gripped it again, white-knuckled.

Seth Adler was afraid. His world was crashing down around him, and mortality was staring him in the face for what had to be the first time in thousands of years. Theo knew the way the story went: the mummy was preserved in order to provide a home and anchor for a part of the soul, and without it, the soul could be lost forever. His weakness was in someone else's hands, and Anhurmose son of Merenptah was scared. He was going to die, and maybe Theo was going to die with him.

But she was mortal. Completely, utterly normal and mortal. She didn't want to die, but it had always been part of the plan—the last act, the final hurrah, the ultimate brushstroke on the canvas of her life. The immortal man feared death because he could avoid it, but the mortal woman knew something he didn't.

She knew that they weren't dead yet.

"I want to try something," she said softly.

Seth was concentrating on his work. "You have an idea?"

"Sort of." The words felt awkward, but they were nothing but words. She leaned over and, as gently as if she had his life in her hands, brushed the fine, dark hair off the nape of his neck. He tensed under her hands, but she pressed a kiss against the skin and the merest tremor ran through the muscles there.

"Theo," he said hoarsely. Raggedly. "I'm trying very, very hard not to take things out of context right now... Ah!"

She wondered if he knew how much that little noise, deep in his throat as she nipped at the jut of his collarbone, meant to her. It sent a deep thrill through her, whispering of control and safety and *don't think, do*. It was a feeling she liked.

"Mr. Adler," she said quietly, her lips brushing against the taut skin, "am I trying to seduce you?"

A laugh broke from him, but it trailed off into a moan as she ran her nails ever so lightly over the softest skin at the base of his ribs. "I think you are," he rasped.

His breath was coming faster and his dark eyes burned as he half turned in his chair, trying to face her. One hand wrapped around her wrist, keeping her fingers from probing farther—for her safety, maybe, but perhaps also for his. There was a glint in the fine, dark hair of his temples where sweat was beginning to gather.

"Theo." Her name was a hoarse whisper on his lips. "Theo, I…I don't know. It's a matter of…"

"If you say 'life and death,' Seth Adler," she said, her own voice rough, "you won't like what I do."

The challenging words broke something in him. Surging up from his chair, he kissed her hungrily, biting on her lower lip and drawing a gasp from her. His arms went around her, hard and strong and demanding, but not tight enough. He was still restraining himself. Words were still left unsaid. And Theo didn't like not having things explained. She shivered as the stubble rasped against her lips, but she pulled him closer.

The words finally came out in low whispers between kisses. "Theo. It's not responsible. We're on the run. I don't have anything. And the magic—the gods—"

"Seth." She laid her hands on the hard planes of his chest, feeling the pounding of his heart through the thin fabric. "I'm clean, you're freshly regenerated, and I've had the implant for months now." She shrugged one shoulder. "It's one less thing I have to worry about in the morning."

"And you say you're not practical," he murmured. He drew Theo into him, letting her cradle her head above his collarbone. She pressed another kiss there, and he arched, the hard lines of his throat standing out under the skin. He was so close to losing his control, and that was what needed to happen.

"Are you sure?" he whispered. "I'm stronger than you. I don't want to hurt you."

"You won't." She nipped at the skin over the pulse point, drawing a moan from him. "Just be with me, Anhurmose…."

His name falling from her lips in a hoarse murmur made him shudder as he held her. She wondered how long it had been since someone had called him by his real name, his birth name—especially a woman in his arms. In that moment he looked stark, lost, and his pain and need were written in raw lines on his face.

"Anhurmose," she whispered. His arms tightened around her, a silent promise.

"Meri tje." His voice was a rumble deep in his chest. He drew her down onto the couch, and there were no more words between them.

CHAPTER THIRTEEN

I have unburdened myself to many priests and wise men
in my time, but none so happily as to a woman who will
bear no foolishness.

– Excerpt from the Jurisprudence of Diokles,
circa 910 BCE (fragment)

It had been a long time for him. Too long.

Seth wet a cloth with bottled water and finished his ablutions. Theo had gone to wash up, and he was once again alone with his gods for a few minutes. He breathed deeply, feeling the blessed emptiness where the fear had once been.

With striking ease Theo, the woman behind the glass, had crossed the final barrier between them. She'd said his name, his real name, and in that moment she'd meant something by it. Half of him was afraid that something was about to go wrong, but the other half felt like throwing a bottle of champagne through a plate-glass window and shouting to the world what had happened.

For a moment his English failed him, and he tilted his head back and poured half the water over his head.

He was sitting cross-legged on the couch, mopping his face, when the door slid open and Theo came light-footed into the room. She smiled awkwardly at him, almost shy. Her cheeks were flushed, her eyes bright and lively. She was a creature of color and vitality, purely human, with no immortal clay in her. How had it happened that she could affect him so much?

Seeing her, Seth rose and offered her the couch. Theo shook her head and gently but firmly pushed him back down. Then she settled in next to him, a fresh bottle of water in hand, legs curled loosely under her as she made herself comfortable.

"All right, we both know how this is going to go," she said softly. "You haven't survived for so long by being careless. You're wondering what kind of a liability I'll be. No, that's not right, is it? You're wondering what's going to go wrong. How I'm going to throw you over, make you realize what a bad idea it was to sleep with me."

So that was how it happened. She called to his shabtis like an artist could, but she was blunter than a bow stave when needed. There would be no more compromising or lying to this one. Gods, what a relief.

Seth leaned forward and slid his fingers into the collar of her T-shirt, gently pulling the material down to expose the bruise he had left on her shoulder. Theo let out a soft breath as he pressed a kiss to the spot.

"I have lived a long time," he murmured, his mouth a bare inch from her skin. "But I know how to hold on to a good thing when I find it."

"Jerk," she said fondly. She glanced up at the shelf of gods. "I wonder if we've scandalized them."

He laughed. "Considering how some of them were worshiped, we may have earned a favor or two."

"It'll make up for the curses the rest of them will be throwing our way." She scooted down on the couch, making herself comfortable against him and taking a sip of water. "They don't look much like the shabtis."

The casualness of her tone didn't quite fool Seth. "Theo," he said softly. "I told you. I don't have any memories for your art."

"I'm not asking for memories, Anhurmose." His eyebrows shot up at that, and she put a hand on his arm. "Please don't…don't think I'm playing a game. This wasn't a scheme to get information." She swallowed. "But I can't *not* ask."

"Ask about what?"

"About the art. The story." She let out a breath she hadn't known she'd been holding, and her hand tightened. "Tell me about the shabtis, Anhurmose. Please."

He looked down at her. His first instinct was to say no—the secret must be protected at all costs, or his too-long life would be ended and the gods would have him. But… "Why?" he said finally.

"Because it's what I love."

He examined her, his eyes hooded in the dim light. Then, with a whisper of blankets and skin on cloth, he gathered her to him. Their bodies fit neatly together, her head against his shoulder, him staring at nothing.

He told her.

Magic had always been a part of his life, because it was part of Kemet itself. People believed in signs, spells, ritual incantations, and the power of names and images. It was said that great priests and kings had known the art of making wax figures of their enemies and then destroying those figures to bring destruction on the enemies. Those who could read, and were high enough to enjoy the privilege, studied in the kingdom's great libraries in hopes of obtaining that kind of power. Whenever the sky clouded and rain fell, everyone who could made ritual offerings to help the barque of the sun overcome the serpent who wanted to swallow it.

But he'd never seen magic happen. Enchanters worked with their little figures and their incantations, but no matter how long he served in the pharaoh's innumerable wars, he'd never seen spells destroy an army. No matter how people behaved when the rain began, the sun always came back. He believed, but in a perfunctory sort of way, the way he believed in the existence of dirt. It just…was. For a man who couldn't read and relied on the priests to handle godly affairs, magic wasn't something to be concerned about.

He'd taken it for granted that his life would go the way he wanted, and that when he died, he'd have a good burial and an afterlife worthy of a loyal servant of the pharaoh.

Then came disease, and Anhurmose had turned to magic when nothing else would help him.

"Hearts," he said. "Wax figures are too mutable; that was part of it, but the spirit needed something to—hold on to, I suppose. We made shabtis that would hold my soul, and we put in the hearts of sacrificial animals."

"A life for a life," she said softly. Their hands were entwined, and she ran her thumb over the edge of his.

"Not quite. They say…" He mulled over his words, searching for the right ones. "They say Khnum made the first people on his potter's wheel. Every one of us is clay, at the bottom of it. But the heart is the center of it, the thing that made us alive. And I think you can't run blood through a heart that's not your own. My brother might know, but after I died, I never saw him again."

He spun out the story for her. Two brothers wrapped up in a race against time, frantically searching for the grain of truth in centuries of religion and mysticism. Testing and refining. Hoping. And finally, a formula and a prayer that could do what was needed.

"Can you tell me?" she said.

With only a second's hesitation he whispered the words of the prayer for her, and he watched her drink them in: "Khnum is my father, Neith is my mother... *Ha ne sah en Merenptah...*"

She sighed and nestled into him.

"I'd like to paint it," she said.

He made a *hrrm* noise, drawing a tired laugh from her.

"Though not if it's going to cost anyone their soul."

"I don't know if it will," he murmured. "But being what I am gives me a healthy appreciation for charms and rituals."

"There are so many thesis papers begging to be written about this." He chuckled at that, and she poked him in the shoulder. "Don't tell me it's never crossed your mind. Even if you published your memories as theories, it could help expand people's ideas of what Egypt—Kemet—was like. Isn't that important?"

"Maybe," he said. "But it's not going to change anything. Not a lot of people actually care what happened four thousand years ago, Theo."

Her face fell. Seth gently brushed back a tousled curl of her hair, looking into her eyes. "I know you do," he said. "But no matter what I do, it's gone, Theo. A god with one worshiper is barely a god at all, and a nation with one citizen isn't much better. I'd rather let people think of Kemet as dead and buried."

"Not dead, maybe," she said, running her fingers over his shoulder. "Moved on. If you're still alive, maybe the afterlife is real too. For them, anyway."

"I almost hope it isn't," he admitted in a low voice. "Maybe this is magic, or science, or...something. I don't like the idea of facing Ammit and Anubis after four thousand years of hiding from them."

She pressed a kiss to his mouth, smiling against the skin as he made a little noise deep in his throat.

He could feel his borrowed heart thumping under her hand, and wondered if she could too.

"Well," she said, "at least you can start your negative confession with 'I have not lied to those who sought knowledge from me.'"

"No, I haven't," he agreed. "It's a nice change."

CHAPTER FOURTEEN

For Set held in his heart great hatred for Osiris, and
would not be swayed by words or by deeds. And when
the rage was upon him, he slew him, and cut him into
pieces to be scattered across the length and breadth of
the land.

- Excerpt from the Rebirth Papyrus,
circa 1390 BCE

He was asleep, but he might have been dead. A strange pall lay over his
left side, and the skin there was sunken and gray. Theo watched in
silence, counting between each shallow breath, wondering if he might
have had a stroke.

No, that couldn't be it. What kind of clay-bleeding mummy man had
a stroke? Carefully she oriented herself. North was that way, so—Ah.

His sickly side faced west. To Egyptians the west was the realm of
the dying sun, where gods of the dead dwelled and souls were brought
for judgment. She remembered the creeping, stalking dog shadow.
Zoology was not her department, but she'd bet anything that it had been
a jackal.

She knew enough to understand that Anubis wasn't an evil god. He
was a guardian of the dead and a patron of mummification, not a satanic
ghoul. But Seth had committed a sin against him and against the cosmic
order of *ma'at*, dodging his influence and the land of the dead entirely.
Maybe there was no specific commandment against living forever, but if
Anubis was real he would be understandably annoyed about it.

Yet Seth had trusted her despite the possibility of divine wrath. She
remembered his low, soft voice reciting the incantation that had brought

him back to life. One of the greatest discoveries in the history of humanity. The museum already had the inscription, the one written on the shabtis, but it was nothing without the prayer that went with it.

Ha ne sah en Merenptah. O Khnum, tjewet it; O Neith, tjewet imawet, ink nefer...

Ha and *ne.* Tangerine and gunmetal. She matched each syllable to a color, turning the poetry of the ancient language into a panorama in her mind.

It would stay there, locked away. The gallery of her mind's eye had no visitors allowed. But knowing it—knowing the truth—meant more to her than she could ever put into words. The words of life *were* art.

Despite everything, a smile crept across her face. If she still had a job when this was over, Dr. Van Allen would be getting a hell of a mural from her.

She wondered, almost idly, what the curator was doing. How would he handle another blow to the department? The first robbery had been bad enough, and now it looked like his trust in Theo (if he'd ever had any) had been misplaced. The exhibit was ruined.

The thought squeezed at her heart. The mummy and the shabtis, not to mention the jewelry.

Jewelry...that was the piece of the puzzle that didn't fit. Mummy and shabtis, yes, united by magic and Seth. Jewelry? There wasn't much jewelry listed among Number Three's grave goods, thanks to what Seth had described as the "secrecy of sacrilege." It was hard to gather valuables for a tomb when there wasn't supposed to be a tomb. What little had been found was cheap clay and faience amulets, stuff that even as antiquities wouldn't fetch much of a price and apparently had no connection to magic beyond the usual protective symbols. The tyet had been noteworthy for its unusual placement, but it wasn't that big of a note.

So why had it been taken? Or had it really been jewels from the burial, and not something else entirely?

Dr. Van Allen wouldn't talk to the press if he could avoid it. Letting people know exactly what had been stolen guaranteed that the thief would take the items apart to prevent their being recognized. Better they be lost to an illegal collection than destroyed entirely. That was how Van Allen would see it, anyway.

She needed to find out what was going on.

Seth had learned to play the long game because it used to be his best option. He was going to outlive everyone and, at least until the mummy was taken, he could have afforded to be patient. It had kept him alive, but it also meant he had learned not to think like a vulnerable human.

Theo couldn't afford to hide forever. She had one lifetime, and she didn't want to spend it as someone else. Falsely accused fugitives on TV always seemed to manage pretty well, but Theo wasn't the A-Team type. There had to be a way to fix this without going that far.

Seth hadn't blinked at the mention of jewelry. It was one more part of a situation he had to escape. But it niggled at Theo, a discordant patch of olive drab in the middle of *Starry Night*. She needed to learn more.

She pressed a kiss to his cool, sunken cheek and slipped off the couch. He didn't stir. If it hadn't been for the slight rise and fall of his chest, he might have been completely dead.

It wasn't a face she'd anticipated when she'd hoped to meet someone, but it wasn't one she regretted.

His keys were in his jacket where he'd dropped it. After a moment's thought, she unlocked the door, then used the keys to weigh down a piece of parchment on the spindly writing desk.

She started to write in English, but stopped and, rearranging her grip on the pen, pieced out a few English words in the hieroglyphic alphabet.

I'm going to ask some questions. Back soon. T.

Then she made a quick bow to the standing gods and slipped the small tyet amulet off the shelf. It was a symbol of resurrection, but it was also a woman's, and she could use the luck. Wearing it would feel strange, but there was nothing wrong with carrying it in her pocket.

Dr. Van Allen was a loner and a night owl. Rumor had it that he lived in a crypt, or possibly a basement laboratory with a body on the slab. With no access to the staff database, she had no way to find out where he lived. But he was also a curator with a pilfered exhibit, and it wasn't even nine o'clock yet. Easy bet that he was still at the museum.

The question was, could she get to him?

But for once she had a stroke of luck. The industrial park around the airport had been built decades ago, and though it didn't see a lot of pedestrians, it did a lot of business. Pay phones had been scattered here and there on the long, unlined streets, and with so little foot traffic, few of the phones had been destroyed by casual vandalism. It'd do.

The block around her was deserted, but she still pulled her collar up and glanced around nervously. She couldn't shake the feeling that some-one was watching her.

An automated voice, a little wavery through the old phone, greeted her, "You have reached the office of Dr. Wayne Van Allen. Who shall I say is calling?"

She pitched her voice down a little. "Sophie Winslow, Clausen Insurance."

"Hold, please," the automated system said. It paid to know whom your boss dreaded.

There was a click, and a familiar voice answered, "This is Dr. Van Allen. Is there a problem?"

"Doctor? I'm sorry to disturb you so late, but this is a very irregular case."

"I understand." Van Allen's voice was oddly worn, and Theo felt a twitch of sympathy for the cold curator. He might not be sociable, but he wasn't a bad person, and she doubted he would enjoy the opportunity to be interrogated about his department's loss. "What is it?"

"The files your office sent for confirmation have been corrupted, and we need to double-check our records for the lost properties." She tried to sound busy and harassed, which wasn't hard. "Can you please confirm the item list?"

There was a moment of silence. Papers shuffled. "I'm surprised. I thought you had that on file, Miss Speer."

Theo almost dropped the phone, but fought to keep her composure. "I'm sorry?"

"I know my employees, Miss Speer. Including those accused of theft." The voice was as cool and flat as ever. "Is there a reason you called?"

"You've got to believe me, sir," she said. "If I'd stolen them, I wouldn't be calling you."

"If so, why did you run from the police?"

"I made a mistake." Was it true? She didn't know. "I got scared."

"And what do you expect me to do?" he said calmly. "I assume you're calling me—and not the authorities—for a reason."

"The jewelry...well...the jewelry doesn't fit the thief's pattern. I wanted to know what it was they stole."

Papers rustled again. "Some rather impressive examples from the

Scythian exhibit."

Theo tried not to slap herself in the face. No wonder—Clausen didn't cover the Scythian stuff. "That doesn't make sense."

"Actually, it's the only thing that does." His calm was slightly eerie. It felt like a conversation they should be having in the cubicles of the loft, not while she was standing in the middle of a deserted industrial block. "The Scythians left us almost no literature, but their jewelry was unparalleled."

"I know, it's gorgeous. I did prep work for the brochure last year."

"It would've been a wonderful exhibit. But then, I've been saying that a lot lately. Who do you think is responsible?"

"You wouldn't believe me if I told you. The Egyptian items were the real goal."

"And why do you think that?"

She laughed, but her heart wasn't in it. "How did I wind up answering your questions instead of asking them?"

"I'm the one asking questions that need answering." She could hear the doctor tapping his pen on the edge of the desk. "If you're telling the truth, Miss Speer, why did he steal the Scythian gold?"

"Cover. Make it look like a regular old burglary." Theo tried to think. "Or maybe for the money, but I wouldn't bet on it. The guy doing most of the robberies seems to be that Collector character, and he doesn't strike me as the type that needs cash on hand. Whoever it is, though, if he knows what I know about Number Three's grave goods, then he's after more than money."

"And what is that, exactly?"

"It's a mess, is what it is." She took a breath as she tried to figure out how to phrase it. "It's...it's big, Doctor. Stolen artifacts, old religion, history being rewritten. Everything we know about Number Three is being turned upside down."

"That sounds suitably mysterious. And unlikely." The doctor's tone remained level. Apparently, being called after hours by an employee on the run didn't really faze him. "Granted, Egyptology spent most of the nineteenth century as scientific plundering, but things have moved along since then. We learn things through careful research and scholarly analysis, not corpse robbing and midnight hijinks."

"Dr. Van Allen, if I could have learned this stuff in an incredibly boring and normal way, I would be thrilled beyond belief. You know how they say that a little knowledge is a dangerous thing?"

A pause. "Do you have proof to offer?"

"Yes." She silently asked Seth to forgive her. "In Number Three's tomb, there's a hidden room behind a panel of Apep. It contains several shabtis and a pretty bad copy of the Coffin Texts. Get the museum's Cairo team to check it out, and I promise you won't be disappointed."

Another pause, longer this time, and she thought she heard the scratching of pen on paper. "It'll take at least twenty-four hours to get a team to the site," he informed her calmly. "Are you going to tell me how you came by this information?"

"I know a guy."

"Miss Speer, you're not precisely instilling me with confidence."

"Sir, I swear if you get our Cairo people on the job, they'll find it." She let out a breath, trying to settle her racing pulse. "But I've learned more. I need to talk to you—I've found some things that could lead us to Number Three." For something to hurt the mummy so badly, it couldn't be in responsible custody. And that meant that Dr. Van Allen, who'd rather see an artifact disappear than risk it being destroyed, didn't know where the mummy was right now.

"I must admit, hostage negotiation was not part of my preparation for this position," he said. Theo could hear more papers shuffling in the background. "But THS203 is invaluable. Where would you like to meet?"

"The museum," Theo said instantly. "I know for a fact that there aren't many cameras in the administrative wing. I'll meet you at the west entrance in one hour." She swallowed her fear and tried to keep her voice steady. "Please believe me—I don't want to see Number Three get hurt."

"It's a little late for that," the doctor responded, his voice steady. "But I believe we share a goal in that respect. One hour."

* * *

The museum campus was dead and dark after nightfall. Dr. Van Allen might not want to see THS203 hurt any more than she did, but that didn't mean she could walk in and ask to see him. Security would be on high alert, and even if there were no cameras in the administrative section, it would be too easy to get caught.

It was probably stupid to come back to the museum. But this new robbery was something out of place, and she needed to see the wrecked collection. Maybe someone who knew about the unnatural aspects of the situation would be able to spot something the police couldn't.

That was the theory, anyway. But as she clambered awkwardly up the iced-over path toward the white building, she forced herself to admit that it was also partially about comfort.

The loft of the Columbian was more like home than her apartment or her parents' place. It was the place where she was safest and happiest, the place that provided her with a bulwark against the rest of the world. Now that everything was going wrong and her life had been violently turned upside down, she wanted to see that place one more time—in case she didn't get a chance to return.

From the outside, the museum was silent and lifeless. Its sleek pillars and high arches seemed to belong to a different time, and with fresh snow covering everything, the building took on the air of an archaeological site. A temple, perhaps. It was as if an ice age had destroyed all life on Earth and the wind was blowing through the shattered stone monuments of a dead species.

Interesting picture. Bad time to be contemplating it, though.

She finally reached the crest of the hill. The reflected light from Soldier Field cast her shadow, thin and wavy, across the main steps of the northern entrance as she passed them by. The north and south sides were for patrons, who would climb shallow steps to a colonnaded entryway and a nineteenth-century-style wrought-iron gate over the modern glass door. The side entrance Theo was aiming for had security doors, a keycard scanner, and a camera perched on the lintel.

Not that she couldn't avoid that. You technically weren't supposed to smoke within one hundred feet of a public building, but the people who had made that policy hadn't realized that they were asking a smoker to give up the broad cover of the museum and go stand in the lake wind when it was below freezing. No matter where the cameras were put, half the art department would be inevitably found wedged into the tiniest blind spot, puffing away like nicotine ninjas. If she'd doubted she was in the right place, she could follow the trail of cigarette butts.

Dr. Van Allen was waiting for her under one of the orange safety lights. The ominous effect of the heavy shadows on his dark suit was somewhat spoiled by the Chicago Bears jacket and scarf he was wearing over it. It occurred to Theo that this was the first time she'd ever seen him wear a coat: on a typical day he would arrive earlier than she would, and often stay later. There were dark circles under his eyes, and he seemed to have shrunk an inch or two in the last few days.

"Miss Speer," he greeted her perfunctorily. "You're going incognito, I see."

"Haven't had much of a choice." She tugged at the edge of her hood, making sure most of her curly brown hair was covered. "Thank you for meeting me, Doctor."

"You made me an offer I couldn't refuse." The curator's tone had a touch of grim humor, which surprised her. She hadn't been aware he could be amused. "I presume you won't consider stepping inside? It's a little chilly out here."

"Actually," Theo said, "I want to see the site of the second robbery."

Dr. Van Allen's eyebrows rose, and she hurried to elaborate. "I'm not going to touch anything or interfere with the site. I won't ask what the cops have told you, or how you think it was done. I need to see it."

The curator looked her over with a strange expression. "You've put a great deal of thought into this," he observed. "I don't recall hiring you for your ability to negotiate a criminal trespass."

Her heart sank. "You didn't. Are we actually going to do anything, Doctor?" The words were sharpened by worry. "Because if you'd rather make fun of me, I can get back to what I was doing and leave you to find THS203 on your own."

"That won't be necessary." Van Allen's lips thinned. "I'm disappointed, though."

"That makes two of us. Not the way I wanted to spend Christmas." Theo gestured to the door. "After you, sir."

After a moment's hesitation, Dr. Van Allen swiped his card through the reader and opened the door. He went first, and Theo followed him, her hood still up to obscure her features.

Granted, nobody was expecting her to return to the scene of her supposed crime. That didn't mean she was going to be careless.

Dr. Van Allen swiped open a new door and the pair of them ducked into the brightly lit back corridors. Theo followed closely, trying not to let her impatience make her get ahead of him. Her heart was thumping painfully under her breastbone. She eyed each corner and door before she reached them.

She knew the shabtis had been divided up. A few were on display;

others had been moved to the secondary prep labs for LoJacking, and if
the news reports had been correct, it was that group that had been stolen.
The rest, a group of twelve or so, were still in Prep A. Thank goodness: if
the little guys had been in one group, they might've all been stolen.

Prep D was a mess. Crime-scene tape roped off the entrance, and
the door hung half-open where the lock had been burned through.
Several clear cases—extra-strength plastic, the toughest available—had
been cleanly broken open, but anything made of glass was smashed. The
sterile tables were scuffed and sooty, with corresponding scorch marks
on the ceiling above them. Theo's eyes widened.

"Did they use dynamite or something?" she said, dumbfounded.
"This isn't a robbery; this is a sack."

"Like Troy," the doctor agreed levelly. "Scorched earth and all."

Theo picked her way through the debris. Several items lay where
they had fallen, cordoned off by the plastic markers the cops used to
label them. An orange-and-black Grecian urn hadn't so much shattered
as crumbled, leaving nothing but a heap of colored chunks. Several less
fragile items, including a stone fertility goddess, were overturned and
flecked with soot. Whatever happened had been quick, messy, and
destructive.

But there was more to it than that. A strange gray pall hung over the
place. Something whispered past her, a familiar-sounding syllable that
was gone when she turned to chase it, and there seemed to be a mistiness
in the air. She twitched, and Dr. Van Allen frowned at her.

She couldn't help it. It was there. It had to be.

Squaring her shoulders, Theo skirted around a caved-in tabletop
and crouched down next to one of the ruined cases. True to her word,
she didn't touch, but she didn't have to. The edges of the plastic were
warped, reflecting the light in smooth spots like flowing oil. It had been
cut with a torch. A nearby particleboard shelf had burned fiercely,
collapsing into splintered ashes that littered the bottom of the cabinet.

The clear plastic was dotted with beads of moisture. Theo swiped a
corner of her sleeve over the cabinet, then sniffed it. It had a faint, rank
odor, like slow-moving water under a hot sun.

A prep room should have been dry.

"Something's going wrong." Theo stood up, trying and failing to
calm her racing heart. Something was already wrong; the shadows were
strange—dark in places where they shouldn't be. The colors were shifting

subtly, but the lighting was staying the same.

Van Allen's eyes narrowed. "Miss Speer, I've been patient. Extraordinarily so, I think. But you're not giving me answers, and paranoia isn't a helpful trait in an employee."

"It's not paranoia if they're really out to get you. Look at the shadows."

The curator looked around the lab. "It's night, Miss Speer. Shadows tend to come out at night. What are you...?" He paused, his brow furrowing. "Wait, what...?"

"Don't you see? The light is wrong." Theo instinctively shifted her feet, bracing as if she were getting ready to run. Maybe she was. "Doc, I think we should get out of here."

"Maybe you're right." Van Allen picked up the phone. "I'll call Security."

"I'm guessing they're going to say everything is okay." Theo backed toward the door, keeping her gaze firmly fixed on the shadows. "Or they won't say anything at all. This is going to sound crazy, but which of these walls faces west?"

"I would say...the one you're looking at." His expression was tightening. "Speer, do you hear something?"

"Whispering?" Yes, yes, she did. "Getting louder?"

"Speer," Van Allen said with inhuman calm, "what the hell is exactly going on here?"

"I'm not sure." Her breathing was shallow, and her eyes watered as she struggled not to blink more than absolutely necessary. Every time she did, the shadows shifted that little bit closer. "But if I had to guess, I think there's a jackal somewhere close."

"Don't be ridiculous." The words seemed to be a reflex.

"Then tell me what that is."

The shadows were coalescing in the doorway. Four paws lightly touched the ground, gliding over the shattered debris on the floor as if it weren't there. The eyes glinting through the darkness were golden, surrounded by sleek blackness.

Theo grabbed a leg from the broken table and hurled it at the eyes. It sailed between them and bounced off the opposite wall of the corridor. The eyes never blinked. Behind her, Dr. Van Allen drew in a breath.

The shadows gathered, and suddenly the eyes winked out. If Theo strained, she could see the darkness draining away, leaking out through the door like dim mist flowing with the air. Heart in her mouth, she pursued it, lunging through the door, and prepared to throw something else if necessary.

Something surged in the dimness of the corridor; the form of a tall, pale man loomed up. His palm slammed against her heart, sending Theo reeling backward. And then came the pain.

Her muscles locked, clenching so tightly that she thought they would rip out through her skin. White-hot agony flooded through her—tearing, wrenching—a knot of pain pulling her inward until she would die or peel her skin off her own bones to escape it. Female voices, four or five of them, were shouting and babbling in her ears as the burning hand wrenched at her heart. She couldn't hold back a scream.

"Ri," one whispered hoarsely against her ear. *"Ata. Ri ata. Hate."*

She gasped for air and as quickly as it had appeared, the pressure vanished. Theo stumbled and sat down hard. Her attacker fell back and hunched over his hand, which was rapidly turning red as if burned. Veins bulged under the skin.

"What—" Van Allen began. His voice came dimly to her ringing ears. Alarmed, the pale man pulled back into the shadows, but it was too late—he'd been spotted. Van Allen leaped forward. "Speer! Are you alive?"

Theo barely managed to make a wheezing noise, her eyes locked on the injured man in the corridor. The face was obscured, but the form wasn't, and through the pounding of her heart she could hear him gasping out strange words in a horribly familiar voice.

Zimmer.

"Why?" she forced out. "Why are you—this—?"

The Security chief lurched forward and grabbed the shoulder of her jacket, dragging her roughly over the threshold. Van Allen's surprised shout was ignored. Theo clawed at his hands, drawing blood, and with a curse he dropped her to the floor.

"Where is he?" he shouted. "What did he give you?"

"He's not here." Theo's words came out as a growl, surprising her. "What are you doing? You set me up!"

Zimmer didn't answer. He turned and ran, his footsteps echoing in the corridor, and Theo staggered to her feet in an effort to follow him. Her knees buckled again, forcing her to grab the lintel for support. The world reeled as if it were trying to shake her off.

"Get back here!" Van Allen shouted. To her surprise, the little curator took off at a respectable sprint, tie flying as he pelted into the darkness after Zimmer.

There was a gasp of pain and a heavy thud. Theo struggled forward, heart in her mouth, but over her own harsh breathing she could only hear one set of footsteps. A dark lump in the shadows resolved itself into Dr. Van Allen lying on his side, one leg askew. The color was draining from his face.

"Dr. Van Allen!" she whispered. The curator cut her off with a grimace and a flail of his hand.

"Not now!" The words were strained, but Van Allen's expression was hard through the pain. "He was heading for the stairs!"

Theo nodded and hurried past the slumped man. She could hear footsteps ahead. Hollow rising echoes as he took the stairs upward. Trying to ignore the burns and aches in her muscles, she pushed herself into a run.

By the time she reached the second landing, she realized where he was heading. Panting, Theo clutched her side and picked up speed. Prep D was close to the ground floors, making it easier to transport artifacts to or from exhibits once they'd been LoJacked and prepared. The rest of the technical floors were above that, but a cut left through Animatronics would get you to Prep A, and that meant shabtis too.

Despite his strange reaction earlier, Zimmer was moving faster than she could. As she skidded through the door to Animatronics, her heart gave a warning twinge and the burning sensation around it spread across her shoulder and collarbone. Heart attack? She hoped not, but she couldn't remember what the warning signs were supposed to be. Everything was a blur.

With an effort, she pushed herself and found an extra burst of speed from somewhere. She couldn't see Zimmer anymore, could just hear the pounding of his footsteps and the occasional crash as he knocked something over. An expensive light table was lying on its side in the middle of the cubicle hallway, its top shattered. Theo skirted it, glass skittering off the treads of her shoes, and braced herself in time to avoid crashing into the wall of the prep lab.

Panting, she leaned against the doorframe. The door had been broken clean off its hinges, but there were no more footsteps. Had he turned around? Missed her in the dark?

She clutched her chest and forced herself to concentrate.

Something was happening in the dimness of the lab, though. There was a strange wet noise, like mud bubbling from a broken sewer pipe. Something creaked; something else shuffled. A damp snap.

Forcing herself to stand up, Theo pushed through and into the lab. Stainless-steel tables and racks of instruments were untouched, and there was no sign of Zimmer. Dim blue security lights flickered from a locked case, and something made a slurping noise as one of the lights died entirely.

The case was full of shabtis. Several had fallen and broken, while others had been knocked aside. Snapped limbs and bits of clay littered the case. But as Theo watched, three of them twitched and began to grow.

Their cracking surfaces bulged and shattered. New clay bubbled up underneath, slick and shiny and glutinous, like wax and blood mixed together. It boiled, trying to form a new crust, then cracked again to make way for fresh clay in an instant. *Half-baked idea,* Theo thought. They were trying to form new bodies but they didn't know how.

In seconds, they were the size of men. Half-liquid fists trailing droplets slammed against the glass and spiderwebbed cracks across the bulletproof material.

They hammered away, pounding on the rapidly splintering glass, their fragile skins reforming with each blow. Chunks of dead clay fell from them and dissolved into dry red dirt, which rose from the case and whirled out on the eddies created by the air conditioner like a dust storm straight from the surface of Mars.

Even as she staggered back, the cracked panel collapsed. Alarms blared as the oozing shabtis burst out of the case, their faces contorted in expressions of pain that their stylized features had never been meant to convey.

Her heart hammered as the shabtis crawled to their feet. They were taller than men and as the clay built up layer by layer, they looked less and less human. Their shells still cracked with each movement, but the glutinous liquid underneath knitted them together again whenever it was exposed. One opened its mouth, letting out a strangled gurgle. Though their bodies twitched and their lavalike cores bubbled with each step, their gazes fixed on Theo.

She wasn't going to wait for them to pull themselves together. She ran.

Her feet skidded awkwardly on the tiled floor, but she kept running. She didn't dare turn around: the wet, sucking noise of liquid clay was following her, and the smell of damp dust suffused the hallways. By the time she reached the staircase, she was moving so fast that she just grabbed the banister and swung around onto the steps without stopping. And they were still following her.

Theo almost tripped over Dr. Van Allen when she reached him. He had pulled himself up against the wall and was leaning back, his eyes closed. Without hesitating, Theo grabbed his arm and hauled him to his one good foot, ignoring the gasp of pain. The smell was growing stronger.

"What is it?" Van Allen said. Theo jerked her head back, and he looked over her shoulder. His eyes widened. "Golems!"

The word was strangled. Theo fumbled frantically for the curator's jacket, trying to grab the ID card that could get them through the security door, but her fingers slipped on the plastic.

"Golems! The etymology is Hebrew, but the legend—perhaps it has roots in Egypt—"

Maybe it was their own unnatural forms resisting them, or maybe the agonized shabtis didn't honestly expect to see a curator theorizing about their connection to Jewish folklore, because the lumbering monsters paused barely long enough. Theo ripped the ID card off Van Allen's jacket and swiped it through the slot, letting out a wordless yelp of triumph as the light turned green. The door slammed shut behind them; a clay hand reaching for Theo's hair crumbled into dust as it was severed.

"The implications..." Dr. Van Allen murmured vaguely, staring at nothing while the door reverberated with blows and Theo pulled hard on his arm. "The implications of, yes, a true automaton...it could offer an alternate explanation for the Antikythera device, for a start..."

Theo urged him forward again, but Dr. Van Allen was dead weight. He descended into random mumblings about gears and folklore and Heron of Alexandria.

With nothing human to vent their rage on, the shabtis howled and attacked anything they could reach. Clay cracked and masonry crumbled, but she could hear glass shattering and the screech of metal as well. There went the windows. Theo pulled harder, hoping that the curator would miraculously develop mobility. He didn't.

A hand landed on her shoulder, and Theo let out a yelp. "Let me go, you son of a—" she began, rounding on her attacker with fists flying.

Instead of dodging, Seth caught her first punch and shifted, throwing her off-balance. Theo stumbled and almost fell, but his grip was like iron and its strength kept her upright.

"What the hell are you doing here?" she gasped out. His arm was rock steady, but there was a faint tremor in the fingers that wrapped around her wrist.

"Followed you," he said tightly. "I was afraid you might do something reckless. Come on, we have to go!"

She would have bristled, but the thunder of the fists on the door made losing her temper a distant second priority. "Wait! We can't leave the doc!"

Seth slung an arm around Dr. Van Allen and lifted him clean off the ground. Theo stumbled at the sudden loss of balance, biting her lip hard as she tried to reorient herself. Van Allen sagged and fell quietly unconscious, and Seth draped him over one shoulder in a fireman's carry.

They ran, and the door burst open behind them. The shabtis screamed as they broke through, a noise like knives on glass, and Theo's heart shuddered in her chest.

The end of the corridor was coming up fast. The urge to escape had been too strong, and the shabtis were between them and the staircase. There were two ways out now: the iron-gated elevator and the security door that led outside. No contest.

Theo grabbed the card and swiped them through the security door, trying to ignore the alarms ringing in the background. She gasped as the cold outside air hit them like a slap in the face.

They were on a fire escape. The steel bars formed a small balcony before turning sharply downward, vanishing into the orange-tinted shadows and creating harsh black lines against the cold white exterior of the building. Snow fell through the gaps in the metal, but ice clung to it, making the footing treacherous. Seth clutched the railing with one hand and balanced the unconscious Van Allen with the other, eyes wild.

"What are we going to do?" Theo panted. Despite the thick security door, she could hear the golems crashing around, making the building shake. They seemed to be bent on destroying everything they touched. "Tell me you know how to kill those things!"

Seth shook his head. "The magic's been twisted. I could sense it a mile off—some kind of spell. I think someone was trying to take over a shabti body." The door vibrated again, knocking icicles free and sending them clattering down the long stairway. "We need to get down, now. Hang on to me and I'll climb."

"Are you crazy? We have to stop them!" Theo's breath caught in her throat. Yuri was on the night shift most of the time. With the alarms blaring, he'd come running, and... Oh God. Not an option. *Think think think.* Magic, Egyptian magic. Shabtis. Seth. Shabtis as magic. Shabtis as Seth...

It was the sight of him, his dark eyes locked on her, that gave her the idea. "Stay here." He grabbed her arm, but she shook him off.

"Theo, don't!"

"No! Stay here." And before he could say anything, she slammed back into the museum.

Wet clay. Wet clay was malleable, and in a creature like that, malleable was dangerous. Two of the three golems had begun to melt into each other, and their howls echoed and re-echoed down the hall as they struggled to separate themselves. The third was smashing every glass case it could get its muddied hands on, leaving streaks of clay on the walls and the carpet. When Theo stopped in the hall, though, their heads turned to follow her.

You spent so much time there, talking to them as if they were real. It had to make an impression.

"My poor little guys," she said.

The golems recoiled. The biggest of them—THS2023, she guessed, judging by the remnants of dark pigment on its head—settled back on itself. Several expressions dragged across its face in quick succession, each feature disconnected from the others in a way that made it impossible for any of the expressions to ever be complete. An angry mouth warped, but the eyes seemed almost afraid.

"Maybe you didn't like it in the prep lab, but at least you were safe," she said, trying not to let her fear show. Her heart pounded and her skin was slick with clammy sweat, but she kept her gaze on the warped face. "Now you're out here, getting clay on the carpet and getting jerked around by magicians. Four thousand is way too old for this kind of thing."

It was like talking to a skittish animal. The words didn't really seem to matter; it was about the tone and the familiar voice, letting them know that there was someone there they knew. She hoped it would be enough.

"I wish this hadn't happened," she continued gently. "I loved you guys so much, seeing you all ready for that exhibit. It's not fair, you getting pushed out here before you get a real chance to shine."

The biggest one clutched its head, its hands sinking into the soft clay. The smaller ones were folding in on themselves as their forms bubbled and shifted. One reached out several pseudopods, temporarily taking on a familiar shape. It was trying to return to its old form.

"It's okay," Theo said, taking a few cautious steps forward. The smallest of the golems tried to reach for her, but fell back, its body spasming. "I'm so, so sorry, guys. I wish I could do something for you right now. But I promise, everything's going to be okay. Whatever happens, there's still gonna be an exhibit, and hundreds and hundreds of people will come by every day to see how amazing and beautiful you are. No one can take that away from you."

The golems shivered. They were losing coherence, their bodies melting into shapeless blobs.

She kept talking, murmuring reassurances, telling them what wonderful things they were, and finally—with a sigh, as if they were giving up—they collapsed. Liquid clay flooded the corridor and began almost immediately to dry into hard patches.

She stumbled back, propping herself against the wall as the golems dissolved. Her eyes stung; she mopped her face with one hand, feeling roughness under her fingers. She, like everything else in the corridor, had been sprayed with quick-hardening ceramic. Clumps were tangled in her hair.

"It's all right," she called out. The alarms were still echoing in the depths of the museum, but to her ears, they seemed to have faded into the background.

The shabtis. Oh God. She leaned against the wall, trying to steady her breathing. The security door creaked open again and Seth appeared in the corner of her eye, a blur of blue copper topped by the dull orange of the doctor's jacket, but she couldn't seem to turn her head to focus on either of them.

Her little survivors. Four thousand years old, those figurines, existing not because of magic or science or preservation labs, but simply because they were works of art that people had chosen to protect. She'd talked to them, teased them, praised them, and maybe loved them a bit. Loved them enough to awaken their link with Seth, and perhaps draw him to her. But she'd never seen them move, and she'd never watched them die. Her vision blurred as tears began to well up.

There was a soft thump as Seth set down the doctor. Van Allen's head lolled, but his eyes were half-open and his color was coming back.

Theo took a deep breath and mopped away the tears with the back of her hand.

"Theo."

Seth took a couple of steps toward her. Theo glanced down as she blotted the last of the tears. She could feel the warmth of him, see his striking colors without looking directly at him, but she wasn't sure what to do now.

He put one hand on her shoulder and gently raised her chin with the other. "Theo," he said softly. "Theo, are you still with me?"

"I'm here." The words came out in a whisper.

"Never do that again," he said. "Please. I don't think my heart can take it."

"Theirs sure couldn't." She closed her eyes and, for a moment, leaned into his touch. She could feel his heart—or something's heart, anyway—under her hands, beating too slowly to be human. Slow, but steady, and she took comfort in its rhythm. He pressed a kiss to her lips, and she wanted to stay there and let herself enjoy it.

But she couldn't. The guards would have responded to the alarms by now if they were able, but even if Zimmer had somehow incapacitated them, the police would be getting the alarm signal too. *Later,* she silently promised herself as she kissed him softly. More of this later. Now, though, she pulled away.

"What happened?" Seth asked, taking the hint.

"I came to see Dr. Van Allen about the second theft." Theo raked a hand through her dirty hair. "Zimmer was here. He grabbed me," she added with a humorless twist of her lips. "His Five-Point Palm Exploding Heart Technique needs work. But he did something to the shabtis and created…that." She busied herself with peeling scraps of hardening clay off her hands, hoping not to meet his eyes.

"He touched you? Where?"

When she showed him, he hooked his fingers into the neckline of her shirt and began to gently tug it down. She tried to push his hand away, but his finger touched something and she winced as another wave of pain flooded through her chest and shoulder. He had torn the neckline, exposing the soft, white cup of her bra and the curve of her left breast. What had been plain skin was marred by a huge fresh burn, bright red with raised, bloodied edges, like a knife had been run over the flesh. It was the size of a man's hand and formed a familiar shape—an ankh with its arms folded inward.

"Tyet," Seth murmured. Blood was draining from his face. "He touched your heart, Theo. He wanted to take your body."

"What?"

Her voice rose in a yelp, and the long hall echoed it back, turning it into a chorus of indignant disbelief. "What do you mean?" she whispered, trying and failing to keep a lid on her surprise. "Tell me that's not what it sounds like!"

"It was...theorized," Seth hazarded. He couldn't meet her eyes. "As an extension of the technique I used. If a soul could be earthed in a shabti, couldn't you find a way to move one soul into another living body? Throw the owner's soul out into the darkness and take his form? But I never..."

"Theorized." Theo swallowed. "By who?"

"Meren." His expression was grim. "My brother."

It took a moment to process. Theo's first thought: *But Mark looks so freaking Irish.* Then her normal thinking caught up and the words left her mouth without being cleared by her brain, "But your brother's dead."

"So am I."

"No, you're not, you're..." She looked for the word and didn't find it. "You said you weren't, Seth. You're in the house when the lights go out."

"I haven't died completely. But I'm supposed to be dead, if things worked the way they should." His gaze flicked over the tyet-shaped burn on her chest. There was a small pink mark next to it, where Seth's teeth had nipped at her breast hours before. "This is magic, deep magic. The kind my brother specialized in."

Theo's hand flew to the pocket of her jacket. The shape of the tyet amulet was still there. Seth's eyes followed her, and his shoulders relaxed a fraction as he saw the outline against the fabric.

"She protected you," he said. "I'll burn a hundred offerings for her. If you hadn't had that, you might not be alive right now."

Theo ran a hand through her hair again and tried not to look him in the eye. The expression there was making her stomach twist. "What now?"

"I have to leave," he said. That got her attention. "I have some books, copies of texts he gave me, in another cache. I might be able to find out if he could have done this. Or if not him, who else."

"Seth," Theo said softly. "Are you rabbiting again?"

"It doesn't matter what I'm planning, Theo. Your involvement ends here." For a moment, Theo wanted to punch him. Or hug him. She wasn't sure which impulse came first. Seth looked like the dead man he was, his expression haunted, his clenched fists white-knuckled. She wanted to scream at him that this wasn't the solution. That she wanted to go with him, or make him stay. With an effort, she made herself speak calmly.

"Going it alone won't solve it," she said, pulling her shirt up to cover the tyet mark. "Please, Seth, think. We need to figure this out."

"Theo," he said, and her name was a harsh whisper. "When I thought this was simply crime, that was one thing. Crime is human. People want gold and antiques for themselves, tombs get robbed—it happens. But this is magic. Gods are involved, Theo. I saw a jackal shadow in the hall—" She couldn't keep her expression neutral, and he flinched. "You saw it too?"

"I...maybe," she said. "I might've been hallucinating."

"Hallucinations only cover so much." The words were bitter. "I know better than anyone that magic is dangerous. Gods, more so. Gods you can't control, especially when they're angry. Someone's going to die, and nobody else in this whole freezing city has bodies to spare!"

He used the word *freezing* like a curse. Theo didn't let his anger touch her. She moved forward and, gently, took his head in her hands. The muscles under the skin stood out like twisted bands of steel, and the skin itself was papery and dry. Stubble scratched at her palms.

She looked him in the eyes and saw desperation.

"Seth," she said. "You didn't do anything wrong."

It was the one thing she could think of to say. But that look in his eyes was so wrong that she wanted, dearly, to wipe it away. A month ago she would've given an arm to be able to paint that desperate fear, to share it with the world. Now she never wanted to see it again.

Seth closed his eyes and leaned into her touch. "I don't know," he murmured, his breath hot against her palm. "I don't know. I did or I didn't. But I've been dodging this for a long time, Theo. I have to go. I can't meet Ammit this way. I can't."

"Then go." The words felt heavy, but they came out in a bare whisper. "But be careful. And take this." She pulled out the tyet amulet she had carried.

When it brushed against his hand, though, Seth jolted back. There was a hiss of burning, and a bright-red mark spread across his palm. Theo gave a startled cry and dropped the amulet, but her own fingers were fine.

"Seth, I'm sorry—" she began.

He shook his head.

"No heart," he said. "Not a human one, anyway. I have to carry Isis's symbol in a cloth; I'm a little déclassé for her since I first died."

"That's her loss." She kissed him. "If you've really got books on this, think about finding them, okay? We're not dead yet."

"From your lips to the gods' ears," he said quietly.

Then he was gone.

Eyes stinging, she turned back to the half-conscious curator. He was slumped against the wall, eyes closed, seemingly unbreathing. For a moment, she wondered if he was in shock. But she moved, and the flat, pale eyes focused on her, pinning her to the spot.

"Miss Speer." The words came out in monotone. "I'm fairly certain that this wasn't supposed to happen."

"No, Doctor," she said. There didn't seem to be another answer. "Are you okay?"

"I seem to have cracked a tibia. Would you mind having a look?" Still barely an inflection, just the dry, stale voice. "I'm having difficulty checking for myself."

Theo pulled up the curator's pant leg. His shin was swollen and purple, the flesh taut and hot. It was flecked with sweat, and when Theo touched it, Van Allen flinched and let out a hiss.

"You broke something," she said, "and the swelling's bad. But I think you're gonna be okay."

"I hope so. We're going to have a lot of cleanup to do." For a moment, the eyes unfocused again. "This could have fascinating repercussions. The account of Israelite slavery in Egypt is often considered apocryphal, since there's been no discernible cultural link between Old Kingdom and, hah, Old Testament. But the mythology…"

"Dr. Van Allen, are you okay?" Theo said, more than a little worried. "You got a pretty bad whack on the head there too. You should probably relax and wait for the police."

"Police?" Van Allen frowned. "Oh. Right. The police will be coming." The bright-blue gaze skewered Theo, and she shifted, unwilling to meet it. "You'd better get moving, I think. You don't want to be caught here."

Theo gawked, momentarily baffled by a sudden rush of love for the sharp curator. Sure, Van Allen was shaken and she'd seen a chink or two in his steely façade, but it seemed that underneath that mask was more steel. So much for academics being soft! Paler than ever and clearly in pain, Van Allen was solid.

"Sir," she said, "you're the best boss ever."

"And don't forget it." Van Allen grimaced as he tried again to move his leg. "And if you see Mr. Zimmer, tell him he's fired."

"With pleasure." Quickly, in case he noticed signs of unprofessionalism, she squeezed his free hand as she stood up. "Thanks."

* * *

A month ago, Theo Speer's most grievous sin had been parallel parking. If you'd asked her to rob a museum, flee from the police, or rendezvous with a man on the run, she would have been completely at sea. To be honest, she still wasn't too strong on most of those things.

But fleeing from police was necessary to save a life. Rendezvousing with a wanted man, ditto. And if she was going to run from someone, the museum was the place to do it. This was her turf.

Marble halls of academe gave way to starkly lit concrete corridors thick with years of paint. She automatically shifted to a flat-footed step, changing her stride to soften the sound of her footfalls. Her breathing seemed unnaturally loud and harsh in her ears.

In the distance, she could hear feet pounding and a rumble of voices. Trying to keep her breaths shallow, she cut a hard left and ducked through the door to Mammal Taxidermy. The doors should have been locked, but Shawn Faroe and his team tended to be slack. Nobody would want to steal dead pine martens, or so the logic went.

From Taxidermy to Insect Preservation. Up one short flight to Tropical Fish. A quick swing from Fish into Herpetology. Kick over the trash can and leave the door to Oversized Herpetology open, in case they thought to check which way she'd gone through. Instead, she swung right and took the fire stairs, clipping out through the safety hatch to wind up in the cleaning corridor behind Cephalopods of the World.

She slipped out through the security door behind the biggest squid and emerged in a maintenance alley almost calf deep in snow.

Her path took her away from the museum campus and down to the lakefront. There, the golden ribbon of Lake Shore Drive resolved itself into eight lanes of high-speed traffic, crossed by occasional pedestrian bridges slick with layers of winter ice. Theo slogged along, keeping to the plowed-up patches of gravel and mud whenever possible.

Far off, she could hear sirens. It took an effort not to panic—there were always sirens in Chicago. It didn't guarantee she was being chased.

But she probably was. The golems had wrecked the place, but who was going to believe that story when there was a convenient rogue employee to blame?

Ten minutes' brisk walk brought her to the Roosevelt subway stop.

The subway was cold but not nearly as cold as outside, and Theo sank down on a bench and loosened her scarf. For the first time in what felt like hours, she had time to breathe and think.

THS2017, 004, and 023. They'd been three of the worst specimens in the collection, battered almost beyond recognition, their chest cavities gaping and empty and their limbs snapped off. But that hadn't seemed to matter when they were being brought to life.

Or had it? Theo didn't know. She only knew that the magician—could she really put that name to Zimmer?—had worked his spell on those three, out of the whole collection. Maybe he really had been trying to take over one of their bodies, but if so, why? And if he was trying to turn them into monsters, why those three? An army of golems would have done the job better.

Hearts? her brain supplied a little helplessly. Hearts were at the center of the Egyptian ritual canon. Having your heart eaten was supposed to be the final destruction. Seth had said they'd put animal hearts in the shabtis, and the tyet hurt him because he was living with a heart not his own.

But the shabtis to rise under the magician's influence had been the ones without hearts. Her gut twisted at the memory of the liquid golems, screaming as they tried to take definite shape. Maybe the magic, whatever it was, didn't work right when there was no heart in the shabtis…

Zimmer touching her heart…

Seth said his brother had theorized about magic. His brother—Mark Zimmer? She didn't know.

Were the guards okay?

Why would Zimmer want to move his soul into her body? Was that what he'd been planning when he came to the museum that night, or had he just seized an opportunity when he learned she was there with Van Allen?

Her head ached; her shoulders burned; blood and clay and sweat stained her. She wanted sleep. She wanted food. She wanted Seth. But Seth was gone now, back to being an ancient Egyptian warrior running from an Egyptian magician. Or worse, actually facing him.

I can't die like this, he'd said. His turf and his mission, so of course he'd follow his own rules.

Except he hadn't been the one to stop the golems. They hadn't been something he'd been prepared to face; the spirit was willing, but the flesh was out of ideas. But she'd won. There was motion there, she'd grabbed it with both hands, and she'd done something that he couldn't.

And she was supposed to *go home?*

Hah. Home. There were probably police watching her apartment. She couldn't go back to Aki—no, she'd risked getting him into trouble already. And she guessed her parents wouldn't be too thrilled to harbor a fugitive daughter.

Parents. A jolt of hope sparked through her. The house in Deerfield! Parents in Taos, a house standing empty. A house that the cops might not be watching. It would take her a couple of hours and several train transfers to get there, and that could help to throw them off her scent.

CHAPTER FIFTEEN

Ammit is the eater of hearts, the great devourer, the final
death. Though each sin burdens your heart, it makes it all
the sweeter to her. Poison yourself with goodness, that
she will not love the taste of your flesh, and pass you by.

- Excerpt from The Commandments of Neferu,
circa 1700 BCE

Deerfield was the kind of suburb where the sidewalks were unimportant. Snow was piled a foot deep on the undisturbed lawns, occasionally tinted coral pink or pale green by Christmas lights and glowing inflatable Santa Clauses. Craftsman houses and pseudo-Victorians stood alongside modern cement-and-glass boxes, but the night blended them together into patches of soft color and shadow. It was a comfortable, quietly wealthy neighborhood where people slept after long days at the office and rarely walked farther than the mailbox.

After a moment, Theo decided not to turn on the lights. No one was supposed to be here, after all. Sighing, she walked stiff-legged up the stairs.

She wanted sleep, badly, but not as much as she wanted a shower. Chicagoans might not stare at a woman smeared with drying clay, but they would still remember her. Faced with the bathroom's array of Italian shampoos and French-milled soaps, though, she balked and settled for a quick sponge bath at the sink. The clay, at least, peeled off easily. Then she wrapped a towel around her damp hair and walked down the hall to her old room.

The room felt sterile. Her locked cupboard of art supplies was in the same place, but everything had been cleaned within an inch of its life.

Her Formula One posters and comics were long gone, replaced by Ansel Adams prints and a throw rug that had clearly never been walked on. It took her almost ten minutes to debone the bed—remove the pillows, shams, and decorative bedspreads—before she could collapse onto it.

The ceiling was layers of shadow. Staring at it did nothing for her.

She lay on a cold bed in a cold house, unable to turn on the lights because she was a fugitive. Her family had no idea where she was, and the man she wanted to be with had been forced away by something dark and evil.

The whole thing had gone further than Theo'd ever imagined. She was exhausted, alone, and had no idea of where to go next or how to help Seth. The world had spun out of control, and she was barely clinging to it.

So much for the greatest discovery in the history of mankind.

Automatically, hungry for a distraction, her mind seized on the thought. What had those words been? Not the shabti inscription but the prayer, the one Seth had recited to her hours before. Concentrating, she called up her paint mnemonic from the depths of her mind. The first colors had been slightly discordant—tangerine and gunmetal, that was it, *ha* and *ne*...

It took almost half an hour to reconstruct the sequence. She stole paper from the printer in her mother's office and scribbled out the syllables, cross-linking them with the colors she had assigned. It was a quick-and-dirty system that had saved her bacon in a few college examinations, but this time it was infinitely more important. If she got a single syllable wrong, who knew what would happen?

No pressure, though.

Once she had the formula, she set it aside and headed for the computer. The only books in her parents' house were coffee-table tomes and histories of political philosophy, but their Internet was top-of-the-line. Theo dove in.

Words streamed past her as she swam from one site to the next, frantically clicking and reading, compiling and adding. Wax models...practices similar to vodoun...ushebtis intended to substitute for the deceased...the power of the name and the image...

An idea began to coalesce. It was insane, but insane had been par for the course for a few days now, and Theo was more than angry enough to take a leap of faith. Wax and clay she didn't have, but there were always other options.

Papier-mâché, for example. Theo ripped open the cupboards, assembling the ingredients she needed. Flour. Salt. Water. Newspaper. Mix and mold.

The object that emerged was crude—she'd never been much of a sculptor. But there it was, a mummiform figure with the bow and dog's leash of a hunter in his hands. Servant of the dead. Tongue between her teeth, she scratched out the hieroglyphs on the damp surface, muttering the incantations as best she could remember and praying that her mnemonic would help her get it right. The damp paper strips bunched and tore under the knife blade as she worked.

There was one ingredient left. She threw the shabti in the oven to harden a little, then snatched a garbage bag and hauled the ladder out of the garage.

It would have been easier at her apartment, where generations of vicious city pigeons lived and died on the roof. Still, the house was a flat-topped International Style box, and Theo remembered how much random junk could collect up there. She scrambled up over the eaves and landed in a snowdrift.

Jackpot! A few dead birds at the edge, one still fresh. From the looks of things, Mom and Dad had been putting out traps to keep the pigeons from crapping on the roof, and the snow had preserved the evidence. Trying not to breathe, Theo scraped the freshest up and shoved it into the garbage bag. If she was going to be doing this a lot, she should really invest in a good chest freezer or something.

Back in the kitchen, it was the work of a few gruesome moments to remove the heart. Murmuring the prayers helped—she could almost imagine she was back in Seth's Egypt, the kitchen an embalmer's work-shop.

Or not. She switched the oven off and ran to throw up in the sink.

Into the shabti went the heart. One final set of incantations, close the hole in the chest with a plug of papier-mâché, and…

…nothing.

Nothing at all. Her disgusting little mixed-media sculpture sat there silent and inert, a testimony to the depths she'd reach, if given the oppor-tunity. Paste and blood on her hands, an amateur autopsy on the kitchen table. Egyptian voodoo.

What would Mom think?

"Not very chic," Theo said aloud, a smile tugging at her lips. What would Amy Clarendon Speer, star of the dinner-party circuit, with her Hermès scarf and English rose complexion, say if she could see her daughter now? She'd probably be outwardly proud her baby girl was expanding her horizons, but inwardly she'd cringe at the thought of dismembering animals. Maybe she'd line up a good shrink. Pretend it was a dream.

The laugh bubbled up inside Theo, hoarse and completely mirthless, a cackle with an edge of hysteria that tore its way out of her dry throat. She laughed and laughed, tears leaking from her reddened eyes, as her crude project sat quietly on the kitchen table in a puddle of fluid and flour paste. Arts and crafts with Leatherface.

She laughed until she had no more breath or tears and staggered into the living room to sleep. Her abortive attempt at black magic lay abandoned on the table.

* * *

Four thousand years was a heavy burden for anyone to carry, but if Seth was lucky, it could help him. He'd been in danger so many times before, and still lasted into the current day with shabtis to spare. What had he done then? What could he do now?

This cache was the biggest he had in the city. It was an old bank building, good turn-of-the-century construction with granite walls and marble floors that he owned through a dummy company. The above-ground floors were abandoned and falling apart—one more piece of urban decay in a city that had seen two hundred years come and go. Underground, though, the cool stone basement and vault were perfect for preserving documents. And other things.

Seth muttered to himself in Kemetic as he pawed through the scrolls. Toulouse? When had he been to Toulouse? As his eyes scanned the parchment, taking in the scrawled lines of hieratic, a dim memory stirred. Oh, 1216, with Fiorentino da Firenze. He hadn't thought about it since he last recopied the scroll in—he checked the tag—1870. About the time Rachid al-Adhur had come to America, in fact.

Fiorentino da Firenze. Nice man. Not that it was going to help Seth now.

Growling, he dropped the scroll and grabbed another one. Volume three: barely fifty years out of time. With a faint sense of disgust, he perused the familiar lines.

I know this is a sacrilege, but I cannot call it anything but an opportunity as well. When I return home, I can present myself to the king under any name I like! Once I've gotten his attention, I can resume my old duties and discover the fate of my children. I can do what I was made to do, and win back some favor into the bargain.

I have all eternity at my disposal. There was never a man who could do what I can! I can conquer death—what's to say I won't also conquer fear? I can be an institution, a nation of men in service of Waset. In another hundred years, I'll be the greatest general of all. I doubt the gods can overlook that.

He'd been so stupid back then. No man, no matter how long-lived, could conquer fear.

Seth, under many names and faces, had fought. He'd fought and died and killed under dozens of banners, and he'd never found perfection or true fearlessness or proof that the gods had forgiven him. And those the gods did not forgive…

The thought ate at him.

And he was still afraid, afraid that he would die, that the tearing, wrenching feeling would return as his mummy was broken again. Magic or not, he was flesh, and flesh had its damn weaknesses.

At least Theo was safe now, he thought with a sneaking sense of relief. A hand had lain on her heart. She had brushed the threat of the magic aside, but Seth knew what it could have done. His enemy had tried to step into Theo's body, replacing her soul and mind. And if it had been done? She would be a true Trojan horse, the perfect weapon against Seth. Thank the gods for the tyet—the thought of her being so used had him shuddering with fear and rage.

He wondered if she'd known what she was getting into, making love to him. Not only that, but she'd done it in full knowledge of what he was. That left a mark.

The memories rose to the surface and Seth took a deep breath, trying to keep focused. In certain ways she was afraid too—worried, determined to be liked and concerned with things he honestly hadn't contemplated in centuries. But Neith knew, there was iron in her somewhere, bright and sharp beneath the smooth, pallid skin, showing in those moss-green eyes that looked right into his soul… Oh gods help him, he couldn't *think*.

It had been a long time since he'd been able to talk so freely with another human being. And a brother or scribe was nothing compared to a woman lying at his side, her voice rough with exhaustion even as she teased information out of him.

And Theo saw things.

He knew in his bones that there was nothing in the world that would last like he did. Everything changed, everything died, and no country or creed or dynasty would endure with real meaning. He had fought and died for causes that went unremembered, served at the right hands of men whose names were disgraced after they passed on, collected the favors of great kings whose monuments had not one stone left atop another. His tomb—and the tombs of far greater and more consequential men—was a dusty old site for bored tourists. The relics of Kemet sat in museums, studied as the flotsam and jetsam of a dead kingdom.

But Theo saw a picture, a creation of the whole. He remembered her stroking the glass as she talked to the shabtis and told them how important they were. Jumbled scraps of tomb goods became, in her eyes, links to a great civilization that had changed the course of the world.

Seth didn't know if she was brilliant, naïve, or insane. But it felt good, he thought, to hope that his lives had meant something.

Egotistic? Oh, definitely. But, godsdammit, couldn't he pretend his life hadn't been a failure? Theo gave him hope. Hope for a future, maybe.

Now memories twisted, fed by that hope. He imagined living one small part of his life completely honestly, worshiping his gods openly and not having to hide behind his stupid, stupid façade of the eccentric loner. Waking up in his penthouse with a rumpled blonde head on the pillows next to his. He turned the image over in his mind: *I need to go to Turkey, Theo. The national institute bought some figurines that might be from my cache. How would you like to see Istanbul today?* The glint in her eyes as she seized on it, the churches and palaces that she wouldn't be able to resist, knowledge he could share with her.

Meri tje, he'd said. *I love you.*

Seth moaned and tried to push the thought out of his mind. The images of long, sleek limbs, barely concealed by folds of smooth, thin cloth, taunted him. She had had to wear white at that first party, hadn't she?

He had to find a solution. Four thousand years on this planet, so many of them recorded on these scraps of paper, couldn't have been lived for nothing. He had to find a way, before his enemy got impatient and decided to damage his mummy again.

Sundown. It came so early in this frigid hellhole; barely past four o'clock, and yet he could feel it in the cold, slithery sensation rippling down his back. His bones ached as the warmth began to bleed out of the world. The borrowed heart in his chest began to slow.

It happened every night. Some were worse than others, and deep winter was the hardest time of all, but he had been facing it for four thousand years. One more night, he could manage that. Survive one more night, steal his mummy back, and then he could sleep soundly again. Perhaps with company.

A jab of pain broke through his thoughts. His left arm, the one closest to the west wall, was beginning to cramp up. Unusual, but not unheard of during long nights. He massaged the tensing muscles and tried to focus on his work.

Then came another jab. Then another. Chilly fingers clawing up his arm to his shoulder, latching on to him with iron-hook claws, digging into the skin and peeling it back. He gripped his shoulder hard, trying to press away the sensation.

Oh Neith, help him. Not again. Not now.

A hand fastened on his heart and he doubled over, stars erupting in front of his eyes. He tried to call out for Neith, but his breath was gone. His heart beat wildly, ready to burst like a ripe grape. Not a single drop of blood spilled, and he was on the ground. He could feel his own skin—not this false substitute, but the dead, dry flesh wrapped in ancient linen—screaming as it was torn.

Breath brushed his ear, the ghost of a ghost of a whisper.

"Hello, dead man."

Not again. Not like this. Seth braced himself against the table and forced himself upright, clawing through the pain that threatened to split him in half. It was coming, and it wanted to kill him, but he couldn't let that happen. Not now—not after four thousand years, and not when he finally had a single fucking thing to look forward to. He snarled something between his teeth (Sabaean, always a good language to curse in) while the voice laughed in his ear.

The shadows were gathering again. He'd seen them in the museum—the pacing jackal and, worse, the lumbering thing with the crocodile head, its nose to the ground as it traced the scent of an old sinner. His enemy had his mummy and was calling on the gods to tear him down.

But Theo had seen the jackal too. Was it visible to those who were purely human and had never worshiped the gods? He clutched the edge of the desk, his fingers white-knuckled, as he stared straight ahead. Sweat beaded on his skin.

Not now.

There was a reason he preferred the bank vault. The cool, dry air was good for paper...wood...metal...

He pulled down the bow stave from its rack and strung it, muscles tearing as he pushed through the creeping cold and pain. The arrows felt good in his hands. Bronze-headed and fletched with ibis feathers, they were perfect copies of the ones carried by Amenemhat's General Anhurmose, known as the Left Hand of Horus, leader of expeditions for the Great House and triumphant victor over the tribes of the far desert.

He probably looked ridiculous, slinging a leather quiver over his rumpled parka and stringing a bow in the basement of an old city bank. He didn't give a damn. Seth Adler didn't have a prayer in this situation, but Anhurmose might.

The shadows were coalescing. There were jackal figures there, and the crocodile-headed monster, but they weren't right.

The first one came crawling out of the darkness, half-formed feet squishing on the bald carpet. Jaundice-yellow eyes faded in and out in sockets that had been crudely scooped out of wet clay. Ceramic bones bulged through the torn skin, which had only raw score marks to show the shape of fur that should have been there. Its knees reversed as it gathered itself up into a crouch. Its teeth were hard, bone-white, and human.

Three more emerged, one from each other wall. Two more jackals and a crocodile-headed, lion-maned figure of Ammit, baring their human teeth and dripping fouled clay as they closed in around him. His fake heart pounded in his chest, so loud that he thought they would hear it and pounce, but he kept his face expressionless and nocked an arrow.

"Puppets and shadows," he called out in old Kemetic. "Is that all?"

"Don't play games with me, corpse," the voice whispered. Cold seized him again as invisible claws curled into the muscle of his shoulder, wrenching and tearing. He barely held back a scream and clutched instinctively at the shoulder again, but there were no marks there.

The jackals raised their heads as one and howled. The sound was eerie but wrong, echoing more deeply and hoarsely than it should have. It was the mournful sound of nightmares in the forests and mountains. Despite the pain, Seth found himself smiling.

"Who's playing games?" he said. "I'm not the one who made a jackal sound like a wolf."

There was a growl from the dimness. "Details are unimportant."

"Details are everything," Seth said. The nearest jackal bared its evil teeth.

It had been lifetimes beyond lifetimes since he'd done drills on the flat red earth of the campsites with his men. But he had returned to life in a new body weeks before, and with it came renewal of the encapsulated memories and skills of his long-lost self. Even as the fake jackal crouched to leap, he loosed the first shaft.

The arrow buried itself in the creature's chest. It howled again, less wolf and more banshee, and bucked as its clay began to fall apart. Seth had another arrow nocked in a fraction of a moment, half turning in place, ears open for movement. The remaining monstrosities were growling in a variety of pitches and beasts' voices, but none of them lunged.

"One more, then!" he shouted. His voice echoed through the stone-lined vaults, and for a moment, exultation overwhelmed fear. They were wrong, cheap imitations made by someone as fallible—as mortal—as he was. He could kill them. He'd never been a magician or a priest, just the Great House's favorite warmaker, but, by the gods, he could kill something and make it stay dead.

His tormentor was less than pleased. It groaned and hissed and clawed at him, but Seth set his teeth and refused to let the shooting pains drive him to the ground again. After so many years of continuous sacrilege, Neith should have turned her face from him, but his aim was still true and he could still make war on his enemies. That gave him hope, and with hope came backbone.

Djed.

"You is make dead," the voice snarled at him. In its anger, its Kemetic had stumbled.

"Thank you," Seth told it tightly. Purely on devilish impulse, he threw in the rhetorical flourishes that the educated men had liked so much. "Now I know you are no servant of the Two Lands," he continued, turning on his heel to survey the circle of monsters. One or two had begun to creep forward, but as his gaze fell on them, they snarled and retreated. "My people knew the power their tongue carried in the service of the red land and the black, and they would never have allowed such degenerate speech."

That got a barely suppressed growl from the voice. Its touch raked at him again and this time Seth staggered, falling to one knee. Seeing him waver, the Ammit started forward. He pinned it to a bookcase with an arrow through the throat, but he was slower on the draw the next time, and the rest of the creatures' eyes were fixed hungrily on him. Icy pain curled into his muscles, raking at his fingers and arms, and he gave a gasp as his left wrist broke.

"You did this to me!" the voice hissed as the bow fell from Seth's suddenly numbed grip. "You stole my shabtis. Broke my head. I could have been a king, but you stopped me. Do you know how many Great Houses I destroyed? I could have been the greatest of them all! But you wouldn't let me! I am always the servant! I hate you! I hate you!"

Seth fumbled for the bow, but his damaged arm wouldn't cooperate. With discordant howls, the clay creatures pounced. Teeth fastened on to the back of his neck. Claws sank into his chest. He tried to draw his wrist knife, but the pain—oh Neith, help him—

He gasped out an obscenity as he died again.

* * *

Theo woke with a start. Her mouth tasted like metal, and a dull ache pulsed at the base of her skull, in time with her racing heartbeat. Why had she been dreaming about churches?

She'd fallen asleep facedown on the leather couch. Blinking aching eyes, she slowly peeled her face off the cushions, grimacing as she did so. The room was dim and unfamiliar, and the pinkish light leaking into it from outside lent it an eerie aspect. A glance at the clock showed that it was after midnight; she'd slept through the whole day, and then some.

"Arise," a man's voice said.

Theo fell off the couch.

There was a man in the living room. She scrambled to her feet and grabbed for the lamp on the end table, but the lamp was a near-solid chunk of brushed steel and she wrenched her arm. The man looked at her steadily, his face expressionless.

His skin was the color of Seth's, but with a warmer undertone. He was bald and wore a white stocking cap pushed far back on his forehead. The rest of his clothes consisted of pale-gray sweatpants, sandals, and white athletic socks. His torso was completely bare. A leash dangled from his left hand, ending at the collar of a steel-colored greyhound that was watching Theo with an expression of near-manic alertness.

"What the hell?" Theo yelped. "Who are you? Get out of here!"

"I am clay," said the man calmly. He knelt, and the dog did likewise, lowering its head. "I am created to serve Anhurmose through you. What is your command, oh my mistress?"

Theo gaped at him. "What?" she said. Her heart was racing, and her arm throbbed painfully as she cradled it. Memories came trickling back: arts and crafts of the damned, failure, falling asleep on the couch. "Wait, I—I made it, but it didn't work."

"I was created to serve Anhurmose in death. He lived." The glassy eyes regarded her calmly. "Then he did not. I rose when he died."

"He died again?" Theo said softly. "How?"

"His enemy is clever. He warped shabti clay and made servants of it to kill him."

"Is it going to happen again?"

"I do not know. It is not my purpose to see the future."

Theo took a deep breath and tried to steady herself. "Prove it," she said. "Prove you're clay."

The man held up one arm and produced a knife from the pocket of his pants. Theo watched, curiously aware of a sense of ritual, as he nicked his arm. Flour paste dripped from the wound.

The breath left her in a great whoosh, and Theo sat down hard on the couch again. The man-golem-thing watched her, his expression utterly level. The dog made a woofing noise but otherwise barely moved. When it blinked, the lids scraped dryly against the hard surface of its eyes.

"How is this my life?" Theo said to nobody. "All I wanted was to get back to work." The shabti failed to respond.

"I can't believe I'm buying this," she told it. Who else was there to talk to? "A mysterious person turns up in front of me with a dog, bleeds paste on my parents' carpet, and I believe that he's the magically created, living version of the shitty art project I made. It's entirely possible that this is a crazy fantasy, and I'm actually safe in a nice padded room somewhere. What do you think?"

There was a stony silence from the pair. Theo raised her head slightly to look the man in the eye, and he stared back, unblinking. She might've called him a robot, but Aki's friend Sandy would be ashamed to produce such lifeless work.

"Do you think?" she added.

The shabti stared. "I am me," he said. He didn't seem inclined to add anything.

"You sure are," Theo muttered. "Great. What's your name?"

"I have no name. I am clay."

"Clay is a lousy name." She tilted her head, examining the unmoving man. "How about Albrecht? Like Albrecht Dürer? You seem like the kind of guy who'd watch the end of the world happening and take notes."

Continued silence. Well, at least he wasn't damning her for a poxy whore or anything. Theo stood again and, taking her courage in hand, moved closer to him. "Your name is Albrecht," she said decisively. "Al for short. What can you do?"

This time, the answer came immediately. "I hunt. I track. I know all that Anhurmose son of Merenptah knows."

Her breath caught in her throat. "So you can find him?"

"I can."

The possibilities were staggering, but Theo forced herself to stay calm. "Does he need to be found?" she said as calmly as she could. Al stared at her again, and she rephrased the question. "You said he died. Is he in pain?"

"He is."

She swallowed. "Does he need help?"

"If he is not to die forever."

No room for equivocation there. The shabti didn't seem to be lying; it probably didn't know how. Seth was in trouble, and the enemy had his mummy. She had to do something.

"One minute," she said breathlessly. The golems stood silent as Theo grabbed her phone and dialed Aki's number.

Voice mail. Of course, voice mail. When had things ever gone right for her in a crunch?

"Aki," she said hastily, clutching the phone so tightly that the plastic creaked under her hands. "Look, it's almost five o'clock right now. If I haven't called you back by noon tomorrow, something bad has happened to me and I think it's Mark Zimmer's fault. Do you under-stand? Mark Zimmer. He's hurting Seth, and I'm trying to find him. He already tried to kill me last night. I can't call the cops; they'll think I'm crazier than I already am, but they'll believe you. Got it? Cops. It's"—a hysterical laugh bubbled to the top—"it's life and death."

There wasn't anything else she could say. She hung up and turned to the statue she had brought to life, staring it right in its dead eyes. "All right," she said, taking a deep breath, "what do you bring on a rescue mission?"

"Weapons," said the voice. "Medicines. More dogs."

"Too bad I'm not a pet person," Theo muttered. But medicines? She could do that. After years of studio work, she'd learned to keep a damn good first aid kit on hand, and her parents had followed her example. She found the kit under the kitchen sink and threw open its lid to check the contents. Still well-stocked—good.

Weapons? Theo had never been a very combative person. She was the queen of passive aggression; her weapons were pointed asides and sharp emails. The supplies she had were art supplies.

Or, if she looked at it another way, she had enough dangerous chemicals to blow up an office building.

Despite exhaustion and fear, a small, grim smile edged its way across Theo's face. Separately, X clearcoat and Y paint thinner were inoffensive, but together they might strip the skin from your hands. Poisons, acid-like industrial solvents, accelerants—all in neat tubes and sold with no questions asked. Even the two-pack-a-day students put out their cigarettes before going into the studio, and it wasn't because you weren't allowed to smoke indoors.

She darted into her old bedroom. The padlock on the cabinet was stiff and coated with dust, and the key was long gone. After wrestling with it for a moment, Theo huffed out an exasperated breath and settled for jimmying it with a thin-bladed screwdriver.

It was disturbing, knowing what she was thinking. But did she have a choice? She just didn't see what else could work.

It was as basic as not combining bleach and ammonia. Theo grabbed an armload of bottles as the voices of her professors echoed in her head: *Be careful with that; it can make you sick. Don't hold an open flame anywhere near it. Make sure you're wearing a mask. Never mix them in the same container!*

She raided her mother's medicine cabinet and makeup kit. Like any experienced traveler in the post-9/11 world, Mrs. Speer kept a large selection of tiny plastic bottles for decanting shampoo, soap, and anything else she might carry on an international flight. Theo mixed two liquids, gave a third a good shaking before sifting in flour from the kitchen, and filled half a dozen containers with her deadly cocktails. One would only last for a couple of hours before the bottle started to melt, but if she was either very lucky or very unlucky, it'd all be over by that point.

The shabti gave the assembled kit a flat stare as she began to pack everything up. "You are going to die," he informed her.

"It's not your purpose to see the future, remember?" she retorted. "Help me carry these."

The eyes focused on the bags. "It is not my purpose to be a porter."

"You've still got hands," Theo said irritably. She jerked open the kitchen drawers and began to root around.

"But it is not my purpose." The stone eyes blinked again as Theo turned, a foot-long bread knife in hand. "Threatening me will not change this."

"I'm not threatening you; I'm being cautious." She shoved the bread knife into one of the bags and added a couple of razor-sharp X-ACTO blades to her pockets. "If you won't help me, then go take your dog out to the garage. There's a blue BMW out there." Remembering her audience, she amended that. "Um, a large blue car. You know what a car is?"

"I am a servant of Anhurmose. I know what he knows." The shabti grabbed his dog's lead, drawing a grating whine from the animal. "This form of machine is inferior to his."

"Good for him," she grunted, picking up the bags.

* * *

It was a strange drive. The shabti-man sat in the front seat with the dog, whose head tracked left and right as it sniffed the air. Orange streetlights and strips of darkness slid over them, picking out corners and edges on features that were too sharply defined to be natural flesh. Anything Theo tried to say died for lack of response.

Sometimes he told her to go left or right. The dog stuck its head out the car window and barked—the sound dry and grating—with each turn; it seemed more eager. Maybe being incarnated was a nice change from its usual routine of nonexistence.

Al watched her calmly from the passenger seat, his flat eyes impassive. The dog wagged its tail, its jaws opening in an unmistakable doggie grin.

"What're you looking at?" she said to him. It. Them.

"You," he said.

"Why?" she snapped. "Shouldn't you be tracking?"

"I know all Anhurmose knows. He thinks you are safe." Albrecht blinked mechanically. "This thought is a comfort to him. It will not comfort him to see you die."

"I'm starting to see why you guys are always kept behind soundproof glass."

They drove for more than an hour, following Albrecht's link and the dog's nose. It took them out of Deerfield and back into Chicago proper, then eastward back toward the lakeshore. Instead of business districts, this area was firmly residential, with streets of small houses in between blocks of storefronts, Asian grocers, and all-night restaurants. They were in Little Vietnam.

She braked. The dog's back was arched, growls rumbling through its thin chest, and Albrecht's spine was stiff as a board. His gaze was fixed on the side of the road.

"This is it," he said. "No farther."

Theo leaned her head against the window, letting her eyes adjust to the scene. No shops here, the sidewalk was bordered by ugly chain-link fencing covered with plastic tarps, and it stretched away up and down the street. A construction site?

She put the car in gear again and followed the curve of the wall. Before long, they found the entrance. Broad, green-painted metal gates chained closed for the night, an anachronism speckled with the glowing reflections of the neon-fronted eatery across the street. A small sign proclaimed this was the Cemetery of St. Boniface.

"A graveyard?" she said to Albrecht.

"A necropolis," he responded hoarsely. There was something in him that seemed to know it was clay, and the clay was beginning to crack. "Old. Good place for ritual; the west is strong there. I am glad to see it."

"Can you help me in there?" she asked softly.

"No." He turned his head to look not at her, but at something past her. "You have raised me to be something, and I have fulfilled my purpose. My hound and I will return to the dust."

"I wish you wouldn't," Theo said. She meant it. She barely knew him, but with him as help and living (in a manner of speaking) proof of the truth, she had something to focus on. Someone to work with.

He blinked, and cracks appeared in the corners of his eyes. "This far, and no farther. I have done the work you wanted," he said. "Go. Help Anhurmose."

"And hopefully not die," she said. With a sigh, she patted the dog's head. "Good boy."

The animal butted her hand with its head. Cracks ran through the rough-sculpted fur. "Very good boy," she amended. He panted.

"Thank you," she added to Albrecht. "You helped me when I was in real trouble. Take care when you get back to the other world, okay?"

He gave her a blank look. "My time is over. There is no beyond for me."

Theo stopped, her hand on the dog's ears. What do you say to that? 'Sorry for creating you'? She blinked, feeling the burning gather in her eyes again.

To her surprise, though, the shabti-man spoke up one more time. "Thank you," he said, "for a name."

"Everyone needs one," she replied softly. "Isn't that right, Lucky?" she added to the dog, who yelped and licked her face with a dry and dusty tongue.

By the time she was out of the car, the tail had stopped wagging. When she put her hand on the cemetery gate and looked back, there was no sign of a man or a dog left in the car.

CHAPTER SIXTEEN

And for the sake of this book of magic, and for the
woman he desired, Khamwaset slew his wife and
children and buried them in the sand.

> *- The Tale of Khamwaset,*
> *as recorded c. 300 BCE*

The gate itself was a problem, but there was always a way around problems. St. Boniface was much older than the neighborhood that
surrounded it and after decades of crumbling, two of the brick guard
walls had simply been demolished to make space for better ones. But no
construction was being done in the middle of December, and the temporary chain fence sagged, the tarpaulins stapled over it flapping in the
wind.

Two broad paths intersected in the middle of the graveyard and
divided it into four roughly equal sections. Signposts pointed the way to
the chapel and the other gates. Theo had to squint to read them: there
were no lamps inside the fence line, probably because nobody was
supposed to be inside at night. The glow from the streetlights at her back
cast long, dim shadows over the ground, blending Theo's outline into
those of a dozen statues and pillar monuments. In the distance, she could
faintly see the gate on the wall to her left.

Grandma Dora hadn't been allowed a standing monument on her
grave. By city law, grave markers had to be flat so the groundskeepers
could easily cut the grass. St. Boniface, more than a century old,
disdained that. It had statues, pillars, monuments of granite, limestone,
sandstone, basalt, or concrete, deep gray touched with orange-white
highlights in the strange ambient gloom of a city night. Here and there

were the occasional telltale flat graves, but St. Boniface had always been an immigrants' cemetery, and, by God, they would have in death whatever they couldn't in life.

She fumbled with the flashlight but managed to get it turned on. The weak beam of light played over the monuments, casting darker shadows this way and that. The pitted face of a limestone angel, etched by the city's tainted air, peered down from its pillar as she examined the historical plaque at its base.

She raised the flashlight and peered into the distance. It was almost impossible to see clearly, with the monuments and pillars casting multilayered shadows and breaking up the line of sight. She might as well have not brought light at all.

With a sigh, Theo lowered the beam of the flashlight to the ground. At least she would be able to see the tombstones before she tripped over them. Bashing her brains out against somebody's great-grandfather's grave marker would be the perfect way to end the evening.

Only the middle of the road was safe to walk on. The road had been plowed recently, but piled-up snow at the edges had frozen into icy hillocks, making the footing treacherous. Theo was barely past the statue of the angel when she slipped and sat down hard, unable to restrain a yelp. Her heavy bags slammed against her hips and ribs, knocking her wind out.

"Maybe I didn't think this through," she muttered, rubbing her aching side.

When she reached the crossroads, she paused, trying to slow her breathing. Her heart was pounding, and every time she took a step the icy gravel crunched loudly underfoot.

Her eyes began to adjust—ever so slightly—to the inconsistent dimness of the cemetery. The farther back she went, the larger and more ominous the monuments were, forming a statue maze of angels, saints, crosses, and mortuary slabs.

The largest, set a little way up a sloping hill, was a huge square mass that looked like a mausoleum. It was one of the only things in the graveyard capable of concealing a full-grown man; the angels and saints fouled the line of sight, but they didn't provide enough cover. Heart in her mouth, Theo crept toward it.

Light leaked over the edge of the strange block.

Three massive marble slabs, pieces of a family plot etched with lists of names and dates, formed a protected plot on the frozen ground. Candles were arranged on one of the headstones, and an old-fashioned oil lamp was burning in front of the central block.

Lying in the hollow formed by the marble slabs were Seth Adler and Anhurmose.

The man was sprawled on his side with his wrists zip-tied behind his back, wearing a T-shirt and jeans. He was rejuvenated, free of gray hairs and oddly plastic in his new youthfulness. Next to him lay an oblong, blanket-wrapped object that might have been a tent or a bundle of luggage, save for the withered feet sticking out one end.

Scraps of ancient bandages littered the dirty snow.

Seth was barely breathing, but there was life in him. In that body, anyway.

Someone had been experimenting. A large plastic tub was propped up against one of the gravestones, and half a dozen unbaked statuettes were scattered around in various stages of completion. One seemed to have exploded, spraying droplets of clay over the surrounding snowy earth. Another looked like it had died at birth and was left sprawling against the tombstone, an eye three times too big bulging out of one socket. More shabtis, real ones from the Columbian's collection, had been set up on various flat surfaces. Two had shattered into pieces, and the third had ballooned into a grotesque, fleshy mass that leaked clay from every crack.

Mark Zimmer knelt next to Seth. He was heavily bundled up in dark colors that blurred his silhouette, and a scarf wrapped around his nose and mouth left red hair, white forehead, and feverish eyes seemingly floating in the air. His hands were bare, and he was kneading a fresh lump of clay and muttering to himself as he worked. As Theo watched, heart in her mouth, Zimmer opened a shallow cut on Seth's arm and hastily dribbled the hardening droplets into his own hands.

"Ri ata," the voice hissed into her ear. *"Ata. Ri ata."*

Again? She tried to wish the voice away and focus on what was going on.

Zimmer was trying to carve symbols into the proto-shabti in his hands. He didn't seem to have much of an idea what he was doing, and the knife slipped, nicking his forefinger and cutting the shabti's head off.

"God fucking dammit!" he hissed, and threw the beheaded statuette at the nearest gravestone. "It's not fair!"

"Ata ri," the voice whispered again. It sounded satisfied this time.

The instant the shabti hit stone, it splattered into an unrecognizable lump. That didn't seem to satisfy Zimmer, though, and as he growled under his breath, he sketched a sign in the air. Blue-white flames instantly licked up and fed on the clay, which crumbled into unrecognizable ash.

Theo's stomach churned as she watched the blue-lit ashes collapse into the snow. Zimmer definitely wasn't happy.

As she watched, silent under the cover of a broad-winged angel, the red-haired man grabbed one of his failures and began molding it into a new shabti. This time he mixed in scraps from the mummy's wrappings before adding the blood, and snatched a small dark-red object from a cooler. It was only when she saw the color dripping between his fingers that she realized it was a heart. By the size of it, it was from a small mammal. Definitely fresh. Bile rose in her throat as she tried not to remember that she'd done the same thing a few hours ago.

There wasn't much she could do against someone who'd tried to steal her body and could set things on fire with a gesture. But if she left him there, he'd keep taking apart both Seths—or, worse, he'd succeed in whatever he wanted to do with the shabtis. She needed to get Seth and the mummy away from him now.

Time for a distraction. While Zimmer swore and threw away the latest attempt, Theo softly picked her way in a wide quarter circle away from the men. Slowly, so slowly, one foot at a time and always wary of the crunch of snow under her boots.

It took her ten minutes to find the right spot. Taking a deep breath, she sorted through her bottles and began to pour a long loop of oily liquid onto the frozen ground.

Well, this would probably catch his attention. Theo twisted an old receipt into a paper stick and lit the tip of it. Then she stepped back and carefully flicked her makeshift match before ducking behind a granite slab.

There was a massive thump and a hot, hissing whoosh, and a wave of heat blossomed in the graveyard. The thick stench of burning gasoline washed over her with a biting acidic component that made her head swim. Mission accomplished.

As Theo scrambled to her feet, a mirthless grin spread across her face. The fire blazed like an open portal to hell. Flames blackened the slick stones with fresh soot and coiled upward in a plume of orange heat that was impossible to miss. Melting snow would choke it out soon enough, but for now it burned furiously on the poisonous fuel she'd mixed for it.

She hoped the residents of the cemetery wouldn't mind what she'd done. After all, the dead would understand what it was like to want to keep someone alive.

Zimmer would probably be coming to check it out. Keeping low, she circled back around, hiding in the shadows of the gravestones.

Her breath caught in her throat as she dropped to her knees beside Seth. He was pallid and sunken-cheeked, his skin drying out. He seemed to be halfway to mummification himself. Theo shook him, but though he mumbled something and shivered, his eyes didn't open.

She pulled out a craft knife and got to work. The zip ties were tough, ribbed plastic, identical to the ones Seth had used on her in the loft...had it really been less than a month ago? She sawed carefully, trying not to accidentally slash Seth's wrists. Killing him might transport his soul to another body, but she had no idea how many shabtis were left.

"Seth," she hissed as the ties parted. "Seth. Come on, Seth, it's Theo. Wake up!"

Snow crunched underneath her. The insistent voice kept whispering but she brushed it aside, annoyed and afraid, and shook him again. Her breath steamed in the air and her fingers ached with cold.

"Wake up," she said. "Wake up, wake up, wake up, come on..."

With agonizing slowness, Seth's eyes opened. He blinked several times and shook his head, scattering the snowflakes that had settled in his hair. "Theo?" he said, his voice cracking. "What's going on?"

"I don't know," she said. She wrapped her arms around him and heaved, trying to help him scramble to his feet. He staggered and wound up leaning against a gravestone, panting shallowly. Blood loss and cold had left his lips tinged blue.

Theo touched the back of her hand to his cheek. The skin was cool, even for Seth, and clammy with sweat. He looked like he had lost a lot of blood. How was that possible? What had Zimmer been doing to him?

"Oh, of course it would be you."

Theo flinched. Seth stiffened. Mark Zimmer emerged from the forest of gravestones, carrying a blazing flame in his open palm.

He was as pale as putty, and in the flickering light from the fire in his hand, deep shadows had turned his face into something skull-like. Behind him, the inferno she had kindled was dying down, leaving the edges of the scene limned with a red-orange glow like the sunset on the last day of the world.

"I didn't think you'd be this much trouble," he told Theo bluntly. He flicked his hand and the ball of fire went flying. It spattered against a nearby limestone pillar and went out, leaving a smear of ash behind. "Does Van Allen know he's employing a budding bomber? I'm surprised you're not on a government watch list."

"Back off!" Theo snapped. "I don't know what you're doing here with this…this black-magic shit, but that's enough. Okay?"

Zimmer's lips twisted. "Really," he said to the world at large. He sounded like Theo had two hours ago, talking to the shabti-man in her parents' house. Tired, disbelieving, and a bit amused despite everything. "That's your plan. An X-ACTO knife. There's a nice, dry mummy lying three feet away from a man who can conjure fire, and you're threatening me with art supplies?"

Her eyes darted to the mummy before she could stop herself—poor old THS203, his bandages completely ruined and his hands and feet mangled, but still seemingly grinning at the ridiculousness of it all. What exactly were you supposed to do in a situation like this? She didn't know.

Before she could formulate a reply, Seth worked up enough breath to speak. He was still bracing himself against the marble, but he squared his shoulders and looked at Zimmer. The dried clay crusting on his wounds cracked and dropped, littering the snow around him with dark fragments.

"Why are you doing this?" he said hoarsely.

Zimmer's jaw tightened. "Don't be cute," he said. He glanced back and forth between Seth and Theo, rolling a fresh spark between his fingertips. "Or is this for her benefit? Should I hang you two upside down over a shark tank and explain my plan in complete detail?"

"I know your plan," Theo interrupted. The sound of her voice surprised herself. "You've gotten hold of old magic somehow. You want to use it, maybe sell it—who wouldn't pay to live forever? So you set me up as Seth's accomplice and robbed the museum."

"Sort of." Zimmer whisked the spark away and picked up the crack-ling mummy. "Money was never part of it. This is just old-fashioned petty revenge."

Seth's expression was stony, but he was beginning to waver a little. Theo quickly moved to his side and wrapped an arm around his waist. After a moment's hesitation, she felt the stiff muscles relax as he leaned into her. "I don't know why," he said finally. "I never did anything to you."

"Of course you didn't, 'Seth.' The past is the past, right?" Zimmer picked a scrap of ancient linen off the corpse and flicked it over his shoulder. "But you took my toys. Maybe you can be reasonable enough to help me get them back."

As he spoke, his fingers tightened on the mummy. Bandages shredded and dry, leathery skin crumpled under his grip. Seth jerked, and Theo couldn't hold back a gasp as she felt one of his ribs collapse into his side. She tightened her grip and braced her feet, barely keeping them both upright.

"I can't," Seth said raggedly. "They were made for me. You might have old magic, but you'll never be able to use them."

"Really," Zimmer responded. "Maybe I'm a little fuzzy on the details after so long, but I remember one part pretty clearly. It was made for *the son of Merenptah*. Two people qualify, and you know it."

Seth's back stiffened, and his jaw worked silently. "You're lying," he said finally. "Meren wouldn't do this. We were brothers. We were friends."

"And then you screwed me over." Zimmer's voice was flat. "You took the shabtis. They were mine and you took them. Do you know where my body is? I don't. I've been in this one for more than thirty years, and you know how much of a pain in the ass it was to get? I've been living this way for millennia, and half the time, I was convinced I was insane! Not all of us get your magic memories!"

He took a deep breath, visibly fighting to keep his temper under control. "I lost my mind because of you, and when I finally tracked you down, you were living the high life thanks to my work. You better believe I'm your brother, because nobody else could hate you as much as I do right now."

Theo's first thought was that he was delusional. Her second thought kicked that first thought hard and pointed out that she was pretty far beyond doubting the potential bizarreness of a situation at this point. She'd accepted Seth, seen him die, made love to him, and built a golem to hunt him down when he was in danger. A long-lost brother—or the soul of one inside the Columbian's head of Security—wasn't impossible anymore.

Not only the head of Security, though. Her stomach lurched at the thought of it. He'd tried to move into her body, back at the museum. And his body—the one that sprang to mind when she thought of him—wasn't his either. He'd lied about everything. He'd lied about his own face.

"I don't believe you," Seth said tightly. "It's not possible."

"Then that's your problem." Zimmer tore a strip of papery bandaging from the mummy's arm. "See, you owe me something, Seth. You owe me a prayer. I didn't let you last this long out of sentimentality; without that prayer, these won't do a thing." He kicked one of his failed statuettes, sending the lump of clay splatting against a tombstone. "I could have been a king, little brother. I want what's mine."

"I"—Seth shook his head—"I can't. Even if you are my brother, you're not the Meren I knew. He made those shabtis to save my life, and you're standing here threatening me." His pulse was wild and erratic under Theo's arm, and she leaned into him a little more, trying to give him some comfort.

He looked down at her for a moment, his eyes dark mirrors in the light of the dying fire. "And you pulled her into it," he added, throwing the words at Zimmer. "I won't help you. Ever."

Zimmer had no answer. For a moment, he struggled to form words— rage and confusion fighting each other in his expression. Theo's heart leaped as seconds ticked past without a reply. Maybe—

Then he shrugged again and snapped off one of the mummy's fingers.

Seth reeled and almost fell. Purple-red stains bloomed under his skin as his right hand wrenched, twisting and breaking of its own accord. He sagged against her, cradling his damaged limb to his chest, pain drawing deep lines on his face.

Theo's first urge was to scream, but she bit down hard and stifled it as she struggled to keep them both upright. Her blood was running cold. Meren-Zimmer had his hands on the trump card, and she wanted to yell, curse, tear the mummy out of his hands, do something, *anything!*

If Zimmer got the shabtis working, her brain whispered, *he wouldn't hurt Seth anymore.* He would have his own supply of bodies and could live forever on his own terms—or whatever he wanted. He wouldn't need to hurt them.

But did that mean he still wouldn't?

He had admitted to stealing bodies. She didn't know how much of his story was fact, but whether or not the accusations he'd aimed at Seth were true, he had still done to someone else what he'd tried to do to her. In his own words, he'd confirmed it—he'd been in that body for more than thirty years. But he was forty, or a little over.

Bile rose in her throat.

If this was true, then he was the kind of man who'd steal a child and put his body on like a new shirt. With Seth dead and the shabtis in his hands, why would he need to change?

The thought hardened like concrete, immovable and impossible to ignore. There was the thing claiming to be Meren, the mind inside the body—and then there was the real Mark Zimmer, the child. The Meren-self was shouting at the slumping Seth now, demanding the secret of the shabtis, and the face, voice, and name he was using had been stolen from someone else. More thoughts whirled: the sacred power of the name, the importance of the body and the heart, the horrible question of how many people had been killed by the man in front of her. How many bodies did you need in order to last four thousand years? Two hundred? Three hundred?

Another finger snapped, and Seth couldn't restrain a scream. Sweat was pouring down his face, and in his pain, he snarled like a dog at his onetime brother.

"Fuck you," Meren said shortly as he dropped the severed finger to the ground. THS203, sprawled facedown over Meren's shoulder, was looking less and less like he had ever been human. Anhurmose was dying twice, at the same time.

She couldn't let that happen. But the way to make him stop was to give up the shabtis, and that would leave the two of them facing a more powerful opponent. Yet shabtis weren't invincible, and if she could bring in help...

Falling to her knees and begging would be too obvious. Meren had known her while he was Zimmer. But he hadn't thought she'd be so much trouble...had seen her as a pawn... How he'd gotten that idea she didn't know, but she had a chance to play to his assumptions.

It took no effort to get the tears started. Letting out a gulping sob, she pushed Seth back against the marble slab and pulled away from him, covering her face. "Oh God," she said. "Oh God, oh God, oh God. I can't do this."

"What are you—" Seth began. His eyes widened. "Theo, don't!"

"You think he's not going to figure it out?" she screamed. "What's going to happen to Aki? Sandy? Dr. Van Allen? I can't believe you didn't tell me this psychopath was following you! You're going to get them killed!"

Seth recoiled. Theo's heart stuttered in her chest as she saw the expression on his face and in his eyes: hurt, surprise, and fear, all plain and unguarded. He wasn't a statue of a pharaoh anymore. Pharaohs were glacial, with a serene countenance and sometimes the merest smile like they knew something you didn't. Now she didn't know who looked worse, Seth or his corpse.

"I didn't know," he managed to say. "Theo, I swear to Neith, I didn't know."

Theo's heart broke again, but she had to keep going. The tears were coming whether she wanted them to or not. "I can't believe this happened. I was so stupid! So much for motion in art!" Her eyes burned, and her fists clenched involuntarily. "If he gets it to work, he'll leave us alone. And I can pretend this never happened, and you can—I don't know—live one more life and die like you were supposed to!"

She turned her back on him, mopping her face with the back of her arm.

"You can't use his shabtis, and you can't make new ones. Not that way." She met Meren's eyes. "But I can."

"Now you're lying," Meren said flatly. Theo's throat tightened. "He won't share the formula with his own brother. You think I'd believe he'd give it to you?"

Her hands were shaking. She jammed them into her pockets.

"'The body of the son of Merenptah,'" she recited. Meren started as the implication of her words hit him. "'Khnum is my father; Neith is my mother. I am pure. I am known to us here as I am known to those who have brought me into this world—'"

"Quiet!" Meren barked. Theo clammed up. "He told you? He told you!"

His eyes were wide, but he didn't seem angry. On the contrary, a grin was appearing on his face. "I take it back. He's the most sentimental moron in the history of humanity. Giving up a sacred formula to the first woman you've fucked in, what, a hundred years?" He shook his head. "You need therapy."

"*Ri ata*," the voice insisted.

"Theo!"

Seth's shout dragged her back to the here and now. "Theo," he continued as she turned reluctantly to face him. "Don't help him. You're going to create a monster. You're going to take a monster and make him *worse*."

"I want it back how it was before," she said. "I can't take this...this magic stuff anymore, Seth. You put my family and my friends in danger by telling me this. I'm going to do what you never could and fix this!"

Theo turned back to Meren, who was certainly enjoying himself. He liked seeing his brother get cut down to size. "You've already got the materials," she said. "I'll make you your shabtis. Then you can leave us alone."

"Okay," he said simply. Theo's heart leaped. "But before we do any-thing impulsive, I have an idea."

There was a rattle and crackle of dry, dusty bones as Meren dropped the mummy of Anhurmose to the ground. "Hey, bro," he drawled, cracking his knuckles as he looked at Seth, Theo momentarily forgotten. "Talk about an out-of-body experience, huh?"

He dipped a hand into his pocket and brought it out again, carrying a fistful of dust. Seth's back stiffened. Meren sprinkled the dust over the mummy, and a light breeze sighed through the graveyard, plucking at their hair and clothes.

"*Da-medu en Meren*," he began. His voice was flat, his eyes distant as he concentrated on the words. He was a schoolboy in front of the board, rattling off the state capitals in a monotone that proved only that he'd done the homework, not understood it.

Harsh syllables tumbled over each other like a collapsing stack of blocks. Seth wavered, streaks of red and purple blooming under his skin as veins burst, still clutching his wounded arm and seemingly struck dumb. His skin had an unnatural sheen and cracks appeared at the corners of his mouth as he tried to speak. The hollows under his eyes were becoming cracks too, and those cracks were widening. Skin shivered and broke. A curl of hair snapped and fell to the ground, where it shattered into a hundred little ridged pieces.

Theo couldn't keep in a scream as Seth Adler collapsed into pieces.

This wasn't like the smooth column of dust he had become in the art room: his body was breaking apart. His stunned expression crumbled in on itself, one staring eye turning brown and cracking in two as it landed in the dirty snow.

And the mummy moved.

No eyes, no tongue, no breath, but it was moving. Its one good arm twitched faintly, a spastic motion that looked like nothing more than the animatronics Sandy cobbled together for fun. Sticklike fingers clutched at the dirty snow.

It. It it it. *Him.*

"If you're going to throw up, don't do it here," Meren said. "The groundskeepers don't like finding puke on graves."

Theo lurched and forced herself to turn around, leaning her forehead against the cool marble. Vomit splattered against the stone, followed by specks of blood. She'd bitten her own tongue and hadn't realized it.

"Now," said that voice from behind her, "I believe I was promised ushebtis?"

Kill him. Stab him. You've got the knives! Kill him!

But her hands wouldn't move; her fingers wouldn't flex. The thoughts raged in the back of her head, less words and more a half-coherent shriek of rage, but they were wrapped up in a body that couldn't seem to get the message. When she finally pushed herself into motion, all she could do was wipe her mouth.

"Ushebtis?" Meren prompted.

Never.

"…Yes," she managed. Stiff-legged, she shuffled over to the box of art supplies and pulled out a fresh hunk of clay.

"Ata. Ri ata. Ri! Ri!" the wind whispered. The voice badgered her, puffs of breeze batting at her hair and clothes, as she folded her hands around the clay to warm it. *"I want."*

Theo almost dropped the clay. The voice was speaking English? What was it trying to tell her? She rolled the stiff lump between her palms, trying to warm it, and concentrated. "Can you hear me?" she whispered. "What do you want?"

"Shabtis," Meren said promptly. "I thought that was obvious." But behind his words came the little voice, stronger now, swirling around and reaching for her.

"I want. I want. Ata ri. Go home. I want. Ata ri."

Theo swallowed. Meren was rotten with magic and couldn't seem to hear the voice; was she going crazy? He was looking at her oddly, though, and she held up the lump of clay for inspection. "I don't suppose you have a hair dryer?" she said. "This stuff is almost frozen solid."

"Sorry, no," Meren said. "Try this." He dropped a six-inch knife into her hand. "I wasn't able to take over your body before, but I can still burn you like a Fourth of July hot dog. So no creative ideas. Got it?" He grinned. "Besides the shabti, of course. Creativity is important there."

He was standing on a grave. The moon was behind her, but Meren's face and form were in shadow as the massive shape of the marble slabs blotted out most of the light. Her makeshift fire had burned itself out, leaving a smell of smoke in the air. What she wouldn't give to put him in that grave right now.

The knife made it easy to work. Shavings of clay littered the ground around her as she carved, and a crude face and form began to emerge from the shapeless lump. Biting her lip, she etched the symbols into the cold surface, running syllables through her mind. They were keyed to more colors, but she'd copied the inscription so often she barely needed them. Goldenrod, slate blue, kelly green...no. Meren was looking at the mummy. She wiped out the third symbol with her thumb and substituted another. Alizarin crimson, that was the ticket...titanium white...life returned to its home...

She hoped that the gods wouldn't stand on grammar. It was cobbled together out of phrases from exhibition pamphlets and textbooks, but it would have to do.

A rustle and a crack. Faint panting. The sick feeling rose again, and she clamped down on it. *Don't look at it. Don't look at him.*

"And the heart?" she said as she gouged out the space in the clay chest.

"Right here." Meren opened the cooler and pulled out another heart. He passed it to her and wiped his gloved hands in the snow, leaving behind streaks of red.

"Bird?" she asked conversationally.

He shook his head. "Cat."

"Was it dead when you found it?"

"Do you really want to know?"

"No." Theo wiped the cold sweat off her face, leaving behind streaks of dirt and blood. Without flinching, she pushed the squishy lump of flesh into the shabti's body and smoothed the clay. "Finished."

Meren twisted his free hand; the shabti lifted out of Theo's hand and sailed across the small space toward him. He caught it neatly and turned it over, examining it.

"You really do know them," he said softly. "You're okay, Theo." For a moment, his expression eased, and he looked like the Mark Zimmer she'd been used to. "I'm sorry you got pulled into this. Whatever he told you, it's a lie, I promise. He stole them from me."

She looked him in the eye. "I don't believe you," she said, her voice wavering. "But I don't care. I want this to be over."

"It will be soon." He squeezed the shabti tightly. "Unless you've decided to screw me over."

Theo's nails bit into her palms. "I wouldn't," she said.

"Promise me." He pointed to the shuddering mummy, its jaw working as it tried to speak without lips or tongue. The only sound it could make was a dry, rustling noise like autumn leaves. "Promise me," Meren repeated softly, "on his life, because if you've gotten this wrong, he's dead. When the sun rises, the last of that spell will be broken, and my worthless son-of-a-bitch brother gets to cross over whether he likes it or not. If you want to see him out of there before the sun comes, promise."

"On his life," she said, "I promise."

Meren laughed—snickered, more like, a high-pitched sound. His left hand convulsed for a moment. "Good. Speak the words."

Theo sat down on her haunches next to the mummy. Meren knelt on her other side and calmly closed his eyes. Theo laid her left hand on his chest; in her right, she raised the mummiform figure. Meren smiled as she began to speak:

The body of the son of Merenptah. Khnum is my father; Neith is my mother. I am pure. I am known to us here as I am known to those who have brought me into this world. O Anubis and Osiris, pass me by, for I am not dead; I live here within, and walk upon the black earth and the red earth. For behold, I arise here, in the vessel of the son of Merenptah, and stand alive.

My mouth has been opened here. My spirit has been enshrined here. My ka has no need of its wings now, for it has a home well prepared for it by the sacred workers who serve the afterlife. Thus it is for the son of Merenptah, the faithful servant of the Crocodile District, of Waset, and of He Who Has United the Two Lands.

Meren was praying too, she thought, watching his still form. What gods would listen to him? What if he couldn't transfer and he blamed her—

No. There it was. A glow was gathering, a hot, dry, white glow, centered on his chest. His heart.

Her hands burned. She yelped and flung the shabti away, half hoping it would fall apart, but even as it landed on the snow, it was changing. Its crude clay shape flexed and shifted, its surface growing smooth and gleaming, running like melted wax as it began to grow.

Meren's knees buckled, his eyes rolled up, and he fell face-first onto the ground. The shabti's knees flexed too as it pawed at the dirt, its body radiating heat that melted the snow around it. The old body lay sprawled on the dirt, barely three yards from Theo, red hair tangled with sweat, its limbs angled strangely.

The worst part was that the shabti wasn't real. Its shape was unnatural, shiny and liquid, like a cheap CGI effect dropped into the middle of the world. The sheer existence of it twisted in Theo's throat—it was *wrong.* A bad note, a mismatching color, a patch of sandpaper in the middle of an acre of velvet. It was out of sync with the world, and it made her sick to look at it.

The mummy—Seth? Anhurmose?—was trying to move again. Theo looked down at him/it (hmt, shelter/owl/bread, "fare for conveyance," pennies for the ferryman?) and remembered a preparation room where the dry brown form lay quietly and never hurt anyone. Seth had been repulsed by the sight of his own corpse, and Theo couldn't blame him, but she'd never hated the mummy the way he did. Swallowing the remnants of blood on her tongue, she took his fragile hand.

She didn't know if she loved him. Not so soon. But there was a connection in there somewhere, and need, and a fierce protectiveness that kept her back straight and her breathing steady while the clay grotesque oozed its way into life.

And that mix of need and motion had given her the courage to do what she'd done.

The prayer was what Meren had needed. But a human brain can't carry four thousand years of memories. Somewhere along the line, he'd forgotten those crucial words. With his stilted Kemetic, who could've said whether he would understand the shabti inscription? And he wouldn't have thought to check it, either, since it wasn't the thing he'd had so much trouble finding.

But that inscription, the one she'd copied over and over again, was the other half of the puzzle. She'd done what he'd wanted and given Meren a new body. He hadn't specified anything about the leftovers.

Something groaned. She didn't look, not daring to hope. Another groan, louder this time, and a rustle of fabric.

And with a hacking cough, Mark Zimmer came to life.

"Fuck!" he burst out, his voice strangled and breathless. "Fuck! Shit! *Dammit!*"

Shabti-Meren rose up, his features forming out of the liquid clay, and still the old body wasn't dead. Zimmer tried to clamber to his feet, failed, stumbled, and collapsed, clutching the nearest gravestone with clumsy fingers. Theo's heart squeezed in her chest as she fought the urge to shout.

Meren had tried to take over her body, back in the museum. He'd failed. But the voices begging for revenge had stayed with her, whispering in English and Kemetic and so many other languages spoken in the past centuries when Meren had stolen them, and the loudest voice had been the one with a remaining link to the world. The voice that had gotten stronger whenever Meren was near. The voice of Mark Zimmer, a child of the 1980s.

The real Zimmer was alive.

But so was the new Meren, and he didn't seem fazed by the trick.

Meren's new form had softer, kinder features than his brother, more open and less battered, and he sported the clean-shaven head of a priest and long, dark eyelashes. He had a similar nose, though—a little smaller, a little more hawkish, a lot less broken. With sandals, a white kilt, and a leopard-skin cloak, he looked like one of Theo's paintings come to life.

"It's true," he said softly, touching a hand to his chest and feeling the rise and fall of it. For a moment, he was in a world of his own. "I remember. I remember things. Almost. It's there. It's true. It's *true.*"

The crumpled heap of Mark Zimmer raised his head. "Fuck you," he croaked. "I never..." He coughed. "I never got to say...say it before."

Meren frowned. "What are you doing, boy?"

"Not a boy." Zimmer lurched to his feet, shaking. "I was. I was *eight.* All I wanted was an Atari!"

"He's alive!" Theo burst out. Seth would have loved it. Her chest ached with mixed emotions, too many to count or name or even color: fear, pain, anger, strangled affection and loyalty, and the merest shred of triumph. This was work she could be proud of.

The priest turned on his heel, his eyes flicking to the stumbling body. "You snake," he said. "I never thought of that."

Seth had called her a backbone and a crocodile, but it was pretty clear that when Meren called her a snake, it wasn't a compliment.

"Don't look at her!" Mark shouted, staggering and almost falling. "Look at me! I'm the one!"

"This is none of your business."

"No. No, it is." Mark scowled and clenched his fists. His motions were broad and sweeping, like a drunk oversteering himself and walking into a wall. A child in a grown-up's body. "You made this my business. I never got to play my Atari! I never got to say 'fuck'! Ever! *You* got to!"

Meren drew a hand across his face, and Mark recoiled, clutching his mouth. Blood leaked between his fingers.

"Look what you did," Meren said to the staring Theo. "Children shouldn't be allowed into this kind of thing, Theo."

Anger flared up, sudden and unpredictable. "Don't," she snarled. "Don't you dare use my name. I don't know you."

"You do." Meren's tone was even, steady, a hard contrast to Theo's shaking voice. "We worked alongside each other for almost a year, and you trusted me when you needed help against…him." He pointed one long finger at the dead man. "Don't pretend otherwise, Theo. You're old enough to know that actions have consequences. Though I suppose final indulgences are allowed."

She had brought him back, brought Zimmer back, but it was clear that Mark couldn't help her. And now that Meren had the idea of how to make shabtis, he wouldn't want anyone else hanging around with that same knowledge.

He would kill her. There would be a eulogy saying she was taken too soon and a flat marker at Rosehill Cemetery that the gardeners would be able to mow over. Her murderer would never be caught…unless they found poor Mark at the same time and decided he was to blame. Two birds, one stone, some assembly required.

To hell with that.

Somewhere along the line, between making love to a man from a different time and ducking through a security door to escape from liquid-clay golems, she'd grabbed djed with both hands. There were too many memories—too many paintings—too much *motion* to let Meren kill her now. Seth was a mess, trapped in the hell of his own corpse, but there was still breath in that withered husk of a body, and King Tut would turn Presbyterian before Theo let Meren hurt him any more.

As she leaned forward, she pulled the mummy closer to her, putting his back to Meren. One hand, hidden behind the dry husk of a body, dipped through the snow and gathered a half-handful of clayey dirt.

Even while she let tears flow, she used the dirty pad of her thumb to sketch two quick symbols on the mummy's hollow chest. The ankh and the tyet, the signs of life. Seth let out a raspy breath, but the sacred marks didn't seem to be hurting him, and it was the only thing Theo could do for the moment. Half-hunched over the mummy, it looked like she was hugging him or praying. Meren didn't seem fazed by it; she doubted he feared prayers or gods either.

He flicked one hand at her, and something slammed into Theo's chest. Her breath whooshed out of her in one moment; she tumbled backward, gasping for air and clutching her aching ribs. Seth fell with her, his poor skin cracking with the impact, and she tried to steady him.

Mark tried to tackle Meren, but Meren stepped neatly to the side and the child-man crashed face-first into a standing gravestone.

Theo lay curled up on the ground, shielding Seth with her body as best she could. Her head swam and her chest throbbed in pain, each breath a struggle.

The priest didn't seem inclined to give her the time to recover. Stepping over to her, he kicked Theo in the side. While she wheezed, he picked up his brother's withered form and cradled it in his arms.

"I remember," he murmured to the dying man. "I do. I remember…I made them for you. I did. And they worked, and it ruined my life. I touched godhood." He held the body of his brother almost affectionately. "To have that power in your hand, to know that you've defeated death, it's…it's intoxicating, Anhurmose."

There was a faint rattling groan from the mummy, like wind crumpling paper.

"Put him down," Theo said softly. "Please."

Meren shook his head. "No," he said. "I want him to finally meet me, eye to eye." He peered at the withered face. "As much as he can, anyway."

"But if you remember you made them for him, then he was telling the truth." Theo forced herself to sit up. Her vision still swam, and her breathing was shallow. "Please. You're his *brother*."

"And he ruined my life." Meren's words were dispassionate now. He might have been talking about the weather. "Because of him, I learned what I could do. I learned I had the power to be the greatest king Kemet had ever seen. But the gods—well, they're gods. Vicious doesn't begin to describe it." He snapped off another of the mummy's fingers. "I took body after body, trying to get to the throne. Shabtis were just clay; why be a new homemade man when you could take on the body of a king? But circumstances always conspired against me. Hundreds of years, I tried. And I started to forget." Another finger, broken like a twig and dropped in the snow. "He stole my life, Theo. Can you blame me for wanting those shabtis?"

"The Collector," she said slowly. "You were the Collector. Robbing Egyptian antiques collections—gathering shabtis and pieces from his tomb. And destroying things you couldn't use."

Meren smiled mirthlessly. She almost couldn't take it anymore. He was gloating; he was on top of the world; he was winning. She had to do something.

Bringing back Mark hadn't worked. The one thing that had changed was that Meren, once hidden inside a mortal body with a beating heart, was at home in a shabti now. Seth was still going to die; the question was whether his brother would burn him alive (undead?) before the sun rose.

She was out of other options. It was time to do something very, very stupid.

The mummy was out of reach. There was no way she could snatch it from Meren's hands, and he would never bring it close enough to give her a shot. She tried anyway, clambering to her feet and making a clumsy rush for the mummy. Meren didn't bother with his spells; he simply tripped her and watched her crash into the dirty snow.

Head down, she curled up in a ball and let more tears flow. Her hands, safely hidden from Meren, pawed up another handful of dirt. When she wiped the tears away, the warm liquid seeped into the dirt and made mud. It was the work of a moment to do what she had to do before redoubling her sobs.

Meren laughed and took a step closer. "Really?" he said. "That's what you're going to do now? So much for the snake—"

The snake struck. Her hands went around his ankles.

Meren's words were truncated by a scream as the twin tyets, painted in grave dirt on the palms of an artist and a woman, touched his skin. His back arched and his muscles spasmed as his flesh cracked and crisped under her hands.

"Bitch!"

He lashed out, his foot narrowly missing Theo's face, but Theo was already moving. She yanked as hard as she could, fingernails digging into the burned skin, and pulled Meren off his feet. With a roar of rage he went flailing backward, landing hard in the snow.

His second kick wasn't quite so wild—one sandaled foot slammed into Theo's temple, making her head ring and sending her twisting sideways on the ground. The mummy had fallen from Meren's grip and was lying inches away—still twitching—

Meren rose, staggering, with open flames blazing in both hands. He hurled palmfuls of fire at Theo, who ducked her head just in time. The flames sputtered against her cheap parka, crisping the plastic and filling the air with a sickly chemical smell. Plastic melted and warped but didn't burn.

Unlike Seth. Meren palmed another ball of flame, but Theo flung herself forward and tackled him to the ground again. He was stronger than she, a lot stronger, and she struggled to keep him pinned. She could hear Mark yelling something in the background, but she couldn't focus on him.

Meren's hands burned. One stray blow and Theo's head snapped back, her world reeling. Her left eye began to swell shut.

It wasn't enough. Her touch could burn him too, but his shabti body couldn't bleed and it healed too quickly. Sparks showered down, landing dangerously close to the mummy, and Theo's breath hitched in her throat. Meren seized the opening, and this time he grabbed and held on.

White-hot pain lanced through her and Theo couldn't restrain a scream. She reeled back, clawing at Meren's grip, as his unnatural fire turned her sleeves to ashes and seared into her skin. He bent over her, grinning, his teeth bared and flecked with clay. She slammed her forehead into his nose and grinned back through her pain at the crunch of cartilage.

Mark came stumbling through the snowy graveyard, Frankenstein's monster in a body three sizes too big for him. He launched himself at Meren, shoving Theo aside and grabbing the priest around the waist. Meren shouted, his words a tangled garble of languages and curses as Mark tried to pummel him.

The boy wasn't much good at it, but he didn't have to be for long. Even as Meren knocked him away with a burst of green light, Theo was ready. She flailed across the grave and seized Meren by his wrist.

This time, the scream wasn't remotely human. Blood rose, burned off, and vanished as the flesh scorched. The tyet—Isis's knot, a symbol more powerful than the ankh, a woman's sigil and a sign of reproach for a man who should have died a long, long time ago—blazed brightly as it burrowed into his skin.

Theo knew about the power of symbols. A language made of pictures...

"No!" Meren screamed. He tried to lash out at her, but as he jerked, his dying hand broke and crumbled away.

He had no heart of his own, and Theo's soared. He was a clay man who thought he was real. Even the touch of the tyet amulet hadn't hurt Seth this way. But this was the written symbol, based in a magic mixed with art and a religion where a man's written name was his identity. And she was facing someone whose real body was long gone and whose heart was that of a dead cat.

"I'm sorry," she said. Maybe she meant it.

She put her hand on his chest, on the place where his animal heart tried and failed to be the real thing, and Meren burst into flame.

It was a fire never seen before in the city on the lake. Too hot, too fierce, too white—the glare of the desert sun at noon, a tiny supernova in the middle of the graveyard. Heat washed over Theo, prickling her skin, scorching her, overwhelming her. She yelped and tumbled backward, her palm burning as the clay scorched her.

Meren's final words were a drawn-out howl. It cut off abruptly. Ash and clay dust settled over everything.

"Holy shit," Mark whispered.

Silence fell.

The noise of the city rumbled in the background, but around them, nothing moved or made a sound. The orange lights of the graveyard bled all other color from the scene, and the dust and ash melded into the charred earth as if they had always been there. Her hands and face were burned stiff.

Someone had to have noticed that blaze. She winced with pain as she checked her watch, wondering how fast the fire department would respond to a call at this time of night.

Mark sagged to his knees and rubbed his face until the skin turned red. "Holy shit," he repeated weakly. "I want to go home."

"Me too." Theo leaned against a gravestone, closing her eyes. One breath, then another, deep and cold, reminding herself that she was still functional, she was alive, Meren was gone, and she and Mark and Seth would be okay.

Seth.

The mummy-man still lay where he'd been dropped. His bandages were torn to shreds, and his arms and legs were broken. His few remaining fingers twitched weakly in an aborted gesture she couldn't understand.

Theo crouched beside him. Her eyes burned, but there were no more tears. Golems and evil priests and ancient spells, her mind could manage. But seeing Seth like that pushed it over the edge of reaction.

Through the mist, though, she knew one thing. As horrible as the weak twitches of the mummy might be, a good man was trapped inside it. Nobody should die like this.

She had to get him out.

"Seth," she said as she bent down. The mummy writhed, twitching and shuddering as he tried to raise his head. One hand clenched, and Theo laid her own stiff hand on it. "Seth. Seth, listen to me." She gently placed her free hand on the mummy's chest. Her mind was whirling, but in the midst of the chaos an awful, brilliant, terrifying plan was forming. She knew what she had to do, and it scared her to death, but there was no arguing—it needed to be done.

"Seth," she murmured. "I'm going to try and fix you. I think I know what to do. But...but I'm going to need you to trust me."

There was a spasm that might have been a nod. The hand tightened on hers for a moment.

The plastic tub of materials was lying where Meren had left it. There wasn't much clay left, barely a lump the size of a baseball, and Theo dropped to her knees and fumbled for a fresh handful of earth.

Her fingers were clumsy. The burned skin was nearly rigid and the fresh scrapes had begun to scab over, but as she stretched and strained to get the cold material to respond, they broke open again. A dribble of warm blood mixed with sweat, sinking into the clay and lending it a tiny bit of liquidity. Theo let out a hoarse breath and reached for the first words.

"A vessel..." she began raggedly. The clay was cold and hard under her burned fingers, but she dug in as best she could. "A vessel for the son of..."

No. Not that mistake again. Theo squeezed her eyes shut, willing the clay to yield. As it drank in the warmth from her hands, it began to soften ever so slightly, and Theo forced it to move. "A vessel for *Anhurmose*, the son of Merenptah."

It was beginning to move more easily now. The squarish blob elongated, pulled into more of a soft rectangular shape. "A vessel for Anhurmose, son of Merenptah. Khnum is his father and Neith is his mother. He is pure. He is known to us here as he is known to those who have brought him into this world. O Anubis and Osiris, pass him by..."

Theo's watch face glowed: sunup in ten minutes.

The torso emerged, misshapen and indistinct, but definitely more than a random lump. There was no more time for clothes or delicate details of anatomy. What she had here was one step up from third-grade art class, but she clutched it as she worked and thought *Anhurmose* into it. She had to hope it was enough.

She gouged out its chest, readying a place. When she reached into the cooler, though, her stomach dropped. There were no more hearts. Meren had used the last one.

That left her one option. The idea had barely formed before she recoiled from it, but the sun was about to rise, and Seth was dying slowly in an ancient husk. A heart was what she needed.

Hearts were the center of this whole thing. He'd said it in the museum, hadn't he? *Every one of us is clay, at the bottom of it. But the heart is the center of it, the thing that made us alive. And I think you can't run blood through a heart that's not your own.*

This could work. Or it could kill him. But he was already trapped in a dead shell, and Theo had to give him the chance. She knelt next to him again and told him what she had to do.

"I'm sorry," she whispered, her hands splayed on the ancient linen. "I'm so, so sorry. I have to."

Silence. And then, barely, the nod again.

There was no time to be careful or subtle about it. The few remaining bandages were beyond fragile now; it took only a second to tear them, the fabric crumbling into dry fragments in her hands. The chest, sunken and alien, was bared. And there was the incision the embalmers had made so long ago, once stitched closed, now shrunken until it gaped open.

She plunged her hand into his chest.

Movement. Something shuddered under her fingers—erratic, withered, crackling as it moved. It felt like leather covered in parchment, twitching spasmodically as if something alive and frantic was trapped inside it. With her own in her throat, Theo lifted out the shivering, beating, dried heart of a dead man. The mummy's back arched as he went into cardiac arrest.

Hands trembling, she settled the horrible thing into the new shabti. As she smoothed over the clay, she added a prayer of her own. It wasn't orthodox, but she had to try.

Help him, Neith. He's suffered enough.

Light was gathering. It gathered in the shabti, and—oh no no no, not now—it gathered at the horizon as well. The mummy convulsed. Theo smelled soot and ash, chased for a bare second by the hot, dry scent of sand and salt. She dropped the shabti next to the mummy, and it glowed, writhing and pulsing unnaturally as it fought to live.

She prayed.

And with a strangled gasp, Anhurmose, son of Merenptah, rose from the grave.

"Seth," Theo breathed. He convulsed, his muscles straining beneath his skin, but he was there and the flesh was smooth and unmarked where the ancient heart had gone in. He lay next to his own dead body, naked in the snow but alive. The mummy was still and quiet.

Seth gasped for breath. His left hand flexed, then seized hers, almost crushing it in a desperate grip. His eyes opened.

The word came out in a hoarse rattle: *"Theo."*

He tried to raise his right arm and failed. The hand and arm were a crushed mess, bruises purpling under the dark skin. His right leg was twisted, clearly broken, and a milky film covered the iris of his right eye.

The right side. To his left, the sun was rising over the edge of the horizon, casting pinkish-orange light over the desolate scene. She had barely finished in time. His right side was still in shadow, lying in the darkness of the night and the west, and the power of the western realm of death had left its mark.

"Seth, Seth, listen. You're alive. You're...you're a little messed-up, but you're alive," Theo said, pressing a kiss to the one white-knuckled hand he had left. The muscles relaxed a fraction, and he let himself sink down on the frozen ground.

"Theo," he rasped again, his voice barely a croak. Blood stained his teeth and lips—red blood, flowing and smooth, not a single grain of clay or speck of dust. His heart was his own.

"I'm here," she murmured.

"Theo." His eyes focused, vaguely. "Hurts."

"I know, Seth. I know." She squeezed his good hand, hoping he could feel it. His fingers flexed, and he squeezed back, weakly. "They'll be here soon. I promise. We'll get someone here. Need to find a phone..."

Mark stumbled over, his movements jerky and awkward. His hair had fallen into his eyes, and his entire body was sweat-streaked and coated with a fine layer of grave dirt. The gray-green jacket, cargo pants, and boots that Meren had chosen didn't fit the soul who occupied the body; he was gawky and ungainly, like a marionette with one crucial string tangled.

He fell to his knees beside them, almost toppling over. His legs didn't seem to want to bend.

"Is he okay?" he said, eyes wide.

"He'll make it," Theo said. She hoped. "M—you—I dropped my bags over by that grave. There's a medical kit in there. Get bandages—"

Mark tried to stand, but his knees still weren't working, and he fell again. Groaning, he pulled himself to his hands and knees and crawled, scuffling in the dirt. Theo murmured more prayers as she shucked out of her jacket and wrapped it awkwardly around Seth's wrecked arm and ribs. The blood came out in a slow ooze.

"You'll be okay," she whispered to him. "You'll be okay, you hear me? We're not in the Bronze Age anymore, Anhurmose. We can fix anything these days. I'll get you to the hospital, and you don't need to be afraid, because you're bleeding blood." The words flowed like a mantra, coming from some deep place that she couldn't put a name to. "You'll make it. You'll make it, and I'll come visit you in the hospital every day and embarrass you by bringing you something stupid from the hospital gift shop. Maybe a balloon with 'Get Well, Grandma' on it, because hospitals don't have 'Get Well, Maybe-One-Time-Hookup Statue Man' stuff most of the time. So stay with me, okay? I want a chance to kiss you when we're not running for our lives."

Something wailed in the distance. Sirens, rising and falling in a screech that filled Theo with hope. Sweat stood out on Seth's face and chest, but he was breathing deeply and his eyes were open wide. *Just a little longer, just a little longer.*

"You'll be okay," Theo repeated softly.

"Don't push it," Seth gasped. Despite the pain, he managed a strained smile. His good hand tightened on Theo's again, to the point where she thought she heard the bones creak. "Trying too hard."

"This is really not the time for sarcasm," Theo murmured, wiping sweat out of his eyes with the pad of her thumb.

The sirens were growing louder. Behind her, she could hear shuffling and heavy breathing as Mark came crawling back, dragging the medical kit. Behind him, distant but oh-so-welcome, came the sound of footsteps and voices.

CHAPTER SEVENTEEN

Blessed is he who rests here, for the hands of others have
given him life. Blessed is he who rests here, for he only
sleeps. Blessed is he, for a scribe shall wake him.

- Prayer found in the tomb of THS203,
inscribed c. 1975 BCE

They were arrested. Finally.

At least when the officers encountered the tableau in the graveyard,
they were less concerned with handcuffs than paramedics. Seth was
bundled into an ambulance and Theo went down to the nearest police
station in another, a paramedic on one side dabbing ointment on her
burns while an officer on the other asked question after question that
she couldn't answer. She said nothing, only half pretending to be in
shock, while she struggled to come up with an explanation that wouldn't
end with jail time.

She was staring at the wall of the otherwise empty interrogation
room, letting her mind drift and trying to ignore the aches and pains,
when the door opened and a policewoman came in.

"Did Mr. Zimmer think he was an Egyptian priest?" she said. Theo's
jaw dropped.

"How did you know—" she began, before clamping her lips shut.

At which point Dr. Van Allen, seated regally in a brand-new wheel-
chair, was let into the room.

The next few hours passed in a daze. When the cops had followed
Security into the museum the night before, finding a curator with a
broken leg and a mess beyond description in the hallways, they'd
assumed it was the work of the rogue employee. Van Allen had said that

Theo was indeed there but that the guilty party was none other than Mark Zimmer, the Security head, who'd been under the delusion that he was a magician. A check of Zimmer's home found him absent and turned up several items that should have been in the custody of Midwestern museums.

Then they'd received a tip about an apparent explosion in a cemetery in Little Vietnam. When emergency services arrived, they'd found Theo, Seth, and Zimmer in the graveyard, surrounded by explosion markers. Theo was burned and marked with Egyptian symbols; Seth was maimed and naked; and Zimmer was babbling nonsense.

The biggest surprise of all, though, was that Zimmer confessed. He swore he'd done it and begged them to lock him up. Theo was horrified, but Dr. Van Allen reported that the former Security chief seemed remarkably calm about the idea of prison. "He kept saying he was just happy to be himself again," Van Allen said. "As soon as the paperwork is completed, you should be free to go. You'll doubtless need to remain in the city for questioning, but I suspect that will be a welcome alternative to prison."

"I..." Theo was momentarily lost for words. "Sir," she finally said. "Thanks. For standing up for us."

Dr. Van Allen merely peered over his glasses. "Don't thank me yet," he said. "I suspect you're going to have an extremely interesting story to tell me. Aren't you?" The gaze brooked no disagreement.

* * *

A week later, she stood in front of Dr. Van Allen's office door. Christmas had passed quietly, with her splitting time between the Deerfield house and Seth's hospital room. As yet her parents had no idea anything had happened. Theo knew she would have to explain about the "kidnapping" eventually, but now that their car was back in the garage and the blood and papier-mâché had been removed from the house, it was possible they wouldn't question the official story. Still, she wasn't looking forward to that conversation.

Or this one, either. The plain dark door of Dr. Van Allen's office made her think of the principal's office.

Something touched her shoulder, and Theo jumped before remembering. Seth looked down at her with one eyebrow raised, his expression wry.

"Nervous?" he said.

"Never mind me." She put a hand on his good arm, steadying him. He moved slowly now; his right leg was in a heavy black brace, slightly marring the line of the dark-gray suit. The cane he leaned on seemed too old for him. This new body was unlike any he had had before, and the wounds of the west did not heal quickly. "Are you okay with this?" she said.

"I'm alive. That's more than enough for me." The door opened, and they went in.

The curator was sitting behind his desk, his chair angled sideways so that his own broken leg could be propped up on a padded stool. This cast was a crisp, pristine white, but someone had spoiled the effect by drawing a smiley face on the knee. The rest of him was as immaculate as usual, if you discounted the dark circles under his eyes.

"Well," he said, looking Seth and Theo up and down. His gaze particularly lingered on Seth. "Perhaps I should make a pithy comment about the prodigal son returning, but I find that Christianity is not the topic on my mind these days."

"Say anything you like," Seth replied neutrally. "May we sit? It's been a long couple of weeks."

"Yes, you may, and yes, it has." Van Allen nodded to the chairs in front of his desk. Seth motioned Theo forward and then followed, limping. When he came down a little too hard on his right side, Theo grabbed his good arm and steered him to a chair despite his protests. Seth murmured thanks, but his expression was strained. Torture he could handle, but this new, weaker body was something he hadn't dealt with in a long time.

"Nevertheless," Van Allen continued, blithely skating around the mention of Seth's injuries, "you're right. The sons aren't always prodigal, but they tend to vanish anyway. A story springs to mind. The Tale of Sinuhe."

Theo made a soft "oh" noise. Seth's shoulders hunched as the muscles tightened almost imperceptibly, but he maintained eye contact and he seemed calm.

"Supposedly, a man named Sinuhe was a trusted servant and adviser of Pharaoh Amenemhat," Van Allen narrated coolly. "When his master was assassinated, the innocent Sinuhe nevertheless feared for his life and fled Egypt. Though he married a princess in a foreign land, he was never happy until he returned to his home. Amenemhat's son reached out to him: 'Be reminded of the day of burial…you shall not die upon the hill-land or be buried wrapped in a sheepskin. You have wandered for too long; think of your corpse, and return.'"

Seth and Theo exchanged glances. The message was plain. It was a story about what a good death and a decent funeral meant in the ancient world, and what someone would give up to have that. Trust the doctor to question magic by citing historical precedent.

Van Allen adjusted his glasses and nailed Seth to the chair with a stare like a crossbow bolt. "Miss Speer told me parts of a story, Mr. Adler. It sounded completely ridiculous, but, I have to admit, certain aspects of it ring true. The golems, for example, were fairly compelling." Was that the merest touch of humor in his tone? "If you two are lying to me, you've put so much effort into it that I'm tempted to let you off any-way. But for now, lacking evidence to the contrary, let's proceed as if it's the unvarnished truth."

He folded his hands and fixed Seth with a calm stare. "In which case, you sit before me as a citizen of Kemet who neglected to pass on to the afterlife of the Deshret. An ancient Egyptian who, unlike Sinuhe, put his mortal flesh before his immortal soul. And I have to admit, that's the part that confuses me most of all."

"Sinuhe was an ideal," Seth said flatly. "I remember when that story was making the rounds. I was the cause of it."

Van Allen sat back in his chair, his face a polite mask. "Interesting. Were you also responsible for crucifying Jesus and killing Attila the Hun?"

No surprise there: they were, after all, asking him to swallow a completely bizarre story. He could have written the entire thing off, the way she had blamed Seth's disintegration on drugs and dust; instead, he was giving them a chance to explain. "No. But Sinuhe was the perfect example of service to Egypt, and the ideal of putting afterlife over living. Don't you think it's strange that a country already so completely devoted to the gods and their realm would wind up circulating a story like that? A story that says 'forget being a prince; you should be worrying about your mummy'? They knew it already. Why would they need to be reminded?"

"That's a rather spurious line of argument," Van Allen said. "Myth doesn't always originate as a moral example. Some are stories for the sake of being stories. Others are actual recountings of real events. Maybe

Sinuhe was real, and you call him a myth for the sake of propping up
your story."

Seth met him, gaze for gaze. "At this point, Doctor, it's your word
against mine. How exactly do you plan to resolve an argument like this?
Time travel?"

"Maybe later. Tell me more about what you did that supposedly
prompted the creation of Sinuhe. I was under the impression that secret
rituals remained, shall we say, secret?"

"They should have been. But when I got sick, my brother—Zimmer,
as you knew him—helped me with the shabtis and my tomb. We told
everyone that I was going into seclusion and praying for healing. Then, if
the spell worked, I could return and claim the gods had blessed me." He
shook his head. "But you already know that you can't build a tomb with
only an invalid and a priest."

"The servants talked?" Van Allen said.

"Slaves. Don't whitewash it. The markets were flooded with captives
after the campaigning season. We bought them cheap and kept them
loyal with generous payments, plus threats and beatings, if necessary."

Van Allen's gaze flickered to Theo again, as if he was silently asking
her what she thought of that admission. She stared steadily back. Could
she be angry on behalf of people who'd been dead for four thousand
years? Or lose her temper about what had happened before the inven-
tion of steel?

"By the way," she added softly, "I think he knows you're baiting him,
Doc."

Van Allen's poker face was amazing. "I am?"

"The afterlife of the Deshret?" Seth's mouth twisted. "Deshret
means the red earth, the desert, and you know it does. Not the afterlife.
Either you're an incompetent scholar, or you were setting me up to fail
by offering bad information."

"I was," Van Allen agreed, almost amiably. "So the slaves, you were
saying?"

"One of them talked, I heard later. Caused a minor panic. If the story
was true, then what I was doing was sacrilege. Perverting the cosmic
order, upsetting the barque of the sun, consorting with chaos, gaming the
system. Take your pick." Seth leaned forward. "They fought rumor with
rumor. Knowing King Senwoseret, he dreamed it up himself; he always
had a good head for stories, especially when the Great House was on

campaign and he got to spend time with someone besides the palace busybodies." Seth grinned ruefully.

"I followed the news as best I could. I was in my first new body then, lurking around Kush, hoping to come back and claim I'd been healed, once the rumors died down. They didn't, not in his lifetime. I waited forty years for him to die, and I never could shake the idea that he was still a kid sitting on his dad's throne."

As Seth spoke, Theo watched his face. The life was there, vitality and humor and strength forcing their way through a body left sluggish by the failing power that had created it. The emotions animated him, and the smooth ripple of movement added warmth to him. Not just the motion, either. There were healthier tones in his skin now. His veins ran with blood instead of clay and magic, and his eyes were bright.

She transferred her gaze to the curator. If Dr. Van Allen thought Seth was a lunatic or a scammer, he was doing a good job of hiding it. When he asked a question about life in Kush and Seth answered easily, Van Allen's fingers curled against the desk. She recognized the motion—the impulse to grab a pen and start jotting down notes.

Dr. Van Allen was listening. Dr. Van Allen, the one who insisted on absolute precision in everything and publicly called Egyptology his vocation, was calmly listening to a story about mummies and magic and warped golems created out of shabtis. It would have been so easy for him to do what Theo had done originally and try to write the whole thing off as a hallucination, but he'd gone to bat for both of them and accepted a story that should have been kryptonite to a serious scientist.

But this was Dr. Van Allen, who also never left anything to chance and always wanted proofs on his desk as early as possible. A week was more than enough time to get the Columbian's Cairo team down to Thebes for a quick examination of tomb THS2. He would probably have that badly spelled copy of the Coffin Texts on display in a few months.

He caught her staring and merely raised an eyebrow. As usual, his expression gave little away. She shrugged, her own expression innocent—he'd probably know she was onto him anyway.

For a moment, there was silence. Then Dr. Van Allen resettled himself in his chair and, to Theo's astonishment, relaxed.

"Tell me about your life, Mr. Adler."

"What do you want to know?" Seth said.

Van Allen considered the issue for a moment.

"Everything."

Theo's smile widened, and Seth grinned at her fondly before turning back to the curator.

"I was born in Thebes, around 2000 BC…"

EPILOGUE

He's okay. I'm okay. It'll be okay eventually.
Memo: Colors and games.

- Excerpt from the diary of Theodora Speer,
date unknown

The inquest took place on a Monday afternoon. Theo was present, heart in her mouth, as Dr. Van Allen calmly explained that Mark Zimmer had set up Mr. Seth Adler and one of his own staffers to take the fall for a series of robberies. Mark confessed to everything, his tone wobbly as he described how it had been done and the steps he'd taken. His parents, a wan-looking couple in late middle age, wept. One of the cops rubber-stamped a pile of paperwork.

Seth had left immediately after testifying, unwilling to dwell on the story of his brother's death. Theo wondered if he was leaving for good—but he was waiting for her outside, his collar turned up against the cold, the scarf wrapped tightly around him, just as it had been on the day they'd gone to lunch. His cheeks were red with the cold, and his bad hand was tucked into the pocket of his coat.

He smiled, and Theo smiled back, a warm feeling settling in her chest despite the chill of the air and the worry of the hearing. He held out his good hand, gloved fingers enfolding hers and squeezing.

"How did it end?" he said.

"All right," she responded, "I think. Mark said he did it, and with his history…I mean, his mind was thrown out of his body when Meren took over, and his family thought he'd had an aneurysm. There shouldn't be any problems with accepting that there was something wrong with his mind this time too. You've already been cleared, and charges are being dropped against me. Mark'll spend a lot of time in a mental ward, but I don't think he's unhappy about that. He really needs therapy." She shivered, unsure of how to feel. She knew she would never be able to accept the real Mark Zimmer, despite knowing the whole truth. There were bad memories associated with that face.

"I thought so." Seth shook his head. "He'll need to find a new career once he's out. I can help him with that. But for now, at least he has his body back."

Theo nodded. "He had tears in his eyes. Kept describing his 'out-of-body experience' and flexing his hands like he couldn't believe he had them." She swallowed, trying to get rid of the lump rising in her throat. "His parents started crying too. They said they didn't care; they had their son back."

"Long may it last," Seth said.

"Speaking of..." Theo added uneasily. She was certain they were already both thinking it, but she couldn't not ask. "Will Meren..." She shook her head at the thought, and Seth squeezed her hand again. "Will he come back? Will he try to take back Mark's body?" *Is he watching us right now?*

Seth bent his head. Strands of his long, dark hair, flecked with snow instead of gray, fell down over his eyes as he shook his head. "No," he said simply. "Meren's a soul without a form or a heart. The boy's soul stayed because his body was still alive and others may have lingered because of their murder, but Meren challenged the gods directly. He'll be judged and go to the outer darkness beyond the west."

There was weariness in his voice, and Theo squeezed his hand back. Much as she hated Meren for what he had put them through, she knew that Seth was the one who had lost the most. The brother who'd tutored him, helped him, and saved him had tried to kill both Seth and Theo.

"And what about you?" she said quietly. "Are you going to be judged too?"

"I don't know," Seth replied. "But if I'm condemned for wanting to live a long life, then I'll have a lot of company."

He drew her to him. His kiss was soft, sweet, and a little sad; they'd come to a crossroads, she thought, even as she returned the kiss. But she held his gloved hand in hers, remembering the darkness in the halls and the terror of his supposed death, and she knew that she would be joining him on his road for now. She'd learned too much to stop.

As they separated for a moment, their breath clouding in the cold air, Seth looked down at her with those heart-stopping dark eyes. "So am I still crazy?" he said softly. "The last time I tried that in a public place…"

She laughed, and it seemed that a knot was unraveling in her chest. "I can't vouch for your sanity," she said, "but whenever you want to do that, you won't catch me objecting."

"Glad to hear it," he said as he ran his one long-fingered hand through her loose hair. Her eyes burned, seeing again his bleeding limbs and wondering if she could have done it better—but he tilted her chin up and kissed her again, warm and loving and so very, very alive. Her worry melted away in a rush of heat and emotion.

"Don't be sad," he murmured. "You fixed me."

She blinked away her tears and scowled, trying not to let her emotions get the best of her. "I don't remember building psychic powers into you, mister."

"I don't have to be psychic to see what you're thinking," Seth said. "I know you too well."

"Only because you cheated," she told him, gently prodding his good shoulder with her index finger. "If it hadn't been for those shabtis, you wouldn't know me from Alexander the Great."

"You don't think much of my powers of observation, do you?" he said, wrapping his weak arm around her waist. A fresh gust of wind brought a flurry of snowflakes with it, peppering his face and hair and forcing him to muffle a sneeze. Theo laughed and rested her hands on his shoulders.

"Well, I still don't know that much about you, do I? I think I deserve the time to learn." She flicked a couple of snowflakes off his shoulder. Seth twined one loose strand of her hair around his fingertip, the ash-blonde standing out against the black fabric of his glove.

They stood there for a long time. Passersby on the museum campus bridgeway could probably see them—him a tall, inscrutable figure in gray, snow making constellations in his dark hair, and her with her blonde braid and orange parka looking up at him. Theo saw him, saw her, saw the picture they made, and laughed.

Seth looked at her in astonishment, but Theo couldn't suppress her giggles long enough to explain. Yin and yang, male and female, light and dark in figure form. The kind of cheap symbolism that would have made her art teachers kick someone out of class. Her lover shook his head as

CATHERINE BUTZEN

she laughed herself out, and held her while she caught her breath and tried to focus.

"Seth," she managed, "we have to get you some new colors."

"That's what I love about you," he said. "You don't stop. You made me a new body, and now you want to get new clothes on it too?"

His tone was teasing, and she laughed again and pressed a kiss to his lips. "Trust me," she said, "your color palette is all wrong. I'm thinking deep navy, jade green, silver gray, maybe a touch of ivory…"

"No green," he said. "It makes me look like a third wife."

"Fine. No green."

"And before we do anything else, I need your help with something."

"Oh?"

"Yes. Where do you buy an Atari?"

Thinklings

TIMELESS BOOKS • QUALITY AUTHORS

www.ThinklingsBooks.com
Facebook.com/ThinklingsBooks
@ThinklingsBooks

Thinklings Books started out when three speculative-fiction-loving editors—Deborah Natelson, Sarah Awa, and Jeannie Ingraham—got together and formed a writing group. We called ourselves the Thinklings, in honor of C.S. Lewis and J.R.R. Tolkien's group, the Inklings.

Over time, we found ourselves agonizing more and more about how messed-up the publishing industry had become. Why couldn't good books get published? Why were so many bad books published just because their authors had big Twitter followings? We wished there were something we could do about the problem . . . and then we realized there was.

As a developmental editor, a substantive/line editor, and a proofreader, the three of us knew good writing when we saw it—and we knew how to make it even better. We had a lot of experience walking our clients through the publishing process—both traditional and self-publish—and we had contacts with marketing and design experts. We had some amazing unpublished books lined up and ready for production. We had, in fact, everything we needed to make a great publishing company. All that was left was to actually do it.

So we're doing it.

Spectacular Reads. Every Time.

IT'S TIME TO TAKE OVER

Fodder of Humble Village is a soldier for the plot of each new story, and, frankly, he's really sick and tired of getting speared, disembowelled, and decapitated so the good guys can look glorious. In fact, he's not going to take it anymore.

The Plot Bandits
the complete four-book . . . uh, trilogy . . .
by Katherine Vick

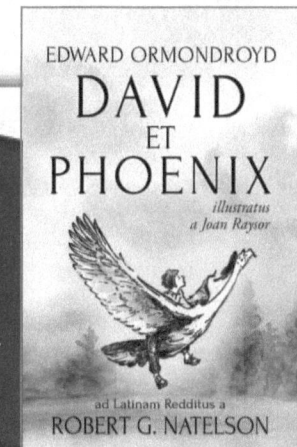

AND YOU THOUGHT COLLEGE WAS TOUGH BEFORE

Try getting bitten by a werewolf. And being hunted by madmen. And being stalked by a very suspicious secret organization.

Hunter's Moon
by Sarah M. Awa

RIDICULOUSLY MAGICAL. MAGICALLY RIDICULOUS.

Crafted as a slave to serve Time, the clockwork man escapes to seek out his imagination, his purpose, and his name.

The Land of the Purple Ring
by Deborah J. Natelson

THE CLOCK IS TICKING

Plans seldom survive contact with the enemy, a truth thrown at Mercedes when an ordinary trip turns into a battle for survival.

Bargaining Power
by Deborah J. Natelson

ABOUT THE AUTHOR

Catherine Butzen was born and raised in Chicago, Illinois. Surrounded by world-class museums and with a family library overflowing with everything from computer manuals to Norse myths, Catherine developed an enduring love for history and writing. Her first book, the horror adventure *Thief of Midnight,* was published in 2010.

Today she lives and works in Madison, Wisconsin. Her interests include sewing, archery, languages, cybersecurity, and being a font of strange but occasionally useful trivia. You can find her at catherinebutzen.wordpress.com, or on Twitter @cjbutzen.

www.ingramcontent.com/pod-product-compliance
Lightning Source LLC
Chambersburg PA
CBHW052045240626
47153CB00006B/2217